Charles Frederick Forshaw

Holroyd's Collection of Yorkshire Ballads

Charles Frederick Forshaw

Holroyd's Collection of Yorkshire Ballads

ISBN/EAN: 9783744777858

Printed in Europe, USA, Canada, Australia, Japan

Cover: Foto ©Andreas Hilbeck / pixelio.de

More available books at **www.hansebooks.com**

HOLROYD'S

COLLECTION OF

Yorkshire Ballads.

WITH SOME REMARKS ON

BALLAD LORE BY W. J. KAYE, M.A.

AND A LIFE OF

ABRAHAM HOLROYD BY WILLIAM SCRUTON.

EDITED BY

CHAS. F. FORSHAW, LL.D.

EDITOR "YORKSHIRE SONNETTERS," "YORKSHIRE POETS, PAST AND PRESENT."
ETC. ETC.

LONDON :
GEORGE BELL & SONS, YORK STREET,
COVENT GARDEN.

———

1892.

TO

GEORGE ACKROYD, Esq. J.P.

NORTH PARK ROAD, BRADFORD.

A TRUE POET, A NOBLE PATRON, A SINCERE FRIEND, AND AN

UPRIGHT CHRISTIAN GENTLEMAN.

———•<•———

HEREWITH I tend the fruit of many pens—
    Rare gems of Yorkshire's choicest poesy!
Rich buds by our loved county's denizens!
    Famed flowers forenamed for fairest fragrancy.
And I am glad—for well I know thy soul
    Rejoiceth at old Yorkshire's deeds of might!
    And he who culled these blossoms of delight
Would joy with us to know that on Time's scroll
His name is writ. He laboured not in vain—
    For now the products of long, weary ages,
    The wit, the wisdom of our bygone sages
Are here to teach, amuse, and entertain.
And it would please his inmost heart to know
That I to thee these records would bestow.

EDITOR.

PREFACE.

—

VERY few prefatory remarks are needful, as anything I might say on ballads and ballad lore, would be quite superfluous after Mr. Kaye's brief, but poignant, article thereon.

It is mainly through the munificent generosity of Mr. George Ackroyd, J.P.,—a valued friend of Mr. Holroyd's—that these ballads, which he collected from almost all available sources, are now before the public—and Mr. Ackroyd will ever receive the warmest thanks of all true-hearted literary men, that these records of Mr. Holroyd's research have been given to posterity in volume form.

After Mr. Holroyd's death Mr. Ackroyd, who, as is well-known, is one of Bradford's sweetest poets, composed the following beautiful and touching tribute to his memory :—

In Memoriam.

—

ABRAHAM HOLROYD,

JANUARY 1ST, 1888.

"Gone to the life beyond,"
Where sorrows are unknown,
Where loving hearts to hearts respond,
And worship near the throne.

No pain nor sickness there.
No weariness of age—
Gone every sigh and every care
Of this world's pilgrimage.

Another life begun,
Where pleasures never cease—
No shadows of a setting sun,
But light, and joy, and peace.

Then shall we mourn thee gone?
Thy earthly travail o'er?
Ah, no! the thought be ours alone,
" Not lost, but gone before."

January 22nd, 1888.

No apology is necessary for its quotation.

A large number of gentlemen, hearing that the work was in progress, sent in their names for copies. Among these may be mentioned the Archbishop of Canterbury, the Right Hon. the Marquis of Lorne, and the Trustees of the British Museum.

To Mr. Kaye for his remarks on " Ballad Lore," and to Mr. Scruton for his sanction to insert his biography of Mr. Holroyd, my thanks are specially due.

Chas F. Forshaw.

WINDER HOUSE, BRADFORD,
6th August, 1892.

Some Remarks on Ballad Lore.

By WALTER J. KAYE, M.A.

PRINCIPAL OF ILKLEY COLLEGE, YORKSHIRE; EDITOR "LEADING POETS OF SCOTLAND."

———

THERE appears to be little doubt in the minds of most writers on ballad lore that in former times, before the days of chronicler, historian, or poet-laureate, ballads served as a convenient method of recording the stirring annals of all countries. Whether a recital of public events, or marked episodes in domestic life, were needed, the ballad was found a ready vehicle for its safe transmission to generations following.

In the early period the story in simple verse of the heroic deeds of our forefathers, their love of the family hearth and prowess displayed in its defence, roused up a martial ardour. The wandering bard oft composed on the spot an impromptu weaving of the simple tale. His ballads embodied too the manners and customs, and modes of thought of the period. The word ballad is derived from the French *baller*, to dance, and thus meant originally in all probability a song accompanied by dancing to the minstrel's harp. But in more recent times, it became the technical term for an old fashioned French poem. It now no longer preserves to us the rehearsal of valorous deeds. But of stories of the wonderful and the wild, of sentiment and passion too, these simple versifyings became an accepted means of conveyance.

Pleasing by their quaintness, and exciting admiration by their rude homely vigour and rugged directness of diction, ballads were readily committed to memory by the professional reciter, minstrel and bard.

The happy reciter of ballads was ever a welcome guest at the festive board in the good old times of our ancestors.

Some writers conclude that ballads have been from one age of bards to another thus handed down since the 11th or 12th century. But what nation in Europe has not its ballads, its popular rhymes, always fresh with each rising generation ? We find them everywhere,—in Greece, Turkey, Russia, Italy, the German Fatherland, Provence, Brittany, and in our own Islands. In this country Lancashire takes a prominent position, and Yorkshire is a keen competitor with its ballad lore. Are we able by any known data to certify on reasonable grounds the authors of our own country's ballads, or to fix upon the exact period of their origin with reasonable approach to certainty? Mr. Andrew Lang says, " It is natural to conclude that our ballads were first improvised and circulated in rustic dances." Thus they have without doubt descended to us from the far off past, and from days of simplicity, untrammelled by modern culture.

It is worthy of remark that the same topics, the same personifying of natural objects, the same ideas, constantly recur in the ballad lore of Eastern and Western Europe. This shows at any rate a strong family likeness, and seems almost to betray a common parentage.

Collections of our national ballads have been made at different times. Notable amongst these are Bishop Percy's ' Reliques,' Evans's ' Old Ballads, Historical and Narrative,' and Ritson's ' Ancient Songs from the time of Henry III.'

Pinkerton, Jamieson and Finlay have collected the Scottish Ballads ; and Sir Walter Scott has immortalised the ' Minstrelsy of the Scottish Border.'

ILKLEY COLLEGE, YORKSHIRE,
25th July, 1892.

LIFE OF ABRAHAM HOLROYD.

By WILLIAM SCRUTON,

AUTHOR OF "THE BIRTHPLACE OF CHARLOTTE BRONTË;" "PEN
AND PENCIL PICTURES OF OLD BRADFORD;" ETC.

THE following article. from the pen of Mr. Scruton. appeared in the
" Bradford Weekly Telegraph " for January 7th, 1888, and by Mr.
Scruton's kind permission it is reproduced in these pages.

" There are few names in the modern literary annals of Yorkshire
more familiar than that which forms the subject of the present sketch,
and no apology can therefore be necessary for the prominence which is
given to it in this issue of the · Weekly Telegraph.'

" Stern death. which comes at last to all. came on Sunday
morning last to a · worthy' whose name will be bound up in the
history of Bradford as long as that history endures. But the · dread
angel ' had no terrors for Abraham Holroyd. His religion (for he was
profoundly religious) was of a practical kind that gave him much
happiness in life, and brought him consolation and courage when face
to face with death. And now · After life's fitful fever he sleeps well.'

" It has been my pleasure and privilege too, to be intimately
acquainted with Mr. Holroyd for more than a quarter of a century.
In my own antiquarian pursuits I have often been indebted to him for
guidance and help, which were ever given freely and unstintedly. for
he was indeed generous to a fault. As the years rolled on, the
acquaintanceship gave place to a close and enduring friendship, and as
a friend I found him firm and true.

" Mr. Holroyd's career had been an eventful and interesting one,
and while in conversation with him he sometimes let fall snatches of it,
enough to satisfy me that it was one well worthy of being · placed on
record.' When I first ventured to hint this to him he did not seem to
fall in with it very cordially. but after a while he broached the subject
himself, and, to my delight, said that, as soon as he could find time, he

would sit down and write out, to the best of his ability, and the powers of his memory, the story of his life. The making of a promise was with Mr. Holroyd as good as its fulfilment, for he was ever a 'man of his word.' And so it came to pass that, after a little patient waiting, I had put into my hands one day a well-written manuscript in Mr. Holroyd's handwriting, of which the following is a copy.

"I was born at the village of Clayton, near Bradford, on the 2nd of April, 1815. My father's name was Isaac Holroyd, and he was born and brought up at a place called Storres, near Thornton Heights. My mother was descended from the Barkers of Clayton on the father's side, and on that of the mother from the Northorps of Bradford-dale. They were both handloom weavers, and as soon as my legs were long enough to reach the treadles they set me to work at the same employment. I received no education at school except one summer my grandfather Holroyd paid threepence a week for me, when I learnt to read. This was at the old Village School, Clayton. My parents were too poor to do anything, as they had four little ones all younger than myself, yet though we were so poor, our family was very much respected and I never knew of anyone saying a bad word of any of us. I picked up my skill in writing at home, practising from slips or copies set for me by a cousin. When I was seventeen years of age I began to pen short poems and rhymes, and these being very much admired, Mr. Wardman, of Bradford, printed a few of them in 1834. In the meantime my father died, and I, still working as a weaver, was employed first by Mr. J. Ackroyd, of Halifax, and then by Mr. Richard Fawcett, of Bradford. Wages, however, in 1836, had become so low that I determined to enter the army and give up weaving. I had been pulled off sixpence a time in six weeks, and so on the 5th of November of that year I enlisted at Leeds into the 32nd Regiment of Foot, then stationed at Montreal, in Canada. On the next day I was sworn before a magistrate at Leeds, and in a day or two I was sent off with others by way of steam packet at Hull to London. Afterwards I was sent by packet to Plymouth to join the depôt of my regiment. Here in the George's Square Barracks I learnt my drill, and in June, 1837, started in the barque Rajah for Quebec, Capt. Birtwhistle—a Skipton man—in command of about a hundred of us recruits.

"When at home in Clayton I had only been able to buy about four books, and these were small volumes for the pocket, with one exception. The books were 'Ossian's Poems,' 'Burns' Poems,' 'Franklin's Works,' and 'The Pilgrim's Progress.' The large book was 'Pope's Works,' with Homer's Iliad and Odyssy. I found some of the recruits on board the ship great scholars. One of them had been educated at Queen's College, Dublin, and he was a man of prodigious memory. On the long and dreary voyage he taught me much for which I am truly thankful. But he was, alas! though the best of friends, a slave to drink.

"At the end of July we reached the St. Lawrence, and passing Quebec were sent on by steamboat to Montreal. I was placed in the 4th Company, and had scarcely got settled ere the news of the death of William the Fourth arrived and the accession of Queen Victoria announced. Troubles were brewing in the Legislature of the Colony and open rebellion was threatened. In January I was sent, along with thirteen others, to secure a bridge over the St. John's River, north of Montreal. Here we stayed two weeks, then met with some rebels at St. Eustache, and a force having come up, an attack was made, and the wooden church and nearly the whole town was burnt to the ground, as well as Grand Brule, another large village. We then returned with almost a hundred prisoners to Montreal, where many of them were executed. My comrade and bed-fellow during the cold weather was shot in the forehead and killed. At the beginning of this action I was told off to the ammunition guard. As soon as we got to Montreal my company was ordered off to Upper Canada, and we travelled in sleighs, with horses, post haste on the ice to Lake Ontario, where we took a steamer for Kingston, but only stayed there long enough to give a man a hundred lashes with the cat o' nine tails for smashing his musket when drunk in a sleigh. Taking steamer again, we were soon at Toronto. From thence we sailed to Hamilton. Thence in sleighs to Ancaster and Brantford. Here arrests were daily made of rebels, the whole being lodged in the jail of that town—I doing duty every second day and night. After the trials were over thirteen men were hanged one morning on one scaffold—a sickening sight. A few days after my company marched to St. Thomas, and the rebellion being ended we were quiet for a time. A lady whom I had befriended by getting her an interview with her husband—a prisoner—met me in the street and with great kindness introduced me to the best people in the place. Her husband had been acquitted as innocent. A gentleman, a friend of hers, offered to advance me £25 to buy my discharge from the army. I to attend a sick son of his for a year and drive him about in their carriage. I therefore bought my discharge, but before the end of the year the young man died, and my master sold all his property and emigrated to Illinois, I going with him and his wife to drive and help in anything that might be needed. On passing through Michigan I took the ague from the swampy state of the land at that time, and in a while, when the summer came on, I became very ill. I was advised to go south to get quit of the ague, and my master, having been appointed Probate Judge of the County, I was sorry to leave Rockford, the place where he had 'settled.' Sick and salivated with quinine I started on foot to Chicago—then a town of only one street.

Striking south I tramped towards the Mississippi river, and after
many days of travelling through that lonely state, I arrived at Peoria,
and found a small steamer ready to sail down to St. Louis. Going on
board I got to that city after much delay, caused by the low state of
the water. Taking steamer at St. Louis I got to New Orleans in
eight days, with two dollars in my pocket, which however, were stolen
that night from my clothes (though under my pillow) at the house
where I had put up to lodge. There I was then, in a strange city, sick,
and with no money. The landlord of the lodging-house advised me
to go to the Charity Hospital until I got well. I went and was
admitted. In eight days I was discharged cured, and left to seek a
living—I knew not where. For three days I had nothing to eat except
some bits of apples which had been thrown out from a steamer as
damaged. At night I hid myself away in new buildings in the course
of erection. On the fourth day a gentleman gave me a job to help in
removing his furniture, and I pleased him so that he offered me money:
as much as I might need until I could get some settled employment.
I took an empty room, furnished it, and in about two months obtained
regular employment with a respectable firm of merchants. There was
always plenty for me to do, for at least the winter half of the year.
My leisure hours I spent in studies, reading the best books I could
borrow, and watching the manners of the people amongst whom my
lot seemed to be cast.

"In the previous years I had gained much knowledge of mankind,
and the earth-mounds of the west had interested me much, and
created in me a love of the ancient in every thing I saw or read of—
hence my love for antiquarian pursuits during the after part of my
life. The company I kept was always the best I could find everywhere,
and I found in the American people—both North and South—warm
hands and loving hearts, without one exception, amongst those whom I
became acquainted with, and I shall ever remember both the people
and the country with feelings of sincere affection.

"In 1846 I married Miss Amelia Jenkyn, of St. Stephen's-in-
Bramwell, Cornwall. She had lately come with a relation to the city.
The clergyman who married us was the Rev. Chas. Goodrich, Rector
of St. Paul's, New Orleans. He was a brother of the famous Peter
Parley, the author of books for young people. When I had been
eight years in my situation my health gave way with the heat of the
climate, and I was obliged to resign it. My English doctor told me
that I must return to my native country if I would save my life. I
and Mrs. Holroyd, therefore, took passage home in May, 1851,
and arrived at Liverpool on the 10th July. After a visit to the
great exhibition, London, we proceeded to Cornwall, where Mrs.
Holroyd remained with her parents for a time, while I went forward

to Bradford to establish myself in some business. For some time after my arrival in this town my cousin, John Tyas, gave me a home with him. He resided at the top of Westgate, and I soon got a shop—some four yards square—opposite the old Zoar Chapel. Here I started business in real good earnest. Mr. William Cook, of Vicar Lane, supplied me with most of what I needed in the way of stationery, periodicals, &c., and the newspapers I got from the publishers. This was in October, 1851. In 1853-54 I published by subscription a large view of Saltaire, but when the engraving was ready, after six months' delay, many of the subscribers were dead or gone away, and I was some £15 short of paying the £63 due for the engraving and printing of it. In my dilemma I wrote to Sir (then Mr.) Titus Salt, and he sent for me, and after I had told him of my luck, he gave me a cheque for the engraver and printer, and I handed over to him all the money I had received. This was my first introduction to Mr. Salt, and ever after he stood by me in whatever I took up. He was to me ever a staunch and true friend. With the shop I had terrible hard struggling to keep my head above water, and my little family increasing, it was at the time fearful hard uphill work, as we say in Yorkshire. In 1854, I determined to strike out in a new direction in the way of publishing. I printed " Eldwick Glen," a crude poem of my own, and soon sold them all. This made me better known, and helped my custom with the new acquaintance.

" The few literary men then in Bradford called on me, such as John James, Ben Preston, Edward Sloane, Stephen Fawcett, Edward Collinson, and a host of others, whose names would fill a column. Here, about the year 1858, I compiled a little book with the quaint title of " Spice Islands passed in the Sea of Reading." This took well also ; and thus encouraged, I took heart, and began to push in the newspapers every good work going on in Bradford, praising the literary efforts of my townsmen, and when opportunity occurred I drew attention to the antiquities of my beloved town of Bradford, and the surrounding district. Almost everything I wrote had my full name at the end. I also tried to give the chapter and verse for all that I sent, for my chief ambition was to be understood by the common people.

" I now began as publisher and editor in earnest. The following is a pretty full list of my projects :—' The Cottage in the Wood,' by the Rev. Patrick Brontë, 1859. ' T' Spicy Man,' ' T' Creakin' Gate,' ' Natterin' Nan,' ' T'Maister o' t' Haase,' these all in 1859, and by my friend Ben Preston. Then ' The Philosophy of Lord Bacon,' by John James, F.S.A. ' The Life of Joseph Lister, of Bradford,' and ' The Rider of the White Horse,' 1860. In this year I began the ' Bradford Historical Almanack,' which I continued for six years. I also in 1860 October started ' The Bradfordian.' (a repository of local talent,) which came out for 27 months, when I was forced to stop, as its publication was bringing me to poverty and heaping difficulties on me pecuniarily. This work gave me the most pleasure of anything I ever did in my life. It brought me into contact with the best men and women of the time then in Bradford and the vicinity. In 1863 I published ' The Physical Geography of Bradford,' &c., by Louis Miall. Also in 1864 the ' Poems and songs of Ben Preston.' These sold off at once, and made me acquainted with the Rev. S. Baring-Gould, and he asked me to assist him in collecting for his book, the Yorkshire Oddities,' which I did. I also had much to write to and for the late Thomas Wright, F.S.A. I then proposed the publishing of my ' Collectanea,' and My good friend the late Sir Titus Salt promised to stand by me until I chose to stop. This he did. For what occurred after this had gone on for some time, see my introduction to the said ' Collectanea,' which I was not able to complete in book form until 1873. After removing to Saltaire I wrote the little work, ' Saltaire and its Founder ' of which there have been sold four editions of, in all, 3,500 copies. Nearly all my others were 1,000 editions, named previously. I wish to add that the people of Bradford, in 1868, presented me with gifts on leaving for Saltaire.

HARMONY COTTAGE.

"In 1873 I edited and published at Saltaire also ' A Garland of Poetry by Yorkshire Authors ' (collected specimens of nearly a hundred writers of my native county), a work which has been greatly admired. I dedicated it to my dear friend Mr. George Ackroyd.

" In 1874. old age creeping on. I retired from business to Eldwick on a small income. where I hope to spend the few remaining days of my life in peace. and in preparation for the entry into another and a better life.

* * * * * *

" Little remains to be added to this simple story of a well-spent life. During his brief residence at Eldwick in the small but comfortable house which he had built there (which. by the way. he thought of calling the ' Hermitage.' but finally gave it the more appropriate name ' Harmony Cottage ') he employed himself in cultivating his bit of garden ; corresponding with literary friends, and in contributing to local and other journals choice articles from his rich archæological treasure-house. The old love of country was strong within him. and here he found pure nature in her various aspects.

His books were rivers. woods and skies.
The meadow and the moor.

" The summit of Gilstead Moor was. however. too cold and exposed for Mrs. Holroyd, who was a native of Cornwall. and Harmony Cottage had to be abandoned as a place of residence. Of late years Mr. and Mrs. Holroyd resided with a married daughter— Mrs. Thornton—at Shipley. and here it was that the venerable author and antiquary closed his career, happily surrounded with every comfort. His spirit passed away to the ' Better Land ' as peacefully and as quietly

' As the dawn glides into day.'

" Much of the good work done by Mr. Holroyd in literature and archæology is not alluded to in the narrative that he has left us of his career. He was too modest a man to say much of himself, and moreover he laboured more to exalt others than himself. Many other of his literary ventures might be mentioned if space allowed. But perhaps this were needless. for are they not already chronicled in the annals of Yorkshire literature ? As a publisher he was most industrious. but as a writer hardly less so.

" From the stores of a ripe intellect and with a well informed mind, he contributed many interesting papers to local journals.

" If from his restricted means he was unable to take great projects in hand, he was untiring in his efforts to do everything that fairly came within his grasp. hence there is scarcely a chapter of local history with which the name of Abraham Holroyd is not associated.

" Mr. Holroyd possessed a keen and intelligent appreciation of good poetry. An ardent admirer of our English ballads, he collected during a long course of years, nearly three hundred choice ballads and songs belonging to Yorkshire alone.

"Mr. Holroyd was a genuine antiquary, but not of the type that sees no merit in a book beyond its antiquity or scarcity. He was too liberal-minded to believe that a book is valueless because it might not happen to be one of a first edition, or that its real worth is depreciated by its abundance or its free and unrestricted circulation among the book-reading public. For the good work that he has done in popularising, by means of cheap reprints, works of a scarce and costly character, he is deserving of public gratitude.

———

"The remains were interred on Wednesday in the burial ground of St. John's Church, Clayton. The funeral, which was of a semi-private character, was only attended by the deceased's most intimate friends. A short service was conducted at the residence, prior to leaving for Clayton, by Mr. Mitchell, a member of the New Church (Swedenborgian), Saltaire, of which Mr. Holroyd was one of the founders. Shortly before one o'clock the *cortege* left for Clayton, and was attended by the Rev. Mr. Rendell (Bradford), and Messrs. Dyson, Armitage, and Stephenson, representing the New Church at Saltaire; and a few local antiquarians, including Mr. W. Scruton, Mr. Wm. Cudworth, and Mr. J. H. Turner. The coffin was made of polished pitch pine, and was borne by a hearse, followed by mourning coaches containing the relatives of the deceased. Mr. T. T. Empsall, the president of the Bradford Historical and Antiquarian Society, and a number of Clayton friends, joined in the procession at that place. The burial service was performed at the church and at the grave side by the Rev. J. E. Gerrard. A beautiful floral cross was placed on the coffin by Mr. George Ackroyd, one of the deceased's oldest friends."

PLACE BALLADS.

Sheffield is a Wonderful Town, O!

Air—*All among the leaves so green, O!*

LADIES and gentles all,
I am ready at your call,
To sing a little song,
And I will not keep you long,
  About the sights of this wonderful town, O!
In Sheffield's praise, tune my lays,
For what 'tis famed shall soon be named,
I'll tell, don't doubt it, all about it,
    Hey down, ho down, derry derry down,
    Sheffield is a wonderful town, O!

For cutlery so famed
None with Sheffield can be named,
Where the people all their lives,
Are making razors, scissors, knives,
  In this very wonderful town, O!
Lots of files, all in piles;
Stones go round, razors ground;
Friday quick, goes boring stick;
Saturday get your pay,
Then regale yourselves with ale.
    Hey down, etc.

Next the market-place survey,
When round comes the market day;
And there such sights you'll see
That, with me, you will agree,
  This Sheffield is a wonderful town, O!
Lots of stalls against the walls,
Make your rambles through the shambles,
Beef and mutton, stuff a glutton,
Butchers cry, 'Who'll buy?'
Dogs and asses, pretty lasses,
If you gain Campo-lane,
Neville's ale, bright and pale,
You will find to your mind.
    Hey down, etc.

B 2

Next a lawyer 'mongst you came,
Lawyer Applebee, his name,
He could get you all estates,
Fill your pockets and your plates,
    For the good of this wonderful town, O !
Points of law, well did draw,
House and land did understand;
Took the chaise various ways
Law profession took possession,
With a nod took up a sod,
In he lets, sweepy bets,
Gets your brass, then, alas !
Off he waddles, then he schedules,
    Hey down, etc.

In the church-yard all the people
Are gazing at the steeple,
Where the man, to point the spire,
Is each moment getting higher.
    To amuse you in this wonderful town, O !
From the crate shows his pate,
See him climb, with stone and lime,
' Lord ! how high,' people cry,
I'd rather he was there than me ;
By gauls, if he falls.
    Hey down, etc.

Last the playhouse in this street,
Where your favourites you greet,
And where actors, funny folks,
Make you laugh with cracking jokes
    For the joy of this wonderful town, O !
Act away, all so gay.
Sights so funny, for your money,
Believe not me, but come and see :
Bell ringing, actor singing,
Then you roar encore,
    Hey down, ho down, derry derry down,
    Sheffield is a wonderful town, O !

This song was written in the early part of the present century.
and is preserved in a three-volume work, entitled : " The Universal
Songster, or museum of mirth." No date, but printed at the Ballan-

tine Press, Edinburgh, by Ballantine and Hanson. It would appear
to have been originally published in parts, and every part is illustrated
on the front by George and Robert Cruikshank. The song was evidently intended to be sung on the stage ; hence the allusions to local
matters and local persons.

Mother Shipton.

To the tune of *Nancy Dawson*.

Of all the pretty pantomimes
That have been seen or sung in rhymes,
Since famous Johnny Rich's times,
    There's none like Mother Shipton.
She pleases folks of every class,
She makes her swans and ducklings pass,
She shows her hog, she shows her ass,
    Oh, charming Mother Shipton !

Near to the famous dropping well,
She first drew breath, as records tell,
And had good beer and ale to sell
    As ever tongue was tipt on :
Her dropping well itself is seen,
Quaint goblins hobble round their queen,
And little fairies tread the green,
    Called forth by Mother Shipton.

Oh, London is a charming place,
Yet grumble not ye critick race,
Tho' Mansion House is seen to grace
    The streets in Mother Shipton.
You think a blunder you decry,
Yet you might see with half an eye
'Tis Mother Shipton's prophecy,
    Oh, charming Mother Shipton.

Come, jolly tars and sailors staunch,
Oh, come with us and see the launch,
'Twill feast your eyes, and fill your paunch,
    As done by Mother Shipton,

The shores give way, the hulk that prop—
Huzza ! the ship is launched—and pop !
'Tis turned into a baker's shop,
    Oh, charming Mother Shipton.

Then after several wonders past,
To Yorkshire all return at last,
And in a coal pit they are cast,
    Oh, wondrous Mother Shipton,
Yet she redeems them every soul :
And here's the moral of the whole—
'Tis Mother Shipton brings the coal,
    Oh, charming Mother Shipton.

It is difficult, at this day, to understand some of the allusions in the above ballad. It is quite possible they may be explained in some of the prophecies attributed to her pen or tongue. Dr. Ingledew appends this note to the song :—" Tradition tells us that near the Dropping Well, at Knaresborough, this famous sybil was born, about the year 1487. She married Tobias Shipton, a carpenter, of Shipton, near York, and from this match derived the name of Mother Shipton. Many tales of her skill in futurity are still related in the country ; the whole of which, including a series of succeeding events, are stated to have been delivered to the Abbott of Beverley, as in the following :—

    " A maiden queen full many a year,
    Shall England's warlike sceptre bear."

Spoken of Queen Elizabeth, that was beloved by her subjects, and dreaded by her enemies, above forty years.

    " The western monarch's wooden horses.
    Shall be destroyed by Drake's forces."

The King of Spain's mighty armada in 1588 was destroyed by the English Fleet.

    " Triumphant death rides London through,
    And men on tops of houses go."

The first line points to the great plague in London in 1665 : the second to the great fire in the year after.

This famous prophetess died in the fifty-ninth year of her age, and fulfilling her own prediction even to the day and the hour. On her tomb was placed this epitaph :—

    Here lies she who seldom ly'd,
    Whose skill so often has been try'd,
    Her prophesies shall still survive,
    And ever keep her name alive.

Æthelgiva.

A LEGENDARY BALLAD OF WHITBY ABBEY.

BY WILLIAM WATKINS.

———

" HERE may'st thou rest, my sister dear,
  Securely here abide ;
Here royal Edelfleda lived,
  Here pious Hilda died.

" Here peace and quiet ever dwell :
  Here fear no rude alarms :
Nor here is heard the trumpet's sound,
  Nor here the din of arms !"

With voice composed and look serene,
  (Whilst her soft hand he press'd,
The maid who trembled on his arm,
  Young Edwy thus address'd.

Blue gleam'd the steel in Edwy's hand,
  The warrior's vest he bore :
For now the Danes by Hubba led,
  Had ravaged half the shore.

His summons at the Abbey gate
  The ready porter hears ;
And soon in veil and holy garb,
  The Abbess kind appears.

" O take this virgin to thy care,
  Good angels be your guard :
And may the saints in heaven above
  That pious care reward.

" For we by fierce barbarian hands
  Are driven from our home :
And three long days and nights forlorn,
  The dreary wastes we roam.

" But I must go—these towers to save ;
  Beneath the evening shade,
I haste to seek Earl Osrick's power,
  And call Lord Redwald's aid."

He said—and turn'd his ready foot ;
  The Abbess nought replies ;
But with a look that spoke her grief,
  To heaven upcast her eyes.

Then turning to the stranger dame—
  " O welcome to this place :
For never Whitby's holy fane
  Did fairer maiden grace."

And true she said—for on her cheek
  Was seen young beauty's bloom,
Though grief, with slow and wasting stealth,
  Did then her prime consume.

Her shape was all that thought can frame,
  Of elegance and grace ;
And heav'n the beauties of her mind
  Reflected in her face.

" My daughter, lay aside thy fears,"
  Again the matron cry'd,
" No Danish ravishers come here,"
  Again the Virgin sigh'd.

The Abbess saw, the Abbess knew,
  'Twas love that shook her breast ;
And thus, in accents soft and mild,
  The mournful maid addrest.

" My daughter dear, as to thy friend,
  Be all thy care confest :
I see 'tis love disturbs thy mind,
  And wish to give thee rest.

" But hark ! I hear the vesper bell,
  Now summons us to prayer :
That duty done, with needful food
  Thy wasted strength repair."

But now the pitying mournful muse
  Of Edwy's hap shall tell ;
And what amid his nightly walk,
  That gallant youth befell.

For journeying by the bank of Esk
  He took his lonely way ;
And now through showers of driving rain
  His erring footsteps stray.

At length, from far, a glimmering light
  Trembled among the trees :
And entering soon a moss-built hut,
  A holy man he sees.

" O father, deign a luckless youth
  This night with thee to shield :
I am no robber, though my arm
  This deadly weapon wield."

" I fear no robber, stranger, here,
  For I have nought to lose :
And thou may'st safely through the night
  In this poor cell repose.

" And thou art welcome to my hut,"
  The holy man replied :
" Still welcome here is he whom fate
  Has left without a guide.

" Whence and what art thou, gentle youth ? "
  The noble Edwy said
" I go to rouse Earl Osrick's power.
  And seek Lord Redwald's aid.

" My father is a wealthy lord,
  Who now with Alfred stays ;
And me he left to guard his seat,
  Whilst he his duty pays.

" But vain the hope—in dead of night
  The cruel spoiler came ;
And o'er each neighbouring castle threw
  The wide devouring flame.

" To shun its rage at early dawn,
  I with my sister fled ;
And Whitby's Abbey now affords
  A shelter to her head.

" Whilst I, to hasten promised aids,
  Range wildly through the night,
And, with impatient mind, expect
  The mornings friendly light."

Thus Edwy spoke, and wondering, gazed
  Upon his friendly host,
For in his form beam'd manly grace,
  Untouched by age's frost.

The hermit sigh'd, and thus he said.
    " Know, there was once a day,
This tale of thine would fire my heart,
    And bid me join thy way.

" But luckless love dejects my soul,
    And casts my spirits down ;
Thou seest the wretch of woman's pride,
    Of follies not my own.

" I once amid my sovereign's train
    Was a distinguish'd youth.
But blighted in my former fame,
    By sorrow's cankering tooth.

" When Etheldred the crown did hold,
    I to this district came :
And then a fair and matchless maid
    First raised in me a flame.

" Her father was a noble lord,
    Of an illustrious race,
Who joined to rustic honesty
    The courtiers gentle grace.

" 'Twas then I told my artless tale,
    By love alone inspired :
For never was my honest speech
    In flattering guise attired.

" At first she heard, or seem'd to hear,
    The voice of tender love :
But soon, the ficklest of her sex,
    Did she deceitful prove.

" She drove me scornful from her sight,
    Rejected and disdain'd :
In vain did words for pity plead,
    In vain my looks complain'd.

" How could that breast which pity fill'd,
    Ever relentless be ?
How could that face which smiled on all,
    Have ever frowns for me ?

" Since that fell hour I in this cell
    Have lived recluse from man ;
And twice ten months have pass'd since I
    The hermits life began."

" O stain to honour ! Edwy cry'd ;
   O foul disgrace to arms !
What, when thy country claims thy aid,
   And shakes with wars alarms,

Cans't thou, inglorious, here remain,
   And strive thyself to hide :
Assume the Monkish coward life,
   All for a woman's pride ? "

With louder voice and warmer look.
   The hermit host rejoin'd,
" Think'st thou vain youth, the chains of fear
   Could here a warrior hold.

" Know boy, thou seest Hermanrick here :
   Well vers'd in war's alarms :
A name once not unknown to fame,
   Nor unrenown'd in arms.

" O Athelgiva ! (yet how dear,
   Did I thy danger know :
Yet would I fly to thy relief,
   And crush th' invading foe."

With fluster'd cheek, young Edwy turn'd,
   At Athelgiva's name :
And " Gracious powers ! it must be he ! "
   He cries, " It is the same !

I know full well, I have not now
   More of thy tale to learn ;
I heard this morn, ere from the wave,
   You could the Sun discern.

" My sister loves thee, gallant youth,
   By all the saints on high !
She wept last night, when thy hard fate
   She told with many a sigh.

" Forgive her then, and in her cause
   Thy limbs with steel enfold !
Was it not Ardolph's daughter, say,
   Who late thy heart did hold ? "

" It was, it was ! Hermanrick cried ;
   I heard her brother's name ;
'Tis said he was a gallant youth,
   Who sought abroad for fame."

Then Edwy sprang to his embrace,
    And clasp'd him to his breast :
" And thou shalt be my brother, too,"
    He said, and look'd the rest.

" But now let honour fill thy mind,
    Be love's soft laws obey'd :
'Tis Athelgiva claims thy sword,
    'Tis she demands thy aid.

" She, with impatient anxious heart,
    Expects thy quick return :
And till again she sees me safe,
    The hapless maid will mourn.

" Then let us fly to seek these chiefs,
    Who promised aid to send :
Earl Osrick was my father's guest,
    Lord Redwald is my friend."

Hermanrick said, " First let us go
    To cheer yon drooping maid ;
Again, I'll wear my canker'd arms,
    Again, I'll draw my blade."

Then from a corner of the cell
    His clashing arms appear ;
But when he mark'd the growing rust,
    The warrior dropt a tear.

Then forth they went—Hermanrick knew
    Each pathway of the wood :
And safe before the Abbey gate
    At break of day they stood.

Now sleep the wearied maiden's eyes
    At length had kindly seal'd,
When at the gate the wandering knights
    Returning day reveal'd.

" Quick, call the Abbess," Edwy said,
    To him who kept the door,
Who watched and prayed the live long night,
    A pious priest and poor.

The Abbess came with instant haste :
    Th' alarming bell was rung ;
And from their matted homely beds
    The sainted virgins sprung.

Fair Athelgiva first the dame,
  Soft speaking, thus address :
My daughter, an important call
  Commands me break thy rest.

" Thy brother at the Abbey gate,
  Appears with features glad ;
And with him comes a stranger knight,
  In war-worn armour clad."

With faltering step and bloodless cheek,
  Young Athelgiva went ;
Confusion, shame, surprise, and joy,
  At once her bosom rent.

When in the stranger knight she saw
  Hermanrick's much-loved face :
Whilst he by generous love impelled
  Rush'd to her fond embrace.

Fain would the muse attempt to paint
  What joy the lover knew,
Who found his long disdainful maid
  At once, fair, kind, and true.

Then Edwy, while entranced in bliss
  The happy pair remained,
Recounted o'er the tale, how he
  Hermanrick lost regained.

But soon, alas ! too soon, was heard,
  To damp their new form'd joys,
The groan of death, the shout of war,
  The battle's mingled noise.

For up the hill, with eager haste,
  A breathless courier came ;
He cries, prepare for dire alarms,
  And shun the approaching flame.

Fierce Hubba, landing on the beach,
  Now drives our feeble band :
Who, far too few to stop his force,
  Fly o'er the crimson'd sand.

What anguish filled the maiden's breast,
  What rage the lover knew,
When looking down the steepy hill,
  They found the tale was true,

Each warlike youth then grasp'd his spear,
  The trembling damsel said.
" O where is now Earl Osrick's power,
  And where Lord Redwald's aid ? "

" Alas, alas ! " the Abbess cries,
  " Far as my sight is borne,
I cannot see the ruddy cross,
  Nor hear Earl Osrick's horn."

Stern Hubba now to direful deeds
  Impell'd his savage crew ;
And o'er the blood empurpled strand
  The golden raven flew.[1]

" Behold," he cries, and waves his lance,
  Where yon proud turrets rise ;
Of those who prove war's glorious toil,
  Let beauty be the prize.

" There gold and beauty both are found,
  Then follow where I lead ;
And quickly know you have not fought
  For honour's empty meed."

He said, and press'd to gain the hill,
  His shouting train pursue ;
And fired by hopes of brutal joys,
  Behold the prize in view.

Young Edwy mark'd their near approach,
  And rushed to oppose their way :
Nor did, with equal ardour fired,
  Behind Hermanrick stay.

Like mountain boars the brother chiefs
  On Denmark's warriors flew ;
And those who held the foremost ranks,
  Their fury overthrew.

Soon pierc'd by Edwy's fatal lance,
  Lay Valiant Turkil here,
There Hardicanute bit the dust,
  Beneath Hermanrick's spear.

But vain is courage, strength, or skill,
  When two oppose an host ;
A dart with sure and deadly aim,
  At Edwy Hubba tost.

His sister, who o'erpower'd by grief,
  Had fainted on the floor,
Recover'd by the matron's care,
  Now sought the Abbey door.

When on the fatal carnaged spot,
  She cast her weeping eyes :
"O blessed Mary !" cries the maid,
  "My brother bleeds and dies."

Then forth she ran and gained the place :
  Where press'd by crowds of foes,
Hermanrick stood—the shades of death
  Her brother's eyelids close.

The furious Dane nor pity knew,
  Nor stayed his vengeful arm :
Nor ought avails that heavenly face,
  Which might a tiger charm.

First on th' unguarded chief he rush'd,
  And bore him to the ground :
The helpless damsel's plaint of woe,
  In war's loud shout is drown'd.

She saw Hermanrick's quivering lips,
  She mark'd his rolling eye ;
She faints, she falls ; before her sight
  Death's visions dimly fly.

" And, O thou dear and much lov'd youth,"
  The dying virgin cried ;
" Howe'er in life I wrong'd thy truth,
  Yet true with thee I died."

She spoke no more—e'en Hubba felt
  The force of love sincere :
Then first his breast confess'd a sigh,
  Then first his cheek a tear.

"And, O my friends, the rage of war,"
  He cries. "Awhile forbear ;
And to their weeping kindred straight,
  These breathless bodies bear."

" Or fear the wrath of Powers Divine,"
  Nor could he further say ;
But quickly with disorder'd march,
  Bent to his ships his way.

For now was heard Earl Osrick's horn,
　Shrill sounding through the dale :
And now Lord Redwald's ruddy cross
　Was waving to the gale.

His tardy aid Earl Osrick brought
　Too late, alas! to save :
And far beyond th' avenging sword
　The Dane now rode the wave.

Grief seized the warriors heart to see
　In dust young Edwy laid :
And stretched by brave Hermanrick's side
　Fair Athelgiva dead.

But on the holy cross he swore
　A brave revenge to take,
On Denmark's proud and bloody sons.
　For Athelgiva's sake.

This vow in Kenworth's glorious field,
　The gallant Earl did pay :
When Alfred's better star prevailed,
　And England had her day.

That day the Dane full dearly paid
　The price of lover's blood ;
That day in Hubba's cloven helm
　The Saxon javelin stood.

The bodies of the hapless three
　A single grave contains,
And in the choir, with dirges dire,
　Are laid their cold remains.

Lord Ardolph on his children's tomb
　Inscribed th' appending verse :
And long the Monk's in gothic rhyme,
　Their story did rehearse.

And often pointing to the skies,
　The cloister'd maids would cry,
" To those bright realms, in bloom of youth,
　Did Athelgiva fly."

　　1. The famous *Reafen*. or Enchanted Standard, in which the
Danes put great confidence. It contained the figure of a raven, which
had been inwoven by the three sisters of Hinguar and Hubba, with
many magical incantations. and which. by its different movements.

prognosticated, as the Danes believed, the good or bad success of any enterprise.

Mr. Ingledew's book, from which I quote, adds as follows :— Oswy, King of Northumberland, being engaged in war with Penda, the Pagan King of Mercia, vowed that if he was victorious, he would dedicate his daughter, Ethelflida, then about one year old, to the service of God in the Monastery Aertesia (Stag Island), of which Lady Hilda, niece of Edwin, first Christian King of Northumberland, was Abbess, and having procured ten hides of land in the place called Strenshalle (Whitby) built, in 657, a Monastery for men and women, dedicated to St. Peter, and Lady Hilda was the first Abbess. This Abbey continued to flourish until 867, when a party of Danes, under Hinguar and Hubba, landed at Dunsley Bay, plundered the country, and destroyed the Monastery. The story, as above, is supposed to begin about this time. (See Appendix Note 1.)

The Barber of Thirsk's Forfeits.

FIRST come, first served—then come not late,
And when arrived keep your sate ;
For he who from these rules shall swerve,
Shall pay his forfeit—so observe.

Who enters here with boots and spurs,
Must keep his nook, for if he stirs,
And gives with armed heel a kick,
A pint he pays for every prick.

Who rudely takes another's turn,
By forfeit glass—may manners learn ;
Who reverentless shall swear or curse,
Must lug seven half-pence from his purse.

Who checks the barber in his tale,
Shall pay for that a gill of yale ;
Who will, or cannot miss his hat
Whilst trimming pays a pint for that.

And he who can but will not pay,
Shall hence be sent half trimmed away ;
For will he—nill he—if in fault,
He forfeit must in meal or malt,
But mark the man who is in drink,
Must the cannikin oh, never, never clink.

As I came through the North countree,
The fashions of the world to see,
I sought for my mery companie,
    To go to the cittie of London :
And when to the cittie of Yorke I came,
I found good companie in the same,
As well disposed to every game
    As if it had been at London.

CHORUS—Yorke, Yorke, for my monie :
        Of all the citties that ever I see,
        For mery pastime and companie,
        Except the cittie of London.

And in that cittie what saw I then ?
Knights, squires, and gentlemen
A-shooting went for matches ten
    As if it had been at London,
And they shot at twenty pounds a bowe,
Besides great cheere they did bestowe,
I never sawe a gallanter showe,
    Except I had been at London,
                Yorke, &c.

These matches, you shall understande,
The Earle of Essex took in hande,
Against the good Earle of Cumberlande,
    As if it had been at London.
And agreede these matches all shall be
For pastime and good companie,
At the cittie of Yorke full merily
    As if it had been in London.
                Yorke, &c.

In Yorke there dwells an alderman, which
Delights in shooting very much,
I never heard of any such
    In all the cittie of London.

His name is Maltbie,[2] mery and wise
At any pastime you can devise,
But in shooting all his pleasure lyes,
   The like was never in London.
                  Yorke, &c.

This Maltbie for the cittie sake,
To shoot (himself) did undertake,
At any good match the Earles would make,
   As well as they do in London.
And he brought to the fields with him,
One Upecke, an archer, proper and trim,
And Smith, that shoote about the pin,
   As if it had been at London.
                  Yorke, &c.

Then came from Cumberlande archers three,
Best bowmen in the North countree,
I will tell you their names what they be
   Well known to the cittie of London.
Walmsley many a man doth knowe,
And Bolton how he draweth his bowe,
And Ratcliffe's shooting long agoe,
   Well known to the cittie of London.
                  Yorke, &c.

And the noble Earl of Essex came
To the field himselfe, to see the same,
Which shall be had for ever in fame,
   As soone as I come at London.
For he showed himselfe so diligent there,
To make a mark and keepe it faire,
It is worthy memorie to declare
   Through all the cittie of London.
                  Yorke, &c.

And then was shooting out of crye,
And skantling at a handfull nie,
And yet the winde was very hie,
   As it is sometimes at London.
They clapt the cloutes so on the ragges,
There was such betting and such bragges,
And galloping up and down with nagges,
   As if it had been at London.
                  Yorke. &c.

And never an archer gave regard
To halfe a bowe and halfe a yarde.
I never see matches go more harde,
    About the cittie of London.
For fairer play was never plaide,
For fairer lays were never laide,
And a week together they kept this trade,
    As if it had been at London.
                Yorke, &c.

The Maior of Yorke [3] with his companie,
Were all in the fields, I warrant ye.
To see good rule kept orderly,
    As if it had been at London.
Which was a dutiful sight to see,
The maior and aldermen there to bee,
For setting forth of archerie
    As well as they do at London.
                Yorke, &c.

And there was neither fault nor fray,
Nor any disorder any way,
But every man did pitch and pay,
    As if it had been at London.
As soon as every match was done,
Every man was paid that won,
And merily up and down dide rome,
    As if it had been at London.
                Yorke, &c.

And never a man that went abroade
But thought his monie well bestowde,
And monie laid in heap and loade,
    As if it had been at London.
And gentlemen there so franke and free,
As a mint at Yorke again should be,
Like shooting did I never see,
    Except I had been at London.
                Yorke, &c.

At Yorke were ambassadours three,
Of Russia—lords of high degree,
This shooting they desirde to see,
    As if it had been at London.

And one desirde to draw a bowe,
The force and strength thereof to know,
And for his delight he drew it so,
　　As seldom seen in London.
　　　　　　　　　　Yorke, &c.

And they did marvaile very much,
There could be any archer such,
To shoote so far the cloute to tutch,
　　Which is no news to London.
And they might well consider than,
An English shaft will kill a man,
As hath been proved where and wan,
　　And chronicled since in London.
　　　　　　　　　　Yorke, &c.

The Earle of Cumberland's archers won
Two matches cleare, ere all was done,
And I made haste a pace to ronne,
　　To carrie these news to London.
And Walmsley did the upshot win,
With both his shafts so near the pin,
You could scant have put three fingers in.
　　As if it had been in London.
　　　　　　　　　　Yorke, &c.

I passe not for my monie it cost,
Though some I spent and some I lost,
I wanted neither sod nor roast,
　　As if it had been in London.
For there was plentie of everything,
Redd and fallow deere, for a king,
I never saw so mery shooting,
　　Since first I came from London.
　　　　　　　　　　Yorke, &c.

God save the cittie of Yorke, therefore,
That hath such noble friends in store,
And such good aldermen send them more,
　　And the like good luck at London.
For it is not little joye to see,
When lords and aldermen so agree,
With such according communaltie,
　　God send us the like in London.
　　　　　　　　　　Yorke, &c.

God save the good Earle of Cumberland,
His praise in golden lines shall stande,
That maintains archery through the land,
    As well as they do at London.
Whose noble minde so courteously,
Acquaints himself with the communaltie,
To the glory of his nobilitie,
    I will carrie the praise to London.
                Yorke, &c.

And tell the good Earle of Essex thus,
As he is now young and prosperous,
To use such properties vertuous,
    Deserves great praise in London.
For it is no little joye to see,
When noble youth so gratious bee,
To give their good wills to their countree,
    As well as they do at London.
                Yorke, &c.

Farewell, good cittie of Yorke, to thee,
Tell Alderman Maltbie this from mee,
In print shall this good shooting bee,
    As soone as I come at London.
And many a song will I bestow
On all the musitians that I know,
To sing the praises where they goe,
    Of the cittie of Yorke, in London.
                Yorke, &c.

God save our Queen, and keep our peace,
That our good shooting may increase,
And praying to God let us not cease,
    As well at Yorke as at London.
This all our countree round about,
May have archers good to hit the cloute,
Which England cannot be without,
    No more than Yorke or London.
                Yorke, &c.

God grant that (once) Her Majestie
Would come, her cittie of Yorke to see,
For the comfort great of that countree,
    As well as she doth at London.

Nothing shall bee thought too deare,
To see her highness' person there,
With such obedient love and feare,
As ever she had in London.

                                        Yorke, &c.

(1.) This valuable historic ballad is from a black letter broadside
in the Roxburghe Collection in the British Museum, and has always
been a favourite chap-book history. The butts and the rifle have now
taken the place of the long bow.

(2.) Christopher Maltby, a draper, was Lord Mayor of York in
1583.

(3.) Thomas Appleyard was Lord Mayor of York in 1584.

In a book very kindly lent me by Mr. Robert Power, of Moor-
head, Shipley, I find some valuable information concerning the author
of the above ballad. It occurs in some notes by J. Woodfall Ebsworth,
M.A. *Cantab*, to a reprint by Robert Roberts, Straight Bar Gate,
Boston, Lincolnshire ; an old and very scarce work entitled, "Choyce
Drollery : Songs and Sonnets." Being a Collection of divers excellent
pieces of poetry of several eminent authors. *Never before printed*.
London, printed by J. G. for Robert Pollard, at the Ben. Johnson's
Head, behind the Exchange, and John Sweeting at the Angel in
Popes-Head Alley. 1656. Then follows, "An Antidote Against
Melancholy : Made up in Pills. Compounded of Witty Ballads,
Jovial Songs, and Merry Catches. Printed by *Mer Melancholicus*, to
be sold in London and Westminster. 1661." The first poem in this
latter work is, "The Ex-Ale-tation of Ale," and contains fifty-seven
verses of wit, satire, and praise of that exalting drink. Of this poem
our editor thus writes :—"Notice the characteristic mention of William
Elderton, the Ballad-writer (who died before 1592), in the thirty-third
verse :—

        "For ballads Elderton never had peer ;
    How bent his wit in them, with how merry a gale,
    And with all the sails up, had he been at the cup,
    And washed his beard with a Pot of Good Ale."

Wm. Elderton's "New Yorkshire Song," intituled "Yorke,
Yorke, for my Monie" entered Stationers' Hall, 16 November, 1582,
and afterwards "Imprinted at London by Richard Iones ; dwelling
neere Holboorne : 1584," has the place of honour in the Roxburghe
Collections, being the first ballad in the first volume. It consequently
takes the lead in the valuable "Roxburghe Ballads" of the Ballad
Society, 1869, so ably edited by William Chappell, Esq. F.S.A. It

also formed the commencement of Ritson's Garland : York, 1788. It is believed that Elderton wrote the " excellent Ballad intituled The Constancy of Susanna." R. Coll. I. 60; Bagford, II. 6 ; Pepys, I. 33. 496. A list of others was first given by Ritson, since by W. C. Hazlitt, in his Handbook. p. 177. Elderton's " I enten Stuff ys come to the Town " was reprinted by F. O Halliwell, for the Shakespeare Society, and Drayton alludes to Elderton in Huth's seventy-nine Black Letter Ballads. Elderton had been an actor in 1552 ; his earliest-dated ballad is of 1553, and he had ceased to live by 1592. Camden gives an epitaph of him in regard to his "thirst complaint," which is thus translated :—

> " Dead drunk here Elderton doth lie ;
> Dead as he is, he still is dry :
> So of him it may well be said.
> Here he, but not his thirst, is laid."

A manuscript possessed by Joseph Payne Collier, mentions in further confirmation :—

> " Will Elderton's red nose is famous everywhere
> And many a ballet shows it cost him very dear ;
> In ale, and toast, and spice, he spent good store of coin ;
> You need not ask him twice to take a cup of wine.
> But though his nose was red, his hand was very white,
> In work it never sped, nor took in it delight ;
> No marvel therefore 'tis, that white should be his hand,
> That ballets writ a score, as you well understand."

— —

The Banks O' Morton O' Swale.

———

As autumn poured her teern o'good,
  And woe had ceased to wail,
Ah wandered forth hard by a woode,
  Upon the banks o'Swale.

And there ah spied a lovely nymph,
  Yan that nean could but hail,
Ah said " Sweet lass come take a trip
  Alang the banks o'Swale.

Wi' looks as sweet as angels wear,
  She soon was in the vale,
And ah was walking by my fair,
  Upon the banks o'Swale.

But ah sall ne'er forget that night,
    Whale life or memory fail,
The hours they passed wi' syke delight,
    Upon the banks o'Swale.

They swifter flew than did the stream,
    That murmered on the vale,
For mah enjoyment was extreme,
    Upon the banks o'Swale.

Ah loved that lass as meh life,
    Ah felt to wish her weal,
Ah asked her to become my wife,
    Upon the banks o'Swale.

Wi' looks bespeaking mind intent
    On what ah ardent tell,
E vain ah wooed her to consent
    Upon the banks o'Swale.

Ah kissed, ah pressed her to gi' way—
    But all of no availe :
She had a wooer far away
    Fra the sweet banks o'Swale.

A drinking ranting wretch was hee,
    As ever was out o' hell,
She took his hand and spurned me
    Far fra the banks o'Swale.

But ah ! when years had rolled away
    Ah met a form full frail,
She recognised me that day
    As fra the banks o'Swale.

Said ah full low, " Can this be she,
    This thing of woe and wail,
That ah yance kissed delightfully,
    Upon the banks o'Swale.

O, heavens it was the very one
    Ah met e' that sweet vale,
But ah the every charm was gone,
    Ah saw on't banks o'Swale.

Wi' sorrow stamped on her brow
    She did her mind unveil,
She told me all she had passed through
    Since on the banks o'Swale.

But O, her history how sad,
  Too sad for me to tell,
T'wad mak a heart o' stone to bleed ;
  Ah mourn ye banks o'Swale.

Then ye nymphs that mak sea free
  Wi' laddies that love all,
Ah think of her that went wi' me
  Upon the banks o'Swale.

And spurn syke wooers that wad woo
  Ye to become their wife ;
For knaw 'e this, if ye do
  Ye'd ruined be for life.

This ballad was communicated to C. J. D. Ingledew, Esq. Ph. D.
for his " Ballads and Songs of Yorkshire," by Mr. William Todd, of
Heckmondwike. Morton o'Swale is a pleasant straggling village, in
the parish of Ainderby Steeple, near North Allerton, on the east
bank of the Swale. Lambard, Bede, and other early writers inform
us that Paulinus, the first Archbshop of York, baptised 10,000 persons
in this river in one day. " By cause at that tyme theare weare no
churches or oratorys yet buylt." (See appendix note 2.)

On Leaving York.

By JOSEPH HARDAKER.

FAREWELL, great York, to all thy scenes adieu ?
  Thy scenes far-famed, thy boasted charms I fly;
I leave them all, for beauties ever new,
  Without a murmur, and without a sigh.

True, thou hast charms that may awhile allure
  The wondering eyes to admiration's height :
But these must fade, while Nature shall endure
  And spread her charms in rich effulgence bright.

Here stand, I grant, the works of cunning art,
  Masonic science spreads its grandeur here ;
Grandeur that doth unrivalled charms impart,
  Excelling far what modern hands can rear.

The sculptor's art, the statuary's skill,
  The builder's strength, the pencil too displayed,
May long untold antiquities reveal,
  While their great founders slumber with the dead.

The marble urns and monuments excel
  In solemn state, all that I knew before ;
But these, alas ! alone survive to tell
  A piteous tale—their owners are not more.

Here while I wander through the winding aisles,
  And round these rich stupendous columns stray,
I know full well these venerable piles,
  Will lose their strength, their beauty too decay.

These massive walls, firm in adhesive lime,
  Whose gates clang with reverberating jar,
Have long withstood the wasting hand of time.
  And braved the ruthless ravages of war.

Oft on these battlements and ramparts strong,
  Cheered by the moon, when roused from soft repose,
The faithful sentinel has paced along,
  And watched the movements of invading foes.

Beneath yon battlements in hapless hour,
  When the dark posterns echoed with alarms ;
And round yon ivy-crested tower
  Full oft were heard the clang of Roman arms.

Here first the ancient bold Brigantes dwelt,
  A fierce and warlike, but a scattered race :
Brave and intrepid in the ensanguined field,
  Hardy, expert, and skilful in the chase.

Oft from yon mote, and long-erected mound,
  In proud display the Roman eagles rose,
Whose conquering legions thundering o'er the ground,
  Spreads desolation 'mong her daring foes.

Here lies, of Roman Emperors, the dust,
  Their warlike deeds in fame alone alive :
Of them remains nor monument nor bust,
  The names of their chief works alone survive.

Here many a Saxon, many a Norman lie,
  And many a haughty, proud, insulting Dane,
Whose ruthless cruelty of deepest dye,
  Whose tarnished deeds their country's annals stain.

The change of time, how amply here displayed!
  Earth must to earth, and dust to dust return ;
The hands which once the imperial sceptre swayed,
  Are pent within the boundaries of the urn.

Beneath the rich majestic Minster's dome,
  In silent, dark solemnity is laid,
Within the narrow limits of a tomb,
  Full many a pious, many a reverent head.

And hoary heads are laid in ashes low,
  That gracefully the studded mitre wore :
And hands that once with reverential awe,
  The sacred badge, the pastoral crosier bore.

Grand, truly grand, the venerable piles,
  Sublimely grand, when the sweet organ's sound
In rich gradations sweep along the aisles,
  While vocal choristers are chaunting round.

Fondly the sense with admiration dwells,
  On scenes like these, and traces with surprise
The winding cloisters leading to the cells.
  And views, astonished, towers that climb the skies.

But cities' scenes, with all their pomp and pride,
  Afford not one alluring charm for me :
Their pomp and pageantry I e'er deride,
  And all their gaudy, vain allurements flee.

Fair Nature's charms surpass the power of art
  Unknown to moth, and uneffaced with rust,
Its pleasing scenes will ecstacy impart,
  When these great towers are crumbled into dust.

Give me the cot, erected on the green,
  To pomp, and pride, and luxury, unknown,
Where pass my moments tranquil and serene,
  In peaceful rest and solitude alone.

Far from the noise and bustle of the great,
  The crush of crowds, the fearful clang of arms ;
Far more delightful is the lone retreat,
  Far more inviting are the village charms.

Free is the air where gentle breezes blow,
  And bright the beverage of the crystal spring ;
Calm is the covert where the hazels bow,
  Where hawthorns bloom, and woodland concerts ring.

There let me dwell. to busy life unknown,
   Where Nature's charms promiscuously blend,
To breathe the fragrance of the florid lawn,
   And share the solace of a social friend.

I have not been able to gather much information regarding the
author of the above lines. They are selected from " Poems, Lyric
and Moral, on various subjects. By Joseph Hardaker, Bradford.
Printed for the author, and sold by T. Inkersley, Bridge Street, 1822."
In 1830, Mr. Aked, of Keighley, printed for him " The Aerapteron ;
or Steam Carriage." To these was added in 1831. " The Bridal of
Tomar and other poems : " printed by Charles Crabtree, of Keighley.
The titles of some of the poems are very curious, as " An Epistle to
my Lady's Lap Dog. Pompey." " To the Author's Fine Collection of
Walking Sticks : or Bundle of Crutches." which last, it appears, were
necessary to him. He lived at Haworth, and it must be noted that all
the Brontë's family were then residing in the village, and probably
knew him. A friend informs me that Mr. Hardaker, during his life,
tried almost every sect of religionists, and that he finally became a
Roman Catholic, and died in that ancient faith. (See Appendix Note 3.)

The Lover's Bridge, near Whitby.

This bridge is beautifully situated amongst the romantic scenery
of the Cleveland Hills, about ten miles west of the town of Whitby.
It consists of an elegant single arch spanning the small river Esk at
the east end of Glaisdale, and almost within a stone's throw of the
North Yorkshire and Cleveland Branch of the North-Eastern Railway,
which crosses the Esk near to where the latter is joined by the Glaisdale Beck. There is a legendary tale told regarding the origin of this
bridge, which is graphically described in the following beautiful lines
of Mrs. George Dawson. A lover was trying to cross the Esk to pay
a farewell visit to his sweetheart on the eve of his departure to a
foreign land, but the river being very much flooded at the time, he was
reluctantly compelled to give up the attempt :—

They talk of dales and hills in Wales
   As the loveliest in our isle :
But the Yorkshire dells and rocky fells,
Where the bright sunbeams on the sparkling streams
   Are all forgot the while,

You may roam for hours 'mid sweet spring flowers,
   With a gurgling beck beneath,
Whilst a rustling breeze just parts the trees
And reveals the sweep of the wild woods deep
   Shut in the darkling heath.

You may hear the note of the blackbird float
   From the top of each tall ash tree,
When he pours his song each evening long :
For in " true love " tales such romantic dales,
   Must needs abundant be.

The dalesmen say that their light archway
   Is due to an Egton man,
Whose love was tried by a whelming tide.
I heard the tale in its native vale,
   And thus the legend ran :—

" Why lingers my loved one ?   Oh ! why does he roam
On the last winter's evening that hails him at home ?
He promised to see me once more ere he went,
But the long rays of gloaming all lonely I've spent—
The stones at the fording no longer I see—
Ah ! the darkness of night has concealed them from me."

The maiden of Glaisdale sat lonely at eve,
And the cold stormy night saw her hopelessly grieve ;
But when she looked forth from her casement at morn,
The maiden of Glaisdale was truly forlorn !
For the stones were engulphed where she looked for them
      last
By the deep swollen Esk that rolled rapidly past ;
And vainly she strove with her tear-bedimmed eye
The pathway she gazed on last night to descry.
Her lover had come to the brink of the tide,
And to stem its swift current repeatedly tried ;
But the rough whirling eddy still swept him ashore,
And relentlessly bade him attempt it no more.

Exhausted he climbed the steep side of the brae,
And looked up the dale ere he turned him away ;
Ah ! from her far window a light flickered dim,
And he knew she was faithfully watching for him.

I go to seek my fortune, love,
  In a far, far distant land ;
And without thy parting blessing, love,
  I am forced to quit the strand.

But over Arncliffe's brow, my love,
  I see thy twinkling light ;
And when deeper waters part us, love,
  'Twill be my beacon light.

If fortune ever favour me,
  Saint Hilda ! hear my vow !
No lover again in my native plain,
  Shall be thwarted as I am now.

One day I'll come to claim my bride,
  As a worthy and wealthy man !
And my well-earned gold shall raise a bridge
  Across the torrent's span.

The rover came back from a far distant land,
And he claimed of the maiden her long-promised hand ;
But he built, ere he won her, the bridge of his vow,
And the lover's of Egton pass over it now.

In writing of this Ballad Mr. William Andrews, of Hull, relates
as follows :—"Mrs. Dawson, in her charming lines, has not given an
altogether correct version of the story. The facts of the case are as
follow :—One Thomas Ferres, it is stated, was born at Egton or
Danby, in the North Riding of Yorkshire. Others give his birthplace
as further north, and say that he came into the neighbourhood of
Danby as a tramp; but all are agreed in the poverty of his origin, and
that he spent some portion of his early life at Danby. There is a
tradition in that neighbourhood, that in crossing by stepping stones
over the river Esk, when swollen by rains, he fell in, and was nearly
drowned, and that, in gratitude for his own preservation, and with
charitable regard for others, for which he was so eminently distinguished
in after life, he made a vow that if ever he was able he would build a
bridge there. He redeemed his vow, and erected an elegant bridge,
having one arch. This bridge is generally known as "Beggar's
Bridge," though sometimes called the "Lover's Bridge." It bears
the initials of Ferres, and the date of 1621. Ten years later, namely,
in 1631, he died, and was, according to the directions contained in his
will, buried in the grave of his first wife, in the north aisle of the choir

of Holy Trinity Church, Hull, where there is in the north wall, a wooden monument to him, containing a portrait. In the trancept of the same church is a handsome white marble structure, by Earle, bearing the following inscription ;—

TO THE MEMORY OF
THOMAS FERRES,
Who died on the 31st day of January, 1630, aged 62 years.
Born in humble and obscure station,
he raised himself to distinction and honour.
He was Master of a ship trading from Hull for several years.
He was admitted a Younger Brother, and subsequently an Elder
Brother of the Trinity House,
and three times elected Warden of that Corporation ;
He was also Sheriff and Mayor of Hull.
In the abundance of his prosperity, he did not forget the needy.
Knowing that "it is more blessed to give than receive,"
and having experienced the perils of the sea, he administered
especially to the wants of the aged and worn-out seamen.
Careful in his lifetime to maintain good works, he
devoted at his death the bulk of his property
to purposes of Christian charity.
To mark their admiration of his character and respect of his memory,
this monument has been erected by the Corporation of
the Trinity House."

In the "History of the Town and Port of Kingston-upon-Hull," by James Joseph Sheahan, published in 1866, will be found a most interesting notice of Alderman Ferres, mainly drawn from a manuscript in the possession of the Secretary of the Trinity House, Mr. E. S. Wilson, F.S.A.

The Sledmere Poachers.

—

COME all you gallant poaching lads, and gang along with me
And let's away to Sledmere woods, some game for to see,
Its far and near—and what they say, its more to feel than see,
So, come my gallant poaching lads, and gang along with me.

On the fifth of November last, it being a starlight night,
The time was appointed, boys, that we were for to meet,
Then at twelve o'clock, at midnight, boys, we all did fire
    a gun,
And soon my boys, it's we did hear the old hares begin to
    run.

We have a dog, we call him Sharp, he in Sledmere woods
    did stray
The keeper, he fell in with him, and fain would him slay,
He fire two barrels at the dog, intending him to kill,
But by his strength and speed of foot, he tripped across
    the hill.

All on one side and both his thighs he wounded him full
    sore,
Before we reach'd home that night, he with blood was
    covered o'er,
Recovering his strength again, revenge for evermore we
    swore,
There's never a hare shall escape him, that runs on Sled-
    mere's shore.

We have a lad, we call him Jem, he's lame of one leg,
Soon as the gun is shoulder'd, and the dog his tail begins
    to wag,
When the gun presented fire, the bird came tumbling down,
This lad he kill'd it with his club, before it reach'd the
    ground.

So as we march'd up Burlington Road, we loaded ev'ry gun,
Saying, if we meet a keeper bold, we will make him for
    to run,
For we are bright Sledmere lads, our names we will not tell,
But if we meet a keeper bold, we'll make his heart to swell.

When we landed in Cherrywoods, we went straight up the
    walk
We pecked the pheasants in the trees, softly we did talk.
We marked all out that we did see, 'till we returned again,
We are going to Cotly Woodbro' to fetch away the game.

Come all you gallant poaching lads, I must have my will,
Before we shoot this night, let's try some hares to kill,
For shooting you well know it makes a terrible sound,
So if we shoot before we hunt it will disturb the ground,

D

We landed into Saddaby fields—to set we did begin,
Our dog was so restless there we could not keep him in,
But when our dog we did let lose, 'tis true we call'd him
    Watch,
And before we left the ground that night we fifteen hares
    did catch.

So it's eight cock pheasants and five hens, all them we
    marked right well,
We never fired a gun that night but down a pheasant fell,
You gentlemen wanting pheasants to me you must apply.
Both hares and pheasants you shall have and that right
    speedily.

So come my poaching lads who love to hunt the game
And let us fix a time when we shall meet again,
For at Cotly Woodbro' there's plenty of game, but we'll
    gang there no more,
The next port shall be Kirbyhill where hares run by the
    score.

So now my lads we'll gang home and take the nearest way
And if we meet a keeper bold his body we will bray,
We are bold Sledmere lads, our names we will not tell,
If we meet a keeper bold we'll make his head to swell.

Armthorpe Bells.

I SING the church of Armthorpe town,[1]
    That stands upon a hill,
And all who in the Fly come down[2]
    May see it if they will.

But there to them it doth appear
    An humble barn, tho' neat,
I wish the rector every year
    Had it choke full of wheat.

I only mean supposing it
    A very barn indeed ;
I'm sure he'd give thereof what's fit
    To them who stand in need.

The steeple then, you may presume,
  Is not like that of GRANTHAM,
For bells and chimes there was no room,
  And now they do not want them.

In vain the Quakers it abuse,
  And with their canting flout it,
Calling this church a steeplehouse,
  There's no such thing about it.

Although no steeple doth appear,
  Yet bells they're not without,
High hung in air aloft they are,
  But where ? Ah ! there's the doubt.

How can this be, for you to tell
  Requires somewhat to think on ;
And yet they serve the folks as well
  As would Great Tom of Lincoln.

The architect, a silly man,
  (And artist too—God wot ;)
Some say, when he drew up his plan,
  The steeple he forgot.

But that was not the cause of it,
  Our wiser rector fancies ;
'Twas not the builder's lack of wit,
  But want of the finances.

To rectify this great neglect,
  Before the cash was spent all,
An useful thing he did erect,
  Both cheap and ornamental.

For he a simple wall did raise
  Upon the west end gable,
And I must own unto his praise,
  It stands yet firm and stable.

And of his skill to give some proof,
  Which he'd not done before ;
He built it up above the roof,
  Some six feet high or more.

Of this, from north to south th' extent
  Was full as long as high,
For doing which his wise intent
  I'll tell you by and bye.

Two holes quite through this wall were seen
    Like windows in a garret,
That two small bells might hang therein,
    For passengers to stare at.

But how to get these bells—alas !
    Much jangling did create,
Much ale, and much tobacco, was
    Consumed in the debate.

One wiser than the rest propos'd
    To draw up a petition,
Begging SIR GEORGE would be dispos'd
    To pity their condition."

That he would gladly grant this boon,
    Unto his tenants all,
The dinner bell that calls at noon
    The vassals to his hall.

When to Sir George they did impart,
    How much they stood in need,
He said he'd give 't with all his heart,
    And sent it them with speed.

Their need by this being half supply'd,
    They wanted now but one,
But that, with judgment great, they cried,
    Should have a shriller tone.

One thought upon a tavern bell,
    Another on a miller's,
Another thought one would do as well
    That tinkles on a thill-horse.

" A fine one's in the Angel bar,"
    Says one, " And I can steal it,
If on the Bible you'll all swear
    You never will reveal it."

The clerk, a simple tailor, cry'd
    He'd never touch the string
Or whatsoever else they ty'd
    To the accursed thing.

The tailor's speech did for some time
    Put all in great combustion,
They said it was no greater crime
    To steal a bell than fustian.

Here they had stuck, had it not been
　For what I shall relate,
A gift to them quite unforeseen,
　Which was decreed by fate.

A neighbouring corporate town who found[5]
　Their crier's bell too small,
To get one with a deeper sound
　Had call'd a common-hall.

The Mayor, for th' honour of the place,
　Commendably was zealous,
And of whate'er might it disgrace
　Was equally as jealous.

Said, "Gentlemen, and brethren dear,
　You need not now be told
That this here town for many a year
　Looked very mean and old,

But so magnificent is grown,
　As know ye all full well ;
That quality from London town
　Chose to come here and dwell.

Our mansion-house, inside and out,
　So elegant doth rise,
That in the nation, round-about,
　'Tis mentioned with surprise.

Of precious time, 'twould be a loss,
　Should I make long preambles
Of pavements, lamps, and butter-cross,
　And of our butcher's shambles.

But here the new-built gaol, I own,"[6]
　Ought not to be forgotten,
A sweeter place in all the town
　No one would choose to rot in.

Yet notwithstanding all our pains,
　Our judgment and expense,
Yet wanting much, one thing remains
　Of weighty consequence.

For what avails our large gilt mace,
　Our full-furr'd purple gowns ?
Our scarlet fiddler's noted race,
　And lord-like pack of hounds ?

What, though our huntsman's clothed well,
    In coat of grass-green plush,
Whene'er I see our crier's bell,
    I vow it makes me blush.

Whene'er we're sitting in this hall,
    The sound on't makes me sick,
For 'tis a great burlesque on all
    Our body politic.

No dignity's thereby conveyed,
    No harmony decorous,
I marvel much no order's made
    It shan't be rung before us.

Then, gentlemen, with decent pride,
    At this our solemn sitting,
Let us agree that we provide
    A bell our town befitting."

The court agreed ; a bell was bought,
    With more melodious tongue,
How much it cost I have forgot,
    But to this day 'tis rung.

Th' offensive bell was laid aside,
    Like statesmen when discarded,
And in a stable did reside,
    Entirely disregarded.

Soon did the news of this event,
    Reach Armthorpe you may swear,
From whence two leading men were sent
    To treat with Mr. Mayor.

Whom they approached with awkward bow,
    And then with sly address
They told his worship, "That as how
    They were in great distress."

Said, " A great work we have in hand,
    In which we've been too rash,
For now it all is at a stand,
    Only for want of cash.

A bell we want, a small one too,
    Would make our business right,
A second-handed bell would do,
    Did we know where to buy't."

By this time he smelt out their drift,
  And generous as a king.
Said, " We have one—to you we'll giv't—
  'Twill be the very thing.

And I'm well pleased, I do protest,
  To save you so much charge.
But I suppose, though you know best,
  Our bell will be too large."

The bell was fetch'd at his command,
  (A sight to them most pleasing,)
Of which to them, with but one hand,
  He livery gave and seizin.

The joy they did at this conceive
  They could not well conceal,
For as they bowed, and took their leave,
  They rang a tingling peal.

Full fast then homeward they did hie,
  (Almost as quick as thought,)
Nor was their speed retarded by
  The weight of what they brought.

But when the town they did descry,
  They rang their bell aloud,
Which their success did signify
  To the desponding crowd.

The townsmen blessed at the event,
  And at their hearts full glad,
Quickly return'd the compliment,
  By ringing that they had.

So when a ship a fort salutes,
  No sooner have they done,
The fort, to obviate all disputes,
  Returns them gun for gun.

Jason, who brought the golden fleece
  Upon the good ship Argo,
Was not more welcom'd home than these,
  Though they did not so far go.

Both bells were in triumphant state,
  With many a rustic grin,
Conducted to the church-yard gate
  And introduced therein.

Where in the shade of two spread yews,
    Like Baucis and Philemon,
Was told at large the joyful news,
    To many a listening yeoman.

There wanted not to mount them high
    A windlass or a gable,
For any lad that stood thereby
    To run them up was able.

The bells, at last, were safely hung
    In their respective holes,
At weddings, where they both are rung,
    At deaths, the largest tolls.

At first they various ways did try
    In vain to make them speak,
At last they did succeed, and by
    Un tour de mechanique.

The clerk right wisely did foresee,
    By virtue of his post,
That he of their good company
    Was like to have the most.

To keep society alive,
    And that they still might please,
Wish'd that some way he could contrive,
    T'' enjoy the same with ease.

For this he cudgelled his brains,
    At length this happy thought
Occurr'd, which, with small cost and pains,
    He to perfection brought.

He found two yard-long sticks would do,
    Which might from westward come,
When each had been well fixed to
    Its *tintinabulum.*

Two strings, for ropes," a name too great,
    From these sticks might depend,
And by two holes made through the slate,
    Into the church descend.

That he, when sitting on his breech,
    (In either hand a string)
By giving an alternate twich,
    With ease might make them ring.

A great example here is seen,
   Of the mechanic power,
Nor has there yet adopted been
   A better to this hour.

Here critics may cry out with spite,
   Lord ! how these verses jingle !
But, otherwise, how could I write
   On bells that only tingle.

1. Armthorpe is a village about three miles from Doncaster. In Hunter's " History of South Yorkshire," there is a long account of it ; and the place is close by the famous chase of Hatfield, celebrated in another ballad. The chase formerly formed a part of the possessions of the Monks of the Abbey of Roche. In Dr. Miller's " History of Doncaster," he says the church was " a very small building, with one bell hanging on the outside of it, and nothing worth noticing within." This was in 1803.

2. The Fly was the name of a coach that began running in the year 1768, from Leeds to London, and the journey was then generally performed in two days and a half; which was then considered quick travelling.

3. Sir George Cooke, of Wheatley ; probably the seventh baronet, 1766-1823.

4. The Angel Inn at Doncaster, upon the sight of which now stands the Guild-Hall.

5. The town of Doncaster.

6. Here is a clue to the age of the ballad. Miller says, page 183, that " the old gaol was taken down and a new one erected." This would be in 1767.

7. The Old Corporation of Doncaster kept a pack of hounds, three fiddlers dressed in scarlet, called waits, who played at feasts, balls, &c., and walked in procession to the church.

8. In 1762, the huntsman wore " a frock of blue shagg, faced with red," the colours of the Corporation Livery.

9. The low common was enclosed in about 1671, when an allotment of 1 acre and 16 poles was given, in lieu of land appropriated from time immemorial to the finding of Church bell-ropes, and is let to the highest bidder.

This witty ballad first appeared in the " Yorkshire Journal," of Saturday, January 19th, 1788, a newspaper at that period printed and published at Doncaster, by Thomas Sanderson. The editor says it was written by a gentleman of the town. Who this man was it has never been ascertained, but it was very likely Mr. Anstey, the author of the Bath Guide, nephew of the Rev. Christopher Anstey, the then ector of Armthorpe.

The Richmondshire Cricketers' Song.

THE ALL ENGLAND CRICKETERS V. 22 OF RICHMONDSHIRE.

Played September 28th, 29th, and 30th, 1857.

By WILLIAM SWAIN.

YE cricketers of Richmondshire,
   Just list to what I say,
Don on your cricket toggery,
   For England comes to-day ;
Gird well your loins as on the course
   You stand and plaudits meet—
Prepare you for the tug of war,
   The race is to the fleet.

     Then bowl away, my jolly boys,
      With bias, break, or spin,
     And show these noble champions
      That Richmondshire can win.

Success to all you racing blades,
   What horses ere were fleeter ?
There's Abdale with Vedette and Skrim,
   And Watson with good Sneta
He showed them how the race to win—
   John Scott with Mare so famous—
For Impericuse came in the first,[1]
   And beat the Ignoramus.

     Then ride away my jolly lads,
      In Cup or T. Y. spin,
     And show the trainers of the south
      That Richmond jocks can win.

Then to the field once more return,
   Let cricket be the fashion,
And talk about the England match,
   And have no more digression.
Let one and all, at duty's call,

Contrive to buy a ticket,
    And come to see the Richmond gents,
    Against England play at cricket.
        Then bowl away, etc.

The bowler then for England,
    Martingell, Willisher, and Jackson
Davies, King, Anderton, Hayward,[2]
    Clark, and Downs for action :
With Mr. Hirst, whose name's the first,[3]
    There Dr. Parr so clever,
He swallowed a box of his uncle's pills,
    And is going to score for ever.[5]
        Then bowl away, etc.

In stepping out to hit a ball,
    Suppose it be a short 'un,
You'll find your reign cut very short
    By Stephenson or Morton,[4]
Whose sole talent you'll quickly see,
    If you happen just to snitch it,
They'll catch, or stump, and say 'how's that ?'
    And thus you'll lose your wicket.
        Then bowl away, etc.

So may we see a glorious match,
    With the twenty-two in favour,
The England men may win the game,
    But Richmondshire I'd rather,
Success to all who field and bowl,
    And those who guard the wicket.
And all those who want good health
    Must come and play at cricket.
        Then bowl away, etc.

1. Lord Zetland's Ignoramus, trained at Richmond was first favourite for the St. Leger, but was beaten by Imperieuse.

2. This was the first match that the late Tom Hayward played in the England Eleven.

3. Mr. Hirst, now Lieutenant-Colonel Hirst, B.R.V.

4. G. Morton, a noted wicket-keeper of Bedale, was stumper for the Twenty-two, and E. Stephenson for the Eleven.

5. The captain, George Parr, was presented with a gold watch by the Eleven during their stay at Richmond.   (See appendix note 8.)

The Craven Churn-Supper Song.

—

God rest you merry gentlemen !
Be not moved at my strain,
For nothing study shall my brain,
        But for to make you laugh.
For I came here to this feast,
For to laugh, carouse, and jest,
And welcome shall be every guest,
        To take his cup and quaff.

CHORUS.—Be frolicsome every one,
                Melancholy none ;
                Drink about !
                See it out,
                And then we'll all go home,
                And then we'll all go home.

This ale it is a gallant thing,
It cheers the spirits of a king,
It makes a dumb man strive to sing,
        Aye, and a beggar play !
A cripple that is lame and halt,
And scarce a mile a day can walk,
When he feels the juice of malt,
        Will throw his crutch away.—Chorus.

'Twill make the parson forget his men,
'Twill make his clerk forget his pen,
'Twill turn a tailor's giddy brain,
        And make him break his wand.
The blacksmith loves it as his life,
It makes the tinckler bang his wife,
Aye, and the butcher seek his knife
        When he has it in his hand.—Chorus.

So now to conclude my merry boys all,
Let's with strong liquour take a fall,
Although the weakest goes to the wall,
        The best is but a play.
For water it concludes in noise,
Good ale will cheer our hearts, brave boys ;
Then put it round with a cheerful noise,
        We meet not every day.—Chorus.

This homely old haytime song was taken down by the late Dr. James Henry Dixon, many years ago; and to it he appends the following note :—

"In some of the more remote dales of Craven it is customary at the close of the hay-harvest for the farmers to give an entertainment to their men. This is called the churn-supper; a name which Eugene Aram traces to 'the immemorial usage of producing at such suppers a great quantity of cream in a churn, and circulating it in cups to each of the rustic company, to be eaten with bread.' At these churn-suppers the masters and their families attend the entertainment, and share in the general mirth. The men mask themselves, and dress in a grotesque manner; and are allowed the privilege of playing harmless practical jokes on their employers. The Churn-Supper Song varies in the different dales, but the above used to be the most popular version. In the third verse there seems to be an allusion to the clergyman's taking tythe in kind, on which occasions he was accompanied by two or three men and the parish clerk. The song has never before been printed. There is a marked resembled between it and a song of the date of 1650, called *A Cup of Old Stingo*. See *Popular Music*, I., 308."

The paper referred to above as by Eugene Aram, is inserted entire in Lord Lytton's novel of *Eugene Aram*, immediately following the preface. It is a very learned composition, and is entitled, "THE MELSUPPER, AND SHOUTING THE CHURN."

A New Song of Hatfield's Chase.

To the tune of *Joys to Great Cezar*.

YE Hatfielders all, sing joy to great Cezar,
The Duke's got a fall in tow'ring too high, etc.
Tho' a nobleman brave, he's protected a knave.
Now his eyes are got open'd, he better will see
How the monster befriended, has been too self-ended,
And thrown him away ; sing joy to great Cezar,
Ten guineas a day to make you comply.

We've got our good cause, sing joy to great Cezar,
We've ty'd up his jaws, now bite if he can, etc.
This crafty Dun Devil, good faith, was not civil,
To entangle his honour so fast in the bryers;
'Twas like a rank villain, no soul can speak well on;
What think you, my friends, sing joy to great Cezar,
We miss of our ends, if he scopes with his ears.

His first new demand, sing joys to great Cezar,
Did only estend to clover in fields, etc.
But then for your berries, your plums, and cherries,
Your cabbage, your carrots, your cucumbers, too,
Nay, I'll give you my word he'd tythe you a,
Could any one say, sing joy to great Cezar,
It ought but to pay, and wou'd call it his due.

The Court of Assize, sing joy to great Cezar,
His impudent lies employ'd a long day, etc.
'The more to content him, brave Bootle did paint him
In colours so natural, all that were there
With horror detest him, to think what possest him,
Releases to sign, sing joys to great Cezar,
To make his fools join in so damm'd an affair.

A wolf was his dam, sing joy to great Cezar, etc.
Then who should we blame, if he lives by his prey,
By plunder and rappin; but now he's caught napping,
His tools and his homagers, all sneak away.
Resolve but to root him, his spaniels will shout him,
Or down with down, sing joys to great Cezar,
The least curr i'th town will bestow a huzza,
Then here honest soul, sing joys to great Cezar, etc.

Let's quaff t'other rowle in a health to the king,
For our customs of old we still have and will hold
For the good of ourselves, and our countrymen too;
When the Devil's Dun has his tether-length run,
We'll buy him a string, sing joys to great Cezar,
With brother to swing, and for ever adieu!

    Though ancient, apparently, there is something enigmatical about
this "New Song of Hatfield's Chase"; and an explanation is highly
desirable. It resembles the "Dragon of Wantley" in its allegory,
and perhaps relates to some law-suit between a parson and his parishioners about tithes.

The Boy of Egremond.

By John Bird.

—

" Rise up, rise up, my noble boy,
   The morn is fresh and fair ;
The laughing rays look out with joy,
   Rich balm is on the air :—
Rise up, rise up, my gallant son,
   Nor let there story be,
That hawk was flown, or heron won,
   Unseen, unheard, of thee."

The boy rose up, that noble boy,
   He knelt down at her knee ;
And oh, it was a sight of joy,
   That lady's joy to see !
She parted back his golden hair,
   She kissed his bonny brow—
"I would each mother's heart might share
   Thy mother's gladness now !

" For thou art fair, and more than fair,
   Gentle in word and thought ;
Yet, oh, my son, brave boy beware
   Of dangers love hath taught ! "
" Trust me," he cried, and smiling went
   To range the valleys green ;
And many as fair and fond intent
   As dark an end hath seen.

Bright on his path the dewdrops lay—
   Rich gems of Nature's court ;
The foot that chased their light away,
   Seemed but to fall in sport—
Seemed but the joy of him whose bound
   Forgot its speed to hear
The warbling lark, or win the hound
   From his own wild career.

And never shone fair Bolton's Vale
  So beautiful as now,
And ne'er beneath the sportive gale
  Did Wharfe so calmly flow.
" Hark ! hark ! on Barden-fell the horn
  Of the blithe hunter rings,
Buscar ! they rouse a stag this morn ;
  Oh, sweet the bugle sings."

Away, away, they speed with joy,
  The frolic hound and he,
Proud Egremond's far boasted boy,
  That gallant chase to see.
Why pause they in their course ?—'tis where
  The stream impetuous flows
Through the dark rocks, that meeting there,
  Its onward path oppose.

Yet, oh, the gush, the fearful gush,
  Of the wild water's strife !
On that loud eddying flood to rush,
  Were but to sport with life !
Yet one true gaze—one gallant bound—
  And the dread gulf is past !
" Be firm and fleet my faithful hound ! "
  That spring—it was his last !

Held in a leash that craven hound,
  Faltered in fear, and gave
His master to the gulf profound—
  A swift and sudden grave !
One flash of light—one look that tells
  Of late and vain remorse—
And a dark mass the current swells
  Far on its rapid course !

Still beautiful is Bolton's vale,
  Still Wharfe's bright waters there
Trace through long years the mournful tale,
  That bids rash youth beware.
There through its chasm the fatal flood
  Still pours the ceaseless wave,
Where the bright boy one moment stood,
  And sprang—to find a grave !

Fair Bolton's Abbey yet records
   The Lady's sorrowing part,
And silent walls e'en more than words,
   May wake the slumbering heart.
Ye, then, who mourn her gentle son,
   Whelmed in the fearful Strid,
Think on a mother's love, and shun
   The paths her lips forbid !

See the ballad, "THE SOUNDING OF BOLTON PRIORY."

The Dragon of Wantley.

OLD stories tell how Hercules
   A dragon slew at Lerna,
With seven heads and fourteen eyes,
   To see and well discern—a :
But he had a club, this dragon to drub,
   Or he had ne'er done it, I warrant ye :
But More of More-hall, with nothing at all,
   He slew the dragon of Wantley.

This dragon had two famous wings,
   Each one upon each shoulder ;
With a sting in his tayl, as long as a flayl,
   Which made him bolder and bolder.
He had long claws, and in his jaws
   Four and forty teeth of iron :
With a hide as tough as any bapp,
   Which did him round environ.

Have you not heard how the Trojan horse
   Held seventy men in his belly !
This dragon was not quite so big,
   But very near I'll tell ye.
Devoured he poor children three,
   That could not with him grapple :
And at one sup he eat them up,
   As one would eat an apple.

F

All sorts of cattle this dragon did eat :
    Some say he ate up trees,
And that the forests sure he would
    Devour up by degrees :
For houses and churches were to him geese and turkeys ;
    He ate all and left none behind,
But some stones. dear Jack, that he could not crack,
    Which on the hills you will find.

In Yorkshire. near fair Rotherham,
    The place I knew it well ;
Some two or three miles, or thereabouts,
    I vow I cannot tell :
But there is a hedge. just on the hill edge,
    And Matthew's house hard by it :
Oh there and then was this dragon's den,
    You could not chuse but spy it.

Some say this dragon was a witch :
    Some say he was a devil,
For from his nose a smoke arose,
    And with it a burning snivel :
Which he cast off when he did cough,
    In a well that he did stand by ;
Which made it look just like a brook
    Running with burning brandy.

Hard by a furious knight there dwelt,
    Of whom all towns did ring,
For he could wrestle, play at quarter staff, kick, cuff, and
    huff.
    Call son of a whore. do any kind of thing ;
By the tayl and the main. with his hands twain,
    He swung a horse till he was dead ;
And that which is stranger. he for very anger
    Eat him up all but his head.

These children, as I told, being eat ;
    Men, women, girls, and boys,
Sighing and sobbing, came to his lodgings,
    And made a hideous noise ;
O save us all, More of More-hall,
    Thou peerless knight of these woods ;
Do but slay this dragon, who won't leave us a rag on,
    We'll give thee all our goods.

Tut, tut, quoth he, no goods I want ;
  But I want, I want, in sooth,
A fair maid of sixteen, that's brisk and keen,
  With smiles about the mouth :
Hair black as sloe, skin white as snow,
  With blushes her cheeks adorning ;
To anoynt me o'er night, ere I go to fight,
  And to dress me in the morning.

This being done, he did engage
  To hew the dragon down ;
But first he went, new armour to
  Bespeak at Sheffield town ;
With spikes all about, not within but without,
  Of steel so sharp and strong :
Both behind and before, arms legs, and all o'er,
  Some five or six inches long.

Had you but seen him in this dress,
  How fierce he look'd and how big,
You would have thought him for to be
  Some Egyptian porcupig :
He frighted all, cats, dogs, and all,
  Each cow, each horse, and each hog ;
For fear they did flee, for they took him to be
  Some strange outlandish hedge-hog.

To see this fight, all people then
  Got up on trees and houses,
On churches some, and chimneys too ;
  But these put on their trowses,
Not to spoil their hose.   As soon as he rose,
  To make him strong and mighty,
He drunk by the tale, six pints of ale,
  And a quart of aqua vitae.

It is not strength that always wins,
  For wit doth strength excell :
Which made our cunning champion
  Creep down into a well ;
Where he did think this dragon did drink,
  And so he did in truth ;
And as he stoop'd low, he rose up and cry'd Boh !
  And hit him in the mouth.

F. 2

Oh, quoth the dragon, poxtoke thee, come out,
 Thou disturb'st me in my drink ;
And then he turn'd, and stank at him ;
 Good lack ! how he did stink ;
Beshrew thy soul, thy body's foul
 Thy dung smells not like balsam ;
Thou son of a whore, thou stink'st sore,
 Sure thy diet is unwholesome,

Our politic knight, on the other side,
 Crept out upon the brink,
And gave the dragon such a douse,
 He knew not what to think ;
By cock, quoth he, say you so, do you see ?
 And then at him he let fly
With hand and with foot, and so they went to't :
 And the word it was, Hey boys, hey !

Your words, quoth the dragon, I don't understand ;
 Then to it they fell at all,
Like two wild boars so fierce, if I may
 Compare great things with small.
Two days and a night, with this dragon did fight
 Our champion on the ground ;
Tho' their strength it was great, their skill it was neat,
 They never had one wound.

At length the hard earth began to quake,
 The dragon gave him a knock,
Which made him to reel, and straightway he thought,
 To lift him as high as a rock,
And thence let him fall.   But More of More-hall,
 Like a valient son of Mars,
As he came like a lout, so he turn'd him about,
 And hit him a kick on the—

Oh, quoth the dragon, with a deep sigh,
 And turn'd six times together,
Sobbing and tearing, cursing and swearing,
 Out of his throat of leather ;
More of More-hall ! O though rascal !
 Would I had seen thee never ;
With the thing at thy foot, thou hast pricked my throat,
 And I'm quite undone for ever.

Murder, murder, the dragon cry'd,
  Alack, alack for grief ;
Had you but mist that place, you could
  Have done me no mischief.
Then his head he shak'd, trembled and quaked,
  And down he laid and cry'd ;
First on one knee, then on back tumbled he
  So groaned, and kick'd, and dy'd.

This very humorous old ballad is allegorical, and refers to a certain lawsuit between Sir Francis Wortley and the parishioners of Penniston, in Yorkshire. There are several versions extant of the ballad, but I have copied from the " Reliques of Ancient English Poetry," first published by Bishop Percy, a very learned man in such matters, and the first editor of our ancient English Lyric and Ballad poetry. The author of " The Dragon of Wantley," is unknown ; but a key was supplied to Bishop Percy by Godfrey Bosville, Esq., of Thorp, near Malton, in Yorkshire, and is printed in the 6th edition of the Reliques. I subjoin a copy.

" Warncliffe-lodge, and Warncliffe-wood, (vulgarly pronounced Wantley), are in the parish of Penniston, in Yorkshire. The rectory of Penniston was part of the dissolved Monastery of St. Stephen's, Westminster, and was granted to the Duke of Norfolk's family, who therewith endowed an hospital, which he built at Sheffield, for women. The trustees let the impropriation of the great tithes of Penniston to the Wortley family, who got a great deal by it, and wanted to get still more ; for Mr. Nicholas Wortley attempted to take the tithes in kind, but Mr. Francis Bosville opposed him, and there was a decree in favour of the modus in 37th Elizabeth. The vicarage of Penniston did not go along with the rectory, but with the copy-hold rents, and was part of a large purchase made by Ralph Bosville, Esq., from Queen Elizabeth in the 2nd year of her reign ; and that part he sold in 12th Elizabeth to his brother Godfrey, the father of Francis, who left it, with the rest of his estate, to his wife, for her life, and then to Ralph, third son of his uncle Ralph. The widow married Sir Lyonel Rowlstone, lived eighteen years, and survived Ralph.

This premised, the ballad apparently relates to the law-suit carried on concerning this claim of tithes made by the Wortley family. " House and churches were to him geese and turkey," which are titheable things the dragon (Sir Francis Wortley) chose to live on. Sir Francis Wortley, the son of Nicholas, attempted again to take the tithes in kind ; but the parishioners subscribed an agreement to defend their

modus, and at the head of the agreement was Sir Lyonel Rowlstone,
who is supposed to be one of "the stones, dear Jack, which the
dragon could not crack." The agreement is still preserved in a large
sheet of parchment, dated 1st of James 1st, and is full of names and
seals, which might be meant by the coat of armour, " with spikes all
about, both within and without." More of More-hall was either the
attorney or councillor, who conducted the suit. He is not distinctly
remembered, but More-hall is still extant at the very bottom of Wantley
(Warncleft) Wood, and lies so low that it might be said to be in a well ;
as the dragon's den (Warncliff Lodge) was at the top of the wood.
" With Matthew's house hard by it." The keepers belonging to the
Wortley family were named, for many generations, Matthew Northall ;
the last of them left this lodge, within memory, to be keeper to the
Duke of Norfolk. The present owner of More-hall still attends Mr.
Bosville's Manor Court, at Ox Spring, and pays a rose a year. " More
of More-hall, with nothing at all, slew the dragon of Wantley." He
gave him instead of tithes so small a modus that it was in effect nothing
at all, and was slaying with a vengeance. " The poor children three,"
cannot surely mean the three sisters of Francis Bosville, who would have
been co-heiresses had he made no will? The late Mr. Bosville had a contest
with the descendents of two of them, the late Sir George Saville's father,
and Mr. Copley, about the presentation to Penniston, they supposing
Francis had not the power to give this part of the estate from the heirs
at law, but it was decided against them. The dragon (Sir Francis
Wortley) succeeded better with his cousin Wordesworth, the freehold
lord of the Manor, (for it is the copyhold that belongs to Mr. Bosville)
having persuaded him not to join the refractory parishioners, under a
promise that he should have his tithes cheap ; and now the estates of
Wortley and Wordesworth are the only estates or lands that pay tithes
in the parish. N.B.—The " two days and a night," mentioned as the
duration of the combat, was probably that of the trial at law.

Henry Carey, author of the charming song, " Sally in Our Alley,"
wrote a burlesque opera called the " Dragon of Wantley "; in imitation
of the Stalien operas of his day, and which had a degree of popularity.
It was founded on the ballad, and first acted at Covent Garden,
London, in 1738. This opera has been reprinted by J. Dicks, 313,
Strand, and is sold for one penny. Carey quotes four verses from the
ballad " In The Land we Live In," the late Mr. Charles Knight
gives his opinion as to who was the author of the ballad, but he
produces no evidence.

Scarboro' Sands.

—

As I was a walking over Scarboro' Sands,
   Some dainty fine sport for to see ;
The lasses were crying and wringing their hands,
   Saying, " The route it is come for the Blues."

Dolly unto her mother did say,
   " My heart's full of love that is true " :
She packed up her clothes without more delay,
   To take the last leave of the Blues.

Our landlords and landladies walk arm in arm,
   And so does the young women too,
You'd have laughed if you'd seen how the lasses flocked in,
   To take the last leave of the Blues.

We tarried all night and part of next day,
   For sweethearts we had got enough,
The times being hard the lasses did spare,
   A glass of good gin for the Blues.

Such sparkling young fellows sure never was seen,
   As the Blues and her Majesty too ;
You may search the world over and all Yorkshire through,
   There's none to compare to the Blues.

The boats being ready these lads to jump in,
   The music so sweetly did play ;
They gave out their voices with three loud huzzas,
   Success to the Queen and her Blues.

From a broadside *penes me.*

—

Spence Broughton.

—

To you my dear companions
   Accept these lines I pray,
A most impartial trial,
   Has occupied this day,

Tis from Spence Broughton,
 To show his wretched state,
I hope you'll make reformation,
 Before it is too late.

The loss of your companion,
 Does grieve your heart full sore
And I know that my fair Ellen,
 Will my wretched fate deplore,
Think on those happy hours,
 That now are past and gone,
Now poor unhappy Broughton,
 Does wish he'd ne'er been born.

One day into St. James's
 With large and swelling pride,
Each man had a flash woman,
 Walking by his side,
At night we did retire,
 Unto some ball or play,
In these unhappy pleasures,
 How time did pass away.

Brought up in wicked habits,
 Which brings me now in fear,
How little did I think
 My time would be so near,
For now I'm overtaken,
 Condemned and cast to die,
Exposed a sad example,
 To all that pass me by.

Oh, that I had but gone,
 To some far distant land,
A gibbet post for Broughton,
 Would never have been mine,
But alas for all such wishes,
 Such wishes are in vain,
Alas it is but folly
 And madness to complain.

One night I tried to slumber,
 And close my weeping eyes,
I heard a foot approach,
 Which struck me with surprise,

I listened for a moment,
   A voice made this reply,
Prepare thyself Spence Broughton,
   To morrow you must die.

O awful was the messenger
   And dismal was the sound,
Like a man that was distracted
   I rolled upon the ground,
My tears they fell in torrents,
   With anguish I was torn,
I am poor unhappy Broughton.
   And I wish I'd ne'er been born.

Farewell my wife and children
   To you I bid adieu,
I never should have come to this
   Had I staid at home with you,
I hope, through my Redeemer,
   To gain the happy shore,
Farewell! farewell for ever,
   I soon shall be no more.

(See appendix note 4.)

An Honest Yorkshireman.

Ah iz i' truth a country youth,
   Nean us'd teea Lunnon fashions ;
Yet vartue guides, an' still presides,
   Ower all mah steps an' passions.
Neea loortly leear, bud all sincere,
   Neea bribe shall ivver blinnd me :
If thoo can like a Yorkshire tike,
   A rooague thoo'll nivver finnd me.

Tho' envy's tung, seea slimly hung,
   Wad lee aboot oor country,
Neea men o' t'eearth booast greter wurth,
   Or mare extend ther boounty.

Oor northern breeze wi' us agrees,
    An' duz for wark weel fit us ;
I' public cares, an' law affairs,
    Wi' honour we acquit us.

Seea gret a maund is ne'er confin'd
    Tive onny shire or nation ;
They geean maist praise weea weel displays
    A leearned iddication.
Whahl rancour rolls i lahtle souls,
    By shallo views disarming,
They're nobbut wise 'at allus prize
    Gud manners, sense, an' learnin.

The above first appeared in a Ballad opera, entitled *A Wonder, or, An Honest Yorkshireman,* by Henry Carey ; performed at the theatres with universal applause. London, printed for Edward Cooke, 8vo., 1736. The second edition was entitled *The Honest Yorkshireman.* London, printed for L. Gilliver, and J. Clarke, 12mo., 1736. See *Notes and Queries,* 2nd Series, volume ix., pp. 126.

The Bishop Blase Festival.

The following is an exact copy of the Bishop Blase Broad Side, used at the Commemoration in the year 1825, and has been in my possession since ; but is now owned by Mr. Wm. Scruton, of Bowling. At the age of ten years I had the pleasure of witnessing the procession into the Holmes, Thornton Road, from the very spot where the Oddfellows' Hall stands at present. (See appendix note 5.)

May the trade of the Staple flourish around,
And Britain and Commerce for ever abound,
May Combers act firmly in union and love,
Be guided in justice with truth from above.

As friendship, love, and unity,
    Compose the bond of peace,
In them may our community,
    Join hands and thus increase.

The Original And Correct
Speech,
To Be Spoken At The
Grand Septennial Festival
At Bradford,
On Thursday, February 3rd, 1825,
In Commemoration Of
BISHOP BLASE,
With the Order of Procession, etc.
THE SPEECH:

HAIL to the Day, whose kind auspicious rays,
Deign'd first to smile on famous Bishop Blase!
To the great Author of our Combing Trade,
This day's devoted, and due honour paid,
To him whose fame thro' Britain's Isle resounds,
To him whose goodness to the poor abounds;
Long shall his name in British annals shine,
And grateful Ages offer at his Shrine?
By this our Trade are daily thousands fed,
By it supplied with means to earn their bread,
In various forms our trade its Work imparts,
In different methods and by different arts,
Preserves from Starving, indigents distress'd,
As Combers, Spinners, Weavers, and the rest,
We boast no gems, or costly garments vain,
Borrow'd from India, or the coast of Spain;
Our native soil with Wool our trade supplies,
While foreign countries envy us the prize.
No foreign broil our common good annoys,
Our country's product all our arts employs;
Our fleecy flocks abound in every bale,
Our bleating lambs proclaim the joyful tale.
So let not Spain attempt with us to vie,
Nor India's Wealth pretend to soar so high;
Nor Gason pride him on his Colchian spoil,
By hardships gain'd, and enterprising toil,
Since Britons all with ease attain the prize,
And every hill resounds with golden cries.
To celebrate our Founder's great renown,
Our Shepherd and our Shepherdess we crown;
For England's Commerce and for George's sway,
Each loyal Subject give a loud HUZZA.
        HUZZA.

PROCESSION.

Herald bearing a Flag.
Woolstapler on Horseback, each horse caparisoned with a Fleece.
Worsted Spinners and Manufacturers on Horseback, in White.
Stuff Waistcoats with each a Sliver over the Shoulder, and a White
Stuff Sash, the horses Necks covered with Noils made of thick Yarn.
Merchants on Horseback with coloured Sashes.
Three Guards.   Masters' Colours.   Three Guards.
Apprentices and Masters' Sons on Horseback, with Ornamented Caps,
Scarlet Stuff Coats, faced with bright Mazarine blue, white Stuff
Waistcoats, and blue Pantaloons.
Band.
Mace-bearer on Foot.
Six Guards.   King.   Queen.   Six Guards.
Shepherd and Shepherdess.
Shepherd's Swains.
Guards.   Jason.   Princess Medea.   Guards.
Woolsorters on Horseback, with Ornamental Caps, And Various
Coloured Slivers.
Bishop's Chaplain.
Bishop.
Comb Makers.
Charcoal Burner.
Combers' Colours.
Woolcombers, with Wool Wigs, etc.

The Procession to be formed in Westgate, proceed down Kirkgate
to the bottom of Darley Street, up that street and Rawson's Place,
Round by Manor Row down Skinner Lane, then along Well Street
and High Street to Mr. Garnett's Mill, return to Vicarage, along Vicar
Lane, up to Mr. Duffield's, return down Bridge Street, on Tyrrel
Street, to Mannville, and back to the Holme, there to partake of re-
freshment, then to Little Horton, down Bowling Lane, on Tyrrel
Street, and Market Street, up Kirkgate, down Ivegate, to the Sun
Inn, and there to dismiss.

R. Blackburn, Printer, Westgate, Bradford.

On the right-hand side of the sheet, or Broadside, at the top there
is a woodcut of the Bradford Arms, neatly done. On the left-hand
side a print of the Bishop, with an open book in his left hand, and a
comb in the other such as the combers used at that period. Between
these there is a view of the interior of a combing shop with the men
at work, and below a ship in full sail.

The Dallowgill Hunt.

—

ALL who delight to see and hear
The fox and hounds in full career,
Attention give unto my song
Of what was done—'t won't keep you long—
By men and hounds in Dallowgill,
Which Yorkshire scarce can parallel.

A few true lovers of the sport
Early one morning did resort,
Before bright Phœbus did appear,
Unto a place still call'd Ray Car,
Where from a pile of lofty rocks
They soon unearthed a noble fox.

Away across the vale he went
The dogs they followed him by scent;
And now to you I will expound
The name of every gallant hound
Which ran this long and tedious chase,
The like in Yorkshire never was.

Wonder and Plato the first I shall name,
Ringwood and Chaser—both true game,
Music and Comely, and Kilbuck also,
Famous and Younker—each swift as a doe,
The last is old Trudger, who drives up the rear,
And who makes up the number just half a score.

Away went the fox to Wanley Gill,
The hounds they followed with free good will,
Then over the hills as fierce as fire,
To Arnagill in Mashamshire;
But Reynard could not there abide,
So crossed Coombe Fell by Benjy Guide.

Right into Backstone Gill he goes,
Thinking himself free from his foes,
But they were all so near his scut
He was quickly forced to get out,
And leave his ancient castle there,
Which he'd frequented many a year,

Those dogs laid such strong siege to him,
That river Nidd he was forced to swim :
From river Nidd to Blayshaw Scroggs,
Where Harrison saw both fox and dogs,
And he on horseback followed them,
But they were far too swift for him.

Tantivy still—away they went
Both tooth and nail o'er Ramsgill Bent,
From Ramsgill Bent to Reygill House,
With such a vengeance and carouse,
From Raygill House unto Bougill,
But there was no continuance still.

Right over Heathfield Bents he goes,
Those dogs they gave him such a close,
They viewed him over Greenhow Hill,
Where people ran admiring still,
To see those dogs in such a chase,—
The like in Yorkshire never was.

A sunter's wife thought him a hare,
Cried to her husband—" Run ! I swear,
For they will kill her out of hand,
She is not able long to stand."
Next Reynard crossed the Craven bounds,
Hard chased by those gallant hounds.

From Nursa House to Burnsall Bridge,
As fast as ever he could tridge,
And Lupton followed for to see
What the event of it could be,
Expecting that he could not 'scape
Those hounds—they kept so near his back.

Right into Hebden he did fly,
And earthed there immediately,
Where, in strong castle of wide bounds,
He safely did defy the hounds ;
And after all the toils they'd passed,
They were forced to leave him there at last.

O'er hills and dales, mountains and rocks,
These noble hounds and gallant fox,
Without a pause, without a stay,

Ran more than fifty miles that day;
Though they had their labour for their pain,
They only wish he would come again.

Here's a health to the lord of this manor free,
The noble and honourable Aislabie;
We know he will be glad to see
The hounds that ran so gallantly;
And they will be kept at Dallowgill,
To be a plague to foxes still.

I am indebted to a small tract, published by Mr. Thomas Thorpe, of Pateley Bridge, for the copy of this somewhat unequal ballad; yet, such as it is, it has evidently been the delight of the north country people for a hundred years at least. The Right Hon. Aislabie, lord of the manor of Kirkby Malzeard, mentioned in the last verse, died in 1781, and we must infer that it was written during his lifetime. Dallowgill is in the parish of Kirkby Malzeard, in the West Riding of Yorkshire, from which village it is distant three miles to the westward. It is not a village, but a district of scattered houses along the sloping sides of the river Laver. There is a church, a school, and some fine scenery. Ray Car is the name of two small farms in the lower part of Dallowgill. Wanley Gill is a narrow glen on the moorlands, to the north of Dallowgill. Arnagill is a romantic glen at Moorheads, in the parish of Masham. Coombe Fell is a heathy ridge. Benjy Guide is an upright pillar on the top of it, and Backstone Gill is the name of a brook near the road leading from Masham to Lofthouse, in Nidderdale. Blayshaw, Ramsgill Bents, Raygill House, Bougill, and Heathfield, are all places on the south side of the river Nidd. Greenhow Hill is the well-known mining village of that name, between Pateley Bridge and Skipton. Craven Keld is the boundary between Nidderdale and Craven. Nursa House is also between Pateley and Skipton, near a conical hill, Nursa Knott, 1274 feet high. Burnsall is on the river Wharfe, and Hebden is on the road to Grassington from thence. It is said (also in a note) that the hounds were so fatigued with their long chase that they sunk down at Greenhow Hill, upon the road, and were then "taken in and done for" by the villagers, and that it was two or three days before all the dogs reached home at Dallowgill.

Wedding O' Trust.

SAID TO HAVE HAPPENED AT LEEDS.

A MAN and a maid, last month 'tis said,
At Leeds Old Parish Church were wed:

The ceremony both did say,
Then to the vestry went straightway
To get it there registered down,
That afterwards it might be shown,
If any in their course of life,
Should say they were not man and wife :
His name he wrote just in one line,
And in the next she her's did sign.
Then the priest to them did say,
" Now four and six pence you must pay : "
The man replied " hard is my lot,
I'm sure no money, sir, I've got ;
But if you grant a little trust,
I'll pay you what is right and just."
" We have no trust I say, you clown,
So come and pay the money down."
His colour rose, his words came quicker,
When luckily in came the Vicar,
Who asked whate'er could be the matter,
That made the curate thus to chatter ;
" The matter, sir, enough," said he,
" That married man won't pay the fee,"
The Vicar, turning to the man,
Said, " Friend, come pay us, if you can,
You know the money must be paid,
We have no credit in our trade."
The man in answer said, " You must
To me, sir, grant a little trust,
For I no money have indeed,
Or from your debt I'd soon be freed ;
Next Saturday, at night I'll come,
And pay you when you are at home."
The Vicar (looking very sad)
Said, " where nought is, nought can be had,
Howe'er, I say, then don't forget,
To come and pay your honest debt."
The man declared upon his oath,
He'd not forget,—they parted both,
The married man then homeward hied,
His loving partner by his side ;
In mirth and glee the day was spent,
When night approach'd to rest they went,
When former strife took wing and fled,

And pleasure crown'd the marriage bed ;
Next morn they rose, for work prepar'd,
And all the week they labour'd hard,
And earned the stipulated fee
By Saturday with decency.
Thus, having gained their promised point,
He went at night to buy his joint,
And though his wages were but small,
For groceries, dues, and joint, and all,
Still he resolved the marriage fee,
To pay with punctuality.
He walk'd the shambles thro' and thro',
At length a good sheep's head or two,
His quick attention caught : the price
He ask'd and bought one in a trice :
Then put it in his little wicker,
And truged along to pay the Vicar,
His house he found, and soon began
To rap aloud—the servant ran,
And ask'd him what he pleased to want ?
" To speak to master : " " but you can't,
We have a party here to-day,
Hence master cannot come this way,
But if you'll just relate your message,"—
I'll slyly tell him in the passage,"--
" You're very kind, indeed, my dear,
Pray will you whisper in his ear,
That such a man,—has brought his dues,
He'll come, I think, at such good news."
Away she went—and master came ;
" Well John! pray how is your loving dame ?"
" She's pretty well (I thank you, sir),
Considering how we've had to stir
This week betimes to earn the fee,
Which now I'm come to pay, you see,"
" Well John, I'm really glad to find
That you possess an honest mind :
May heaven smile upon your trade,
I see you've got your markets made."
" Yes sir, I have, but you must know,
This week I've had to buy them low : "
" But still I hope you've got to eat,
As labourers should, some useful meat."

F

"Yes sir, and coming to the point,
I just gave eight-pence for my joint ;
'Twas all I had besides the dues,
And you may see it if you choose."
Surpris'd ! his reverence view'd the wicker,
For John had really "capt the Vicar."
A joint so cheap made him amaz'd,
Howe'er the cloth he gently rais'd,
When lo ! within his basket laid
John's Sunday joint—a good sheep's head.
Struck with the sight, his worship thought
This case would please his friends, no doubt,
If they but knew the tale complete,
It certainly would be a treat,
So with John's leave he went and told
The circumstance to young and old :
And as a proof to what he says,
Held up to view, John's fine sheep's head.
They instant, (having heard the cause)
Said he deserved their warm applause.
Nay more, rejoined a worthy chief,
Such honesty should have relief :
And quickly threw a shilling down,
Which all observed and followed on :
And when the sum they came to count,
(As rumour says) it did amount
To thirty shillings,—which was paid
To John, who then approach'd and said.
"Ye gentlemen, and ladies too,
Most humble thanks I give to you,
For such a gift, I think 'tis right,
Since I'm unworthy of your sight :
With gratitude my heart doth swell,
But gratitude forbids its thoughts to tell,
God bless you all, so now adieu !"
He said, and instantly withdrew,
The Vicar followed to the door,
And said, "Now John since you're so poor,
I freely will forgive the fee,
Rewarding thus your honesty ;
Go home unto your loving wife,
And may you lead a happy life ;
Improve your Sabbaths, do not lurch

At home, but always come to church,
Your Bible read and study well,
In every gospel truth excel ;
Then when your pulse shall cease to beat,
Your soul will rise to bliss complete."
He ceas'd—then homeward John did hie,
First, having wish'd them all " good bye ! "

The Sisters' of Beverley.

THE tapers are blazing, the mass is sung
  In the chapel of Beverley,
And merrily too the bells have rung ;
  'Tis the eve of our Lord's nativity ;
And the holy maids are kneeling round,
While the moon shines bright on the hallow'd ground.

Yes, the sky is clear, and the stars are bright,
  And the air is hush'd and mild ;
Befitting well the holy night,
  When o'er Judah's mountains wild
The mystic star blazed bright and free,
And sweet rang the heavenly minstrelsy.

The nuns have risen through the cloister dim,
  Each seeks her lonely cell ;
To pray alone till the joyful hymn
  On the midnight breeze shall swell :
And all are gone save two sisters fair.
Who stand in the moonlight silent there.

Now hand in hand, through the shadowy aisle,
  Like airy things they've passed,
With noiseless step and with gentle smile,
  And meek eyes heavenward cast ;
Like things too pure upon earth to stay,
They have fled like a vision of light away.

F 2

And again the merry bells have rung,
  So sweet through the starry sky;
For the midnight mass hath this night been sung,
  And the chalice is lifted high,
And the nuns are kneeling in holiest pray'r,
Yes, all, save these meek-eyed sisters fair.

Then up rose the abbess, she sought around,
  But in vain for these gentle maids :
They were ever the first at the mass bell's sound,
  Have they fled these holy shades ?
Or can they be numbered among the dead ?
Oh ! whither can these fair maids be fled ?

The snows have melted, the fields are green,
  The cuckoo singeth aloud,
The flowers are budding, the sunny sheen
  Beams bright through the parted cloud,
And maidens are gathering the sweet-breath'd May,
But these gentle sisters, oh, where are they ?

And summer is come in rosy pride,
  'Tis the eve of the blessed Saint John,
And the holy nuns after vespertide,
  All forth from the chapel are gone ;
While to taste the cool of the evening hour,
The abbess hath sought the topmost tower.

" Gramercy, sweet ladye ! and can it be,
  The long lost sisters fair
On the threshold lie calm and silently,
  As in holiest slumber there !
Yet sleep they not, but entranced they lie,
With lifted hands and heavenward eye.

"O long lost maidens, arise ! arise !
  Say when did you hither stray ?"
They have turned to the abbess with their meek blue eyes,
  "Not an hour hath passed away,
But glorious visions our eyes have seen ;
Oh sure in the kingdom of heaven we've been !"

There is joy in the convent of Beverley,
  Now these saintly maidens are found.
And to hear their story right wonderingly,
  The nuns have gathered around
The long lost maidens, to whom was given
To live so long the life of heaven.

And again the chapel bell is rung,
  And all to the altar repair,
And sweetly the midnight lauds are sung,
  By the sainted sisters there;
While their heaven-taught voices softly rise
Like an incense cloud to the silent skies.

The maidens have risen, with noiseless tread
  They glide o'er the marble floor;
They seek the abbess with bended head—
  "Thy blessing we would implore,
Dear mother? for ere the coming day
Shall burst into light, we must hence away."

The abbess hath lifted her gentle hands,
  And the words of peace hath said,
Ovade in pacem, aghast she stands,
  Have their innocent spirits fled?
Yes, side by side, lie these madens fair,
Like two wreaths of snow in the moonlight there.

List! list! the sweet peal of the convent bells,
  They are rung by no earthly hand,
And hark how far off melody swells
  Of the joyful angel band,
Who hover around surpassingly bright,
And the chapel is bathed in rosy light.

'Tis o'er! side by side in the chapel fair,
  Are the sainted maidens laid;
With their snowy brow, and their glossy hair,
  They looked not like the dead;
Fifty summers have come and passed away,
But their loveliness knoweth no decay!

And many a chaplet of flowers is hung,
    And many a bead told there,
And many a hymn of praise is sung,
    And many a low-breathed pray'r;
And many a pilgrim bends the knee
At the shrine of the sisters of Beverley.

In the south aisle of the nave of Beverley Minster is an altar tomb, covered with a slab of Purbeck marble, placed under a groined canopy, adorned with pinacles and surmounted with figures, without inscription, or indeed anything to lead to a knowledge of its occupants. Tradition assigns it to two maiden sisters (daughters of Earl Puch, of Bishop Burton, and in whose household St. John of Beverley is said, on the authority of Bede, to have effected a miraculous cure), who are said to have given two common pastures to the freemen of Beverley.— POULSON'S *Beverlac*.

The Fisher Lad of Whitby.

My love he was a fisher-lad, and when he came ashore
He always steer'd to me, to greet me at the door;
For he knew I loved him well, as any one could see,
And O but I was fain when he came a courting to me.

It was one lovely morning, one morning in May,
He took me in his boat to sail out on the bay;
Then he told me of his love, as he sat by my side,
And he said that in a month he would make me his bride.

That very afternoon a man of war came in the bay;
And the press-gang came along and took my lad away;
Put irons on his hands, and irons on his feet,
And they carried him aboard, to fight in the fleet.

My father often talks of the perils of the main,
And my mother says she hopes he will come back again;
But I know he never will, for in my dreams I see
His body lying low at the bottom of the sea.

The ships come sailing in, and the ships they sail away,
And the sailors sing their merry songs out on the bay;
But for me, my heart is breaking, and I only wish to be,
Lying low with my lover deep down in the sea.

When the house is all still, and every one asleep,
I sit upon my bed, and bitterly I weep:
And I think of my lover away down in the sea.
For he never, never more, will come again to me.

"During the closing years of last century, when George the Third
was king, the press-gang was a fearful reality,—not a memory of the
past, as it is with us to-day,—and many brave-hearted mariners were
torn from home and friends, and exposed to the dangers of homicidal
strife, perhaps in many instances in violation of their own honest prin-
ciples, and to the prejudice of their interests. The north-east coast of
Yorkshire, with its hardy mariners, was a rich field from which to gather
fresh victims for those bloody French wars, and we can easily imagine
the deep alarm that spread through village and town when the press-
gang came rushing up; great bludgeons in the hands of officers and
sailors, and cutlasses by their sides. The hunted men vainly attempted
escape by concealment or flight; or sometimes turning upon their
ruffianly assailants made a fierce struggle for dear liberty, only to be
dragged away, bruised and bleeding, and subjected to the tyrannical
discipline that ruled in his Majesty's fleet."—"The Press-gang in
Yorkshire," in *Yorkshire Tragedy and Romance*, by E. LAMPLOUGH,
Hull.

The Lads' of the Tees'.

OLD Sagittarius, stuck in the sky
To serve as a watchman as well as a spy,
On finding our archers excell those above,
In envious spite gallop'd off to tell Jove.
"Great king of the gods can you bear to look down
And see your great favorites of old so outdone?
No more will your Trojans and Grecians please,
When eclips'd by the feats of these 'Lads of the Tees.'"

Jove rose in a rage and call'd out for Apollo,
And entreated that he would old Fourlegs follow
And examine if what he'd reported was true ;
Then away to the banks of the Tees the god flew ;
It happen'd the arrow was shot for that day,
When the archers appeared in their nicest array ;
Their sports and their mirth did his godship so please,
He resolved to stop with the " Lads of the Tees."

Next morning old Jupiter sent out his scout,
Winged Hermes to know what Apol was about :
Who swift as an eagle, headlong dashed forth
To enquire why the god staid so long upon earth ;
Oh ! I've found, cried Apollo, some lads to my mind,
They're gentle, they're courteous, they're social and kind ;
They shoot like us gods, and their songs me so please ;
I'll never more quit these brave " Lads of the Tees."

With the god of the bow and of music so near,
Triumphant our course, for no rival we fear ;
With so splendid a model of grace and of art,
Emulation alone do we need on our part ;
Now let us avoid all vain squabbles and strife,
And our science will gild the dull evening of life ;
And hoary old age feel a glow when he sees
His sons are enrolled 'mong the " Lads of the Tees."

This is an admirable archery song, and is evidently the emanation of some superior mind whose name is to me unknown. It appears in that excellent selection of sporting lyrics—Charles Armiger's *Sportsman's Vocal Cabinet.* 1830.

Roseberry Topping.

The story of the tragic fate of Prince Oswy has been told in another ballad. But the legend runs how the mother " mourned with such inconsolable grief that she soon followed him to his grave in Tivotdale Church (Osmotherley), and was, at her own desire, laid by her tenderly beloved child." The heads of the mother and son, cut in stone, may be seen at the east end of the church ; and from a saying of the people, " Os by his mother lay," Tivotdale goes by the name of Osmotherley.

Ah! why do the walls of the castle to-day
   No longer resound with the strains of delight,
And why does the harp of the minstrel so gay
   Now rest in the gloom and the stillness of night?

But late as I traversed these valleys along,
   How high 'mid the air streamed the banners of joy!
While the birth of Prince Oswin, the boast of the song,
   Gave mirth to each heart, as it beamed in each eye.

What stranger art thou, who, in Cleaveland so fair,
   Of the fate of Prince Oswin canst yet be untold?
How an old hoary sage had foreshown the young heir
   By water should die when half a year old!

His mother all eager her offspring to save,
   To Ottenberg high, with the morn did repair,
Still hoping to rescue her son from the grave,
   For well did she know that no water was there.

But how powerless and vain is a mortal's design,
   Opposed to that will which can never recede;
Who shall pull down the bright orb of heaven divine,
   And raise up a Meteor his rays to exceed!

Fatigued, and by ceaseless exertion opprest,
   At length they arrived near the brow of the hill,
In whose shades on the moss they resign them to rest,
   Now fearless of fate as unconscious of ill.

Not long in soft slumbers the fond mother lay,
   Ere aroused by a dream which dire horrors betide,
But, O God, who can paint her wild grief and dismay,
   When she saw her loved babe lie drowned by her side!

On the proud steep of Ottenberg still may be found,
   That spring which arose his sad doom to complete;
And oft on its verge sit the villagers round,
   In wonder recording the fiat of fate.

For this do the walls of the Castle to-day,
   No longer resound with the strains of delight;
And for this does the harp of the bard once so gay,
   Now rest in the gloom of the stillness of night.

The Pin Well at Brayton.

It is dawn : and far in the purpling East
  Is rising the ruddy morn,
And his glinting beams, with warmth increased,
Have roused from his dewy lair each beast,
  And gold-tipped the waving corn :
And the milkmaid, as she saunters along,
Is blithely trolling her matin song.

A merry dame and of joyful mien
  Is that laughing village maid,
As the best and brightest that may be seen
In the May-day dance, or when mistletoe green
  Mocks swains in the hall's deep shade ;
But though belle of the vill, and unrivalled she,
There is room in her heart for jealousy.

And under the giant oak's broad crest,
  That stands at the foot of yond hill,
Are the lazy kine with flowing breast,
Urged on to their wonted place of trest,
  By the maiden's merry trill :
It is there they know they must yield the juice
That God has given to man's best use.

With arching back and with curling tail
  They raise a kindly moan,
As the maiden drops her milking pail ;
But this morning their greeting has no avail,
  For away has their mistress gone !
And through bracken green and the heather-bell
She climbs the hill to the Fairy's Well.

She had dreamt as she lay in her lowly cot
  That the fairies would be kind :
And for one bright pin or a shining groat
  Dropt into the well, if it did not float,
  In its place she would speedily find
The sweet vision of him whom her heart most craves
Rise clear to her view on the rippling waves.

The shining groat lay in her palm,
  And a deep sigh swelled her breast ;
Could that tiny piece bear such a charm ?
And without Our Lady's succouring balm,
  Set her fluttering heart at rest !
So the fairies said ; and so forth she threw
The bribe that should bring either reck or rue.

It danced on the bright pellucid wave.
  Then the ripples closed over its sheen :
"O Virgin mild ! it has found a grave
And the fairies will give me the thing I crave,
  Then hail to thee, heavenly Queen !"
And she peered on the ripples with anxious eye
But no vision comes, and the ripples die !

It is e'en and the vesper bell has tolled
  And the western sun is low ;
The kine are gathered to the fold,
Or spread abroad on the grassy wold,
  And the old folk homeward go ;
But the young remain, and in the choir
  Await the priest and the sacred fire.

Then the bells ring out a merry peal
  Of clattering, gladsome song ;
And their chimes o'er the silent hamlet steal,
Far away to the hill that the elves may feel
  'Tis their own death knell that's rung ;
And southward come, with helping glee,
The mighty tones from the monastery.

And it is the time, so the young folks say,
  When the fairies abroad would start
Their mischievous snares for youth to lay,
Or their sad mad pranks on age to play,
  Or the cattle to maim or smart :
It is then the best time that could arise
These troublesome sprites to exorcise.

So the censer swings before the priest,
  And the banner floats on high ;
Ere the course at the Syren's haunt has ceased
The hymn of praise has its sound increased,

By the voice of the passer-by ;
And as they stand round the Fairies' Well,
It is cursed by candle, book, and bell.
Then the Holy Virgin they implore
    To give it her sacred name—
To be held henceforth for evermore,
For love-sick maid or for leper sore,
    To the fairies' bitter shame.
Yet now, though no Syren's name they tell,
Still the pin is dropt in Our Lady's Well !

Brayton Barf is a solitary hill but little more than a mile south-west of Selby. It is a very conspicuous object, rising to a height of some 150 feet above the surrounding flatness of the Vale of Ouse, and extends the view to the towers of York, to the hills of North Lincoln-shire, the Yorkshire Wolds, and the western range up to Pomfret and Leeds. The hill is now nude, but until some thirty years ago it was covered with timber, which was one of the last relics of the original wood extending to the brink of the Ouse, into which Abbot Benedict cut when he started the Abbey of Selby. It is a circumstance of singularity that on the crest of this hill there is a pit or well in which water is found, but the fluid is never of the most tempting quality; what it would be if the well were properly cleansed I cannot say. It is variously called " Lady Pin Well " and " Our Lady's Well "; and it has been a custom from time immemorial for those who visited that well to drop a pin or coin therein to propitiate Our Lady or the fairies, with hopes and results that the foregoing ballad describes. The custom is a remarkable survival of extreme antiquity ; and it is not the least curious feature of its history that, notwithstanding the interposition of Our Lady, the fairies still remain the presiding deities, as they are likely now to continue. Scott in the introduction to his " Vision of Don Roderick," tells us—

    Decayed our old traditionary lore,
        Save when the lingering fays renew their ring,
    By milkmaid seen beneath the hawthorn hoar,
        Or round the marge of Minchmore's haunted spring.

And he adds in a note that "a belief in the existence of nocturnal revels of the fairies still lingers among the vulgar in Selkirkshire. A copious fountain upon the ridge of Minchmore, called the Cheesewell, is supposed to be sacred to these fanciful spirits, and it was customary to propitiate them by throwing in something upon passing it. A pin was the usual oblation, and the ceremony is still sometimes practised, though rather in jest than in earnest." The same custom prevails to this day at Brayton. The origin of the complex title of our well at Brayton seems to be found in the piety either of one of the olden vicars of Brayton, as stated in the ballad, or in one of the abbots of Selby, who were owners of the Barf. The superstitious peasantry while traversing the monks' wood for windfall firewood, and occasionally, no doubt, for a bit of poaching, would cast their pin into the well under the impulse of their wish, and so transmit the legend to their children. The monk, seeing beauty and piety in the simple custom, and wishful at the same time to remove the pagan superstition in favour of his own creed, substituted Our Lady for the fairies in the name of the well, and so gave to the object of his own intense adoration the blind and soulless devotion that had for so many centuries flowed in another channel. And yet how little have his efforts succeeded, for though he has added the name of Our Lady, he has not destroyed the tradition of the fairies.—Mr. Wm. Wheater, in the *Leeds Mercury*, July 19th, 1884.

The Wensleydale Lad.

AN OLD YORKSHIRE SONG, IN THE LOCAL DIALECT.

WHEN I were at hoam, wi' me feyther an' mother, I niver
    had na fun ;
They kept ma goin fro morn to neet, so I thowt frae them
    I'd run.
Leeds Fair were comin', and I thowt I'd have a spree,
So I put on ma Sunday cooat, and went right merrily.

First I saw wer't factory—I never seed one afore ;
There were threads and taapes, and taapes and silks to sell
    by mony a score.
Owd Ned turn'd every wheel, and every wheel a strap :
"Begor!" says I to t'maisterman, "Owd Ned's a rare
    strong chap."

Next I went to Leeds Owd Church—I wor niver i' one i'
    me days,
An' I wor maistly ashamed o' mysel, for I didn't knaw ther
    ways :

There were thirty or forty fooak, in tubs and boxes sat,
When up comes a saucy ould fellow, says he, "Noo, lad,
    tak' off thy hat!"
Then in thear cooms a gret Lord Mayor, and over his
    shooders a club,
An' he gat into a white sack-poke, and gat into t' topmost
    toob ;
An' then thear cooms anither chap, I thinks they cawd
    him Ned,
An' he got into t' bottommost toob, and mock'd all t' other
    chap said.
So they began to preach and pray—they pray'd for George,
    oor King,
When up jumps t' chap, in t' bottommost toob—says he—
    "Good folks, let's sing."
I thowt sum sang varra weel, while others did grunt and
    groan ;
Every man sang what he wad, so I sang "Darby and Joan."
When preaching and praying were over, and folks wor
    gangin' away,
I went to t' chap i't' topmost toob—says I, "Lad, what's
    to pay ?"
"Why, nowt," says he, "my lad." Begor I were right fain ;
So I clickt hod o' me gret cloob stick and went whistlin
    oot again.

A Prayer of St Leonard.

MADE AT YORK.—FROM A M.SS. OF THE 15TH CENTURY.

No. 42 in Halliwell's Yorkshire Anthology.

REST and refuge to folk disconsolate,
    Father of pity and consolation,
Called recomfort to folks desolate,
    Sovereign Saviour in tribulation,
Virtuous visitor to folks in prison,
    Blessed Leonard ! grant of thy goodness,
To pray Jesu with whole affection,
    To save thy servants from mischief and distress.

Remember on them that lie in chains bound,
  On folk exiled far from their contre,
On such as lie with many grievous wound,
  Fettered in prison and have no libertie.
Forget them not that plain in poverte,
  For thirst and hunger constrained with sickness
Pray to Jesu of merciful pitie,
  To save all those who call thee in distress.

Let thy prayer and thy grace avail,
  To all those that call thee in their need,
And specially to women that travail,
  To ache of bones and diseases that spread :
Help staunch veins which cease not to bleed.
  Help feverous folk that tremble in their access,
And have in mind of mercy and take heed,
  To pray for all that call thee in distress.

Sober and appease such folks as fall in fury,
  To trist and heavy do mitigation,
Such as be pensive make them glad and merry,
  Distraut in thought reform them to reason ;
Relieve the poor from all false oppression
  Of tyranny, and extort brutalness ;
Take them in mercy in thy protection,
  And save thy servants from mischief and distress.

These signs grounded on perfect charity,
  In thy person increasing aye by grace,
O glorious Leonard ! pray Jesu on thy knee,
  For thy servants resorting to this place,
That they may have lisure time and space,
  All cold surfeits to reform and redress,
Housel and shrift, or they hence pace,
  With thee to reign in eternal gladness.

Merciful Leonard ! gracious and benign !
  Show to thy servants some palpable sign,
Passing this vale of worldly wretchedness,
  With thee to reign in eternal gladness,
There to be fed with celestial manna,
Where angels are wont to sing Hosanna !

This prayer (says Mr. William Grainge, of Harrogate), addressed to the Deity through the mediation of St. Leonard, who was patron saint of a large and wealthy hospital in York, is admirable for its spirit of universal charity and sympathy with all suffering.   The expression of ideas is remarkably clear, and free from ambiguity, and the whole piece must be ranked as one of the choicest treasures of early Yorkshire poetry.   (See appendix note 6.)

Howell Wood; or the Raby Hunt in Yorkshire,
February, 1803.[1]

To the Tune of *Ballynamonaora.*

" Let those ride hard who never rode before,
And those who always rode, now ride the more."

WHILST passing o'er Barnsdale I happened to spy,
A fox stealing on and the hounds in full cry ;
They are Darlington's, sure, for his voice I well know
Crying forward—hark forward : from Skelbrook[2] below,
      With my Ballynamonaora,
      The hounds of old Raby for me.

See Binchester leads them, whose speed seldom fails,
And now let us see who can tread on their tails ;
For, like pigeons in flight, the best hunter would blow,
Should his master attempt to ride over them now.
      With my, &c.

From Howell Wood come, they to Stapleton go,[3]
What confusion I see, in the valley below ;
My friends in black collars,[4] nearly beat out of sight,
And Badsworth's old heroes in sorrowful plight.
      With my, &c.

'Tis hard to describe all the frolic and fun,
Which, of course, must ensue, in this capital run,
But I quote the old proverb, although trite and lame
That—" The looker-on sees most by half of the game."
      With my, &c.

Then first in the burst, see dashing away,
Taking all on his stroke, on Ralph the grey ;
With *persuaders* in flank, comes Darlington's peer,
With his chin sticking out, and his cap on his ear.
   With my, &c.

Never heeding a tumble, a scratch, or a fall,
Laying close in his quarter, see Scott of Wood-hall,
And mind how he cheers them, with " Hark to the cry ! "
Whilst on him the peer keeps a pretty sharp eye.
   With my, &c.

And next him on Morgan, all rattle and talk,
Cramming over the fences, comes wild Martin Hawke,
But his neck he must break, surely sooner or late,
As he'd rather ride over than open a gate.
   With my, &c.

Then there's dashing Frank Boynton, who rides thorough-
  breds,
Their carcases nearly as small as their heads :
But he rides on so hard that it makes my heart ache,
For fear his long legs should be left on a stake.
   With my, &c.

That eagle-eyed sportsman, Charles Brandling behold,
Laying in a snug place which needs scarcely be told ;
But from riding so hard my friend Charley forbear,
For fear you should tire your thirty pound mare.
   With my, &c.

And close at his heels see Bob Lascelles advance,
Dressed as gay for the field, as if leading the dance,
Resolved to die hard, nor be counted the last,
Pretty sure of the speed of his favourite Outcast.
   With my, &c.

Next mounted on Pancake, see yonder comes Len,
A sportsman, I'm sure, well deserving my pen ;
He looks in high glee, and enjoying the fun,
Though truly I fear that his cake's overdone.
   With my, &c.

On Methodist perched, in a very good station,
Frank Barlow behold, that firm prop of the nation,

G

But nothing could greater offend the good soul,
Than to *Coventry sent* from the chase and the bowl.
        With my, &c.

Then those two little fellows, as light as a feather,
Charles Parker and Clowes come racing together,
And riding behind them see Oliver Dick,
With Slapdash half blown, looking sharp for a nick.
        With my, &c.

On Ebony mounted, behold my Lord Barnard,
To live near the pack, now obliged to strain hard ;
But mount my friend Barney on something that's quick,
I warrant my lads he would show you a trick.
        With my, &c.

Then Bland and Tom Gascoigne, I spy in the van,
Riding hard as two devils as catch as catch can,
But racing along to try which can get first,
Already I see both their horses are burst.
        With my, &c.

Then smack at a yawner comes my friend Billy Clough,
He gets up, stares round him, faith ! silly enough ;
While Pilkington near him, cries " Prythee, get bled."
" Oh no, never mind, sir, I fell on my head."
        With my, &c.

But where's that hard rider, my friend Colonel Bell ?
At the first setting off from the cover he fell ;
But I see the old crop, thus the whole chase will carry,
In respectable style, the good-tempered Harry.
        With my, &c.

With very small feet, sticking fast in the mud,
Frank Hawksworth I see on his neat bit of blood ;
But pull up, my friend, say you've lost a *fore-shoe*,
Else *bleeding*, I fear must be shortly for you.
        With my, &c.

To keep their nags fresh for the end of the day,
Sir Edward and Lascelles just canter away ;
Not enjoying the pace our Raby hounds go,
But preferring the maxim of " Certain and slow."
        With my, &c.

At the top of his speed, sadly beat and forlorn,
Behold Captain Horton is steering for Baln :
For accustom'd at sea both to shift and to tack,
He hopes by manœu'vring to gain the fleet pack.
   With my, &c.

The two Lee's, Harvey Hawke, Francis South'ron, and all,
Are skirting away for Stapleton Hall ;
Whilst far in the rear behold Alverley Cooke,
Endeavouring to scramble o'er Hampale's wide brook.
   With my, &c.

Far aloof to the right, and opening a gate,
There's a sportsman by system who never rides straight,
But why, my good Godfrey thus far will you roam,
When a pack of fine beagles hunt close to your home.
   With my, &c.

Safe over the brooks—but where's Captain Danser ?
Oh ! he stopping to catch Sir Rowland Winn's prancer ;
But what is the use of that my friend Winn,
If on foot you attempt it, you'll sure tumble in.
   With my, &c.

On his chestnut nag mounted in flank,
At a very great distance behold Bacon Frank ;
So true's the old maxim, we even now find,
That " Justice will always come limping behind."
   With my, &c.

See Starkey and Hopwood so full of their jokes,
From Bramham Moor come, to be quizzing the folks ;
And when they return the whole chase they'll explain,
Though they saw little of it—to crony Fox Lane.
   With my, &c.

Lost, spavin'd, and wind-galled, but showing some blood,
For from Coxcomb's poor shoulders it streamed in a flood ;
Behold Mr. Hodgson how he fumes and he frets,
With his black lays entangled in cursed sheep nets.
   With my, &c.

If his name I passed over, I fear he would cavil,
I just wish to say that I saw Mr. Saville ;
And with very long coat on, (a friend to his tailor)
With some more Wakefield heroes behold Mr. Naylor.
   With my, &c.

A large posse see in the valley below,
Who serve very well to make up a show;
But broad as the brook is, it made many stop,
It's not every man's luck for to get to the top.
With my, &c.

Johnny Dalton so sure at Went made a slip,
His nag tumbled in and he cried for his whip;
His groom coming up found his master so cross
Why curse your fine whip what's become of the horse.
With my, &c.

Now all having passed, I'll to Ferrybridge go,
Each event of the day at the club I shall know;
Where bright bumpers of claret enliven the night,
And chase far away hated envy and spite.
With my, &c.

Then forgive me, my friends. if you think me severe,
'Tis but meant as a joke, not intended to sneer;
Come, I'll give you a toast in a bumper of wine,
Here's success to this club, and to sport so divine,
And the hounds of old Raby for me.

1. Howell Wood is situated about ten miles west of Doncaster.
Amongst the possessions of the Priory of St. Oswald at Nostel that
passed to Dr. Leigh, the original grantee from the crown, on the 22nd
of March, 31 Henry VIII., 1540, were a capital messuage, called
Holewell, or Hovel-hall, in the Parish of Thurnscoe, with a wood of
160 acres.

2. The district called Barnsdale begins at a short distance north-
wards of Robin Hood's Well. It is situated about midway between
Doncaster and Ferrybridge, or Doncaster and Pontefract, and is
celebrated for having been one of the favourite haunts of the " Bold
Robin Hood." *See the Robin Hood Ballads.*

3. Skelbrook is situated about seven miles from Doncaster, and in
the vicinity of Barnsdale, and close to the well of Robin Hood, kept
up a lingering remnant of ancient forestry, in the maintenance here, of
a small park of Deer, but which has been discontinued. See Dr.
Miller's History of Doncaster, p 343.

4. The members of the Raby Hunt wear black velvet collars with
a gold fox thereon, courant, to their scarlet coats.

Remarkable Circumstance at Bretton Hall.?

AT Bretton Hall, near Wakefield, known so well,
Sir William Wentworth Blackett once did dwell;
That mansion was his own,—there, with his bride,
In pomp and splendour, he did once reside;
Yet, in the midst of all that he possessed,
A rambling mind disturb'd Sir William's breast.
His lady and his home he left behind,—
Says he ' The end of this wide world I'll find;
The earth's extensive, but you may depend on 't,
Before e'er I return I'll find the end on 't.
So he embark'd on board a ship we find,
And, sailing, left her ladyship behind,
Who, oft in sorrow did his absence mourn,
And, sighing said, 'O that he would return,
For be his voyage rough or smooth at sea,
It is a cruel, bitter blast to me.'
Sir William, he rolls on through winds and waves;
Undaunted, he all kinds of weather braves;
Nor his strange project ever relinquish'd he,
Till one and twenty years he'd been at sea;
Then, p'rhaps he thought, ' Good lack the world is round,
The end is nowhere, so it can't be found;
And as I'm weary of this wild-goose chase,
At home again, ere long, I'll show my face.'
Then off he set, but little was aware
What would transpire on his arrival there:
For, while Sir William roved, as here express'd,
Another ' Sir' his lady thus address'd :—
' Sir William's gone, ne'er to return again,
Past this world's end, which long he sought in vain;
There's not a doubt he's found the end of life.
But don't be troubled, you shall be my wife.'
She listened, till at length she gave consent,
And straightway, then, to church this couple went.
Sir William does about this wedding hear,
As he unto his journey's end draws near;
And thus, he does within his mind reflect—
' This sly usurper I shall now detect;
Soon shall he know (though much against his will),
At Bretton Hall I have dominion still.

Those woods and fertile fields my own I call,
With this magnificent, this splendid hall;
And now I come to claim them as my own,
Though by my dress not from a beggar known,
My clothes are turned to rags; and, by the weather,
My skin is tann'd till it resembles leather;
So now I'll act the beggar, bold and rude,
And at this wedding boldly I'll intrude;
And though admittance I may be denied,
I'll rob the merry bridegroom of his bride.'
Then at his own hall door one rap he gave,
Resolv'd the inmates charity to crave;
So he presented his request, 'tis said,
And they presented him a crust of bread!
The bread he took, and then, to their surprise,
He ask'd the servants for some beer likewise.
'No, no,' said they ' beer we shall give you none,
You saucy, drunken vagabond, begone!'
At length (with much ado) some beer he got,
And quickly he returned the empty pot;
And straightway then into the hall went he,
And said, he wished her ladyship to see.
'You can by no means see her,' answered they,
'She is newly married! 'tis her wedding day.'
'Married!' the feigned beggarman replied,
'Then I'll not go till I have seen the bride,'
Then towards the dining-room his course he bent:
The servants quick pursued with one consent,
And seized him, with intent to turn him out.
'Come back, you villain; what are you about?'
'About my business, to be sure,' quoth he;
'The room I'll enter and the bride I'll see.'
'We'll see you out of doors,' the servants said!
And now of course, a clam'rous din they made.
Just then, the bride, on hearing such a clatter,
Open'd the door to see what was the matter.
This noble beggar thus obtained a sight
Of her who erstwhile was his heart's delight,
He viewed her in her nuptial garments dress'd,
And did of her a glass of wine request,
Which she denied—who little did suppose
The ragged stranger was her wealthy spouse.
Then straight into the dining-room he went,

And down he sat among the guests, content.
Says he, 'You'll grant me my request, I know;
A glass of wine I'll have before I go.'
The bride, at length, complied with his request,
Thus thinking to dispatch their ragged guest,
But when he did this glass of wine obtain,
He drank and filled, and drank and filled again.
The guests, astonished and disgusted, view'd,
While he proceeded to be far more rude;
Around the bride's fair neck he threw his arm,
And gave a kiss, which did her much alarm.
On him she frown'd, and threaten'd him with law,
Says he, 'your threats I value not a straw;
My conduct to reprove is all in vain,
For what I've done I mean to do again.
Madam, your bridegroom's in an awkward case,
This night I do intend to take his place.'
And, while upon her countenance he pores,
The guests agree to kick him out of doors.
'The deuce is in the beggarman,' they cried;
'He means to either beg or steal the bride.'
'No, no,' says he, 'I mean to claim her as my own.'
He smil'd, and then he did himself make known;
Saying, 'William Wentworth Blackett is my name
For my long absence I am much to blame;
But safe and sound I have returned at last,
So let's forgive each other all that's past.'
The bride did her first bridegroom recognize,
With joy transported, to his arms she flies:
And, whilst they each other tenderly kiss,
The disappointed bridegroom they dismiss;
Who inwardly did his hard case lament,
Hung down his head, and out of doors he went,
'I'm robb'd of this fair jewel, now,' thinks he;
'How cruel is this tender spouse to me!'
Awhile he scratched his head, then heaved a sigh:
Then eyed the hall again, and wiped his eye.
Sir William freely did forgive his wife;
They lived together to the end of life.
My honest story I must now conclude;
Which may by some, be as a fiction view'd;
But, Sirs, the boots in which Sir William went,
Are kept in memory of that event;

The very hat he wore, preserved has been
At Bretton Hall—where they may yet be seen.

The Lord of Saltaire.

BY ABRAHAM HOLROYD.

WRITTEN ON THE OPENING OF THE SALTAIRE WORKS,
SEPTEMBER 20TH, 1853.

ROLL on gentle Aire in thy beauty,
  Familiar in story and song ;
The subject of many a ditty
  From Nicholson's musical tongue.
But a greater than he hath arisen,
  Who has linked thy name with his own ;
He will render thee famous for ages,
  And thou wilt to millions be known.

CHORUS :—Then let us all join in the chorus
    And sing of the qualities rare,
  Of one who by nature is noble !
    And hail him the Lord of Saltaire.

He has reared up a palace to labour !
  Will equal the Cæsars of old ;
The Church and the School and the Cottage !
  And lavished his thousands of gold—
Where the workman may live and be happy,
  Enjoying the fruit of his hand ;
In contentment, and comfort, and plenty,
  Secure as a peer of the land !

CHORUS :—Then let us all join in the chorus,
    And sing of the qualities rare,
  Of one who by nature is noble !
    And hail him the Lord of Saltaire!

From Peru he has brought the Alpaca ;
  From Asia's plains the Mohair ;
With skill has wrought both into beauty,
  Prized much by the wealthy and fair.
He has Velvets, and Camlets, and Lustres ;
  With them there is none can compare ;
Then off, off, with your hats and your bonnets,
  And hurrah for the Lord of Saltaire !

CHORUS :—Hip, hip, and all join in the chorus,
        And sing of the qualities rare,
        Of one who by nature is noble !
        And hail him the Lord of Saltaire.

A Song of Saltaire.

BY ABRAHAM HOLROYD.

WRITTEN ON THE OPENING OF THE SALTAIRE INSTITUTE,
JANUARY, 1871.

REAR high thy towers and mansions fair,
Thou gem of towns, renowned Saltaire !
Long may thy Fanes and Spires arise
In beauty, pointing to the skies ;
For labour dwells ennobled here,
Our homes to bless, our hearts to cheer ;
From morn to eve, the sun I ween,
Shines not upon a sweeter scene.

Sequestered in this lovely dale,
Here Art and Wealth at length prevail ;
Blent with the hum beside thy walls,
Aire's gentle river murmuring falls :
At eve thy bells in silver chimes
Ring out the dawn of happier times,—
The Reign of Love, in Cot and Hall,
When men to men are brothers all.

If the "true pathos and sublime,"
Of life's "a happy fireside clime,"
This long-wished end, it seems to me,
May surely yet be solved in thee.
When Truth shall everywhere abound,
And Peace on every hearth be found,
When learning finds a fitting home,
And helpless Age no more shall roam.

Then shall thy sires rest free from cares;
The heritage of virtue theirs.
Thy youths and maidens, too, shall prove,
The bliss which flows from constant love.
In all thy pleasant streets each day,
Thy children shall in hundreds play;
Or chant in song their hopes and fears,
As time unrolls the future years.

Honours be thine, whose active mind,
This earthly paradise designed;
For doubtful conquests Kings may war,
Thine is a nobler conquest far:
As rivers soon return in rain,
So, good deeds shall come back again.
And thou shalt know within thy breast—
Who blesses, shall himself be blest.

The Milkin Time.

(A CRAVEN SONG.)

MEET meh at the fowd at the milkin-time;
Whan the dusky sky is gowd, at the milkin-time;
    When the fog is slant wiv dew,
    An the clocks going hummin thro'
The wick-sets, an the branches ov the owmerrin yew.

Weel ye knaw the hour of the milkin-time;
The gert bell sounds frev t' tower at the milkin-time;
    But as t' gowd suin turns to grey,
    An ah cannot hev delay,
Dunnat linger bi the way at the milkin-time.

Ye'll finnd a lass at's true at the milkin-time,
Shoo thinks ov nane but you, at the milkin time ;
    Bud my fadder's gittin owd,
    An hes gien a bit ta scowd,
Whan ah's owre lang at the fowd, at the milkin-time.

Happen ye're afear'd at the milkin-time,
Mebbe loike ye've heer'd, at the milkin time
    The green-folk shak their feet,
    Whan t' moon on Heesides breet,
An it chances soa ta-neet, at the milkin time.

There's yan, an he knaws weel whan it's milkin time :
He'd feace the varra deil at the milkin-time ;
    He'd nut be yan ta wait
    Tho a bargest war i't' gate,
If the word, ah'd nobbut say 't, at the milkin time.

James Henry Dixon, Esq., LL.D., the author of this dialect poem, is a native of Craven, and has written several works of a local character. He is the author of " Slaadburn Faar—bein t' Adventures o' Jack and Nelly Smith, o' Girston." Also of " The Ballad of Flodden Field," with a " List of Craven Men who followed Lord Clifford (The Shepherd Lord) to the Battle, in September, 1513." He has also in the press, " Ballads and Songs of the Peasantry of England; " Griffin & Co. He has also just published, " The Felon Sewe of Rokeby and The Freeres, of Richmonde," a Metrical Romaunt, with an introduction and notes. London : Frederick Pitman, 20, Paternoster Row, price 6d. A valuable re-print of an ancient Yorkshire poem.—See Appendix Note 7.

The Banks of Aire.

By Benjamin Milner.

HER drooping form and care-worn face,
    So downcast, sad, and pale,
Was once the seat of every grace,
    The pride of all the vale :—
As oft she wander'd, free from care,
With William on the Banks of Aire.

Then would he hold her hand in his,
And call the hosts above
To witness that no time or change,
Should ever change his love ;
No joys or sorrows e'er impair,
His vows made on the Banks of Aire.

But love, familiar to his tongue,
Was stranger to his heart,
While, like the fiend in Eden once,
He played the serpent's part,
And spread temptation's treacherous snare,
For Mary on the Banks of Aire.

His vows are broken : her's are firm,
And true she will remain :
Although he scorns her constant heart,
She loves her faithless swain :
And still she whispers many a prayer.
For William on the Banks of Aire.

And oft with streaming eyes she strays,
And lingers where they sat.
When hours. like minutes sped away,
In love's alluring chat ;
But now her minutes of despair,
Seem hours on the lone Banks of Aire.

See Appendix Note 9.

The Bilberry Moors.

By John Swain.

SONG.

Come ! will you not go where the bilberries grow,
On their beautiful bushes of green :
Whose ruby bells smiled, in the desolate wild,
On the far away, moorland scene ?
We are up and away, at the dawn of the day,
Young cottagers moving in scores,
Ere the dawn of the day we are up and away—
Away to the bilberry moors.

With basket and tin, with provision therein,
  And light of heart, ready for song ;
Like the birds of the air, in our freedom from care,
  Right merrily move we along.
Nor future, nor past, bringeth shadow or blast,
  And what if the bright call us boors ?
We need no police to look after the peace,
  As we march to the bilberry moors.

The wealthy man's wall bounded not what we call
  The common, and bilberry ground ;
His broad-acred lot—nay, we covet it not—
  Ye wealthy keep all that ye bound !
But the bilberry blue oweth nothing to you—
  It groweth for the rich and poor :
Oh ! mean were the might that would question the right
  To roam on the bilberry moors.

Ye free English hills, with your purest of rills,
  Your purple, and berries of blue,
How stern was the tone, that your solitude lone,
  In the winterly tempest-time knew :
But listen to-day, for as merry a lay
  As ever was sung out of doors—
The warble of glee, the delight of the free,
  The song of the bilberry moors.

Mr. Swaine was born in 1815, and is, I am informed, an inspector in the General Post Office. His books are—" Gideon's Victory," 1835 ; " Harp of the Hills," 3rd. ed., 1851, '57, '58 ; " Cottage Carols, and other poems," 1860 ; " The Tide of Even, and other poems, with tales and songs," 1864. They are all richly gilt—backs, sides, and edges.—See Appendix Note 10.

Come to the Abbey.

COME to the Abbey at eventide,
I love thee to wander at my side,
On Aire's green banks at the close of day,
When the wild bird's song hath died away :

The violet grows like a hermit flower,
Under the shade of the lanthorn tower;
On that lone spot in the twilight dim,
Oh! there will we chaunt our evening hymn.

Come to the Abbey at eventide,
Like an angel sent to be my guide;
The mouldering pile shall our temple be,
And the heavens our glorious canopy:
How tranquil the moon's saluting smile,
When silence reigns in the roofless aisle,
And the ivy's trembling leaf on high
Seems to commune with the quiet sky.

Come to the Abbey at eventide,
When calmly the Aire's deep waters glide;
When the past its mournful story reads,
Clad in a mantle of moss and weeds:
But soon as the glistening night dew falls,
Like clustering pearls on the Abbey walls,
We'll bid adieu to the ruined towers,
And wander home over dewy flowers.

J. Bradshaw Walker is a Yorkshire poet of ability, as may be seen by the specimen which we give above. He is a self-taught man. Having at an early age found employment in the woollen manufacture at Leeds, where he was born, he diligently applied himself to the improvement of his mind, and in a few years was able to undertake the not less laborious task of a schoolmaster, by which vocation he tries to maintain a large family. His published works are " Wayside Flowers, or Poems, lyrical and descriptive," printed in 1840, and a volume of prose and poetry, entitled " Spring Leaves." We believe Mr. Walker was born about the year 1805. For purity of thought and sweetness of diction, the foregoing will compare favourably with any lyric or song in the English language. Kirkstall Abbey is indicated. (See appendix note 11.)

ROBIN HOOD BALLADS.

The Bishop of Hereford's Entertainment by Robin Hood and Little John in Merry Barnsdale.;

———

In the reign of King Richard I., Robin Hood ditties were very popular, and an immense crop of them were produced. Ritson has made a large collection of these, which fill a goodly-sized volume. The ballad which I give is evidently more modern than the first specimen. Merry Barnsdale was a favourite haunt of Ebenezer Elliott, the Sheffield poet. Old Leland, in his Itinerary, says of it:—"A III. miles of betwixt Milburne and Ferribridge I saw the wooddi and famose Forrest of Barnesdale; whar they say that Robyn Hudde lyvid like an outlaw." (See appendix note 12).

SOME they will talk of bold Robin Hood,
     And some of barons bold ;
But I'll tell you how he served the Bishop of Hereford,
     When he robbed him of his gold.

As it befel in Merry Barnsdale,
     All under the greenwood tree,
The Bishop of Hereford was to come by,
     With all his company.

"Come kill a ven'son," said bold Robin Hood,
     "Come kill me a good fat deer,
The Bishop of Hereford is to dine with me to-day,
     And he shall pay well for his cheer."

"We'll kill a fat ven'son," said bold Robin Hood,
     "And dress it by the highway side ;
And we will watch the Bishop narrowly,
     Lest some other way he should ride."

Robin Hood dressed himself in shepherd's attire,
     With six of his men also ;
And, when the Bishop of Hereford came by,
     They about the fire did go.

H

"O, what is the matter?" then said the Bishop,
  "Or for whom do you make this ado?
Or why do you kill the King's ven'son,
  When your company is so few?"

"We are shepherds," said bold Robin Hood,
  And we keep sheep all the year,
And we are disposed to be merry this day,
  And to kill of the King's fat deer."

"You are brave fellows," said the Bishop,
  "And the King of your doings shall know;
Therefore make haste, and come along with me,
  For before the King you shall go."*

"O, pardon! O, pardon! said bold Robin Hood,
  "O, pardon! I thee pray;
For it becomes not your lordship's coat
  To take so many lives away."

"No pardon! No pardon!" said the Bishop,
  "No pardon! I thee owe:
Therefore make haste and come with me,
  For before the King you shall go."

Then Robin set his back against a tree,
  And his foot against a thorn,
And from underneath his shepherd's coat
  He pulled out a bugle horn.

He put the little end to his mouth,
  And a loud blast did he blow,
Till threescore and ten of bold Robin's men
  Came running all on a row;

All making obeysance to bold Robin Hood,
  'Twas a comely sight for to see:
"What is the matter, master," said Little John.
  "That you blow so hastily?"

"O, here is the Bishop of Hereford,
  And no pardon we shall have."
"Cut off his head, master," said Little John,
  And throw him into his grave."

"O, pardon! O, pardon!" said the Bishop,
  "O, pardon, I thee pray;
For if I had known it had been you,
  I'd have gone some other way."

"No pardon! no pardon!" said bold Robin Hood,
 "No pardon I thee owe;
Therefore make haste, and come along with me,
 For to Merry Barnsdale you shall go."

Then Robin he took the Bishop by the hand,
 And led him to Merry Barnsdale;
He made him to stay and sup with him all night,
 And to drink wine, beer, and ale.

"Call in a reckoning," said the Bishop,
 For methinks it grows wondrous high:"
"Lend me your purse, master," said Little John,
 "And I'll tell you by-and-bye."

Then Little John took the Bishop's cloak,
 And spread it upon the ground,
And out of the Bishop's portmantua
 He told three hundred pound.

"Here's money enough, master," said Little John,
 "And a comely sight 'tis to see;
It makes me in charity with the Bishop,
 Though he heartily loveth not me."

Robin Hood took the Bishop by the hand,
 And he caused the music to play;
And he made the Bishop to dance in his boots,
 And glad he could so get away.

* In Manwood's "Forest Laws," is stated as follows:—A.D.
1194. King Richard I., being a hunting in the Forrest of Sherwood,
did chase a hart out of the Forrest of Sherwood into Barnesdale, in
Yorkshire, and because he could not there recover him, he made proclamation at Tickill, in Yorkshire, and at divers other places, that no
person should kill, hurt, or chase the said hart, but that he might
safely retorne into forrest againe; which hart was afterwards called
"A hart royall proclaimed."
    In the old ballad of "Robin Hood and Guy of Gisborne," occurs
the verse as under:—

        "My dwelling is in this wood," says Robin:
         "By thee I set right nought;
        I am Robin Hood of Barnsdale,
         Whom thou so long hast sought."

The Jolly Pinder of Wakefield.?

This ballad is from an old black-letter copy in Anthony à Wood's collection, and it has been compared with others in the British Museum. Some of the lines of this ballad are quoted in the two old plays of the "Downfall" and "Death of Robert, Earl of Huntingdon," 1601, 4to black-letter, but acted many years before that date. Shakespeare also alludes to it in his "Merry Wives of Windsor," Act 1, Scene 1 ; and again in the second part of "King Henry IV.," Act 5, Scene 3.

In Wakefield there lives a jolly Pinder,
   In Wakefield all on a green,
   In Wakefield all on a green :
"There is neither knight nor squire," said the Pinder,
   "Nor baron that is so bold,
   Nor baron that is so bold,
Dare make a trespass to the town of Wakefield,
   But his pledge goes to the pinfold,
   But his pledge goes to the pinfold."

All this be heard by three witty young men,
   'Twas Robin Hood, Scarlet, and John :
With that they espy'd the jolly pinder,
   As he sat under a thorn.

"Now, turn again, turn again," said the pinder,
   For a wrong way you have gone ;
For you have forsaken the King's highway,
   And made a path over the corn."

"O, that were a shame," cried jolly Robin,
   "We being three and you but one,"
The pinder then leapt back thirty good foot,
   'Twas thirty good foot and one.

He leaned his back fast unto a thorn,
   And his foot against a stone,
And there he fought a long summer's day—
   A summer's day so long ;
Till that their swords on their broad bucklers
   Were broke fast into their hands,

"Hold thy hand, hold thy hand," said bold Robin Hood,
  "And my merry men every one;
For this is one of the best pinders
  That ever I tried with sword.

"And wilt thou forsake thy pinder's craft,
  And live in the greenwood with me?"
"At Michaelmas next my cov'nant comes out,
  When every man gathers his fee:

"Then I'll take my blew blade all in my hand,
  And plod to the greenwood with thee."
"Hast thou either meat or drink," said Robin Hood,
  "For my merry men and me?"

"I have both bread and beef," said the pinder,
  "And good ale all of the best."
"And that is meat good enough," said Robin Hood,
  "For such unbidden guests."

"O, wilt thou forsake the pinder his craft,
  And go to the greenwood with me?
Thou shalt have a livery twice a year,
  The one green, the other brown."

"If Michaelmas day was come and gone,
  And my master had paid me my fee,
Then would I set as little by him,
  As my master doth by me."

(Date about 1557.)

The Bold Pedlar and Robin Hood.

Mr. Dixon, alluding to the following Nottinghamshire Ballad, says he took it down from the oral recitation of an aged female living at Bermondsey, London; the old dame assured him that she in turn had often heard her grandmother sing it, and to the best of her belief it had never appeared in print; it appears to have escaped the notice of Ritson, Percy, and other collectors of Robin Hood ballads:—

THERE chanced to be a pedlar bold,
　A pedlar bold he chanced to be;
He rolled his pack all on his back,
　And he came tripping o'er the lee
　　　　Down, adown, adown, adown,
　　　　　Down, adown, adown.

By chance he met two troublesome blades,
　Two troublesome blades they chanced to be;
The one of them was bold Robin Hood,
　And the other was Little John, so free.

Oh! pedlar, pedlar, what is in thy pack,
　Come speedilie and tell to me?
I've several suits of grey-green silks,
　And silken bow strings two or three.

If you have several suits of the gay green silk,
　And silken bow-strings two or three,
Then it's by my body, cried Little John,
　One half your pack shall belong to me.

Oh! nay, oh! nay, says the pedlar bold,
　Oh! nay, oh! nay, that never can be:
For there's never a man from fair Nottingham
　Can take one-half my pack from me.

Then the pedlar he pulled off his pack,
　And he put it a little below his knee,
Saying, if you move me one perch from this,
　My pack and all shall gang with thee.

Then Little John he drew his sword;
　The pedlar by his pack did stand:
They fought until they both did sweat,
　Till he cried, pedlar, pray hold your hand.

Then Robin Hood he was standing by,
　And he did laugh most heartilie,
Saying, I could find a man of a smaller scale,
　Could thrash the pedlar, and also thee.

Go, you try, master, says Little John,
　Go, you try, master, most speedilie,
Or by my body, says Little John,
　I am sure this night you will not know me.

Then Robin Hood he drew his sword,
  And the pedlar by his pack did stand.
They fought till the blood in streams did flow,
  Till he cried, pedlar, hold your hand !

Pedlar, pedlar, what is thy name ?
  Come speedilie and tell to me :
My name, my name, I ne'er will tell,
  'Till both your names you have told to me.

The one of us is bold Robin Hood,
  And the other Little John, so free :
Now, says the pedlar, it lays to my good will,
  Whether my name I chose to tell to thee.

I am Gamble Gold, of the gay green woods,
  And travelled far beyond the sea :
For killing a man in my father's land,
  From my country I was forced to flee.

If you are Gamble Gold, of the gay green woods,
  And travelled far beyond the sea,
You are my mother's own sister's son :
  What nearer cousins then can be ?

They sheathed their swords with friendly words,
  So merrily they did agree,
They went to a tavern and there they dined,
  And bottles cracked most merrilie.

Mr. J. P. Briscoe, of Nottingham, informs me that the above is included in Tegg's edition of Gutch's Robin Hood, 1867, pp. 310—11 —12.

Robin Hood and the Curtal Friar.

In the summer time, when leaves grow green,
  And flowers are fresh and gay.
Robin Hood and his merry men
  Were all disposed to play.

Then some would leap, and some would run,
    And would use artillery ;
Which of you can a good bow draw,
    A good archer to be ?

Which of you can kill a buck ?
    Or who can kill a doe ?
Or who can kill a hart of greece
    Five hundred feet him fro ?

Will Scarlet he kill'd a buck,
    And Midge he kill'd a doe,
And Little John kill'd a hart of greece
    Five hundred feet him fro ?

God's blessing on thy heart, said Robin Hood,
    That shot such a shot for me ;
I would ride my horse one hundred miles
    To find one to match thee lead.

That caused Will Scarlet to laugh,
    He laugh'd full heartily ;
There lives a friar in Fountain Abbey
    Will beat both him and thee.

The curtal friar in Fountain Abbey
    Well can draw a good strong bow ;
He will beat both you and your yeomen,
    Set them all on a row.

Robin Hood took a solemn oath,
    It was by Mary free,
That he would neither eat or drink,
    Till the friar he did see.

Robin Hood put on his harness good,
    And on his head a cap of steel,
Broadsword and buckler by his side,
    And they became him well.

He took his bow into his hand,
    (It was of a trusty tree)
With a sheaf of arrows by his side,
    And to Fountain Dale went he.

And coming to fair Fountain Dale,
    No farther would he ride ;
There was he aware of a curtal friar
    Walking by the water side.

The friar had a harness good,
  And on his head a cap of steel,
Broadsword and buckler by his side.
  And they became him well.

Robin Hood lighted from off his horse.
  And tied him to a thorn :
Carry me over the water, thou curtal friar,
  Or thy life shall be forlorn.

The friar took Robin Hood on his back,
  Deep water he did bestride,
And spake neither good word nor bad
  Till he came to the other side.

Lightly leap'd Robin off the friar's back,
  The friar said to him again,
Carry me over the water, fine fellow,
  Or it shall breed thee pain.

Robin Hood took the friar on his back,
  Deep water he did bestride,
And spoke neither good nor bad,
  Till he came to the other side.

Lightly leaped the friar off Robin Hood's back,
  Robin said to him again,
Carry me over the water, thou curtal friar,
  Or it shall breed thee pain.

The friar he took Robin Hood on his back again,
  And stepped up to his knee :
Till he came to the middle of the stream
  Neither good nor bad spake he.

And coming to the middle of the stream
  There he threw Robin in ;
And choose thee, choose thee, fine fellow,
  Whether thou will sink or swim.

Robin Hood swam to a bush of broom,
  The friar to the willow-wand ;
Bold Robin Hood he got to the shore,
  And took his bow in his hand.

One of the best arrows in his bill
  To the friar he did fly ;
The curtal friar, with his steel buckler,
  Did put his arrow by.

Shoot on, shoot on, thou fine fellow,
  Shoot as thou hast begun :
If thou shoot here a summer's day
  Thy mark I will not shun.

Robin Hood shot so passing well,
  Till all his arrows all were gone :
They took their swords and steel bucklers,
  They fought with might and main.

From ten o'clock that very day
  Till four in the afternoon :
Then Robin Hood came on his knees
  Of the friar to beg a boon.

A boon, a boon, thou curtal friar.
  I beg it on my knee :
Give me leave to set my horn to my mouth,
  And to blow blasts three.

That I will do, said the curtal friar,
  Of thy blasts I have no doubt :
I hope thou will blow so passing well,
  Till both thy eyes drop out.

Robin Hood set his horn to his mouth,
  And he blew out blasts three :
Half-a-hundred yeomen, with their bows bent,
  Came running over the lea.

Whose men are these, said the friar.
  That come so hastily ?
These are mine, said Robin Hood.
  Friar, what's that to thee ?

A boon, a boon, said the curtal friar.
  The like I gave to thee :
Give me leave to set my fist to my mouth,
  And whute whutes three.

That I will do, said Robin Hood.
  Or else I were to blame :
Three whutes in a friar's fist
  Would make me glad and fain.

The friar he set his fist to his mouth,
  And he whuted him whutes three :
Half-a-hundred good bay dogs
  Came running over the lea.

Here is for every man a dog,
  And I myself for thee :
Nay, by my faith, said Robin Hood,
  Friar, that may not be.

Two dogs at once to Robin did go,
  The one behind, the other before :
Robin Hood's mantle of Lincoln green
  Off from his back they tore.

And whether his men shot east or west,
  Or they shot north or south,
The curtal dogs, so taught they were,
  They caught the arrows in their mouth.

Take off thy dogs, said Little John,
  Friar, at my bidding thee :
Whose man art thou, said the curtal friar,
  That comes here to prate to me ?

I am Little John, Robin Hood's man,
  Friar, I will not lie :
If thou take not up thy dogs anon,
  I'll take them up and thee.

Little John had a bow in his hand,
  He shot with might and main :
Soon half a score of the friar's dogs
  Lay dead upon the plain.

Hold thy hand, good fellow, said the curtal friar,
  Thy master and I will agree :
And we will have new orders taken,
  With all haste that may be.

If thou wilt forsake fair Fountain Dale,
  And Fountain Abbey free,
Every Sunday throughout the year,
  A noble shall be thy fee.

Every Sunday throughout the year,
  Chang'd shall thy garments be,
If thou wilt to fair Nottingham go,
  And there remain with me.

The curtal friar had kept Fountain Dale,
  Seven long years and more :
There was neither knight, lord, or earl,
  Could make him yield before.

From an old black letter copy in the collection of Antony A. Wood; corrected by a much earlier one in the Pepysian Library; printed by H. Gosson, about the year 1600. The full title is "The Famous Battell betweene Robin Hood and the Curtall Fryer. To a New Northerne Tune." Curtal friars were so called from the cord or rope which they wore to whip themselves with. The friar here mentioned was very probably so called from the curs which he was the keeper of ; in fact being no friar at all, but only a monk of Fountains Abbey.

Fountains Abbey is said to be the most splendid ruin in England, and was founded in the year 1132, by Thurstan, Archbishop of York, the following account of which I copy from the descriptive catalogue of Richardson's drawings of the monastic ruins of Yorkshire :— "Thirteen Benedictine Monks of St. Mary's, near York, says Tanner, left their house A.D. 1132, with design to observe a more strict and reformed rule, whereupon Thurston, Archbishop of York, gave them a place near Ripon, on which was founded an abbey of the Cisterian order, in honour of the blessed Virgin Mary. Several of the authorities of the Cathedral of York were the earliest benefactors to Fountains Abbey; and their possessions having much increased, it was rendered one of the most important abbeys of the north. It appears that the buildings were commenced about the year 1204, the former monastery having been destroyed, and speedily became one of the most grand. Privileges of various natures were conferred on them by several of the kings and Archbishops of York, and the landed estates of the monastery large. It was surrendered by Marmaduke Broadelay or Bradley, suffragan Bishop of Hull, and the last abbot A.D. 1540. The revenue of the monastery were valued at £998 6s. 8¼d." The air of solemnity which hovers around this celebrated fabric is truly grand. The imposing effect of the abbey and the scenery round about it baffles all description. The abbey has been justly supposed to remain in a better state of preservation and to illustrate the monastic economy more completely than any other similar ruin in the kingdom. It is four years since I saw it last ; but I feel that the impressive effect can never be effaced from my memory. There is a feeling comes over you at the time you are walking along under those dark cloisters that can never be rightly described. With what feelings do you look back upon the time when the monks used to walk through this old ruin chanting their evensong, and comparing their religion with that of the present day. The monks exhibited towards their fellow-man a feeling of brotherly love which is never reached in the modern times, and which can only be seen by visiting the old abbeys of the country and observing the way in which the men helped one another to build these places without wages, as it were, and only receiving as much as was sufficient to keep body and soul together.

The Noble Fisherman: or Robin Hood's Preferment.

———

This is undoubtedly a very old ballad, and shows off Robin Hood in a new character. He leaves the forests of Sherwood and Merry Barnsdale, and goes to fight the French on the high seas off Scarborough. We can easily imagine how popular this ballad would be amongst the people of England centuries ago. Our copy has been collated with one in the British Museum; one in a private collection; and one in Antony A. Wood's collection.

In summer time, when leaves grow green,
   When they doe grow both green and long,
Of a bold outlaw, called Robin Hood,
   It is of him I sing this song :—

When the lily leafe and cowslip sweet
   Both bud and spring with a merry cheere,
This outlaw was weary of the wood side,
   And chasing of the fallow deere.

" The fishermen brave more money have
   Than any merchants two or three ;
Therefore I will to Scarborough go,
   That I a fisherman brave may be."

This outlaw called his merry men all,
   As they sate under the greenwood tree :
" If any of you have gold to spend,
   I pray you heartily spend it with me."

" Now," quoth Robin Hood, " Ile to Scarborough go,
   It seems to be a very fair day."
He took up his inne at a widdow woman's house,
   Hard by upon the water grey.

Who asked of him, " Where wert thou borne ?
   Or tell to me where dost thou fare ? "
" I am a poor fisherman," said he then,
   " This day entrapped all in care."

"What is thy name, thou fine fellow,
  I pray thee heartily tell it to mee ?"
"In my own country where I was borne,
  Men call me Simon over the Lee."

"Simon, Simon," said the goodly wife
  "I wish thou mayest well brook thy name."
The outlaw was aware of her courtesie,
  And rejoyced he had got such a dame.

"Simon, wilt thou be my man ?
  And good round wages Ile give thee :
I have as good a shippe of my own
  As any sails upon the sea.

Anchors and planks thou shall not want,
  Masts and ropes that are so long."
"And if you thus do furnish me,"
  Said Simon. "Nothing shall go wrong."

They pluckéd up anchor and away did sayle,
  More of a day than two or three ;
When others cast in their bated hooks,
  The bare line into the sea cast he.

'It will be long," said the master then,
  "Ere this great lubber do thrive on the sea :
I'll assure you he shall have no part of our fish,
  For in truth he is in no part worthy."

"O, woe is me !" said Simon then,
  "This day that ever I came here ;
I wish I were in Plompton Parke,
  In chasing of the fallow deere.

For every clown laughs me to scorne,
  And they by me set nought at all ;
If I had them in Plompton Parke,
  I would set as little by them all."

They pluckt up anchor, and away did sayle,
  More of a day than two or three ;
But Simon espied a ship of warre,
  That sayled towards them most valourously.

"O, woe is me !" said the master then,
  "This day that ever I was borne ;
For all our fish we have got to-day
  Is every bit lost and forlorne.

For these French robbers on the sea,
   They will not spare of us one man,
But carry us to the coast of France,
   And ligge us in the prison strong."

But Simon said, " Do not fear them,
   Neither master, take you no care :
Give me my bent bow in my hand,
   And never a Frenchman will I spare."

" Hold thy peace, thou long lubber,
   For thou art nought but brags and boasts :
If I should throw thee overboard,
   There's nought but a simple lubber lost."

Simon grew angry at these words,
   And so angry then was he,
That he took his bent bow in his hand,
   And in the ship hatch goe doth he.

" Master, tye me to the mast," said he,
   " That at my mark I may stand fair,
And give me my bent bow in my hand,
   And never a Frenchman will I spare."

He drew his arrow to the very head,
   And drew it with all might and maine,
And straightway, in the twinkling of an eye,
   To the Frenchman's heart the arrow's gane.

The Frenchman fell down on the ship hatch,
   And under the hatches down below,
Another Frenchman that him espyed,
   The dead corpse into the sea did throw.

" O, master, loose me from the mast," he said,
   " And for them all take you no care :
For give give me my bent bow in my hand,
   And never a Frenchman will I spare."

Then straight they boarded the French ship :
   They lying all dead in their sight :
They found within their ship of warre,
   Twelve thousand pounds of money bright.

" The one half of the ship," said Simon then,
   " I'll give to my dame and her children small :
The other halfe of the ship I'll bestow
   On you that are my fellows all."

But now bespoke the master then,
    " For so Simon it shall not be :
For you have won it with your own hand,
    And the owner of it you shall be."

" It shall be soe as you have said,
    And, with this gold, for the opprest,
An habitation I will build,
    Where they shall live in peace and rest.

Perhaps the oldest record of the hero of Barnsdale is entitled " A Lyttle Geste of Robin Hood." The word geste is from the Latin *gesta*, and means deeds or actions. An edition of this, in black letter, was printed by Wynken de Worde, probably about the year 1489, and there was an edition printed in Edinburgh in 1508. It is generally agreed that this long poem, which is in eight parts, was written about the time of Geoffrey Chaucer; that is between 1377 and 1413. Without doubt it is of great historical value. The little chap-book, entitled " Robin Hood's Garland," was printed in 1670, and contained only sixteen ballads, and these are evidently by various hands. In editions published after that time the number varies. That old worthy York printer and rhymer, Thomas Gent, affixed to his collection the following sonnet :—

TO ALL GENTLEMEN ARCHERS.

This garland has been long out of repair,
The songs that are lost no less than number four;
Yet now, at last, by most industrious care,
The sixteen new songs amount to twenty-four.
With the large additions, needs must please, I know,
All the bright ingenious yeomen of the bow,
To read how brave Robin Hood and Little John,
Brave Scarlet, Stutely, valient, bold, and free,
Each of them did bravely, fairly, play the man,
While they did all reign beneath the greenwood tree,
Bishops, friars, and monks, likewise many more,
Parted with their gold for to increase their store,
But ne'er would be guilty of robbing the poor.

This last line of Gent's points out a characteristic of these renowned freebooters, which is also mentioned by Stow, the antiquary and author of "The Survey of London." He says :—" These renowned thieves continued in the woods, despoiling and robbing the goods of the rich. They killed none but such as would invade them, or by resistance for their own defence. The said Robin entertained

100 tall men, good archers, with such of the spoils and thefts as he got, upon whom 400 (were they ever so strong) durst not give the onset. He suffered no woman to be oppressed, violated, or otherwise molested; poor men's goods he spared, abundantly relieving them with that which by theft he got from abbeys and the houses of the rich earles."

Robin Hood's Death and Burial.

When Robin Hood and Little John
  Went over yon bank of broom,
Said Robin Hood to Little John,
  "We have shot for many a pound.

"But I am not able to shoot one shot more,
  My arrows will not flee;
But I have a cousin lives down below,
  Please God, she will bleed me."

Now Robin is to fair Kirkley gone,
  As fast as he can wen;
But before he came there as we do hear,
  He was taken very ill.

And when that he came to fair Kirkley Hall,
  He knocked all at the ring;
For none was so ready as his cousin herself
  For to let bold Robin in.

"Will you please to sit down, cousin Robin," she said,
  "And drink some beer with me?"
"No, I will neither eat nor drink,
  Till I am blooded by thee."

"Well, I have a room, cousin Robin," she said,
  "Which you did never see,
And if you please to walk therein,
  You blooded by me shall be."

1

She took him by the lily white hand,
    And led him to a private room,
And there she blooded bold Robin Hood,
    Whilst one drop of blood would run.

She blooded him in the vein of the arm,
    And locked him up in the room ;
There did he bleed all the live long day,
    Until the next day at noon.

He then bethought him of a casement door,
    Thinking for to be gone,
He was so weak he could not leap,
    Nor he could not get down.

He then bethought him of his bugle horn,
    Which hung low down at his knee,
He set his horn unto his mouth,
    And blew out weak blasts three.

Then Little John, when hearing him,
    As he sat under the tree,
" I fear my master is near dead,
    He blows so wearily."

Then Little John to fair Kirkley is gone,
    As fast as he can dree ;
But when he came to Kirkley Hall,
    He broke locks two or three ;

Until he came bold Robin to,
    Then he fell on his knee :
" A boon, a boon," cried Little John,
    " Master, I beg of thee."

" What is that boon," quoth Robin Hood,
    " Little John, thou begs of me ? "
" It is to burn fair Kirkley Hall,
    And all their nunnery."

" Now nay, now nay," quoth Robin Hood,
    " That boon I'll not grant thee,
I never hurt fair woman in my life,
    Nor man in woman's company.

I never hurt fair maid in all my time,
 Nor at the end shall it be ;
But give me my bent bow in my hand,
 And a broad arrow I'll let flee ;
And where this arrow is taken up,
 There shall my grave digged be."

" Lay me a green sod under my head,
 And another at my feet ;
And lay my bent bow by my side,
 Which was my music sweet :
And make my grave of gravel and green,
 Which is most right and meet."

" Let me have length and breadth enough,
 With a green sod under my head ;
That they may say when I am dead,
 Here lies bold Robin Hood."

These words they readily promis'd him,
 Which did bold Robin please ;
And there they buried bold Robin Hood,
 Near to the fair Kirkley's.

Hargrove, in his " Anecdotes of Archery," 1792, has the following account of the death of Robin Fitz-ooth, or Robin Hood :—"At
length, being closely pursued, many of his followers slain, and the rest
dispersed, he took refuge in the Priory of Kirklees, in Yorkshire, the
prioress at that time being a near relation.   Old age, disappointment,
and fatigue brought on disease. A monk was called in to open a vein,
who, either through ignorance or design, performed his part so ill that
the bleeding could not be stopped.   Believing he should not recover,
and wishing to point out the place where his remains might be
deposited, he called for his bow, and discharging two arrows, the first
fell in the river Calder; the second falling in the park, marked the
place of his future sepulture."

Ritson, a painstaking antiquary, gives the following account, in
the collection by him, of the Robin Hood songs :—" Having for a
long series of years maintained a sort of independent sovereignty, and
set kings, judges, and magistrates at defiance, a proclamation was
published, offering a considerable reward for bringing him in either
dead or alive ; which, however, seems to have met with no success.

At length, the infirmities of old age increasing upon him, and desirou
to be relieved in a fit of sickness by being let blood, he applied fc
that purpose to the Prioress of Kirkleys Nunnery, in Yorkshire, b
whom he was treacherously suffered to bleed to death. This even
happened on the 18th November, 1247, the 31st year of King Henr
III., and if the date assigned for his birth, A.D. 1160, be correct, i
the 87th year of his age. He was interred under some trees at
short distance from the house (or nunnery), a stone being placed ove
his grave." The date on this stone is said to be the 24th December
1247, as preserved by Dr. Gale, of York.—A.H.E.

PATRIOTIC BALLADS.

Battle of Marston Moor.

To horse! to horse! Sir Nicholas; the clarion's note is
    high!
To horse! to horse! Sir Nicholas; the big drum makes
    reply!
Ere this, hath Lucas marched, with his gallant cavaliers,
And the bray of Rupert's trumpets grows fainter in our ears.
To horse! to horse! Sir Nicholas! White Guy is at the
    door,
And the raven whets his beak o'er the field of Marston
    Moor.

Up rose the Lady Alice from her brief and broken prayer,
And she brought a silken banner down the narrow turret
    stair;
Oh! many were the tears that those radiant eyes had shed
And she traced the bright word " Glory," in the gay and
    glancing thread,
And mournful was the smile which o'er those lovely
    features ran,
And she said: " It is your lady's gift; unfurl it in the van! "

" It shall flutter, noble Wench, where the best and boldest
    ride,
Midst the steel clad files of Skippon, the black dragoons
    of pride;
The recreant heart of Fairfax shall feel a sicklier qualm,
And the rebel lips of Oliver give out a louder psalm,
When they see my lady's gewgaw flaunt proudly on their
    wing,
And hear her loyal soldiers shout, For God and for the
    King! "

'Tis soon ! The ranks are broken ! along the royal line
They fly, the braggarts of the court ! the bullies of the
    Rhine !
Stout Langdale's cheer is heard no more, and Astley's
    helm is down.
And Rupert sheathes his rapier with a curse and with a
    frown ;
And cold Newcastle mutters, as he follows in their flight,
" The German boar had better far have supped in York
    to-night."

The Knight is left alone, his steel cap cleft in twain,
His good buff jerkin crimson'd o'er with many a gory
    stain ;
Yet still he waves his banner, and cries, amid the rout,
" For Church and King, fair gentlemen ! spur on, and
    fight it out ! "
And now he wards a Roundhead's pike, and now he hums
    a stave,
And now he quotes a stage play,—and now he fells a
    knave !

Heaven aid thee now, Sir Nicholas ! thou hast no thought
    of fear ;
Heaven aid thee now, Sir Nicholas ! for fearful odds are
    here :
The rebels hem them in, and, at every cut and thrust,
" Down, down," they cry, " with Belial ! down with him
    to the dust ! "
" I would," quoth grim old Oliver, "that Belial's trusty
    sword
This day were doing battle for the Saints and for the
    Lord ! "

The Lady Alice sits with her maidens in her bower,
The grey-haired Warder watches from the castle's topmost
    tower ;
" What news ? what news ? Old Hubert ? " The battle's
    lost and won
The royal troops are melting, like mists before the Sun !
And a wounded man approaches—I'm blind and cannot see,
Yet, sure I am, that sturdy step my Master's step must be ! "

" I've brought thee back thy banner. Wench, from as rude
and red a fray
As e'er was proof for soldier's thew, or theme for minstrel's
lay !
Here, Hubert, bring the silver bowl, and liquor quantum
suff,
I'll make a shift to drain it yet, ere I part with boots and
buff—
Though Guy, through many a gaping wound, is breathing
forth his life,
And I come to thee a landless man, my fond and faithful
wife.

" Sweet ! we will fill our money bags, and freight a ship
for France,
And mourn in merry Paris, for this poor land's mischance ;
For if the worse befall me, why, better axe and rope,
Than life with Lanthall for a king, and Peters for a pope !
Alas ! alas ! my gallant Guy ! curse on the crop-eared boor
Who sent me, with my standard, on foot from Marston
Moor ! "

WILLIAM MACKWORTH PRAED.

(See appendix note 13).

Saxon Grit.

WORN with the battle, by Stamford town,
  Fighting the Norman, by Hastings Bay,
Harold the Baron's sun went down,
  While the acorns were falling, one autumn day,
When the Norman said, " I am Lord of the land,
  By tenure of conquest here I sit ;
I will rule you now with the iron hand ; "
  But he had thought of the Saxon grit.

He took the land and he took the men,
  And burnt the homesteads from Trent to Tyne,
Made the freemen serfs by the stroke of his pen,
  Eat up the corn and drank the wine ;

And said to the maiden pure and fair,
  "Thou shalt be my leman, as is most fit,
Your Baron churl may rot in his lair ;
  But he had not measured the Saxon grit.

To the merry green-wood went bold Robin Hood,
  With his strong hearty yeomanry ready for the fray,
Driving the arrow into the marrow
  Of all the proud Normans who came in his way ;
Scorning the fetter, fearless and free,
  Winning by valour, or foiling by wit,
Dear to our Saxon folk ever to be,
  This merry old rogue with the Saxon grit.

And Kett, the tanner, whipt out his knife,
  And Watt, the smith, his hammer brought down,
For ruth of the maid he loved better than life,
  And by breaking a head made a hole in a crown.
From the Baron heart rose a mighty roar,
  "Our lives shall not be by the king's permit ;
We will fight for the right—we want no more ! "
  Then the Norman found out the Saxon grit.

For slow and sure as the oaks had grown
  From the acorns falling that autumn day,
So the Saxon manhood in thorpe and town
  To a nobler stature grew alway.
Winning by inches, holding by clinches,
  Standing by law and the human right,
Many times failing, never once quailing,
  So the new day came out of the night.

When rising afar in the Western sea,
  A new world stood in the morn of the day,
Ready to welcome the brave and free
  Who could wrench out the heart and march away,
From the narrow contracted dear old land,
  Where the poor are held by a cruel bit,
To ampler spaces for herd and band—
  And here was a chance for the Saxon grit.

Steadily steering, eagerly peering,
  Trusting in God, your fathers came,
Pilgrims and strangers, fronting all dangers,
  Cool-headed Saxons with hearts aflame ;

Bound by the letter, but free from the fetter,
  And biding their freedom in Holy Writ,
They gave Deuteronomy hints in economy,
  But made a new Moses of Saxon grit.

They whittled and waded through forest and fen,
  Fearless as ever of what might befall ;
Pouring out life for the nurture of men ;
  In faith that by manhood the world wins all.
Inventing baked beans, and no end of machines ;
  Great with the rifle and great with the axe—
Sending their notions over the oceans,
  To fill empty stomachs and straighten bent backs.

Swift to take chances that end in the dollar,
  But open of hand when the dollar is made,
Maintaining the meeting, exalting the scholar,
  But a little too anxious about a good trade ;
This is young Jonathan, son of old John,
  Positive, peaceable, firm in the right,
Saxon men all of us, may we be one,
  Steady for freedom and strong in her might.

Then, slow and sure, as the oaks have grown
  From the acorns that fell on that old dim day,
So this new manhood, in city and town,
  To a nobler stature will grow alway ;
Winning by inches, holding by clinches,
  Slow to contention, and slower to quit,
Now and then failing, but never once quailing,
  Let us thank God for the Saxon grit!

This noble poem, spoken from the heart of a true Yorkshireman, was read by the author at the Forefather's Celebration in New York City, the 22nd day of December, 1879.

"From Wharfedale to the shores of Lake Michigan, from the village forge to the City pulpit, from the Methodist Church to the Unitarian, are changes as great as any one man need expect to experience in a lifetime. Robert Collyer passed through them all. He was born at Keighley, December 8th, 1823, but spent most of his boyhood and early manhood within sound of the Old Church bells at Ilkley—the Olicana of the days of the Emperor Severus. Few men have been nurtured in the presence of more lovely or varied scenery. It is a pleasant picture to imagine the blacksmith's boy bursting out from his father's smithy at Blue-berry houses, or from Ow'd Jacky Birch's forge at Ilkley, with a touch of grime here and there on his ruddy cheeks, to learn his earliest lessons at the feet of nature ; lessons about the Fair and the Beautiful, about Freedom and Purity, which were dropped as lightly as thistledown into his growing soul, there to germinate in after times and under distant skies.

Robert Collyer left England for the United States of America, in May, 1850, taking with him a wife who had been wedded one day. Up to that time he had been a working blacksmith, and continued to be for years afterwards, filling up the intervals of toil with the studies of nature, local antiquities and books. Mr. Collyer was a member of the Methodist Church when in England, and continued so for some years after he reached America. In both countries he was an earnest and popular lay preacher, but his views of Christian doctrine, which had been gradually diverging in some respects from the views held by Methodists, became at last so different that he was compelled to abandon his fellowship with them. He joined the Unitarians, or as they love to style themselves in America—the Church of the Liberal Faith. On leaving Philadelphia he was called to take charge of a mission in Chicago, in the beginning of the year 1859. By his eloquence, sympathy with progress, genial disposition, and broad charity, he soon became widely known and honoured. Ten years afterwards his Mission Room becoming too small, Unity Church was built for his growing congregation. This was burnt down by the great fire of 1870. Standing amid the ruins on the Sunday following the fire, surrounded by his homeless flock, the Pastor read the words of the prophet Isaiah—"Our holy and our beautiful house is burned up with fire, and all our pleasant things are laid waste." The second Unity Church rose above the ashes of the former, larger, handsomer, and untrammelled by debt ; Robert Collyer, its minister, is one of the foremost preachers in America."

Such is the vivid account of his career (evidently written by some friendly hand) affixed to a volume of sermons by Robert Collyer, published in London, in February, 1877. In 1880 the pastorate of the Church of the Messiah, in New York, was offered to him, and he accepted it. He has published three volumes of sermons, which may be procured in England. They are entitled "Nature and Life," "The Life that now is," and "The Simple Truth." I have never had the pleasure of seeing him, but from having seen a large photograph of him, I should suppose him to be a man possessed of vast energy and strength, and a good specimen of a "Dalesman." His sermons are brimful of pathos, couched in vigorous Saxon and Old English phrases and idioms, and he deserves the title of the "Poet Preacher of America."

NUTSHELL AUTOBIOGRAPHY OF ROBERT COLLYER.

A correspondent contributes the following quaint autobiographical sketch of the Rev. Robert Collyer, of New York—formerly of Yorkshire, as we all like to remember, and as he was proud to say—taken from a private letter :—" Born at Keighley, in Yorkshire, December, 1823. Father a blacksmith, who moved with us to Fewston in January, 1824, to do the blacksmith work in a great linen factory. Got some schooling at Fewston before I was eight years old, then had to work in the factory until I was turned fourteen. Dreadful old factory-bell used to ring me in at six in the morning and out at eight in the evening, with an hour's rest at noon—hated that bell ever since. Corporation of the great town of Leeds bought the river (Washburn) on which the factory stood, to supply Leeds with water, and pulled the factory down. Asked a gentleman in the Town Council to keep his eye on that bell when it was broken up, and beg me a bit for a paper weight. Council voted me the bell, and Councillor sent it over last fall to New York. Left the factory in 1838 to learn the craft of blacksmith at Ilkley, in Yorkshire (Olicana of Ptolemy), with the man who taught my father. Learned the trade, buried the blacksmith and his wife, managed the place awhile : got married, joined the Methodists in 1848, became a local preacher among them in 1849 ; found the land too strait for me, and emigrated in April, 1850. Got work at once at Shoemaker town, Pennsylvania, to make hammers : stuck right there until 1859. In January of that year the Methodists declined to renew my license to preach ; reasons, heresy and abolitionism. Only heresy was given. Unitarians in Chicago heard of me, and invited me to quit the anvil and come out to take charge of a mission to the poor. Went out February, 1859. Unity people heard me preach and said, " Be our minister." Built the little wooden church that year, big stone church 1867. Fire 1871. Went to New York 1879.

The Mariner's Church.

(From the *Bradfordian*.)

—

Banks of the Humber ! afar and on high—
Masts, like a pine forest, crowding the sky !
Crowds on the waters ! and crowds on the shore !
This way and that way, a rush and a roar,
Steamboat and omnibus, each with its load,

Churning the billow, and shaking the road !
Crowds, like dead leaves, by the whirlwind uplifted,
Hitherward, thitherward, hurried and drifted ;
Hubbub and tumult for ever and ever,
Dust on the highway, and foam on the river.
Pleasure boats start to the sound of the fife,
Friends of dear friends take the last look in life :
Labourer's sweat-drop, and Emigrant's tear,
Fall down together, and darken the pier ;
Harlots in satin, with graces untold,
Offer you friendship, love, all things for gold :
Harlots in tatters too !—smelling of gin—
Wrecked long ago on the breakers of sin !
Merchant ! whose warehouse is half of a street,
Passing poor Lazarus, crouched at his feet.
Ladies and dandies perfuming the air ;
Troops of rank sweaters all heated and bare ;
Numbers unnumber'd, and mixed with the throngs,
Men of all nations, and kindreds, and tongues !
Spot on the world's deck, where pass in review
Types of the races that make up her crew !
Messmates that still through Time's watches employed,
Man the great Air Ship that sails thro' the void.

Thro' the dense multitudes—handsome and brave—
Moved a stout sailor boy, fresh from the wave,
Dealing out freely the jest or the curse ;
Joy in his countenance—gold in his purse—
Riot, wild revel, and brawl in his plans,
Daring the sea's wrath, and laughing at man's !
Onward he goes till a sound in his ears
Startles his soul and he bursts into tears ;
Suddenly, softly, steal forth into air
Words of thanksgiving, repentance, and prayer !
Low near his feet, like a dove on her perch,
Sits on the still wave, the Mariner's Church !
There some poor seamen, each finding a brother,
Sing of Christ Jesus, the God of his mother ;
Sing, too, the words that in life's dawning years
Lips, silent now, sweetly sang in his ears !
Enters the prodigal, leaving without
Laughter and uproar, the curse and the shout !
Enters, and humbled, and melted and shaken,

Turns to the Father, forgotten, forsaken ;
Heeding not, hearing not, what men are saying,
Down on his knees he is weeping and praying;
Weeping and praying, while lovingly o'er him
Hovers an angel, the mother that bore him ;
She, whose delight was to shield and caress him,
She, whose last words were a whispered "God bless him."

Home of the homeless one—found without search—
Blessings rain on thee, O Mariner's Church !
Friend of the friendless one, found without search,
Stand thou for ever a Mariner's Church.

(See appendix note 14).

Back to Winchester ; or, The Yorkshire Volunteer's Farewell to the good Folks' of Stocton.

A NEW SONG.

Tune, "*Push about the Jorum.*"

YE Stocton lads and lasses too,
  Come listen to my story,
A dismal tale, because 'tis true,
  I've now to lay before ye ;
We must away our route is come,
  We scarce refrain from tears, O !
Shrill shrieks the fife, rough roars the drum,
  March Yorkshire Volunteers O.
      Fal-lal-ral.

Yet ere we part, my comrades say,
  Come, Stockhore, you're the poet.
If ere you'd pen a grateful lay,
  'Tis now the time to show it;
Such usage kind, in these good towns,
  We've met from age and youth, sirs ;
Accept our heartfelt thanks, and once
  A poet sings the truth, sirs,

Ye lasses too, of all I see,
  Ye're fairest in the nation ;
Sweet buds of beauty's blooming tree,
  The top of the creation ;
Full many of our lads, I ween,
  Have got good wives and true, sirs ;
I wonder what our leaders mean,
  They have not done so too, sirs.

Perhaps, but hark ! the thundering drum
  From love to arms is beating :
Our country calls, we come, we come,
  Great George's praise repeating :
He's great and good, long may he here
  Reign, every bliss possessing,
And long may each true volunteer
  Behold him Britain's blessing.

Our valient Earl shall lead us on,
  The nearest way to glory,
Bright honour hails her darling son,
  And fame records his story ;
Dundas commands upon our lists
  The second, tho' on earth, sirs,
No one his second to, exists,
  For courage, sense, and worth, sirs,

No venial muse before your view,
  Next sets a veteran bold, sirs,
The praise to merit justly due,
  From Paul she cannot hold, sirs ;
His valour oft has bore the test,
  In war he's brisk and handy ;
His private virtues stand confest,
  In short, he's quite the dandy.

Brave Mackerall heads his Grenadiers,
  They're just the lads to do it,
And should the dons or lank Monsieurs
  Come here, he'll make them rue it,
He'll roar his thunder, make them flee,
  With a row, row, row, row, rara,
And do them o'er by land, at sea,
  As Rodney did Langara.

Young Thompson and his lads so light
  Of foot, with hearts of steel, O,
His country's cause shall nobly fight,
  And make her foes to feel, O,
For should the frog-fed sons of Gaul,
  Come capering a la Francois,
My lads, said he, we'll teach them all
  The light-bob country dance a.

Our leaders all, so brave and bold,
  Should I in verse recite, a,
A baggage waggon would not hold
  The songs that I could write, a ;
Their deeds so great, their words so mild,
  O take our worst commander,
And to him Cæsar was a child,
  And so was Alexander.

Such men as these we'll follow thro'
  The world, and brave all danger ;
Each volunteer is firm and true,
  His heart's to fear a stranger ;
Good folks, farewell, God bless the King,
  With angels sentry o'er him ;
Now, hark ! to Winchester, we'll sing,
  And push about the jorum.
        Fal lal lal la ral.

Stockton : Printed for the author, Herbert Stockhore, private in Earl Fauconburg's Yorkshire North Riding Volunteers.

The Sword-Dancers' Song.

The spectators being assembled in the best or largest room in the house, a clown enters, and after drawing a circle with his wooden sword on the floor, walks round it, and calls in the actors in the following lines, which are sung to the accompaniment of a fiddle, played either outside or behind the door ;—

K

THE first that enters on the floor,
  His name is Captain Brown ;
I think he is as smart a youth
  As any in the town ;
In courting of the lasses gay
  He fixes his delight.
He will not stay from them all day,
  And is with them all the night.

The next's a tailor by his trade,
  Called Obadiah Trim :
You may quickly guess by his plain dress,
  The hat of broadest brim,
That he is of the Quaking sect,
  Who would seem to act by merit
Of yeas and nays, and hums and hahs
  The motions of the spirit.

The next that enters on the floor,
  He is a foppish knight ;
The first to be in modish dress,
  He studies day and night.
Observe his habit round about,
  Even from top to toe,
The fashion late from France was brought,
  He's finer than a beau !

Next I present unto your view
  A very worthy man,
He is a vintner by his trade,
  And Love-ale is his name,
If gentlemen propose a glass,
  He seldom says 'em nay,
But does always think it's right to drink,
  While other people pay.

The next that enters on the floor
  It is my beauteous dame,
Most dearly I do her adore,
  And Bridget is her name.
At needlework she does excel
  All that e'er learnt to sew,
And when I choose, she'll ne'er refuse
  What I command her do.

And I myself am come long since,
  And Thomas is my name,
Though some are pleased to call me Tom,
  I think they're much to blame ;
Folks should not use their betters thus,
  But I value it not a groat,
Though the tailors, too, that botching crew
  Have patched it on my coat.

I pray, who's this we've met with here,
  That tickles his trunk-wame ?
We've picked him up as here we came,
  And cannot learn his name :
But sooner than he's go without,
  I'll call him my son Tom ;
And if he'll play, be it night or day,
  We'll dance you—Jumping Joan.

Trunk-wame is the cant term for a fiddle, but in its literal sense it means trunk—or box-belly. Jumping Joan is a well-known old country dance tune.

"Sword-dancing is not so common in the North of England as it was a few years ago : but a troop of rustic practitioners of the art may still be occasionally met with at Christmas time, in some of the most secluded of the Yorkshire dales. The above is a copy of the introductory song, as it used to be sung by the Wharfedale sword dancers. It has been transcribed from a manuscript in the possession of Mr. Holmes, surgeon, at Grassington, in Craven. At the conclusion of the song a dance follows, and sometimes a rustic drama is performed."—See J. H. Dixon's "Ballads and Songs of the Peasantry of England."

The simple and innocent customs of our forefathers are now fast falling into disuse, and many of the old sports, games, pastimes, and frolics are rarely seen. True, there are a few of them in vogue still, such as football and cricket, but these are games in which the weak cannot engage. All this is regrettable, and leads us to ask the question —Is the " Merry England " of the olden times to be Merry England no longer ? The belief in ghosts, boggards, fairies, phantom horses, gytrashes, and such spiritual beings who used to haunt our lonely roads and lanes, is also fast dying out. All this is, I think, very regrettable, as the whole poetical side of life is lost, and is not replaced by anything better. As a nation we are more serious and sadder.

A writer in the *Gentleman's Magazine,* for May, 1811, deposes that in the North Riding of Yorkshire the Sword Dance is performed from

K 2

St. Stephen's Day till New Year's Day. The dancers usually consist of six youths dressed in white, with ribbons, attended by a fiddler, a youth with the name of " Bessy," and one who personates a doctor. They travel from village to village. One of the six youths acts the part of king. in a kind of farce, which consists chiefly of singing and dancing, when the Bessy interferes, while they are making a hexagon with their swords, and is killed. Olaus Magnus calls this a kind of gymnastic rite, in which the ignorant were successfully instructed by those who were skilled in it ; and thus it must have been preserved, and handed down to us. This dance was, till very lately, performed with few or no alterations in Northumberland and the adjoining counties. One difference, however, is observable in our northern sword dancers, that when the swords are formed into a figure, they lay them down upon the ground, and dance round them. Wallis writes that the Saltatio Armata of the Roman Militia on their Festival Armilustrium, celebrated on the 19th of October, was practised by the country people in the neighbourhood of Northumberland on the annual festivity of Christmas, the Yule-tide of the Druids. " Young men march from village to village, from house to house, with music before them, dressed in an antic attire, and before the vestibulum or entrance of every house entertain the family with the motus incompositus, the antic dance, or Chorus Armatus, with sword or spears in their hands, erect and shining. This they call the Sword Dance. For their pains they are presented with a gratuity in money, more or less, according to every householder's ability ; their gratitude is expressed by firing a gun. One of the company is distinguished from the rest by a more antic dress ; a fox's skin generally serving him for a covering and ornament to his head, the tail hanging down his back. This droll figure is their chief or leader. He does not mingle in the dance." As to the Fool and Bessy, they have probably been derived to us from the ancient Festival of Fools, held on New Year's Day.—H.M.K.

Colonel Thompsons Volunteers.

From a broadside, printed by Forth, Pocklington.

As we marched down to Scarbro' on the fourteenth of June,
The weather it was warm, and the soldiers in full bloom ;
There it was my good fortune to meet my dearest dear,
For my heart was stole away by Colonel Thompson's
  volunteer.

My father and my mother confined me in my room,
When I jumped out of the window and ran into the town,
Where it was my good fortune to meet my dearest dear,
The man that stole my heart was Colonel Thompson's
    volunteer.

Then in came George Etherington all with his bugle horn,
He said he'd seen the prettiest girl that ever the sun
    shone on,
Her cheeks they were like roses, she is beautiful and fair,
And she says she'll march with none but Colonel
    Thompson's volunteer.

Then in came Captain Carter, and unto them did say,
That he had seen the prettiest girl of any there that day,
Her eyes were black as jet, and her hair it hung so tight,
And she says she'll march with none but Colonel
    Thompson's men this night.

Our officers are loyal, they are men of courage bold,
Their clothing is of scarlet and turned up with gold,
It's I could wash the linen to please my dearest dear,
When I was in the field with Colonel Thompson's
    volunteer.

Our ladies they love music, our captain gives command,
They play the prettiest music of all the royal bands,
They play the sweetest music that ever my ears did hear,
For my heart was stole away by Colonel Thompson's
    volunteer.

I'll bid adieu to father, likewise to mother too,
I'll never forsake my soldier, but unto him prove true,
And I'll range the country over with the lad that I love
    dear,
Since I'm bound in Wedlock's bonds to Colonel
    Thompson's volunteer.

Paul Jones, The Cumberland Militia, and Scarbrough Volunteers.

COME each loyal Briton of courage so bold,
As annals can show you would ne'er be controlled,

It vexes my patience, I'm sure, night and day,
To think how that traitor Paul Jones got away.
Derry down, etc.

As soon as this rebel near our shore did come,
From all parts of the town the inhabitants run,
They all stood amazed his fire to see,
But this never daunted our brave Militia.

Our two noble colonels they straight gave command,
Brave Lowther[1] and Fleming,[2] two Parliament men,
They marched through the ranks, and to the men did say,
" Brave boys, have your arms in good order we pray."

Our brave officers all, of every degree,
Took care every man provided should be,
With powder and ball, then each took command,
Said, " Boys for the honour of Cumberland.

Then straight we on guard to the Spaws sent with speed,
To prevent Paul's landing in case there was need ;
The call him Paul Jones, but his name is John Paul,
And if ever we catch him he shall pay for all.

The Serapis and Countess of Scarbrough brave,
Five hours and a half they did bravely behave :
Only two against six the whole time in the fight,
And so with reluctance was forced to strike.

In Whitehaven this brat served his time to the sea,
He was born and bred in the shire of Galloway :
He lived with Lord Selkirk a servant some time,
But committing murder to gaol was confined.

He was try'd for the same and condemned to die,
But broke his confinement, by means cunningly ;
A traitor he stands for the American cause,
And join'd with the French for to pull down our laws.

The inhabitants of Scarbrough to work straight did fall,
In order to protect them from all such as Paul,
And rais'd up a volunteer company with speed,
To defend the town in case there was need.

So now they are provided with everything new,
There hearts they are good, and their clothing is blue,
They'll join our Militia without dread or fear,
For to flog Jackey Paul, should he chance to come here.

I wish every city and town would with speed,
Raise a volunteer company in time of such need ;
To assist our Militia round the British land,
And imitate Scarbrough who has laid them a plan.

So here is a health for to drink great and small,
Success to our militia and volunteers all,
May they all prove loyal and true to their King,
And all such as Paul in a halter soon swing.

From a broadside in the Roxburgh collection. Another on this
event is published by J. Forth, of Pocklington.

1. Sir James Lowther, baronet, of Saleham, Middlesex, son-in-
law to the Earl of Bute, lieutenant and custos-rotulorum of Cumberland and Westmoreland, and Alderman of Carlisle.

2. Sir Michael le Fleming, baronet, M.P. for Westmoreland.

The inhabitants of the Yorkshire coast were frequently, about the
year 1779, thrown into a state of alarm by that intrepid Anglo-
American buccaneer, Paul Jones. This man had formerly been in the
service of the Earl of Selkirk, whence he was expelled with disgrace,
and having repaired to America he volunteered to make a descent on
the British Coast. Being entrusted with the command of a privateer,
he effected a landing at Whitehaven, and set fire to some shipping in
the harbour. He sailed for Scotland, where he landed on the estate of
the Earl of Selkirk, and plundered his house of all the plate. These
services ensured his promotion, and procured him the command of the
Bon Homme Richard, and the Alliance, each of forty guns ; the
Pallas of thirty-two guns ; and the Vengeance, armed brig. With
force he made many valuable captures, insulted the coast of Irelaand
and even threatened the city of Edinburgh. On Monday, the 20th
September, 1779, an express arrived at Bridlington, from the bailiffs of
Scarborough, with intelligence that an enemy was cruising round the
coast. On Thursday a fleet of merchantmen arrived from the Baltic,
under the convoy of the Serapis, and the Countess of Scarborough,
with sixty-six guns, and the first care of Captain Piercy and Captain
Pearson were to place themselves between their enemy and the convoy.
A two hours engagement ensued, and the English being over-powered
were compelled to surrender. The enemy purchased this victory at a
high price, for the loss, 300 men on the Richard alone, and that vessel
received so much injury that she sunk the next day, with many of the
wounded on board. Captain Pearson was knighted for his gallant
conduct, and the freedom of the borough of Scarborough was presented to him and his gallant colleague, in two boxes of " heart of
oak," ornamented with silver.

𝕿𝖍𝖊 𝕮𝖍𝖚𝖗𝖈𝖍 𝖔𝖋 𝕺𝖚𝖗 𝕱𝖆𝖙𝖍𝖊𝖗.

ROBERT STORY.

ENCIRCLED by trees, in the Sabbath's calm smile.
The church of our fathers—how meekly it stands !
O villagers gaze on the old hallowed pile—
It was dear to their hearts, it was raised by their hands !
Who loves not the place where they worshipped their God ?
Who loves not the ground where their ashes repose ?
Dear even the daisy that blooms on the sod,
For dear is the dust out of which it arose.

Then say, shall the church that our forefathers built,
Which the tempests of ages have battered in vain,
Abandoned by us from supineness or guilt,
O say, shall it fall by the rash and profane ?
No ! perish the impious hand that would take
One shred from its altar, one stone from its towers !
The life-blood of martyrs hath flowed for its sake,
And its fall, if it fall, shall be reddened by ours.

ROBERT STORY, OF GARGRAVE.

Robert Story was born at Wark, in Northumberland, but he first
became prominent as an author and a poet during his residence at
Gargrave, where he was schoolmaster and parish clerk, and where
he remained for twenty years. The history of his literary life is a most
interesting one, but I have not room here to give more than a resumé
of it. Born on the 17th October, 1795, he married Ellen Ellison at
Gargrave, on the 17th of May, 1823, with whom he lived happily, and
they had ten children. For the information which follows I am indebted
to the author of the " History of Bradford," who was intimate with
the poet.

At Gargrave by far the best of his poems and songs were written;
and, indeed, his poetical reputation may be said to have begun there.
In 1825 he published a volume of poetry entitled " Craven Blossoms."
In 1827 he again came out as an author ; the work had the quaint title
of the " Magic Fountain." During the agitation before the passing
of the Reform Bill, he took an active part in politics on the Conservative
side, and wrote songs and other poems for his party. In 1836 he
published, by subscription, " Songs and Lyrical Poems," which was
well received, and went into a second edition. Then followed in 1838
his " Outlaw," and " Love and Literature " in 1842. During the

general election of that time he took an active part in the contest for the representation of the West Riding. This was very unfortunate for him, as it brought him into antagonism with Mr. Wilson (now Sir Mathew Wilson), who had, along with Miss Currer, been a main supporter of his school. Added to this, Mr. Story obtained the post of collector of rates for the Gargrave district, and from this period his school rapidly declined, and, in short, his life became irksome at Gargrave, and, like many another, he saw that he must change his quarters. In 1843 Sir Robert Peel, through the influence of the Earl of Ellesmere and Lord Wharncliffe, gave him the situation of a clerk in the audit office, Somerset House, at a salary of ninety pounds a year. He settled with his family of twelve at Lambeth, in an unhealthy district, and his children took the fever, and seven of them died. This was a terrible blow, not to mention the heavy charges of doctor's bills and funeral charges in London. Here he remained 17 years, and the inspector of the audit office stated that Story was never known to be late or absent, although his residence was five miles from Somerset House. This is great praise to a poet. Every year he had a month's holiday, and this he spent in rambles in Yorkshire or on "Sweet Beaumont Side," in Northumberland. But he always visited Bradford before his return to London, for he had troops of friends there, namely, John James, Edward Collinson, William Hector Hudson, and the Reaneys at the George Hotel, Market Street. There he was always a welcome guest.

In the year 1857, the Duke of Northumberland, who was always to him a generous patron, assisted him to bring out a gorgeous edition of all his poems and songs, but I have never had the good fortune to see a copy of this latter book. In 1859 Story was invited to Ayr, and was vice-chairman at the Burns centenary celebrations, and he recited his beautiful ode on Burns. It was seen in that year that his health was failing, and in the spring he caught cold, which he neglected; disease of the heart set in, and he expired on the 7th of July, 1860.

Robert Story was a genial soul, seldom made an enemy; he was a kind and affectionate husband and father, and amid all his reverses, disposed to look on the bright side of life. Mr. James says:—" He stands high among the minor poets of Great Britain, and many of his sweet lyrics will most assuredly descend to, and be admired by posterity, and by none more than Yorkshiremen." After the death of Mr. Story, a selection of his poems was made by Mr. James, who added a well-written life of him, and it was published by Mr. Charles Stansfield, No. 3, Westgate, Bradford, for the benefit of the poet's widow. A fine portrait of Story was engraved as a frontispiece to the book by the late William Overend Geller, a native of Bradford.

The longest and most pretentious of his poems was published in 1853, when he resided in London—" Guthrum, the Dane (a tale of the

Heptarchy), in six cantos." The dedication is as follows :—" To Miss Reany, of Bradford, in the county of York, this poem is proudly and gratefully inscribed by the author." At the end of this volume he had added a large number of historical notes, and a few poems and songs.

The King of the Factory Children.

Friends, stop and listen unto me,
While I give you a brief history,
Of one who's gained his liberty,
   The king of the factory children.
Of Richard Oastler now I sing,
Let all good men their laurels bring,
And deck them round their old tried king,
   The king of the factory children.
Let each one with his neighbour vie,
And shout his praises to the sky,
For labours past to gratify,
   The King of the factory children.

CHORUS:—Rejoice, rejoice, the time has come,
            The captive's left his dungeon gloom
            Amongst his subjects for to roam,
            The king of the factory children

His sterling worth I can't unfold,
He's made oppression lose its hold,
His labours can't be bought for gold,
   The king of the factory children.
A terror to tyrants and to knaves,
Protector of the factory slaves,
To pluck them hence from premature graves,
   The king of the factory children.
His time and talents he did spend,
His factory subjects to defend,
To save them from a cruel end,
   The king of the factory children.
            Rejoice, &c.

To limit the hours of factory toil
He stood undaunted 'midst the broil
Of those who strove the work to foil
   Of the king of the factory children.
But infant's labour was assailed,
And petty tyrants writhed and wailed,
With oaths and curses they assailed
   The king of the factory children.
But gratitude the chain has broke,
Which bound him to the tyrant's yoke,
The prison house no more's the walk
   Of the king of the factory children.
         Rejoice, &c.

The " Bastile Laws " he did oppose,
For he foresaw the poor man's woes,
He therefore stood to plead their cause,
   The king of the factory children.
For man and wife to parted be,
Against Almighty God's decree,
For no " crime " but poverty,
   He could not tamely sit to see :
He told the rich with all his might
To rob the poor they had no right,
Which thundered down the tyrant's spite
   At the king of the factory children.
         Rejoice, &c.

The " Lord of Fixby " him confined
Four years to burk his noble mind,
But all could not the influence bind
   Of the king of the factory children,
His " Fleeters " flew from south to north,
To east and west they issued forth,
And each proclaimed the sterling worth
   Of the king of the factory children.
Now from his prison-house he's come
His arduous labours to resume,
And tyrants they will hear their doom
   From the king of the factory children.
         Rejoice, &c.

Now, loyal subjects all agree,
And cheer your king with three times three,
That's now restored to liberty,
    The king of the factory children.
And show the men of high estate
'Tis not the wealthy and the great,
But those your rights who advocate,
    Whose labours you do appreciate ;
Let sons of toil unite to sing,
And each their humble tribute bring
To cheer the heart of their old tried king,
    The king of the factory children.
            Rejoice, &c.

From a broadside, "Sold by W. Midgley, bookseller, Russell Street, Halifax."

The name of Richard Oastler will long be held in remembrance by the factory operatives of Bradford, and of all England. It was not until the year 1830 (according to Mr. William Scruton) that the movement for a ten hour's factory bill began. And it was first suggested at the venerable building known as Horton Hall, Bradford, then the residence of Mr. John Wood, better known as of the firm of Messrs. Wood & Walker, manufacturers. Mr. Scruton says :—"Mr. Oastler, who was at this time on a visit to Horton Hall, was deeply affected when told that little children were worked from fourteen to eighteen hours a day in some mills without a single moment being set apart for meals. After a long and impressive interview, Mr. Wood concluded by saying : ' I cannot allow you to leave me without a pledge that you will use all your influence in endeavouring to removed from our factory system the cruelties which are now regularly practised.' The pledge was given, and how faithfully it was kept is shown by the monument that was reared in Bradford by thousands of operatives to the memory of their greatest benefactor, Richard Oastler." This is not the place in which to give a history of the factory agitation, but a few notes of memoranda may not be out of place. Mr. Oastler's first move was a letter in the *Leeds Mercury* on "Yorkshire Slavery in Mills," dated September 29th, 1830. On the 25th of August, 1838, he was escorted into Huddersfield by 100,000 workpeople. On the 9th of December, 1840, he was sent to the Fleet Prison for debt at the instance of Mr. Thornhill, of Fixby Hall, where Mr. Oastler had been steward; but he was set free on the 12th of February, 1844, his friends in Yorkshire and Lancashire having collected and paid for him the sum of £3,243 15s. 10d. On the 1st of June, 1847, the Ten Hours' Bill passed; and the Queen signed it on June 8th. The "King of the Factory Children" was at the time laid on a bed of sickness, when tens of thousands were rejoicing at the result of his labours. The Earl of Shaftesbury unveiled the monument near the Midland Station, Bradford, May 15th, 1869.

Sir Miles Stapilton's Scrutiny.

To the tune of *Glorious Charles of Sweden.*

On the joyful news of Sir Miles Stapilton's gaining conquest at the late Scrutiny in the Parliament House.

> YE Yorkshire souls who love your King,
>   The Church, and English nation,
> With me rejoice, and let us sing
>   Upon this blest occasion.
> Sir Miles the Great (tho' little) Knight,
>   Of whom we well may bragg-on,
> We'll read his story with delight,
>   As George who slew the dragon.
>
> His family, our histories tell,
>   In Edward's days were mighty,
> For wit and valour did excell,
>   The thoughts of which delight me.
> From such a spring came late Sir John,
>   As clear streams from a river,
> And hence proceeded his bright son,
>   Sir Miles, Sir Miles for ever!
>
> To see what Providence can do
>   Is certainly amazing;
> To Sir John Kaye we were most true,
>   Who is to us so pleasing,
> Altho' since in election crost
>   By strange or mad behaviour,
> We made amends for what he lost,
>   And now he's in our favour.

Sir Miles's father, through mischance,
  By fall from horse expired ;
No doubt the country would advance
  The knight they so admired.
But since his fate to proper state,
  His active son doth enter,
Knight of the shire, most him desire,
  And so began th' adventure.

What means some us'd to pull him down,
  Were base, beyond denyal ;
Whose mercy, like great Kaye's, was shown
  Upon a solemn tryal ;
By numbers far he did exceed,
  Which made his foes to grieve-a ;
To see him chair'd their hearts did bleed,
  So much they lov'd Geneva.

Hugh Bethell, that most worthy's Squire,
  Such justice did each party,
That every one did him admire,
  And wish'd him joys most hearty ;
Who plac'd Sir Miles upon the chair,
  As gaining the election ;
Once more th' high sheriff be our care,
  To drink his health with affection.

Who can describe that happy day,
  Extatic joys so great, sir ;
Each soul did bear elastic sway,
  Continually replete, sir,
The noble Finch did grace the sight,
  Huzzas and trumpets sounding ;
The city's fill'd with true delight,
  And happiness abounding.

O Wortley ! we must thee admire,
  Like Nestor in contriving !
Who did Sir Miles so much inspire,
  Knew how his foes were driving ;
For sure the balance had outweighed
  And robb'd our knight of glory,
Had not thy skill their arts betrayed,
  And so quite turn'd the story.

But after this, alas! we heard
　　The dread and fierce petition,
And then, as though of souls debarr'd,
　　We seem'd in sad condition!
Nature itself did seem to frown,
　　Scarce pastime was a pleasure,
Our cups could not our sorrows drown,
　　Our hearts were fill'd 'bove measure.

That Miles should out! O dismal tone!
　　What have we all been doing?
Why shall we vote to be undone,
　　Or brought almost to ruin?
Be disaffected call'd, what not,
　　By Quakers, Presbyterians,
As though our church should go to pot,
　　Or we prove Oliverians.

But our good king, he knows full right
　　We are for church and crown, sir;
And he stood by the little knight,
　　Unto his high renown, sir:
At news of which the bells did ring,
　　And bonfires were ablazing;
The country folks who smile and sing,
　　Drink loyal healths most pleasing.

We've got, they cry, "Our dear delight,
　" Sir Miles, and no excuse, sir;
" Let diff"rence now be banished quite,
　" All loving prove and wiser.
" May plenty charm us like Heaven's smiles,
　" And trade spread o'er the nation;
" Health to King George, Sir John, and Miles,
　" To keep us in right station."

From Halliwell's " Yorkshire Anthology."

The Oak and the Ivy.

(From " Spice Islands passed in the Sea of Reading.")

BEN PRESTON.

It was Spring when I saw them in beauty and pride :
The Oak was a Bridegroom, the Ivy a Bride ;
Tall trees stood around them, some fairer than he,
But she twined round him only, so faithful was she,
No stranger with them mingled tendril or spray,
No neighbour might part them, so loving were they ;
Though fragile the ivy, how mighty the oak,
The tempest I ween will be foiled in its stroke.

It was winter :—I saw them, 'mid trouble and strife,
The Oak was a Husband, the Ivy a Wife ;
The arms of the warrior were bared for the fight ;
For the whirlwind rushed o'er him, and storms in their might.
But he loved his own Ivy, and stood to the last ;
Though the whirlwind was sudden, and lengthened the blast.

Then the frost, like a serpent, came after the storm :
But the Ivy her mantle threw over his form ;
His branches the snow and the icicles bore,
But the blight of the winter-wind touched not his core.
Thus lived they—thus bore they—the trials of life,—
The Oak was the Husband, the Ivy the Wife.

Again I beheld them, the storm-cloud was nigh ,
The Oak stood up proudly defying the sky ;
The Ivy clung round him 'mid thunder and rain ;
But the bolt fell, and ah ! he was riven in twain.
In vain she weeps dew-drops, in vain twines around
The form of the loved one, to close up the wound ;
His branches are blackened, all blasted his core ;
The Ivy's a Widow, the Oak is no more.

The Elm is beside her in beauty and pride ;
Say, will she embrace him, once more be a bride ?
Oh no ! oh no ! never : her leaves are all dim ;
She has bloomed, she will fade, she will perish with him.
The Spring comes again, and the forest is gay ;
But the bride and the bridegroom, alas ! where are they ?
O see where they slumber, the sere leaves beneath,
In life undivided, embracing in death.

TRAGIC BALLADS.

The Murder near Leeds.

The tune is— *The Bleeding Heart, &c.*

ALAS, what times here be
For men to live so sinfully ;
Nothing but wickedness doth reign
In people's hearts, we find it plain :
The Devil prompt men unto sin,
And to amend they'll not begin.
Till justice overtake them streight :
Then they repent when 'tis too late :
   God grant us Grace, and keep us free
   From murther and adultery.

But now my subject to indite,
It doth my muses sore affright,
And forceth me to shed a tear,
For me to write what you shall hear.
'Tis of a young man, I may say,
Which did his parents not obey ;
But like a crafty, cunning elf,
Despis'd his friends, ruin'd himself :
   God grant, &c.

This man to lust was so inclin'd,
And for to satisfy his mind
Did covit strait another's wife,
For which, no doubt, he'll lose his life :
Her husband having gone to sea,
He often kept her company,
And night and day was at her still,
His wicked mind for too fulfill,
   God grant, &c.

Alas, quoth she, this must not be,
My husband being now at sea,
And I but lately married am,
Pray don't a weak woman trapan.
Qth he, my dear, there's none shall know
My tender love, which I will show ;
If thou lov'st me, as I do thee,
Thou ever shalt live happily.
>   God grant, &c.

I pray, good sir, your suit forbear,
And henceforward come not me near ;
I would not for riches great store,
You should come nigh me any more ;
Although she often said him nay,
No rest she took from him night nor day,
Until a promise she exprest
To satisfie his wickedness.
>   God grant, &c.

Quoth he, my dear, do not you fear,
Travel with me into Yorkshire ;
There I have means for to maintain
Both thee and I from friends' disdain ;
For none shall know where we do go,
I will secure thee from grief and woe ;
Such flattering words she did not deny,
But went with him in a strange country.
>   Then God grant, &c.

Where they some time lived free from strife,
All took them to be man and wife ;
The woman she grew big with child,
By him which had her thus beguiled.
She often charg'd him to take heed,
Pray don't forsake me in time of need ;
Remember now your oaths to me,
And loving be in my extremity.
>   Then God grant, &c.

He valli'd not her words that time,
But studied an inhuman crime ;
The devil tempts him night and day,
How for to take her life away ;

He had her to a private place,
And being void of fear and grace,
Into her throat he put a knife,
Which ended this poor woman's life.
　　　Then God grant, &c.

He cuts her mouth from ear to ear.
Not thinking vengeance was so near,
Then out her eyes he straight did bore,
Also her tongue in pieces tore,
Her womb he ript open so wide,
Then laid the baby by her side.
This wicked wretch having so done,
Takes horse and speedily was gone.
　　　Then God grant, &c.

But murder, which cries loud on high
For vengeance, takes him speedily,
And brings him back at that same time
To answer for his bloody crime.
Unto a justice he did confess
His bloody deed of wickedness,
Then to York Castle he was sent,
God give him grace for to repent.
　　　God grant, &c.

Young maids and wives, I pray ye all,
Take warning by this woman's fall,
Don't yield to flattering speeches fair,
And of lewd young men have a care ;
Also you that husbands have,
Yield to no tongue that comes to crave
You to defile your marriage bed ;
Take warning here, be not misled.
　　　God grant us grace, and keep us free
　　　From murther and adultery.

Finis.

Printed for F. Coles, T. Vere, S. Wright, and J. Clarke. [From
Wood's Collection of printed Ballads in the Ashmolean Museum at
Oxford, E. 25, F. 102.]
INHUMAN AND CRUEL BLOODY NEWS FROM LEEDS, IN
YORKSHIRE.—Being a true relation of a young man which intict
another man's wife from London down into the country, which, after

some time, he most barbarously murthered in a most frightful manner
in a desert place, near Leeds, cutting her tongue and her eyes out of
her head, her throat being cut from ear to ear; and after all this,
being not satisfied, rip her open, and takes a child out of her womb,
laying it down by her side. This being done, he took horse and was
coming for London; but the murther being found, he was pursued
and taken, and sent to York Castle, where he must lye till the next
Lent Assizes, and then receive his due punishment. This being
written in the meantime for a warning piece to all young women, to be
careful how they be trepann'd by false and deceitful young men. With
allowance, Jan. 4, Ro. L'ESTRANGE.''

I have copied the above old ballad from the "Yorkshire
Anthology," edited by James O. Halliwell, Esq. It is an excellent
specimen of the kind got up and sold on broad sheets, in the days of
King James and the first Charles; and is most likely founded on some
real circumstance, as it was licensed by Roger L'Estrange.

The Leeds Tragedy;

OR, THE BLOODY BROTHER.

GOOD Christian people all, I pray
  Awhile to me draw near,
And such a story I will tell
  You ne'er before did hear.

For ever since the world began,
  Such a thing was never known;
When you have heard it you will say
  'Twill melt the heart of stone.

At Leeds in Yorkshire, as we hear,
  A noble lord did dwell;
He had a son and daughter fair,
  As many know full well.

His lady happening to die,
  Each was his chiefest care;
His daughter he loved best, they say,
  Both dutiful and fair.

Lords and knights they courted her,
  But she did them deny,
Saying, I am resolved
  A maid to live and die.

Her fame among the country rang,
  So dutiful was she ;
Her brother fell in love with her,
  Which caused this tragedy.

So was he struck in love with her,
  As to his bed he went ;
He'd many things, but all in vain,
  He could have no content.

For to speak he was asham'd,
  And so he well might be ;
Sure such a thing was never known
  Or heard by none but me.

One day he to his sister sent,
  So up to him she came ;
Cries he, dear sister, 'tis for you
  I'm in this burning flame.

She hearing him say so reply'd,
  Come brother, tell to me
What I can get to save your life,
  And I will get it free.

Poor soul, she, little thinking then
  What was his base intent,
Kept urging him to tell her straight,
  What would give him content.

At last, this wicked rogue ! he said,
  If I could go with thee,
Of my pains I should be free,
  And satisfied will be ;

Your beauty has so charmed me.
  If you do me deny,
By gazing at thy fair body,
  I instantly must die.

Soon as these words to her he spoke,
    Unto him she did say :
You wicked, vile, and cruel wretch !
    Forbear these words I pray :

O brother, once I lov'd you well,
    As any sister sure ;
But now my love is turn'd to hate,
    I cannot you endure.

You are the worst of creatures, sure,
    And so deserve to burn !
And was not you my brother dear,
    You out of doors should turn.

For now you're hateful in God's sight,
    And all will you disdain ;
How can you thus offend the Lord,
    In being so prophane ?

So from him then she quickly goes,
    But yet lov'd him so well
That of the thing which he had said,
    Her father would not tell.

When she was gone, he then did say,
    Reveng'd on her I'll be ;
For I will get my will of her,
    The first opportunity.

She hearing him for to say so,
    No rest at all could take ;
With grief and woe her tender heart
    Was ready then to break.

And to the Lord, poor soul, she pray'd,
    Upon her bended knees,
For to turn this ingrate's heart
    That she might be at ease.

Now he was plotting all the time
    Of her to get his will,
And afterwards he was resolv'd
    Her precious blood to spill.

Her father kept a noble park,
   One evening she did go,
And as her brother was gone out,
   She walked to and fro'.

Long in the park she had not been,
   Before that he came in,
And missing of his sister dear,
   He to the park did run.

If she is there, I'm safe enough,
   Reveng'd on her I'll be ;
When I have had my will of her,
   I'll murder her, said he.

But as he came unto the place
   Where the poor creature sat,
With a dissembling smile, he said,
   My sister dear, well met !

But when she turn'd and found him there,
   The rose her face forsook,
And, trembling, to him she did say,
   I do not like your look :

For you have mischief in your heart,
   As I can plainly see,
But your desire you shall not have,
   I am resolved, of me.

He said, Sister, you do guess right,
   To be with you I'm come ;
So this base wretch most eagerly
   Unto her arms did run.

But she cry'd out with might and main,
   Good Lord, look down, I pray !
She struggled till her strength was spent,
   And then she swoon'd away.

This cursed stony-hearted wretch
   Of her did get his will,
And afterwards he was resolv'd,
   Her precious blood to spill.

As soon as ever she did revive,
  Said he, I'll end thy life,
Crying, this knife shall end the smart,
  And none shall know the strife.

I'll stab it in the strumpet's heart,
  So pray make no dispute.*

His sister hearing him say so,
  Unto the Lord she cry'd,
O had it been Thy blessed will,
  That I before had dy'd.

Sure I should never then have felt,
  The torments I go through ;
Sure thou can'st ne'er my brother be,
  And thus to use me so.

I that am your flesh and blood,
  Don't use me so severe :
Since you've defil'd me, spare my life,
  For Christ's sake, brother dear.

He said, these words will not prevail,
  But here I'll have your life :
Then to her breast as white as snow
  He put the hateful knife.

The tears did trickle down her cheeks,
  Her life of him she crav'd :
Oh ! don't forget the judgment day !
  How will you then be saved ?

No longer will I stay, he said,
  Then gave the fatal blow ;
Her precious blood upon her breast
  Did like a fountain flow.

This did not turn his stony heart,
  Undaunted still was he ;
He straightway went and dug a grave,
  To hide her fair body.

Now when that he this grave had dug,
  And laid her in the ground,
He went and covered her blood,
  For fear it should be found.

---

* Two lines apparently wanting, but so in MS.

Such heinous things cannot be hid
 From God's most piercing sight :
For, in short, this wicked crime
 Was brought to open light.

Her aged father long did mourn
 For her, but could not hear
What had become of his sweet child.
 Whom he did love so dear.

The wicked wretch, her brother, did
 With him seem to moan :
His father little thought that he
 The wicked deed had done.

His father said to him one day.
 We will a hunting go :
Since thy dear sister can't be found,
 I'll strive to ease my woe.

Full six months her body did lay there,
 Covered with dust and mold :
And, most strangely, as you shall hear,
 The murder it was told.

Just as the sport it did begin.
 And in this place did come.
The hounds all on a sudden stopp'd,
 And would no further run.

Now he then amazed stood,
 So did the nobles all :
And the son turn'd as pale as death.
 And from his horse did fall.

The lord unto the rest did say.
 What ails my dearest son ?
My heart doth flutter in my breast :
 Sure some bad mischief's done !

The place was open'd instantly,
 Where they soon her found,
The body of his daughter dear,
 Laid in that spot of ground.

At last when they had him reviv'd ;
  And to his senses come ;
His father said, I fear you have
  This cursed action done.

So straightway to the corpse he went,
  And kiss'd her lips like clay,
Saying, this is my child, of whom
  I took such care alway !

He kiss'd her lips till floods of tears,
  Down from his cheeks did flow :
Since her dear body now is found,
  I mean the truth to know.

But when he tax'd him with the same,
  He could it not deny ;
And when he had the story told,
  He made him for to cry—

Father, where shall I go ? said he,
  Or whither shall I run ?
You shall to prison go, said he,
  And there receive your doom.

No compassion at all you had
  Upon your sister dear ;
The worst of deaths you do deserve,
  For being so severe.

She was to me as dear as you,
  Nay, I did love her best.
The Lord receive my soul, said he,
  For here I cannot rest.

He order'd him for to be seiz'd,
  And unto prison sent—
Until the assizes there he lies—
  Lord send he may repent.

His father instantly ran mad,
  And in his bed was ty'd ;
None did expect him for to live
  Until his son was try'd.

We hope this will a warning be
    To wicked, lustful men !
For such a thing sure ne'er was known
    Since first the world began.

This old ballad is very scarce, and is copied from J. O. Halliwell's
Yorkshire Anthology, of which only 130 copies were printed.

The Bowes Tragedy; or, The True Lovers.

GOOD Christian people, pray attend
    To what I do in sorrow sing ;
My bleeding heart is like to rend
    At the sad tidings which I bring
Of a young couple, whom cruel fate
Designed to be unfortunate.

Let Carthage Queen be now no more
    The subject of your mournful song ;
Nor such odd tales which heretofore
    Did so amuse the teeming throng ;
Since the sad story which I'll tell
All other tragedies excel.

Yorkshire, the ancient town of Bowes,
    Of late did Roger Wrightson dwell,
He courted Martha Railton, who
    In virtuous works did most excel ;
Yet Roger's friends would not agree
That he to her should married be.

Their love continued one whole year,
    Full sore against their parents' will ;
But when he found them so severe
    His royal heart began to chill ;
And last Shrove Tuesday took his bed
With grief and woe encompassed.

Thus he continued twelve days' space
　　In anguish and in grief of mind ;
And no sweet rest in any case
　　The ardent lover could he find.
But languished in a train of grief,
Which pierced his heart beyond relief.

Martha, with anxious thoughts possest,
　　A private message to him sent :
Acquainting him she could not rest
　　Until she had seen her loving friend ;
His answer was, " Nay, nay, my dear,
Our folks will angry be, I fear."

Full frought with grief she took no rest,
　　But spent her time in pain and fear,
Until few days before his death
　　She sent an orange to her dear ;
But's cruel mother, in disdain,
Did send the orange back again.

Three days before her lover dy'd
　　Poor Martha, with a bleeding heart,
To see her lover hy'd
　　In hopes to ease him of his smart ;
Where she's conducted to the bed,
In which this faithful young man laid.

Where she with doleful cries beheld
　　Her fainting lover in despair ;
Which did her heart with sorrow fill,
　　Small was the comfort she had there :
Tho' his mother show'd her great respect
His sister did her much reject.

She stay'd two hours with her dear
　　In hopes for to declare her mind ;
But Hannah Wrightson stood so near
　　No time to do it she could find ;
So that, being almost dead with grief,
Away she went without relief.

Tears from her eyes did flow amain,
   And she full oft wo'd sighing say,
" My constant love, alas ! is slain,
   And to pale death become a prey.
Oh ! Hannah, Hannah, thou art base ;
Thy pride will turn to foul disgrace."

She spent her time in godly prayers,
   And quiet rest from her did fly,
She to her friends full oft declares
   She could not live if he did die ;
Thus she continued till the bell
Began to sound his fatal knell.

And when she heard the dismal sound,
   Her godly book she cast away,
With bitter cries would pierce the ground,
   Her fainting heart began to decay :
She to her pensive mother said,
" I cannot live now he is dead."

Then after three short minutes' space,
   As she in sorrow groaning lay,
A gentleman did her embrace,
   And mildly unto her did say,
" Dear melting soul, be not sad,
But let your passions be allayed."

Her answer was, " My heart is burst,
   My span of life is near an end :
My love from me by death is forced,
   My grief no soul can comprehend."
Then her poor heart did soon wax faint
When she had ended her complaint.

For three hours' space, as in a trance,
   This broken-hearted creature lay,
Her mother, waiting her mischance,
   To pacify her did essay ;
But all in vain, for strength being past,
She seemingly did breathe her last,

Her mother, thinking she was dead,
  Began to shriek and cry amain,
And heavy lamentations made,
  Which call'd her spirit back again,
To be an object of hard fate,
And give to grief a longer date.

Distorted with convulsions, she
  In dreadful manner gasping lay,
Of twelve long hours no moment free,
  Her bitter groans did all dismay;
Then her poor heart, being sadly broke,
Submitted to the fatal stroke.

When things were to this issue brought,
  Both in one grave were to be laid:
But flinty-hearted Hannah thought
  By stubborn means for to persuade
Their friends and neighbours from the same,
For which she surely was to blame.

And being asked the reason why
  Such base objections she did make,
She answered thus scornfully,
  In words not fit for Billingsgate:
"She might have taken fairer on,
Or else be hang'd." Oh, heart of stone.

What hell-born fury had possest
  Thy vile inhuman spirit thus?
What swelling rage was in thy breast
  That could occasion this disgust,
And make thee show such spleen and rage,
Which life can't cure nor death assuage?

Sure some of Satan's minor imps
  Ordained were to be thy guide;
To act the part of sordid pimps,
  And fill thy heart with haughty pride:
But take this caveat once for all,
Such devilish pride must have a fall.

But when to church the corpse were brought,
  And both of them met at the gate,
What mournful tears by friends were shed,
  When that, alas ! it was too late !
When they in silent grave were laid,
A constant youth and constant maid.

You parents all, both far and near,
  By this sad story warning take,
Not to your children be severe
  When they their choice in love do make ;
Let not the love of cursed gold
True lovers from their loves withhold.

The late Mr. Denham says :—"The Bowes Tragedy was, I understand, written immediately after the death of the lovers, by the then
master of Bowes Grammar School. His name I never heard. My
father, who died a few years ago (aged eighty), knew a younger sister
of Martha Railton's, who used to sing the tragedy to strangers passing
through Bowes. She was a poor woman, advanced in years, and her
vocalism earned her many a piece of money."

The tragic death of these two lovers suggested to the poet David
Mallet the beautiful ballad of "Edwin and Emma," to be found in his
works. Mallet's poem is by far the best of the two, and the following
particulars are worth quoting. He thus begins his narrative :—

Far in the windings of a vale,
  Fast by a sheltering wood,
The safe retreat of health and peace.
  A humble cottage stood.

There beauteous Emma flourished fair,
  Beneath a mother's eye ;
Whose only wish on earth was now
  To see her blest and die.

Long had she filled each youth with love
  Each maiden with despair,
And, though by all a wonder owned.
  Yet knew not she was fair.

Till Edwin came, the pride of swains,
  A soul devoid of art ;
And from whose eye, serenely mild,
  Shone forth the feeling heart,

M

Edwin's father and sister were bitterly opposed to their love. The poor youth pined away. When he was dying Emma was allowed to see him, but the cruel sister would not allow her a word of farewell. As Emma returned home she heard the passing-bell toll for the death of her lover.

> Just then she reached, with trembling step,
>   Her aged mother's door—
> "He's gone!" she cried, "and I shall see
>   That angel face no more.
> "I feel, I feel this breaking heart
>   Beat high against my side "—
> From her white arm down sunk her head ;
>   She, shivering, sighed and died.

The lovers were buried on the same day, and in the same grave. A simple but tasteful monument was erected to their memory in 1848, by F. Dinsdale, LL.D., author of "The Teesdale Glossary," and other works. It was against the west end wall of the church, under the bell turret, where the lovers were buried. The monument bears the following inscription :—

> "Roger Wrightson, jun., and Martha Railton, both of Bowes, buried in one grave ; He died in fever, and upon tolling his passing bell, she cry'd out My heart is broke, and in a few hours expired, purely through Love,
>   March 15, 1714-15.
> Such is the brief and touching Record
> contained in the parish Register of Burials.
>   It has been handed down
> by unvarying traditions that the grave
>   was at the west end of the church,
>   directly beneath the bells.
> The sad history of these true and
> faithful lovers forms the subject of
>   MALLET'S pathetic ballad of
>   EDWIN and EMMA."

A vast amount of information, literary, personal, and typographical, connected with the poem of "Edwin and Emma," is given in the "Ballads and Songs, by David Mallet," edited by Dr. Dinsdale. (See appendix note 15).

Poor Mary, the Maid of the Mill.

THERE came to the mill stream, her pitcher to fill
One eve, gentle Mary, the maid of the mill ;

The gay waters ran swiftly, the wheel it went round,
Like snow wreaths the meal fluttered down as it ground ;
When Mary, half giddy, dipped her pitcher at last,
Strange phantoms of death o'er her young vision passed ;
Has the current grown stronger ? has her arm grown too
    weak ?
Hark ! one heavy plunge, and one wild, thrilling shriek !

She's gone down the mill-stream, and under the wheel,
It stops but to tear her—the wood and the steel !
The miller within felt that terrible shake,
Scarce a bone of poor Mary the wheel did not break !
When he looked from his lattice how fearful the sight,
There floats a dull corpse on the waters so bright ;
They lift out the body, they wring out the hair,
The face of poor Mary, though crushed, is still fair.

Then one spoke as follows, " 'Tis strange, but she said
Yester morn, as she carried her pail on her head,
That she dreaded the mill-stream, it haunted her so,
Some day she should drown there, and feared much to go."
" Last night," said the miller, " I dreamt she was drowned,
And thought of that dream when the wheel stayed its
    round,
And terribly shook as the fell deed was done.
Ere I reached it to stop it all smoothly it run ;
And this body was floating so lifeless and torn,
O'er the bright, heaving streamlet now sluggishly borne."

Alas for poor Mary, the maid of the mill !
Thy song will not wake with the lark's on the hill :
What damsel will venture thy pitcher to fill ?
Who can gaze on yon arch, or the dark currents gleam,
On yon wheel in its round, tossing spray o'er the stream,
Where the mill runs so fast, and the green waters glide,
Nor think of poor Mary, how sadly she died ?

    William Henry Leatham, of Hemsworth Hall, near Pontefract,
who is the author of the above ballad, informs me in a letter that it is
formed on a real circumstance which happened in the year 1847. The
girl went to draw water from a mill stream, and looking on the water
too earnestly, fell in, and lost her life as related.

This name must be placed with the best of our Yorkshire poets. A lover of poetry, he has wooed the muses to a good purpose. Born at Wakefield, July 6th, 1815; it was there he wrote and published all his earlier poems. These comprise :—A Traveller's Thoughts," &c., 1841; "The Victim," 1841; "Sandal in the Olden Time." 1841; "The Siege of Granada," 1841; "Strafford, a Tragedy," 1842; "Oliver Cromwell, a Drama," 1843; "Henrie Clifford and Margaret Percy," 1843; "Emilia Monterio," also "The Widow and the Earl, a ballad of Sharlston Hall," 1843; "The Batuccas and other Poems," 1844; "Montezuma, a Ballad of Mexico," "The Red Hand, and other Poems," 1845; "Life hath many mysteries," 1847. To these may be added "A Ballad of Newby Hall Ferry, and other Poems." 1869. In 1855 he published "Selections from the Lesser Poems of William Henry Leatham." London : Longmans. Also in 1858, "Tales of English Life and Miscellanies," Arthur Hall, Virtue, & Co., London : Two Volumes. (See appendix note 16).

———

Luke Hutton's Lamentation.

WHICH HE WROTE THE DAY BEFORE HIS DEATH, BEING
CONDEMNED TO BE HANGED AT YORK FOR HIS
ROBBERIES AND TRESPASSES THEREABOUTS.

To the tune of *Wandering and Wavering.*

——

I am a poor prison'r condemned to die :
  Ah, wo is me! wo is me! for my great folly :
Fast fetter'd in irons, in place where I lye ;
  Be warn'd young wantons, hemp passeth green holly.
My parents were of good degree,
By whom I would not ruled be ;
Lord Jesus receive me ; with mercy relieve me,
Receive, O sweet Saviour, my spirit unto Thee.
My name is Hutton—yea, Luke, of bad life ;
  Ah, wo is me, &c.
Which on the highway, did rob man and wife :
  Be warn'd, &c.
Intic'd by many a graceless mate,
Whose council I repent too late :
Lord Jesus forgive me, &c.

The same refrain occurs in every verse, which it is needless to repeat.

Nor twenty years old (alas) was I.
When I began this fellony,
With me went still twelve yeomen tall
Which I did my twelve Apostles call.
There was no Squier nor Baron bold.
That rode by the way, with silver and gold,
But I and my Apostles gay
Would lighten their load e'er they went on their way.

This news procured my kinsfolk grief,
That, hearing I was a famous thief,
They wept, they wail'd, they wrung their hands,
That thus I should hazard life and lands.

They made me jaylor, a little before,
To keep in prison offenders sore.
But such a jaylor was never known;
I went and let out every one.

I wis this sorrow sore grieved me,
Such proper men should hanged be :
My office then I did defie,
And ran away for companie.

Three years I lived upon the spoil,
Giving many an Earle the foyl :
Yet did I never kill man or wife,
Though lewdly, long, I led my life.

But all too bad my deeds have been,
Offending the country and my good Queen ;
All men in Yorkshire talk of me ;
A stronger thief there could not be.

Upon St. Luke's day was I born,
Who want of grace has made me scorn ;
In honour of my birthday, then,
I robb'd, in bravery, nineteen men.

The country were to hear this wrong,
With hues and cries pursued me long ;
Though long I 'scap'd, yet loe at last
In London I was in Newgate cast.

At last the Sheriff of Yorkshire came,
And in a warrant he had my name,
Quoth he, " At York thou must be try'd,
With me, therefore, hence must thou ride."

Like pangs of death his words did sound,
My hands and arms full fast he bound ;
" Good sir," quoth I, " I had rather stay,
I have no heart to ride that way."

When no entreaty would prevail,
I called for beer, wine, and ale ;
And when my heart was in woful case,
I drank my friends with smiling face.

With clubs and staves I was guarded then
I never before had such waiting men ;
If they had ridden before me amain
Beshrew if I had call'd them again.

But when unto York I was come,
Each one on me did cast his doom ;
And whilst you live this sentence note—
Evil men can never have good note.

Before the judge then I was brought,
But sure I had a direful thought,
Nine score indictments and seventeen
Against me there were read and seene.

And each of these were fellony found,
Which did my heart with sorrow wound,
What should I herein longer stay ?
For this I was condemned this day.

My death, each hour, I did attend
In prayers and teares my time did I spend,
And all my loving friends that day
I did intreat, for me to pray.

I have deserved my death long since,
A viler sinner liv'd not than I
On friends, I hoped life to save
But I am fitted for the grave

Adieu, my loving friends, each one,
Think on me, lords, when I am gone,
When on the ladder you do me view,
Think I am nearer Heaven than you.

Formerly the York theatrical season commenced in the assize week, and the York mobs would congratulate themselves in anticipation, saying, "Eh, lads! there'll be rare fun next week; players is comin', and men's to be hang'd,"—the latter probably being the more delectable sport of the two. At this time, however, none scarcely, excepting common rascals, such as turnip-stealers, pickpockets, sheep-stealers, burglars, and murderers, were hanged. The days of the Farnley Wood Plot, the Rising in the North, the Pilgrimage of Grace, and of Jesuit-hunting, were past, when men of high degree were turned off the ladder by the hangman, and dismembered and disembowelled on the block before the eyes of the populace. Glorious days those, when they could see a nobleman or a country gentleman thus butchered by the hangman. But now the most exciting spectacle was the execution of a bold highwayman, who tripped up the ladder with a nosegay in his bosom, bowed gracefully, or made a speech to the mob, and then nonchalantly threw himself off, the people sympathising with him, looking upon him as a hero, and making his plucky death the theme of conversation and admiration for long after. Those of the former class were traitors generally, of noble or high-born families, and proud is that family which can boast of having had an ancestor excuted for treason.

In the year 1598 the York mob had a special gratification, unique in York, and, perhaps, in Europe, in witnessing the hanging of an Archbishop's son, not for treason, heresy, or any other high crime for which it is a glory to die—but as a common malefactor, for a robbery on the highway.

Luke Hutton was a younger son of Matthew Hutton, Archbishop of York, the elder of the two Archbishops of that name and of the same family. Fuller says that he was not the son of the Archbishop, but of Robert Hutton, a Canon of Durham; in which statement he is followed by Thoresby of the Ducatus and Hutchinson, the historian of Durham, evidently without further research, for Canon Hutton was a Fellow, and consequently a bachelor, at Cambridge in 1589, rendering it clear that he could not have a grown-up son, who had finished his collegiate education, nine years afterwards. Still, he might not have been the son of the Archbishop; but his Christian name, Luke, seems to be a confirmation of the assertion that he was, as the Archbishop had two sons born previously to the date of Luke's birth, who were named Matthew and Mark.

He was well educated, and passed through college with a reputation for scholarship, and displaying abilities for poetical composition, which gave promise of future excellence; but through idleness in his studies, or irregularity in his life, he left without taking a degree. He had led a dissipated life at college, and, on leaving, went to London

and associated himself with evil characters, and frequently got into
trouble through his malpractices; but eventually a fit of repentance
came over him, and he resolved to lead a better life. At that time he
published a poem, entitled "Luke Hutton's Repentance," which he
dedicated to the Earl of Huntingdon. There is no known extant copy
of the printed work; but the MS., which was in Thoresby's collection,
is still in existence. It consists of eighty-one six-line stanzas, and is not
bad poetry, but is written in a dreamy, visionary style that is scarcely
intelligible. The following stanza will give an idea of its character ;—

> Lay'd on my bed I 'gain for to recount
> A thousand things which had been in my time—
> My birth, my youth, my woes—which all surmount ;
> My life, my losse, my libertie, my crime,
> Then, where I was unto my mind recalling,
> Methought earth gap'd, and I to hell was falling.

The first edition is supposed to have been published in 1596 or 1597,
and it was reprinted in 1612, and again in 1638, to the latter being
added a " Dialogue on Coney Catching."

Unfortunately, his repentance did not last long ; he soon again
fell into his old practices, was apprehended, cast into Newgate, tried,
as it would appear, before Lord Chief Justice Popham, and acquitted.
Whilst in prison he composed another work, which was published
without date. It was entitled, "The Blacke Dogge of Newgate, bothe
pithie and profitable for all readers. *Vide, Lege, Cane.* Time shall
trie the Trueth. Dedicated to the Honble. Sir John Popham, Kt.,
Lord Chiefe Justice of Englande. All encrease of honour and happiness. Signed, Lvke Hvtton." In the prefatory address, he says his
chief object is to expose " a great number of bad fellowes, who vnder-
neath the couller of office and service doe mightily abuse both Justice
and Justices, which in this booke is largely discouered, and that yovr
honovr being certified, such bad fellowes shall be the sooner look't
into, and their outrages quallified." The work was dramatised by
Day, Hathway, and Smith, and brought out on the stage in 1602.

Even this narrow escape was not sufficient to reclaim him from his
evil life ; but finding London too hot for him, he went into Yorkshire
and took to the highway, committing several robberies. At length he
was apprehended, committed to York Castle, tried on a charge of
highway robbery at the ensuing assizes, condemned, and executed. It
appears his father might, by his influence, have saved him and his
family from the ignominy of a public execution ; but with Spartan-like
rigour he allowed the law to take its course.

In the year of his execution (1598) there was published a broadside,
a copy of which is in the British Museum, assuming to have been
written by Hutton when lying in the condemned cell, which may or may

not have been his composition, but which bears internal marks of its
authenticity. It is entitled "Luke Hutton's Lamentation, which he
wrote the day before his death, being condemned to be hanged at
York for his robberies and trespasses thereabouts; to the tune of
"Wandering and Wavering."

Bill Brown, the Poacher.

In seventeen hundred and sixty-nine
   As plainly doth appear then,
A bloody scene was felt most keen
   Till death it did draw near then :
Of poor Bill Brown, of Brightside Town,
   A lad of well-known fame then,
Who took delight, both day and night,
   To trace the timid hare then.

With wires strong they marched along,
   Unto brave Thriberg town then,
With nut-brown ale that ne'er did fail,
   And many a health went round then :
Bright Luna bright did shine that night,
   To the woods they did repair then,
True as the sun their dogs did run,
   To trace the lofty hare then.

A lofty breeze amongst the trees,
   With shining he came on them,
Like Cain he stood seeking for blood,
   With his bayonet and his gun then ;
Then he did charge with shot quite large,
   George Miller did him spy then ;
This rogue's intent was fully bent,
   One of us poor lad's should die then.

His cruel hand he did command
   That instant for to fire then,
And so with strife took poor Brown's life:
   Which once he thought entire then.

His blood aloud for vengeance cried,
   The keeper he came on then,
Like cruel Cain up to him came,
   And so renewed his wounds then.

Now this dear soul ne'er did controul
   Nor think that man no ill then ;
But to Dalton Brook his mind was struck,
   While his clear blood did spill then ;
For help he cried but was denied,
   No one there nigh him stood then ;
And there he lay till break of day,
   Dogs licking his dear blood then.

Farewell dear heart, now we must part,
   From wife and children dear then ;
Pity my doom, it was too soon,
   That ever I came here then ;
Farewell unto the brave dear lads
   Whoever range the fields then,
This cruel man's murdering hand,
   Has caused me for to yield then.

In grief and pain till death it came,
   To embrace his dear soul then,
Who took its flight to heaven straight,
   Where no man can controul them.
The country round heard of the sound,
   Of poor Brown's blood being spilt then
'Twas put in vogue to find the rogue,
   That justice might be done then.

With irons strong they marched along
   Unto York Castle fair then ;
In a dark cell was doomed to dwell,
   Till the judge he did appear then ;
George Miller bold. as I've been told,
   Deny it here who can then,
He ne'er was loth to take his oath,
   Brown was a murdered man then.

There was a man who there did stand,
   Whose heart did shake amain then ;
But gold did fly they can't deny,
   Or at Tyburn he'd been hung then.

They'd ne'er been bold to hear it told,
  To hear of Shirtly's doom then;
The judge put it off to God on high
  Or they might have judged him soon then.

There was brave Ned Greaves never did fail,
  To crown poor Bill Brown's name then,
George Miller brave defies each knave,
  That travels o'er the plain then;
With sword and gun now we will run,
  Though the law it doth maintain them,
Yet poor Brown's blood lost in the wood
  For vengeance cries amain then.

Bold Nevison, the Highwayman.

Did you ever hear tell of that hero,
  Bold Nevison was his name?
He rode about like a bold hero,
  And with that he gained great fame.

He maintained himself like a gentleman,
  Besides he was good to the poor;
He rode about like a bold hero,
  And he gained himself favour therefore.

On the twenty-first day of last month,
  Proved an unfortunate day;
Captain Milton was riding to London,
  And by mischance he rode out of his way.

He called at a house by the roadside,
  It was the sign of the Magpie,
Where Nevison he sat a drinking,
  And the captain soon did he espy.

Then a constable very soon was sent for,
  And a constable very soon came;
With three or four more in attendance,
  With pistols charged in the King's name.

They demanded the name of this hero,
    "My name it is Johnson," said he,
When the captain laid hold of his shoulder,
    Saying, "Nevison," thou goest with me.

Oh! then in this very same speech,
    They hastened him fast away ;
To a place called Swinnington Bridge,
    A place where he used to stay.

They called for a quart of good liquor,
    It was the sign of the Black Horse,
Where there was all sorts of attendance,
    But for Nevison it was the worst.

He called for a pen, ink, and paper,
    And these were the words that he said,
" I will write for some boots, shoes, and stockings,
    For of them I have very great need."

'Tis now before my lord judge,
    Oh ! guilty or not do you plead :
He smiled unto the judge and the jury,
    And these were the words that he said.

" I've now robbed a gentleman of twopence,
    I've neither done murder nor killed,
But guilty I've been all my lifetime,
    So, gentlemen, do as you will."

' Its when that I rode on the highway
    I've always had money in great store ;
And whatever I took from the rich
    I freely gave it to the poor."

But my peace I make with my Maker,
    And with you I'm quite ready to go ;
So here's adieu ! to this world and its vanities,
    For I'm ready to suffer the law."

FROM A BROADSIDE.

The stories of this freebooting "hero" are very contradictory,
and also the dates of his arrest. The Rev. Oliver Heywood, in his diary,
writes as follows :—" Upon Thursday, March 6th, 1683-4, one Mr. J.
Hardcastle, of Penthorp, near Wakefield, understanding that John

Nevison, the highwayman, was drinking at an alehouse near Sandal
Castle, took some with him, and so arrested Nevison, and brought
him to Wakefield. Mr. White made him a Mittimus, sent him to
York, midst of the assizes, the judge proceeded on his former con-
viction, condemnation some years ago, he had a pardon, but it was
conditional if he would leave the kingdom, but he had stayed, so forfeited
his life, the judge told him he must dye, for he was a terrour to the
country, pronounced the sentence, which was executed on March 15,
(my baptism day) 1683-4—he was something stupid, yet at the gallows
confessed that he killed Fletcher, (the constable) near Hooley (Howley),
in his defense, but did not betray his companions, thus at last he is
found out, and taken to his mischief, his time was come, but he had a
long reign, he was born at Wortley. Mistress Cotton knew his
parents and him when young, they were brought up prophanely."

A True and Tragical Song, Concerning Captain John Bolton.

To the tune of *Fair Lady Lay your costly Robes Aside.*

A true and tragical song concerning Captain John Bolton, of
Bulmer, near Castle Howard, who, after a trial of nine hours, at York
Castle, on Monday, the 27th of March, 1775, for the wilful murder of
Elizabeth Rainbow, an Ackworth girl, his apprentice, was found
guilty, and immediately received sentence to be executed at Tyburn,
near York, on Wednesday following, but on the same morning he
strangled himself in the cell where he was confined, and so put a period
to his wicked and desperate life. His body was then pursuant to his
sentence, given to the surgeons at York Infirmary, to be dissected and
anatomized.

GOOD Christian people all, both old and young,
Pray give attention to this tragic song ;
My days are shortened by my vicious life,
And I must leave my children and my wife.

When I was prisoner to York Castle brought,
My mind was filled with dismal pensive thought
Conscious of guilt, it filled my heart with woe,
Such terrors I before did never know.

When at the bar of justice I did stand,
With guilty conscience and uplifted hand,
The court straightway then unto me they said,
What say you Bolton, to the charge here laid ?

In my defence I for a while did plead,
Sad sentence to evade (which I did dread),
But my efforts did me no kind of good,
For I must suffer and pay blood for blood.

To take her life I did premeditate,
Which now has brought me to this wretched fate ;
And may my death on all a terror strike,
That none may ever after do the like !

Murder prepense it is the worst of crimes,
And calls aloud for vengeance at all times ;
May none hereafter be like me undone,
But always strive the tempter's snares to shun !

By me she was seduced in her lifetime
Which added guilt to guilt and crime to crime ;
By me she was debauched and defil'd,
And then by me was murder'd and her child.

Inhuman and unparalled the case,
I pray God give all mortal man more grace ;
None's been more vile, more guilty in the land ;
How shall I at the great tribunal stand !

I should have been her guardian and her friend,
I did an orphan take her for that end,
But Satan did my morals so subdue,
That I did take her life and infant's too.

To poison her it was my full intent,
But Providence did that design prevent ;
Then by a rope, fast twisted with a pipe,
I strangled her and took her precious life.

My council I did hope would get me clear,
But such a train of proofs there did appear,
Which made the Court and jury for to cry,—
He's guilty, let the wicked culprit die !

When I in fetters in York Castle lay,
The morning of my execution day,
For to prevent the multitude to see
Myself exposed upon the fatal tree.

I then did perpetrate my last vile crime,
And put a final end unto my time ;
Myself I strangled in the lonesome cell,
And ceased in this transit world to dwell.

(See appendix note 17).

The Cropton Murders.

—

IN the quiet village of Cropton,
    Among the Yorkshire farming grounds,
A cruel murder, sad and startling,
    Has aroused the country round.
One Joseph Wood, a well-known farmer,
    In seclusion there did dwell,
His son and him they lived together,
    Their sad fate we now must tell.

No one pities the cruel monster,
    For the deed that he has done,
Although he killed the poor old farmer,
    Why didn't he spare the helpless son ?

These two poor victims have been missing
    Since nearly six months ago,
There cruel relation, Robert Charter,
    A Liverpool letter he did show.
The letter said the poor old farmer
    And his son had gone away
From Liverpool to cross the ocean,
    And would return some other day.

There were many had their own suspicions
    That some foul play had been done,
But nothing could be found to prove it,
    Or bring it home to the guilty one.

He took this letter immediately,
And read it o'er while she stood by;
Then he did this letter burn,
Left her in grief to make her mourn;
She wrung her hands and tore her hair,
Crying I shall fall into despair,
O fatal death, come pity me,
And ease me of my misery!

The Hartlepool Tragedy.

In the year 1727, a merchant of Northallerton, in the county of York, committed a barbarous murder on a young woman named Mary Fawden, who was pregnant to him. The name of this man was William Stephenson; and to gain his end he persuaded her, under a promise of support and protection, to go with him to Hartlepool, in the Bishopric of Durham; and he then threw her over the cliffs upon the sea shore. He was, however, soon arrested, and was hung at Durham on the 26th of August, 1727. The lines below are said to have been composed by himself, and were taken down from his own lips in gaol on the night before his execution. In the parish register of Hartlepool there is an entry as follows:—" Mary Farding, a stranger, who by a coroner's inquest was found to be murdered, was buried June 7th, 1727." In the churchwardens' accounts there is a charge " For making Mary Farthing's grave: 1s. 10d." The reader will notice that in this matter the unfortunate woman's name is spelt in three different ways, a specimen of careless spelling very common in parish matters formerly.

Good Lord, I'm undone, Thy face I would shun,
    I have angered my God, and displeased His Son;
I dare not come nigh Thy great Majesty,
    O! where shall I hide my poor soul when I die.

Thy vengeance I dread on my guilty head,
    All hopes of Thy mercy from me now have fled;
My poor sinful soul is filthy and foul,
    And terror and horror in my conscience roll,

The shame of my race, and mankind's disgrace,
  My actions all over were wicked and base ;
No devil in hell, that from glory fell,
  Can now with my guilty soul parallel.

Her affections I drew, how could I embue
  My hands in her blood ?   Oh ! my God, I do rue
The curst hellish deed.   I made her to bleed
  That never did wrong, in thought, word, or deed.

I used my whole art till I stole her heart ;
  I swore to befriend her, and still take her part ;
Thus by my treachery she was beguil'd,
  Which made her weep sorely, but I only smil'd.

With sighs and with groans, with tears and with moans,
  She offer'd such plaints as would soften flint stones :
Oh ! where should I hide my shame ? oft she cry'd ;
  Dear sir, take some pity, and for me provide.

I fear'd she'd breed strife 'twixt me and my wife,
  And that all my friends would lead me a sad life ;
Then Satan likewise did join each surmise,
  And made me an hellish contrivance devise.

I promised her fair, that I would take care
  Of her and her infant, and all things prepare,
At Hartlepool town, where she should lie down :
  Poor soul ! she believed me, as always she'd done.

Thus wickedly bent, with her then I went,
  She little expecting my bloody intent ;
We then drank some ale, and I did prevail
  With her to walk out, which she did without fail.

We then took our way to the brink of the sea,
  And there, like a fury, to her I did say—
" You impudent wretch, that coverts my store,
  I'm fully resolved you shall plague me no more."

She, dreading her fate, alas ! when too late,
  Did call out for mercy, whilst I did her beat
With the whip in my hand ; she, not able to stand,
  Ran backwards, and fell from the rock to the strand.

N 2

He took this letter immediately,
And read it o'er while she stood by :
Then he did this letter burn,
Left her in grief to make her mourn ;
She wrung her hands and tore her hair,
Crying I shall fall into despair,
O fatal death, come pity me,
And ease me of my misery !

The Hartlepool Tragedy.

In the year 1727, a merchant of Northallerton, in the county of
York, committed a barbarous murder on a young woman named Mary
Fawden, who was pregnant to him. The name of this man was
William Stephenson ; and to gain his end he persuaded her, under a
promise of support and protection, to go with him to Hartlepool, in
the Bishopric of Durham ; and he then threw her over the cliffs upon
the sea shore. He was, however, soon arrested, and was hung at
Durham on the 26th of August, 1727. The lines below are said to
have been composed by himself, and were taken down from his own
lips in gaol on the night before his execution. In the parish register
of Hartlepool there is an entry as follows :—" Mary Farding, a stranger
who by a coroner's inquest was found to be murdered, was buried June
7th, 1727." In the churchwardens' accounts there is a charge " For
making Mary Farthing's grave : 1s. 10d." The reader will notice
that in this matter the unfortunate woman's name is spelt in three
different ways, a specimen of careless spelling very common in parish
matters formerly.

Good Lord, I'm undone, Thy face I would shun,
    I have angered my God, and displeased His Son ;
I dare not come nigh Thy great Majesty,
    O ! where shall I hide my poor soul when I die.

Thy vengeance I dread on my guilty head,
    All hopes of Thy mercy from me now have fled ;
My poor sinful soul is filthy and foul,
    And terror and horror in my conscience roll.

The shame of my race, and mankind's disgrace,
    My actions all over were wicked and base ;
No devil in hell, that from glory fell,
    Can now with my guilty soul parallel.

Her affections I drew, how could I embue
    My hands in her blood ? Oh! my God, I do rue
The curst hellish deed. . I made her to bleed
    That never did wrong, in thought, word, or deed.

I used my whole art till I stole her heart ;
    I swore to befriend her, and still take her part ;
Thus by my treachery she was beguil'd,
    Which made her weep sorely, but I only smil'd.

With sighs and with groans, with tears and with moans,
    She offer'd such plaints as would soften flint stones ;
Oh! where should I hide my shame ? oft she cry'd ;
    Dear sir, take some pity, and for me provide.

I fear'd she'd breed strife 'twixt me and my wife,
    And that all my friends would lead me a sad life ;
Then Satan likewise did join each surmise,
    And made me an hellish contrivance devise.

I promised her fair, that I would take care
    Of her and her infant, and all things prepare,
At Hartlepool town, where she should lie down ;
    Poor soul! she believed me, as always she'd done.

Thus wickedly bent, with her then I went,
    She little expecting my bloody intent ;
We then drank some ale, and I did prevail
    With her to walk out, which she did without fail.

We then took our way to the brink of the sea,
    And there, like a fury, to her I did say—
" You impudent wretch, that coverts my store,
    I'm fully resolved you shall plague me no more."

She, dreading her fate, alas! when too late,
    Did call out for mercy, whilst I did her beat
With the whip in my hand ; she, not able to stand,
    Ran backwards, and fell from the rock to the strand.

In the hopes that the sea would wash her away,
  I hastened homeward without more delay,
But was taken soon, to have my sad doom,
  And must perish shamefully just in my bloom.

Which makes my heart ache and ready to break,
  I pray, my dear Saviour, some pity now take
On sinners the worst, lewd, bloody, and curst,
  Who owns his damnation both righteous and just.

But, oh! my God, why should my Saviour die,
  If not to save sinners as heinous as I ;
Then come cart and rope, both strangle and choke,
  For in my Redeemer I still trust and hope.

Let all men beware, when married they are,
  Lewd women are surely a dangerous snare :
Then love your own wives, those men only thrive
  That are the most pious and chaste in their lives.

Some particulars of this wilful deed may be found in "Th
History and Antiquities of Northallerton ; by C. J. Davison Ingledev
Esq., of the Middle Temple. London : Bell and Daldy, 1858, p. 352.

The Eland Tragedy : Revenge upon Revenge.

No worldly wight can here attain,
  Always to have their will ;
But now in grief, sometimes pain,
  Their course they must fulfil.

For when men live in worldly wealth,
  Full few can have that grace
Long in the same to keep themselves
  Contented with their place.

The Squire must needs become a Knight,
  The Knight a Lord would be :
Thus shall you see no worldly wight
  Content with his degree.

For pride it is that pricks the heart
  And moves men to mischief;
All kind of pity set apart
  Withouten grudge or grief.

When pride doth reign within the heart
  And wickedness in will,
The fear of God quite set apart;
  Their fruits must needs be ill.

Some cannot suffer for to see
  And know their neighbour thrives
Like to themselves in good degree,
  But rather seek their lives.

And some must be possessed alone,
  And such would have no peer,
Like to themselves they would have none
  Dwell nigh them anywhere.

With such like faults was foul infect
  One, Sir John Eland, Knight;
His doings made it much suspect
  Therein he took delight.

Sometime there dwelt at Crosland Hall
  A kind and courteous Knight;
It was well known that he withal
  Sir Robert Beaumont hight.

At Eland Sir John Eland dwelt,
  Within the Manor Hall,
The town his own, the parish held,
  Most part upon him all.

The market town was Eland then,
  The patent hath been seen,
Under Edward's seal certain,
  The first Edward, I wean.

But now I blush to sing for dread,
  Knowing mine own country,
So basely stored with Cain, his seed
  There springing plenteously.

Alack! such store of witty men,
  As now are in these days;
Were both unborn and gotten then
  To stay such wicked ways.

Some say that Eland, Sheriff, was
    By Beaumont disobeyed,
Which might him make for that trespass
    With him the worse affraid.

He raised the country round about,
    His friends and tenants all :
And, for this purpose, picked out
    Stout, sturdy men, and tall.

To Quarmby Hall they came at night,
    And there the lord they slew ;
At that time, Hugh of Quarmby hight,
    Before the country knew.

To Lockwood then, the self-same night,
    They came and there they slew
Lockwood, of Lockwood, that wily knight,
    That stirred the strife anew.

When they had slain thus suddenly
    Sir Robert Beaumont's aid
To Crosland they came craftily ;
    Of naught they were afraid.

The hall was watered well about,
    No wight might enter in :
Till that the bridge was well laid out,
    They durst not venture on.

Before the house they could invade,
    In ambush they did lodge ;
And watch'd a wench with wily trade,
    Till she let down the bridge.

A siege they set : assault they made
    Heinously too the hall ;
The knight's chamber they did invade
    And took the knight withal.

And this is for most certainty
    That, slain before he was,
He fought against them manfully,
    Unarmed as he was.

His servants rose, and still withstood,
    And struck with might and main :
In his defence they shed their blood,
    But all this was in vain.

The lady cried and shriek'd withal,
  When as from her they led
Her dearest knight into the hall,
  And there cut off his head.

But all in vain, the more pity,
  For pity had no place,
But craft, mischief, and cruelty,
  These men did most embrace.

They had a guide that guided them—
  Which in their hearts did dwell,
The which to this that moved them,
  The very devil in hell.

See, here, in what uncertainty
  This wretched world is led,
At night, in his prosperity:
  At morning slain and dead.

'Twas a woeful house there was,
  The Lord lay slain and dead,
Their foes then eat before their face
  Their meat, ale, wine, and bread.

Two boys Sir Robert Beaumont had,
  There left alive unslain,
Sir John of Eland he then bade
  To eat with him certain.

The one did eat with him truly;
  The younger it was, I think;
Adam, the elder, sturdily,
  Would neither eat nor drink.

" See how this boy," said Eland, " see,
  His father's death can take,
If any be, it will be he,
  That will revengement make ;

But if that he wax wild anon,
  I shall him soon foresee,
And cut them off, by one and one,
  As time shall then serve me."

The first fray here now you have heard,
  The second doth ensue ;
And how much mischief afterward
  Upon these murders grew ;

And how the mischief he contrived
His wicked heart within.
Light on himself shall be described,
Mark! for I now begin.

The same morning two messengers
Were sent to Lancashire,
To Mr. Townley and Brereton,
Their help for to require.

Unto the mount beneath Marsden,
Now were they come with speed ;
But, hearing that their friend was slain,
They turned again indeed.

When Eland with his wilful ire
Thus Beaumont's blood had shed,
Into the coasts of Lancashire
The Lady Beaumont fled.

With her she took her children all
At Brereton to remain ;
Sometimes also at Townley Hall
They sojourned certain.

Brereton and Townley friends to her
They were, and of her blood,
And presently it did appear
They sought to do her good.

They kept the boys, till they increased
In person, and in age
Their father's death to have redrest
Still kindled their courage.

Lacy and Lockwood were with them
Brought up at Brereton Green
And Quarmby ; kinsman unto them,
At home durst not be seen.

The feats of fence they practised
To wield their weapons well
Till fifteen years were finished
And, then it so befell

Lockwood, the eldest of them all,
Said " Friends, I think it good
We went into our country all
To 'venge our father's blood.

If Eland have this for well done,
  He will slay me indeed :
Best were it then we slew him soon,
  And cut off Cain, his seed.

I saw my father Lockwood slain.
  And Quarmby in the night.
At last of all, they slew certain,
  Sir Robert Beaumont, Knight.

O Lord ! that was a cruel deed,
  Who could their hands refrain,
For to pluck out such wicked weed,
  Though it were to their pain,"

To this the rest then all agreed,
  Devising, day by day,
Of this their purpose how to speed.
  What was the readiest way.

Two men that time from Quarmby came,
  Dawson and Haigh, indeed,
Who then consulted of the same,
  Of this how to proceed.

These countrymen, of course. only,
  Said Eland kept alway.
The Turn at Brighouse certainly,
  And you shall know the day.

To Cromwell-bottom you must come,
  In the wood there to wait ;
So you may have them all, and some,
  And take them in a strait.

The day was set ; the Turn was kept
  At Brighouse by Sir John ;
Full little wist he was beset
  Then, at his coming home.

Dawson and Haigh had played their parts
  And brought from Brereton-green
Young gentlemen with hardy hearts
  As were well known and seen.

Adam, of Beaumont, there was laid,
  And Lacy with him also,
And Lockwood, who was nought afraid,
  To fight against his foe.

In Cromwell-bottom woods they lay
  A number with them mo,
Armed they were in good array,
  A spy they had also ;

To spy the time John Eland came
  From Brighouse turn that day,
Who plays his part and shows the same
  To them as there they lay.

Beneath Brookfoot a hill there is
  To Brighouse on the way ;
Forth came they to the top of this,
  There prying for their prey.

From the lane end then Eland came,
  And spied these gentlemen ;
Sore wondered he who they could be
  And vail'd his bonnet then.

" Thy courtesy vails thee not, Sir Knight,
  Thou slew my father dear,
Sometime Sir Robert Beaumont hight,
  And slain thou shalt be here."

Said Adam Beaumont, with the rest,
  " Thou hast our father slain ;
Whose deaths we mind shall be redrest,
  Of thee and thine certain."

To strike at him still they did strive,
  But Eland still withstood,
With might and main to save his life,
  But still they shed his blood.

They cut him from his company,
  Belike at the Lane-end ;
And there they slew him certainly,
  And thus he made an end.

Mark here the end of cruelty,
  Such fine hath falsehood, lo !
Such end, forsooth, himself had he
  As he brought others to.

But Beaumont yet was much to blame,
  Tho' here he played the man ;
The part he played not in the same
  Of a right Christian.

A pure conscience could never find
  A heart to do this deed :
Tho' he this day should be assign'd
  His own heart's blood to bleed.

But kind, in these young gentlemen,
  Crept, where it could not go,
And, in such sort, enforced them
  Their father's bane to slo.

The Second Fray now here you have,
  The Third now you shall hear :
Of your kindness no more I crave
  But only to give ear.

When Sir John Eland thus was slain,
  Indeed the story tells,
Both Beaumont and his fellows then
  Fled in Furness fells.

O, cruel Mars, why wert thou not
  Contented yet with this ?
To shed more blood but still thou sought
  For such thy nature is.

Their young conscience corrupt by thee
  Indeed could never stay,
Till, into extreme misery
  They ran the readiest way.

For Cain, his seed on every side,
  With wicked hearts disgraced :
Which to show mercy hath denied,
  Must needs be now displaced.

In Furness fells long time they were,
  Boasting of their misdeed :
In more mischief contriving there
  How yet they might proceed.

They had their spies in this country
  Nigh Eland, who then dwelled,
Where Sir John Eland lived truly
  And there his household held.

Mo gentlemen then were not there
  In Eland, who then dwelled,
Where Sir John Eland lived truly
  And there his household held.

He kept himself from such debate,
   Removing thence withal,
Twice on the year by Savile-gate
   Unto the Bothom-hall.

Adam of Beaumont, then truly
   Lacy, and Lockwood eke,
And Quarmby came to their country
   Their purpose for to seek.

To Cromwell-bottom wood they came,
   There kept them secretly:
By fond deceit there did they frame
   Their crafty cruelty.

This is the end, in sooth to say,
   On Palmson E'en at night
To Eland miln they took their way,
   About the mirk midnight.

Into the milnhouse there they brake,
   And kept them secretly:
By subtilty thus did they seek
   The Young Knight for to slay.

The morning came, the miller sent
   His wife for corn in haste:
These gentlemen in hands he hent,
   And bound her hard and fast.

The miller sware she should repent,
   She tarried there so long;
A good cudgel in hand he hent
   To chastise her with wrong.

With haste into the miln came he,
   And meant with her to strive:
But they bound him immediately,
   And laid him by his wife.

The young Knight dreamt the self-same night
   With foes he were bested,
That fiercely settled then to fight
   Against him in his bed.

He told his lady soon of this;
   But, as a thing most vain,
She weighed it light and said, " I wis;
   We must to church certain,

And serve God there this present day,
  The Knight then made him bown,
And by the milnhouse lay the way
  That leadeth to the town.

The drought had made the water small
  The stakes appeared dry,
The Knight, his wife, and servants all
  Came down the dam thereby.

When Adam Beaumont thus beheld,
  Forth of the miln came he,
His bow in hand with him he held
  And shot at him sharply.

He hit the Knight on the breastplate,
  Whereat the shot did glide.
William of Lockwood, wroth thereat,
  Said " Cousin, you shoot wide."

Himself did shoot and hit the Knight
  Who nought was hurt by this,
Whereat the Knight had great delight
  And said to them, " I wis

" If that my father had been clad
  With such armour, certain
Your wicked hands escaped he had,
  And had not so been slain.

" O Eland town," said he, "alack
  If thou but knew of this,
These foes of mine full fast would flee
  And of their purpose miss."

By stealth to work they needs must go,
  For it had been too much
The town knowing, the lord to slo
  For them, and twenty such.

William of Lockwood was adread,
  The town should rise indeed,
He shot the knight right through the head,
  And slew him then with speed.

His son and heir was wounded there,
  But yet not dead at all,
Into the house conveyed he were,
  And died in Eland hall,

A full sister forsooth had he,
  An half-brother also :
The full sister his heir must be,
  The half-brother not so.

The full sister his heir she was,
  And Savile wed the same,
Thus lord of Eland Savile was,
  And since in Savile name.

Lo ! here the end of all mischief
  From Eland, Eland's name
Despatched it was, to their great grief
  Well worthy of the same.

What time these men such frays did frame
  Deeds have I read and heard,
That Eland came to Savile's name
  In Edward's days the Third.

But as for Beaumont and the rest,
  They were undone utterly ;
Thus simple virtue is the best
  And chief felicity.

By Whittle Lane End they took their flight,
  And to the old Earth-yate ;
Then took the wood, as well they might,
  And speed a privy gate.

Themselves conveying craftily
  To Anneley Wood that way,
The town of Eland manfully
  Pursued them that day.

The lord's servants throughout the town
  Had cried with might and main,
" Up, gentle yeomen, make you bown
  This day your lord is slain."

Whittle, and Smith, and Rimmington,
  Bury, with many mo,
As brimme as boars they made them bown
  Their lord's enemies to slo.

And, to be short, the people rose
  Throughout the town about ;
Then, fiercely following on their foes
  With hue, and cry, and shout.

All sorts of men show'd their good-wills,
 Some bows and shafts did bear,
Some brought forth clubs, and rusty bills,
 That saw no sun that year.

To church, now, as the parish came,
 They join'd them with the town,
Like hardy men to stand all same,
 To fight now they were bown.

Beaumont, and Quarmby saw all this,
 And Lockwood, where they stood :
They settled them to fence, I wist,
 And shot as they were wood.

Till all their shafts were gone and spent,
 Of force then must they flee ;
They had dispatched all their intent,
 And lost no victory.

The hardiest man of them that was,
 Was Quarmby, this is true :
For he would never to turn his face,
 Till Eland men him slew.

Lockwood, he bare him on his back,
 And hid him in Aneley Wood.
To whom his purse he did betake
 Of gold and silver good.

" Here take you this to you," said he,
 " And to my cousins here,
And, in your mirth remember me,
 When you do make good cheer.

If that my foes should this possess,
 It were a grief to me ;
My friend's welfare is my riches
 And chief felicity.

Give place with speed, and fare you well
 Christ shield you from mischief.
If that it otherwise befal
 It would be my great grief."

Their foes so fiercely followed on,
 It was no biding there ;
Lockwood, with speed, he went anon,
 To his friends where they were,

With haste, then, towards Huddersfield,
  They held their ready way—
Adam of Beaumont the way he held,
  To Crosland Hall that day.

When Eland men returned home,
  Through Aneley Wood that day,
There found they Quarmby laid alone
  Scarce dead as some men say.

And then they slew him out of hand;
  Despatch'd him of his pain;
The late death of their lord Eland,
  Inforced them certain.

Learn, Savile, here, I you beseech,
  That in prosperity,
You be not proud, but mild and meek,
  And dwell in charity.

For by such means your elders came
  To knightly dignity.
Where Eland then forsook the same,
  And came to misery.

Mark here the breech of charity,
  How wretchedly it ends.
Mark here how much felicity
  On charity depends.

A speech it is to every wight,
  Please God who may or can;
It wins always, with great delight,
  The heart of every man.

Where charity withdraws the heart
  From sorrow and sighs deep,
Right heavy makes it many a heart,
  And many an eye to weep.

You, gentlemen, love one another,
  Love well the yeomanry;
Count every Christian man his brother,
  And live in charity.

Then shall it come to pass truly,
  That all men you shall love;
And after death then shall you be
  In Heaven with God above.

> To whom, always, of every wight,
> Throughout all years and days,
> In Heaven and earth, be day and night,
> All honour, laud, and praise.

Ealand, Eland, or Elland Hall was situate on the opposite side of the Calder to the village of the same name, near Halifax, and, according to tradition, was the scene of the deadly affray by which the name became extinct. The metrical record of that hereditary feud was transcribed by Hopkinson about the year 1650, and has little but internal evidence to support the truth of the sad story it relates. It has been supposed by some to be fiction, but Whitaker, in his " Loidis and Elmete," says :—" In my opinion the poem authenticates itself. Let the reader turn to the following transcript from Dodsworth's MSS. of that time, and he will find that though the estate passed by marriage of a sister of the last of the Eland's to the Savile's, there was a brother Henry. . . . The poem informs us that Henry was a brother of the half-blood, and therefore the immediate ancestor having died he could not succeed. This could not be invented. Then, again, the story is so circumstantial, the places, dates, &c., so specific and so consistent, that I cannot conceive it a fable. . . . Hopkinson has given it an air of modernism to which it is not entitled, by having altered the spelling. I am inclined to refer it to the end of the reign of Henry the VIII., when, from several other specimens, it appears that a humour of versifying prevailed in this country. The hint given to ' Savile not to lose the good graces of the people by pride may well suit Sir Henry Savile, who died in 1558, but would have been impertinent had it been addressed to his long-lived son, Edward Savile. I suspect the whole to be the expansion of a much more ancient and perhaps contemporaneous ballad now irretrievably lost.' " The date of the copy in my possession is 1789, and is entitled " Revenge upon Revenge, or an Historical Narrative of the Tragical Practices of Sir John Eland, of Eland, High Sheriff of the county of York, committed upon the persons of Sir Robert Beaumont, and his alliances in the reign of Edward the Third, King of England : together with an account of the Revenge which Adam, the son of Sir Robert Beaumont, and his accomplices, took upon the persons of Sir John Eland and his Posterity, &c."

Another account :—In the reign of Edward III., Sir John Elland, of Elland, instigated by some unexplained cause of hostility, raised a body of his friends and tenantry, and placing himself at their head, sallied forth by night for the Manor Hall, and attacked and slew Hugh of Quarmby, Lockwood of Lockwood, and Sir Robert Beaumont, of Crossland : the latter of whom was torn from his wife, and beheaded in the hall of his own house ; the whole of these were murdered in the presence of their families. On the perpetuation of these sanguinary murders, the younger branches of the Beaumonts, the Quarmby's, and the Lockwoods fled into Lancashire, and found an asylum under the roofs of the Towneleys and the Breretons. It was not till the eldest son of the three outraged families had grown up to manhood that retribution was sought and obtained for the blood of their parents. With this purpose the three young men placed themselves in a wood, at Cromwell-bottom, and as Sir John Elland was returning from Rastrick they met him beneath Brookfoot and slew him. Not satisfied with this act of justice, they determined to extirpate the name of Elland, with which sanguinary intention they placed themselves in a mill, near which the young knight, with his lady and their son, had to pass to church. On the approach of the family over the dam, the murderers rushed forth, and shot an arrow through the head of the father, and wounded his only child so desperately that he died soon after in Elland Hall. The name of Elland now became extinct, and the daughter of Sir John having contracted marriage with one of the Saviles, the property passed into that family. The murder of the young knight and his infant son roused the town of Elland to arms, and they advanced *en masse* to punish the murderers. For some time, Beaumont, Quarmby, and Lockwood, whose arms vengeance had nerved, stood their ground, and defended themselves with distinguished valour against the unequal numbers by which they were assailed, but being at length overpowered, Quarmby fell dead upon the field, and his comrades only escaped the same fate by the fleetness of their horses. These startling events are supposed to have occurred in the year 1327.

HUMOROUS BALLADS.

The Fair.

YE loit'ring minnits faster flee,
Ye're all ower slaw behawf for me,
   That wait impatient for the moornin' ;
To-moorn's the lang, lang wish'd for fair,
Ah'll try to shine the fooremost there,
   Mysen i' finest cleeas adoornin',
               To grace the day.

Ah'll put mah best white stockings on,
An' pair o' new cawf-leather shoon,
   My cleean-wesh'd goon o' printed cotton ;
Aboot my neck a muslin shawl,
A new silk hankercher ower all,
   Wi' sike a careless air ah'll put on.
               Ah'll shine that day,

My partner Ned, ah knaw, thinks he,
" He'll mak' his sen secure o' me,"
   He's ofens se'd he'd treeat me rarely ;
But ah sal think ov other fun,
Ah'll aim for sum rich farmer's son,
   An' cheeat our simple Neddy fairly,
               Sea sly that day.

Why mud ah nut succeed as weel,
An' get a man full oot genteel,
   As awd John Darby's dowghter Nelly ;
Ah think mysen as good as she,
She can't mak' cheese or spin like me,
   That's mare 'an beauty, let me tell ye,
               On onny day.

Then hey! for spoorts an' puppy shows,
An' temptin' spice-stalls, rang'd i' rows,
  An' danglin' dolls, by t' necks all hangin',
An' thoosand other pretty seeghts,
An' lasses, traill'd alang the streets,
  Wi' lads, to t' yal-house gangin'.
            To drink that day.

Let's leeak at winder,—ah can see 't,
It sceams as tho' 'twas growin' leeght,
  The cloods wi' early rays adoornin',
Ye loit'ring minnits faster flee,
Ye're all ower slaw behawf for me
  'At wait impatient for the moornin',
            O' sike a day.

Here is a specimen of rich Yorkshire humour. The fair one
it will be seen is very worldly-minded. She is evidently in a fever of
expectation, and looks "for spoorts an' puppy shows" with the eager
anticipation that flutters the heart of many a city's daughter on the
prospect of the first drawing-room day. The verses are from "A
Garland of New Songs," no printer's name.

I'm Yorkshire Too.

By the side of a brig that stands over a brook
  I were sent betimes to school,
I went wi' the stream as I studied by book,
  And was thought to be no small fool ;
I ne'er yet bought a pig in a poke,
  To gie Old Nick his due,
Yet I ha' dealt wi' Yorkshire folk,
  But I were Yorkshire too.

I were pretty weel liked by each village maid
  At races, wake, or fair,
For my feyther had addled a vast in trade,
  And I weer his son to heir ;

And seeing I did not want for brass
  Gay maidens came to woo,
But, though I liked a Yorkshire lass,
  Yet I were Yorkshire too.

Then to Lunnon by feyther I were sent,
  Genteeler manners to see :
But fashion's so dear—I came back as I went,
  And so they made nothing o' me ;
My kind relations would soon ha' found out
  What 'twur best wi' my money to do,
But, says I, my dear cousins, I thank ye for naught,
  I's not to be co'sened by you.

Unfortunate Miss Bailey.

—

A captain bold in Halifax,
  Who dwelt in country quarters,
Seduced a maid, who hanged herself
  One morning in her garters ;
His wicked conscience smited him,
  He lost his stomach daily,
He took to drinking ratafia,
  And thought upon Miss Bailey.
    Oh, Miss Bailey! Unfortunate Miss Bailey.

One night, betimes, he went to rest,
  For he had caught a fever,
Says he, " I am a handsome man,
  But I am a gay deceiver."
His candle, just at twelve o'clock,
  Began to burn quite palely,
A ghost stepped up to his bedside
  And said, "Behold Miss Bailey ! "
    Oh, Miss Bailey ! &c.

"Avaunt, Miss Bailey, then he cried,
  "Your face looks white and mealy."
"Dear Captain Smith," the ghost replied,
  "You've used me ungenteely:
The crowner's 'quest goes hard with me,
  Because I've acted fraily,
And Parson Biggs won't bury me,
  Though I am dead Miss Bailey."
      Oh, Miss Bailey! &c.

"Dear corpse," said he, "since you and I,
  Accounts must once for all close,
I've got a one-pound note
  In my regimental small-clothes:
'Twill bribe the sexton for your grave."—
  The ghost then vanished gaily,
Crying, "Bless you, wicked Captain Smith,
  Remember poor Miss Bailey."
      Oh, Miss Bailey! &c.

The above humourous song made its first appearance in 1805, in Colman's play, "Love laughs at Locksmiths." There is also a Latin version of this song in the *Gentleman's Magazine* for August, 1805, written by the Rev. G. H. Glasse. The allusion to Halifax is nothing more than a poetic licence, and means no more than does that of Goldsmith, when he named his immortal novel, "The Vicar of Wakefield." Some years ago I met with a song having the same title as the above, and which I believe is of the same date, which I give below:—

Miss Bailey's Ghost.

The dog had ceased to bark,
  The silver moon shone bright,
When in the lone church yard
  Stood poor Miss Bailey's sprite,
Oh, what will become of me?
  Ah, why did I die?
Nobody coming to bury me,
  Nobody coming to cry!

The first time I saw Captain Smith
   I was *fair*, though he treated me *foul*,
So here *tête-a-tête* with the moon
   All night will I bellow and howl.
Oh, what can the matter be,
   My own ghost in the cold *must expire*,
While wicked Smith o'er his ratafie,
   Is roasting his shins by the fire.

The last time I saw my deluder
   He gave me a shabby pound note,
But I borrowed his best leather breeches,
   To wear with my wooden surtout.
And it's oh, to be cover'd in decency,
   For a grave I the parson did pay,
But Captain Smith's note was a forgery,
   And I was turned out of my clay.

And here am I singing my song
   Till almost the dawning of day ;
Come, Sexton, come, Spectre, come, Captain,
   Will nobody take me away ?
But hold, yet I've one comfort left,
   Delightful to most married fair.
Though cold, and of all joy bereft,
   Yet still I've the breeches to wear.

The first of these songs is given in Dr. Ingledew's " Ballads and
Songs of Yorkshire ; " but they are both inserted in " The Universal
Songster, or Museum of Mirth," vol. 1, printed at the Ballantyne
Press, Edinburgh ; no date.

The Merchant's Son: and the Beggar Wench of Hull.

You gallants all, I pray draw near,
And you a pleasant jest shall hear,
How a beggar wench of Hull,
A merchant's son of York did gull.
   Fal, la, &c.

One morning on a certain day,
He clothed himself in rich array,
And took with him, as it is told,
The sum of sixty pounds in gold.

So mounting on a prancing steed.
He towards Hull did ride with speed,
Where, in his way, he chanc'd to see
A beggar wench of mean degree.

She asked him for some relief,
And said with tears of seeming grief,
That she had neither house nor home,
But for her living was forced to roam.

He seemed to lament her case,
And said, thou hast a pretty face ;
If thou wilt lodge with me, he cry'd,
With gold thou shalt be satisfy'd.

Her silence seemed to give consent,
So to a little house they went :
The landlord laughed to see them kiss
The beggar wench, a ragged miss.

He needs must have a dinner drest,
And call'd for liquor of the best,
And there they toss'd off bumpers free,
The jolly beggar wench, and he.

A dose she gave him as 'tis thought,
Which by the landlady was brought ;
For all the night he lay in bed,
Secure as if he had been dead.

Then she put on all his cloaths,
His coat, his breeches, and his hose ;
His hat, his perriwig likewise,
And seis'd upon the golden prize.

Her greasy petticoat and gown,
In which she rambled up and down,
She left the merchant's son in lieu,
Her bag of bread and bottle too.

Down stairs like any spark she goes,
Five guineas to the host she throws,
And smiling then she went away,
And ne'er was heard of to this day.

When he had took his long repose,
He look'd about and mist his cloaths.
And saw her rags lie in the room,
How he did storm, nay fret and fume.

Yet wanting cloaths and friends in town,
Her greasy petticoat and gown
He did put on, and mounted strait.
Bemoaning his unhappy fate.

You would have laugh'd to see the dress
Which he was in, yet ne'ertheless
He homewards rode, and often swore,
He'd never kiss a beggar more.

Printed and sold in Aldermary Churchyard. Bow Lane, London.

Jack's Alive; or. the Amphibious Yorkshireman.

WHEN I lived in the North I could handle a flail.
But I'd sooner by-half had a cup o' good ale.
I ne'er could abide work, unless hard set for meat :
I'd sooner by half gaped up and down t' street,
And made love to each damsel I chanced for to meet,
As for beauty they all owned I ne'er could be beat.

I first lived in one place and then in another :
Wur turned out of all, so I then lived wi' brother.
But he said I wur lazy, and turned me off too,
And that for his purpose I never should do.
So I went to the fairs with a straw in my mouth :
But it wouldn't do there, so I came up to the South :

At walking I always were good as most folk.
But I'd much sooner ride, sirs—I'ze sure I don't joke.
As I didn't know gainest rood up to this town,
I'd com'd in a ship for a pound and a crown :
But instead of famed Lunnon, they stopt in the Downs.
Where a man-of-war pressed me, them hungry hounds.

As I crawl'd up ship's side, I were terribly 'fraid :
Thinks I, down at home now I'd much better stayed.
A man shook my hand when I com'd up to the top,
And he put me to work with a thing like a mop :
Then he played on a whistle, just like a great boy,
Sung a song like a raven, about " All Hands A-hoy,"

No sooner he'd done than I heard a great noise,
When he sung out again " Bear a hand boys."
Says I, " What's to do ?" but the de'el a man spak,
And a chap came and laid a cain over my back,
Saying, " Lubber stand by, we want none syke as you ;"
" I'm quite of your mind, so pray let me go."

This hurry and bustle, I found very soon,
Was not a new joke and a very old tune :
A Frenchman they tell'd me had come alongside,
I ax'd which was him, for I thought they had lied ;
And I found I wur right, for instead of one man
I'll be hanged if they hadn't two hundred to one.

They bade me pluck up, says I, " Pluck up yersen,
For I've come fra the North, where we've fought now and
      then :
Though no sailor, I've got British blood in my veins,
So you take and manage your ropes and your reins ;
I've fought wi' an Englishman often 'ere now,
And it's hard if I cant lick a Frenchman or two."

" You must fight a great gun," said a young man to me.
" I'll be shot if I do, for I'd sooner fight thee."
But the gun fought the French from a hole in the ship's
      side,
Till they called out they'd done, and a vast of 'em died.
Then the sailors they bade me go wash off my muck ;
" Yes," said I, " but let's give 'em one more shot for luck."

The captain informed me the Frenchmen had struck,
" Why, then, strike him again," said I, all of a ruck.
So they sent me aboard wi' a sword in my hand,
And there I kept guard till we came to the land ;
Then they paid me my wages, no longer I'll roam,
And plough no more seas, but mind ploughing at home.

Songs like the above were very popular during the wars with the French, in the latter part of the last century and the beginning of the present. They appear to have been composed to be sung in the minor or lower-class theatres. There is not much that is elevated in them, but they were, no doubt, suited to the popular taste of the time. One is surprised to find so many of these ditties relating how Yorkshiremen went up to London ; and how they were "fleeced" or robbed, and endured strange mishaps during their stay in the city ; and suggesting the idea that this kind of song was the composition of some Cockney.

Tommy Towers and Abraham Muggins: or, the Yorkshire Horse Dealers.

HARD by Clapham town-end lived an old Yorkshire tyke,
Who in dealing in horses had never his like :
'Twor his pride that i' aw the hard bargains he'd pit,
He'd bit a gort mony, but never got bit.

This oud Tommy Towers* (bi that name were knaan)
He'd an old carrion tit that were sheer skin and baan :
Ta hev killed him for t' curs wad hev bin quite as well,
But 'twor Tommy's opinion he'd dee on himsel !

Well ! one Abey Muggins†, a neighbourin' cheat,
Thowt ta diddle oud Tommy wod be a rare treat ;
He'd a horse too, 'twer war than oud Tommy's, ye see,
Fort' neet afore that he'd thowt proper to dee !

Thinks Abey, t'owd codger'll never smell t' trick ;
I'll swop wi' him my poor decad horse for his wick,
And if Tommy I nobbud can happen to trap,
'Twil be a fine feather i' Aberram's cap.

Soa ta Tommy he goes, an' the question he pops :
"Between my horse and thine, prithee, Tommy, what swops ?
What wil't gi' ma ta boot, for mine's better horse still ?"
"Nout," says Tommy ; "I'll swop even hands an' ye will !"

Abey preacht a long time about summat ta boot,
Insistin' that his was the liveliest brute :
But Tommy stuk fast where he first had begun,
Till Abey shook hands, and said, " Done Tommy, done ! "

" Oh, Tommy ! " said Abey, " I'se sorry for thee,
I thowt thaa'd a hed mair white i' thee e'e ;
Good luck's wi' thy bargain, for my horse is dead."
" Hey," says Tommy, " my lad, soa is mine, an' its fleead."

Soa Tommy got t'better o't bargain, a vast,
An' cam' off wi' a Yorkshireman's triumph at last ;
For tho' 'twixt deead horses, there's not mich ta choose,
Yet Tommy war richer by t'hide an' fower shoes.

* This song is copied from a broadside, which has the usual
chorus at the end of each verse, of " Derry down, &c." It was
formerly very popular in Yorkshire, and in some parts it is still a great
favourite.   The descendants of Tommy Towers were residents of
Clapham within the last few years, and used to take great pleasure in
relating the adventure of their ancestor.   Clapham is on the highroad
between Skipton and Kendal, in the West Riding of Yorkshire.
    † It has generally been supposed that Abey Muggins was a
soubriquet for a then popular innkeeper of Clapham.

The Yorkshireman in London.

Oh ! gentle folk, what do you think ?
    Oh ! where do you think I've been ?
I'm sure I ne'er shall sleep a wink,
    I'se so pleased with the sights I ha' seen.
It grows very late, you'll all say,
    And its time we were all gang'd to bed,
But my feet carried me to the play,
    And I can't get it out of my head.
            Sing tal de rol, &c.

Odzooks ! what a nation fine place !
  And what waundy fine people go there :
I was never before in such case,
  For I didn't know which way to stare !
On one side I see'd the gay beaux,
  On 't 'other the ladies so fair !
Who, I'm sure takes no pride in their cloaths,
  For they scarce provide any to wear !
          Tol de rol, &c.

But soon as the play was begun,
  Which they call'd the " Bold stroke for a wife :
I was up to my elbows i' fun,
  Such as I ne'er see'd before i' my life :
For the Quakers they stuck us so prim,
  So humble, yet so full of pride !
So solemn, yet so full of whim
  That wi' laughing I thought I'd ha' died.
          Tol de rol, &c.

In the farce of the " Devil to pay,"
  Mr. Jobson, a huge clever chap,
Made his wife every order obey,
  By the power of his wonderful strap !
So I find them that wander and roam,
  Learn something from all that they see :
I'll speak to our cobler at whoam,
  And get him to make one for me.
          Tol de rol, &c.

Now I'm com'd to the end of my story,
  I reckon it's time to gie o'er,
Though I'd like you to hear what a woory
  And scrawging they made at the door ;
Yet to tell you the whole of the rout,
  It's too late in the night to begin ;
So to cut my tale short, I'm com'd out,
  But the dewl knows how I got in.
          Sing tol de rol, &c.

Yorkshireman in London.

———

WHEN first in London I arrived
  On a visit, on a visit ;
When first in London I arriv'd,
  'Midst heavy rain and thunder,
I spied a bonny lass in green,
The bonniest lass I'd ever seen ;
I'd oft heard tell of a beauteous Queen :
  Dash me, thinks I I've found her.

I look'd at her, she looked at me,
  So bewitching, so bewitching,
I look'd at her, she look'd at me,
  I looked so very simple.
Her cheeks were like the blooming rose,
Which on the edge neglected blows ;
Her eyes were black as any sloes,
  And near her mouth a dimple.

I stood stock still, she did the same,
  Gazing on her, gazing on her ;
I stood stock still, she did the same,
  Thinks I I've made a blunder ;
Just then her cheeks turn'd deadly pale,
Says I, my love, what do ye ail ?
Then she told me a dismal tale,
  That she was scared with thunder.

Madame, says I, and made my bow,
  Scraping to her, scraping to her ;
Madame, says I, and made my bow,
  I'd quite forgotten t'weather ;
But if you will permission give,
I'll see you home where-e'er you live.
So she popt her arm right through my sleeve,
  And off we went together.

A bonny wild-goose chase we had,
  In an' out, Sir, in an' out, Sir ;
A bonny wild-goose chase we had,
  The bollar stones so galled me,

At last she brought me to a door
Where twenty lasses—nay, or more—
Came out to have a better glore
    At t'bumpkin, as they called me.

Walk in, said she, kind sir, to me,
    Quite politely, quite politely;
Walk in, she said, kind sir, to me,
    Poor chap, say they, he's quite undone.
Walk in, says she, no, no, says I,
For I've got other fish to fry;
I've seen you home, so now, good bye,
    I'm Yorkshire, though in London.

My pockets soon I rummish'd over,
    Cautious ever, cautious ever;
My pockets soon I rummish'd over,
    Found there a diamond ring, sir;
For I had this precaution took,
In each to stick a small fish hook, a small fish hook;
So in grappling for my pocket book,
    The barb had stripped her finger.

Three weeks I've been in London town,
    Living idle, living idle;
Three weeks I've been in London town,
    It's time to go to work, sir;
For I've sold the ring, and here's the brass,
I have not played the silly ass;
It will do to toast a London lass,
    When I get back to Yorkshire.

    I have copied the above from "The Yorkshire Anthology, a
collection of modern ballads, poems, and songs," collected by James
A. Halliwell, 1851. I have another copy, a little altered, which I
found in the "Museum of Mirth," in which the second verse is
omitted. The other is entitled "Quite Politely." The allusion above
to bollar stones is new. Perhaps boulder stones or cobble stones is
here meant. Mr. C. G. D. Ingledew prints his copy from "A Garland
of New Songs," printed by G. Marshall, in the Old Flesh Market,
Newcastle-upon-Tyne, 1870."

Ould Malley's Voluntine.

———

Ould Malley threw her knitting dewn
   And stood awhile a'th floor,
Starin at summot t'post hed browt
   Unto hur cottage door.
Ther' shap o't Queen stuck on o't neuk,
   An summot else beside,
'At wakkend up ould Malley's pluck
   To see what wor inside.

Hoo opppend it, bud what hoo saw,
   It made hur varry queer;
Thear lots o varses up an dewn,
   An picturs here an theer.
Hoo cudd'nt read it, bud hoo said,
   "Aw think aw'st goa to'th skoil,
An get th' ould man to read it me,
   At learnin awm a fooil."

Soa Malley donn'd hur bonnet on,
   Hur shoin an Sunday gewn;
An off hoo set, it wor not long
   Afore hoo clapt it dewn,
Upo ould Johnny's writin' desk,
   Who said, "thew cuts a shine,
Who's sent ta this? awm fain ta see
   Thee, get a Vuluntine."

"A Voluntine," hoo said, "Who'll send
   A Voluntine to me?
Aw think they're wrang i' they're top lock,
   To day awm fifty three,
An neaw to hev a voluntine,
   Awd nivver one afore;
An noabdy's whisperd love to me,
   Fur twenty year an more."

"Well what o' that," ould Johnny said,
   "Its nut to lat to mend,
Aw sent tha this to let tha knaw
   I want to be thi friend.

Beside aw knew thaa'd bring it here
    For me to read to thee,
Soa pray tha doff thi bonnet off,
    An tak a cup o' tea :

An we will mak it up to day,
    If thee hes bud a mind ;
Aw connot live be'th dead thew knaws,
    Soa dunno be unkind ;
Bud tak ma neaw for what awm worth,
    Awm nawther rich nor fine ;
An mak ma what aw want to be,—
    Thi love, thi Voluntine."

Ould Malley shamed an hung hur heead,
    An blushing gav consent ;
Then went an doft hur bonnet off,
    An sat hur deawn content.
So they wer wed i Easter wik,
    The day wer varry fine ;
An oft sin then they've laft and taukt,
    Abewt that Voluntine.

A New Song, called Robert Wilson and John West.

As for our misfortunes, our spirits revive,
This night for our lodgings let us contrive ;
Drink about then, says Robert, and let us be glad
For as long lives the merry heart as those who are sad.

Our Scarbro' is an ancient seaport town of request,
There lives one Robert Wilson and another John West ;
Both men of great courage, and soon you shall know
How this confounded marriage has brought them so low.

P 2

As fortune doth favour, it seldom doth fail,
We are met together both in love and good ale ;
Drink about, then, says Robert, and lets not be mice,
For I know you can give the best of advice.

Advice and to reason let me understand ;
If I know your wants I'll do what I can ;
Adzooks, man ! says Robert, I am in great strife ;
Was there ever a man so perplex'd with a wife ?

Says John unto Robert, if you will resign,
Give me your wife, and I will give you mine ;
Adzooks, man ! says Robert, you talk very strange ;
Pray what will you give, and we'll make an exchange.

To exchange for an old one I never intend,
For mine is a young scold, perhaps she will mend :
Yours is an exclaimer, and she's grown very strong ;
There's no man can tame her, she's reign'd too long.

I am vexed to think that my money's all gone,
Two hundred pounds and some odds I have owing,
Some forty shillings, some others a crown,
But now it is noised all Scarbro' roun.

Adzooks, man ! says John, I wish it was mine,
Let it come when it will, it will come in good time,
Good time, then, says Robert, as the proverb doth run,
There's a time for everything under the sun.

There's a time for to laugh, and a time to cry,
There's a time for to live, and a time for to die,
There's a time for to borrow, I dare well to say,
But never a time for me to have pay.

Before that I stay here in Scarbro in want,
I'll go to the sea for my country to fight ;
No great ship of war that ever did run,
Can fight me so sore as my wife she has done.

The Will of Whitehead's Pig.

John Calcutt, a weaver, of Knaresborough, wrote the following
ngular piece many years ago, and after long passing about in manu-
ript from hand to hand, at last found a place in the corner of a local
ewspaper. We never heard of anything else that "Poor Jack" did
any way except his building a row of cottages with some money
hich he had won in a prize in a lottery, and they are to this day
illed, "Calcutt Houses."

Now that I am about to die,
To make my Will I needs must try ;
To little Tom, who runs about,
I freely give my ugly snout :—
And the two ears upon my head,
I gave them both to Dirty Ned.

And I declare in this my Will,
My liver all belongs to Bill ;
My curly tail so trim and hairy,
I leave to Betsy and to Mary :
To kind Maria and to Jane,
Who oft relieved my hungry pain ;

In token of my great regard,
My " hearts of hearts " I do award
To Frank, who gently did me tether,
I leave my gall, and eke my bladder ;
And to my master and his man,
To each I give a Side and Ham.

Then to our neighbour, Mrs. Pratt,
I give a thumping lump of fat ;
To Bella Lambert, saucy slut,
I only leave a dirty gut :
But to her neighbour, Holmes, the tailor,
I leave my paunch—and 'tis a *Wailer!*

To Walker, who lives in the ark,
And to his daughter, Mrs. Clark,
I leave my trotters all save one,
Which I shall give away anon.

And in this Will I do declare
Bob Corker shall have all my hair,
That as my dying knell he whistles
He may reward himself with bristles.

For Mrs. Simpson, careful soul,
I'll have my blood caught in a bowl,
Hoping, when in a proper posture,
She will invite poor Roger Foster
To have a bit—'twill be so nice,
When she has seasoned it with spice.

And now, my friends, I must resign
To death this worthless life of mine ;
But yet, before I pass the gate,
To meet my sad, my solemn fate,
Ingratitude I deem a crime—
For making of my Will in rhyme,
I give my last remaining foot,
In payment, unto JACK CALCUTT."

Dolly Dugging.

LOVE's like I deant knaw what,
    Deevil cannot match it,
Auld, young, and middle aged,
    I's sartain sure ta catch it ;
I catched it yance mysen,
    It made me quite uneasy,
And when I gat a wife
    By gum she set me crazy.

Dolly Dugging I teak ta be my wife, Sir,
    I did noutt but cry she led me sic a life, Sir,
I nivver efter smiled nor spent yan hour i' laughter.
    She wor a angel forst, but she proved a deevil efter.

happened on a time I axed a friend ta dinner,
I needed some mysen I'd growed sae mickle thinner,
oll bought some ribs o' beef when doon sits I an Davy,
She gave us beans to pick while she tuk meat and gravy

    Aboot a week fra this,
        Our Dolly d' getten collick,
    Now thinks I ta mysen,
        This is time for frollick.
    Dolly prayed neet and day,
        As lang as she prayed I swer,
    She prayed she might live,
        But I prayed she might dee, sir.

    Sud Bonyparte cum
        I'd fit him for his folly,
    For I couldn't wish him warse,
        Than wedded tiv our Dolly ;
    She'd bring his courage doon,
        And him severely handle,
    Ay and mak him soon as fond,
        As ony fardin can'le.

    Printed and sold in Bow Church-yard, London.   See Horace
odd's *Garland*, in the British Museum.

Harry the Tailor.

WHEN Harry the tailor was twenty years old,
He began for to look with courage so bold ;
He told his old mother he was not in jest,
But he would have a wife as well as the rest.

Then Harry next morning, before it was day,
To the house of his fair maid took his way.
He found his dear Dolly a making of cheese,
Says he, "You must give me a buss, if you please !"

She up with the bowl, the butter milk flew,
And Harry the tailor looked wonderful blue.
"O, Dolly, my dear, what hast thou done?
From my back to my breeks has thy buttermilk run."

She gave him a push, he stumbled and fell
Down from the dairy into the draw-well.
Then Harry, the plough boy, ran amain,
And soon brought him up in the bucket again.

Then Harry went home like a drowned rat,
And told his old mother what he had been at,
With buttermilk, bowl, and a terrible fall,
O, if this be called love, may the devil take all!

This song was taken down some years ago from the recitation of
a country curate, who said he had learned it from a very old inhabitant
of Methley, near Pontefract, Yorkshire. Mr. Dixon says it was not
before in print.

———————

King James First and the Tinkler.

—

AND now, to be brief, let's pass over the rest,
Who seldom or never were given to jest,
And come to King Jamie, the first of our throne,
A pleasanter monarch sure never was known.

As he was a hunting the swift fallow dear,
He dropped all his nobles, and when he got clear,
In hope of some pastime away he did ride,
Till he came to an ale-house, hard by a wood-side.

And there with a tinkler he happened to meet,
And him in kind sort he so freely did greet:
"Pray thee, good fellow, what hast in thy jug,
Which under thy arm thou dost lovingly hug?"

"By the mass," quoth the tinkler, "its nappy brown ale,
And for to drink to thee, friend, I will not fail ;
For although thy jacket looks gallant and fine,
I think that my twopence as good is as thine."

"By my soul ! honest fellow, the truth thou hast spoke,"
And straight he sat down with the tinkler to joke ;
They drank to the King, and they pledged to each other,
Who'd seen 'em had thought they were brother and brother.

As they were a-drinking the King pleased to say,
"What news, honest fellow ! come, tell me, I pray ?"
"There's nothing of news, beyond that I hear
The King's on the Border, a-chasing the deer.

"And truly, I wish, I so happy may be,
Whilst he is a-hunting, the King I might see,
For although I've travelled the land many ways,
I never have yet seen a King in my days."

The King, with a hearty brisk laughter replied,
"I tell thee, good fellow, if thou canst but ride,
Thou shalt get up behind me, and I will thee bring
To the presence of Jamie, thy Sovereign King."

"But he'll be surrounded with nobles so gay,
And how shall we tell him from them, sir, I pray ?"
"Thou'lt easily ken him when once thou art there ;
The King will be covered, the nobles all bare."

He got up behind him, and likewise his sack,
His budget of leather, his tools at his back ;
He rode till he came to the merry greenwood,
His nobles came round him, bareheaded they stood.

The tinkler, then seeing so many appear,
He slily did whisper the King in his ear :
Saying, "They'e all clothed so gloriously gay,
But which among them is the King, sir, I pray ?"

The King did with hearty good laughter reply,
"By my soul ! my good fellow, it's thou or it's I ;
The rest are bareheaded, uncovered all round ; "
With his bag and his budget he fell to the ground,

Like one that was frightened quite out of his wits,
Then on his knees he instantly gets,
Beseeching for mercy ; the King to him said,
" Thou art a good fellow, so be not afraid.

" Come, tell me thy name ? " " I am John of the Dale,
A mender of kettles, a lover of ale ; "
" Rise up, Sir John, I will honour thee here,
I make thee a knight of three thousand a year ! "

This was a good thing for the tinkler indeed ;
Then unto the court he was sent for with speed,
Where great store of pleasure and pastime was seen,
In the royal presence of King and of Queen.

Sir John of the Dale he has land, he has fee ;
At the court of the King, who so happy as he ?
Yet still in his hall hangs the tinkler's old sack,
And the budget of tools which he bore at his back.

The present version of this ballad is a traditional one, taken down
as here given, by the late Dr. James Henry Dixon, from the recital of
the late Francis King : of whom he gives the following account :—
" This poor minstrel was born at the village of Rylston, in Craven, the
scene of Wordsworth's *White Doe of Rylstone*.   King was always
called ' The Skipton Minstrel,' and he merited that name, for he was
not a mere player of his jigs and country dances, but a singer of heroic
ballads, carrying his hearers back to the days of chivalry and royal
adventure, like the Kings of England called up Cheshire and Lancashire to fight the King of France, and Monarchs sought the greenwood
trees, and hob-a-nobbed with tinkers, knighting these John's of the
Dale as a matter of poetical justice and high-sovereign prerogative.
Francis King was a character.   His physiognomy was striking and
peculiar ; and, although there was nothing of the rogue in its expression,
for an honester fellow never breathed, he might have sat for Wordsworth's ' Peter Bell.'   He combined in a rare degree the qualities of
the mime and the minstrel, and his old jokes and older ballads and
songs always ensured him a hearty welcome.   He was lame in
consequence of one leg being shorter than the other, and his limping
gait used to give occasion to the remark that ' few Kings had had
more ups and downs in the world.'   He met his death by drowning on
the night of December 13th, 1844.   He had been at a merry-making
at Gargrave, in Craven, and it is supposed that owing to the darkness

of the night he mistook the road and walked into the river Aire. As a musician his talents were creditable, and his name will long survive in the village records.   The minstrel's grave is in the quiet churchyard of Gargrave." Further particulars of him may be found in Dixon's *Stories of the Craven Dales*, published some years ago by Tasker and Son, of Skipton.

The ballad was probably written in the reign of King James the First, or soon after his death. Bishop Percy mentions it in his *Reliques of English Poetry*, but did not insert it; neither is it to be found in any other collection than *Bell's English Poets*. It is to be found only in broadsides and chap-books of modern date. Mr. Dixon states that the ballad is very popular on the border, and throughout all the dales of Cumberland, Westmoreland, and Craven.

Dick and the Devil.

From the *Notes and Queries*.

ROBIN a devil he sware a vow,
    He swore by the *sticks*[1] in hell—
By the yelding that crackles to mak the *lowe*[2]
    That warms his namsack[3] well.

He *leaped* on his beaste, and he rode with heaste,
    To *mak* his black oath good :
'Twas the Lord's day, and the folk did pray,
    And the priest in *cancel* stood.

The door was wide and in does he ride,
    In his clanking *gear* so gay :
A long keen brand he held in his hand,
    Our Dickon for to slay.

But Dickon good hap he was not there,
    And Robin he rode in vain,
And the men got up that were kneeling in prayer,
    To take him by might and main.

Rob swung his sword, his steed he spurred,
    He plunged right through the thrang
But the stout smith Jock, with his old mother's crutch,[1]
    He gave him a woundy bang.

So hard he smote the iron pat,
    It came down plume and all ;
Then with bare head away Robin sped,
    And himself was *fit* to fall.

Robin a devil he *wayed*[3] him home,
    And if for his foes he seek,
I think that again he will not come
    To *late*[6] them in Kendal Kirk.[7]

1. The unlettered bard has probably confused "styx" with the kindling, "yelding," of hell-fire.
2. Flame.
3. Evidently namesake.
4. Probably crock, to rhyme with Jock.
5. "He way'd me home" is yet used.
6. "Too late" is "to seek;" from *lateo*.
7. Kirk is a poor rhyme for seek. I think it should be written, "search," and "church."

The above was communicated by a person signing the initials of Y. A. C.; and he says they were picked up from some nursery rhymes recited by one Martha Kendal, who was a native of "the dales" of Yorkshire.

- -

The Butcher Turned Devil.

—

COME neighbours draw near and listen awhile,
I will sing you a song, it will cause you to smile :
It's concerning Old Nick, he's the father of evil,
He has long been well known by the name of the devil.

In the village of Empsall, near to Wakefield town,
To an old woman through the chimney he came down ;
If you'd been there to see him, you would have thought it
    funny,
But he frightened the old woman, for he wanted all her
    money.

Says he, "Woman take warning, for now I tell you plain,
To morrow night at twelve o'clock, I'll visit you again :
One hundred bright sovereigns for me you must prepare,
Or else with me you then must go, to a place you may
    guess where.

Then up through the chimney he vanished from her sight,
And she went to the Wakefield bank as soon as it was light:
" You must pay me one hundred pounds," to the bankers
    she did say :
" You ought to give us notice, you can't have it to-day."

O then she wept most bitterly and told them her tale
How the devil he would fetch her, or her money without
    fail ;
Says the banker, " I will help you, though I beg you will
    be still,
And I'll apprehend the devil, and send him to the tread-
    mill."

At Empsall a great thundering noise, was heard again that
    night,
The devil down the chimney came with his long horns and
    a light :
Two men that were in readiness seized him in a trice,
And they held the devil just as fast as if he'd been in a vice.

Next day great crowds of people went to see the devil there,
But they say he changes shape, and so it did appear;
For when he found the old woman safe, and found he
    could not touch her,
He lost his horns and tail, and turned out to be a butcher.

The devil has been blamed when innocent, 'tis true,
But now he is caught in the fact, they will give him his due ;
And since he bears such a bad name, there's no doubt but
    they will
Keep him prisoner as long as he lives, at Wakefield tread-
    mill.

From a broadside, printed by J. Harkness, of Preston.

The Crafty Plough Boy.

If you please to draw near till the truth I declare,
I'll sing of a farmer who lived in Hartfordshire.
A pretty Yorkshire boy he had for his man
For to do his business; his name it was John.

One morning right early he called his man,
And when he came to him he thus began—
"Take this cow," he said, "this day to the fair;
She is in good order, and her I can spare."

The boy went away, with the cow in a band,
And came to the fair, as we understand;
In a very short time he met with two men,
And sold them the cow for six pounds ten.

They went to his master's host's house for to drink,
Where the farmer paid to the boy down his clink.
The boy to the landlady then he did say,
"Oh, what shall I do with my money, I pray?"

"I'll sew it in the lining of your coat," said she,
"For fear on the road you robbed should be."
Thus heard a highwayman, while drinking of wine
Who thought to himself, "The money is mine."

The boy took his leave and homeward did go;
The highwayman he followed after also,
And soon overtook him upon the highway:
"Oh, well overtaken, young man," he did say.

"Will you get up behind me?" the highwayman said;
"But where are you going?" inquired the lad;
"Above four miles farther, for aught that I know."
So he jumped up behind, and away they did go.

They rode till they came to a dark, dark lane;
The highwayman said, "I must tell you plain,
Deliver your money without any strife,
Or else I will surely deprive you of life."

He found there was no time to dispute,
So jump'd off behind him without fear or doubt,
He tore from his linings the money throughout,
And among the long grass he strewed it about.

The highwayman instantly jumped from his horse,
But little he dreamed it was for his loss.
Before he could find where the money was sown
The boy got on horseback and off he was gone.

The highwayman shouted, and bid him to stay,
The boy would not hear him, but still rode away
Unto his own master and to him did bring
Saddle and bridle and many a fine thing.

When the maid-servant saw Jack come riding home,
To acquaint her master ran into the room.
The farmer he came to the door with a curse,
" What a plague ! Is my cow turned into a horse ? "

The boy said, " Good master, the cow I have sold,
But was robbed on the road by a highwayman bold,
And while he was putting it into his purse,
To make you amend I came home with his horse."

His master laughed till his side he did hold,
And said, " For a boy thou hast been very bold ;
And as for the villain, you served him right,
And has put upon him a true Yorkshire bite."

They open'd the bags and quickly was told
Two hundred pounds in silver and gold,
With two brace of pistols ; the boy said, " I vow
I think, my good master, I've well sold your cow."

Now, Jack, for his courage and valour so rare,
Three parts of the money he got for his share ;
And since the highwayman has lost all his store,
Let him go a robbing until he get more.

This ditty has often been reprinted on broadsides during the last
hundred years, and may be traced back as far as 1780. Hardly any
two are alike. The copy which I have adopted is from Logan's
Pedler's Pack of Ballads and Songs, 1869, which differs from the copy
in Dr. Ingledew's collection of Yorkshire Ballads, published in 1860.
There is in it a great likeness to the ballad, " Saddle To Rags."

The Sweeper and Thieves.?

A TALE BY D. LEWIS.

This tale is founded on fact, and happened at Leeming Lane,
a few years ago.

A Sweeper's lad was late o' th' neeght,
His slap-shod shoon had lecam'd his feet :
He call te see a good awd deeame,
'At monny a time had trigged his weeame ;
(For he wor then fahve miles fra yam,)
He axed her i' t' lair te let him sleep,
An' he'd next day their chimlers sweep.
They supper'd him wi' country fare,
Then shewed him tul his hooal i' t' lair.
He crept intul his streehy bed,
His pooak o' seeat beneath his heead ;
He wor content, nur cared a pin,
An' his good friend then locked him in.
The lair fra t' house a distance stood,
Between 'em grew a lahle wood ;
Aboot midneeght or nearer morn,
Twea theives brak in te steal ther coorn ;
Heving a leeght i' t' lantern dark,
Seean they te winder fell te wark ;
An' wishing they'd a lad ta fill,
Young Brush, whea yet hed ligg'd quite still,
Thinkin' 'at men belanged te t' hoose,
An' that he noo mud be of use,
Jumped down directly onte t' fleear,
An' t' thieves beeath ran oot at deear,
Nor stop at owt, nur thin nur thick,
Fully convinced it wor owd Nick.
The sweeper lad then ran reeght seean,
Te t' hoose, an' telled em what wor deean ;
Maister an' men then quickly raise,
An' ran te t' lair wi' half ther cleeas ;
Twea horses, secks, and leeght they fand,
Which hed been left by t' thievish band ;
These round i' t' neighbourheead they cried,

But nut an awner e'er applied ;
For neean durst horses awn ner secks,
They wor seer freeghtened o' ther necks ;
They selled the horses, and of coorse,
Put awf the brass i' Sooty's purse ;
Desiring when he com that way,
He'd always them a visit pay,
When harty welcum he sud have,
Because he did ther barley save.
Brush clinked the guineas in his hand,
An' oft te leeak at 'em did stand,
As heeam he wistling teak his way,
Blessin' t' awd deeame wha let him stay,
An' sleep i' t' lair, when late at neeght,
His slap-shood had leem'd his feet.

The Yorkshireman.

My feyther, who always knew what he were at,
  A cunning and good-natured elf,
Bid me take care of this thing and take care of that,
  But, says I, I'll take care o' myself.
So I ventured fra Yorkshire to better my lot,
And since 'twas my fortune to come to this spot,
I'm vastly weel pleased wi' the place I ha' got,
      Where I sing fal de ral, &c.

Since money, they say, makes the mare for to go,
  Getting money must be the best plan,
And as Yorkshiremen understand horseflesh you know,
  On my hobby I keep while I can.
This ground is all fair, and I fear not a jot,
There'll be no falling off if I don't spur too hot,
And when luck doesn't gallop, she's welcome to trot
      While I'm singing fal de ral, &c.

And when I get married, for marry I must,
  As soon as I find out a lass,
She'll meet wi' a pretty good husband, I trust,
  And wi' her I'll ha' plenty o' brass.

Q

I'm not hard to please when I'm choosing, d'ye see,
She mun come o' good kin, and besides she mun be,
For beauty, why—just such another as me.

This eighteenth century song is copied from an old work printed at
the Ballantine Press, Edinburgh, no date, entitled, "The Universal
Songster, or Museum of Mirth." The whole is comprised in three
volumes, royal octavo, and contains thousands of English, Irish, and
Scotch lyrics. The illustrative engravings are by George and Robert
Cruikshank.

Old Wicket and his Wife.

O ! I went into the stable,
    To see what I could see,
And there I saw three horses stand,
    By one, by two, and by three ;
O ! I called to my loving wife,
    And, "Anon, kind sir," said she ;
" O ! what do these three horses here,
    Without the leave of me ? "
" Why you old fool ! blind fool !
    Can't you very well see,
These are three milking cows
    My mother sent to me ? "
" Ods bobs ! well done !
    Milking cows with saddles on !
The like was never known ! "
Old Wicket a cuckold went out,
    And a cuckold he came home !

O ! I went into the kitchen,
    And there for to see,
And there I saw three swords hang,
    By one, by two, and by three ;
O ! I called to my loving wife,
    And, " Anon, kind sir, quoth she ;

"O! what do these three swords do here
    Without the leave of me?"
"Why you old fool! blind fool!
    Can't you very well see,
These are three roasting spits
    My mother sent to me?"
"Ods bobs! Well done!
    Roasting spits with scabbards on!
The like was never known!"
Old Wicket a cuckold went out,
    And a cuckold he came home!

O! I went into the parlour,
    And there for to see,
And there I saw three cloaks hang,
    By, one, by two, and by three;
O! I called to my loving wife,
    And, "Anon, kind sir," quoth she;
"O! what do these three cloaks do here,
    Without the leave of me?"
"Why you old fool! blind fool!
    Can't you very well see,
These are three mantuas
    My mother sent to me?"
"Ods bobs! well done!
    Mantuas with capes on!
The like was never known!"
Old Wicket a cuckold went out,
    And a cuckold he came home!

O! I went into the pantry,
    And there for to see,
And there I saw three pair of boots,
    By one, by two, and by three:
O! I called to my loving wife,
    And, "Anon, kind sir," quoth she;
"O! what do these three pair of boots here,
    Without the leave of me?"
"Why you old fool! blind fool!
    Can't you very well see
These are three pudding bags
    My mother sent to me?"
"Ods bobs! pudding bags with spurs on!

The like was never known!"
Old Wicket a cuckold went out,
    And a cuckold he came home!

O! I went into the dairy,
    And there for to see,
And there I saw three hats hang,
    By one, by two, and by three:
O! I called to my loving wife,
    And, "Anon, kind sir," quoth she:
" Pray what do these three hats here,
    Without the leave of me?"
" Why you old fool! blind fool!
    Can't you very well see,
These are three skimming dishes
    My mother sent to me?"
" Ods bobs! well done!
    Skimming dishes with hat bands on!
The like was never known!"
Old wicket a cuckold went out,
    And a cuckold he came home!

O! I went into the chamber,
    And there for to see,
And there I saw three men in bed,
    By one, by two, and by three;
O! I called to my loving wife,
    And, "Anon, kind sir," quoth she;
" O! what do these three men here,
    Without the leave of me?"
" Why you old fool! blind fool!
    Can't you very well see,
They are three milking maids
    My mother sent to me?"
" Ods bobs! well done!
    Milking maids with beards on!
The like was never known!"
Old wicket a cuckold went out,
    And a cuckold he came home!

The above copy was obtained in Yorkshire, but similar ditties are
to be met with in all parts of England and Scotland, with considerable
variations. There can be no doubt about its antiquity. When well

sung it cannot fail to "bring down the house," as the phrase goes, and there is no wonder at its being popular in country districts. Mr. Dixon collated the above with one printed at the Aldermary Press, and which is preserved (he says) in the third volume of the Roxburgh Collection. A Scotch version may be found in Herd's Collection, 1769; and also in Cunningham's *Songs of England and Scotland*, London, 1835.

The Beggar's Will.

—

THERE was an antient man, and a beggar by his trade,
Fell sick at his lodging-house, and unto his landlord said,
"Oh, landlord, I am sick, and I find myself very ill,
If you will my witness be, then fain would I make my will.
Fal, lal, &c.

"For there's many men drops away in diseases, I do hear,
Their childer falls out to suit, and that's the thing that I fear;
But what as I have for to leave I'll leave it in such a wise
That when I am dead and gone no strife amongst them rise.
Fal, lal.

"Come hither, my eldest son, and come listen unto me :
My good old leathern bag I will bequeath to thee,
There's in it a good horn spoon, and eke a wooden bowl,
With milk and pottage both, son, which I got at a dole.
Fal, lal.

"The bowl is of ashen wood, and it's season'd well and sure,
The one side of it hath holes three or four ;
It has a check in the side, and it got it, I know when,
And with a good hempen string, son, I sew'd it up again.
Fal, lal.

" Thou'st also have my clogs, and all to them belongs,
There's cappins five or six, and four good leather thongs ;
There is a good ox clea, likewise a tough tup's horn,
That'll mend both heel and toe, son, when as thou seest
      they're worn.
Fal, lal.

" My cap a threefold gelt, with thrums fast together,
To keep thy head warm and dry, I give it thee, in wet
      weather ;
It's lined with dog-skin wool, and it's stitched up before,
All this thou shalt have, son, but thou shalt have no more.
Fal, lal.

" The next place I bequeath to Dick, my younger lad,
My good old russet cloak, which I long time have had :
The groundwork on't was laid when the great frost began,
It's threescore years since, Dick, and it's perish'd many a
      man.
Fal, lal.

" And ever since that time I to't some things did add
Of bits and scraps of clouts, as I found them to be had,
There's never a man in the shire alive that I can name
That's had a new coat e'er since, Dick, but thou'st a piece
      of the same.
Fal, lal.

" My doublet and my slops I'll give to thee, my son,
They were thy grandsire's before the abbey it was pulled
      down,
It is a long time since, Dick, but yet, thou seest, they're
      here,
Though not so good, Dick, as I could wish they were.
Fal, lal.

" In the doublet sleeve there is a fob that doth contain
Things that cannot be got without great care and pain,
There's ends, and thrums, and a button, all made of
      leather,
There's haglets, thrums and thread, and a needle altogether.
Fal, lal.

"Thou'st also have my girdle, it is both strong and good,
My whittle, that hangs thereby, is in a sheath of wood,
My mittens and my gibb I will bequeath to thee,
My blessing—and that is all, Dick, thy portion's like be.
Fal, lal.

"Come hither, my daughter Nell, it's hard that thou
should'st lack,
Thou'st have my begging poke, which I carried on my back;
There is a Lucie in't, and a pair of good knitting sheaths,
And thrums that's worth a groat, as Webster says and
swears.
Fal, lal.

There's mickle pieces four, if they shorter be
They'll get thee money and meal hereafter, thou shalt see;
There's sixpence out at use, and it lies in Webster's hand,
Take thou the rent of that, Nell, but let the old stock
stand.
Fal, lal.

"There's fourpence in a clout, and it is no lesser sum,
Thou mayest tae and lay it out, and bestow it well in
thrums,
And if thou hast good luck, and inkle sell out dear,
Thy groat may doubled be, Nell, once in seven year.
Fal, lal.

"Thou'st also have my kit, and it's seasoned well and sure,
It hath not empty been, Nell, these threescore years and
more,
Of kern milk, blue milk, drink, whey, whig, and perry,
And several sorts of liquor which oft has made me merry.
Fal, lal.

" It's had in it ale and beer, and once it was filled with
wine,
And after it all things relish'd well that came in't for a
long time,
There's a pair of butter-bills, too, made of good ox horn,
That has not empty been twice, Nell, since thou was't
born.
Fal, lal.

"Now I have made my will, and hope you'll see it assigned
And see those things be done, and according to my mind ;
My worldly cares aside, my mind is now at ease,
I offer myself to God ; let Death come when he please."
Fal, lal, &c.

A Yorkshire ballad, obtained from oral tradition, and communicated by Henry Jackson, Esq., of Sheffield, to J. O. Halliwell, Esq. "The foregoing verses," says Mr. Jackson, "were copied from *A Copy* written by an old gentleman who died in 1782. He had been in the habit of singing them for many years, and, as far as I can learn, the chorus was sung with an accompaniment of some particular manipulation, which made the glasses on the table ring. I should imagine, from the account I have, beating one hand upon the other, as a forgeman hammered a bar of steel."

Ballad on the Goodmanham Mule.

This specimen of village humour is selected from "Country Ballads," a tract published by Thomas Thorpe, of Pateley Bridge, in 1869. "John Fowler, huckster, of the village of Goodmanham, having purchased a mule at Beverley fair, when he brought it home the inhabitants of the village expressed the following opinions upon its merits and demerits, which were at once done into rhyme by the poet laureate of the village " :—

> JOHNNY Fowler bowt a mule,
> His wife Hannah thowt it wadn't suit ;
> 'Oh, but I think it will !'
> Says Willy-up-o'-th'-Hill,
>
> 'Give her a sly prick !'
> Says Milner Dick :
> 'Give her a pinchin'!'
> Says David Quinchin.

' How nicely she goes ! '
Says Hatfield and Rose ;
' She's as hard as nails ! '
Says Dicky Dales.

' Know weel or ommas ! '
Says Robert Thomas.
' Why, what's her trade ! '
Says Mistress Wade :
' Carryin' a spice stall ! '
Says Nancy Hall.

' Noo, what's her rate ! '
Says Tommy Tate :
" Seaven mile i'th hoor ! '
Says Billy Moor.

' Ill trot her to Driffil ! ' (Driffield)
Says aud Spip Withill ;
' An' back agean afore dark ! '
Says aud Dan Clark.

' An' I'll trot her to Selby ! '
Says aud Len' Kirby :
' O' bud she's a tightun ! '
Says aud Robert Leighton.

' She gangs like a hoss ! '
Says young Dicky Ross ;
' Mair like an ass ! '
Says Ramskill's lass.

' Thou's a great feal ! '
Says Lizzy Beal ;
' She gangs like a creckit ! '
Says Mister Beckett.

' Just trot her on ! '
Says fine young John ;
' It's nowt bud malice ! '
Says Rhoda and Alice.

' Tee her up to'th church ! '
Says silly Willy Perch :
' An' I'll let her lowse ! '
Says aud Nan Fowse.

He kept himself from such debate,
  Removing thence withal,
Twice on the year by Savile-gate
  Unto the Bothom-hall.

Adam of Beaumont, then truly
  Lacy, and Lockwood eke,
And Quarmby came to their country
  Their purpose for to seek.

To Cromwell-bottom wood they came,
  There kept them secretly :
By fond deceit there did they frame
  Their crafty cruelty.

This is the end, in sooth to say,
  On Palmson E'en at night
To Eland miln they took their way,
  About the mirk midnight.

Into the milnhouse there they brake,
  And kept them secretly ;
By subtilty thus did they seek
  The Young Knight for to slay.

The morning came, the miller sent
  His wife for corn in haste :
These gentlemen in hands he hent,
  And bound her hard and fast.

The miller sware she should repent,
  She tarried there so long ;
A good cudgel in hand he hent
  To chastise her with wrong.

With haste into the miln came he,
  And meant with her to strive :
But they bound him immediately,
  And laid him by his wife.

The young Knight dreamt the self-same night
  With foes he were bested,
That fiercely settled then to fight
  Against him in his bed.

He told his lady soon of this :
  But, as a thing most vain,
She weighed it light and said, " I wis ;
  We must to church certain,

And serve God there this present day,
  The Knight then made him bown,
And by the milnhouse lay the way
  That leadeth to the town.

The drought had made the water small
  The stakes appeared dry.
The Knight, his wife, and servants all
  Came down the dam thereby.

When Adam Beaumont thus beheld,
  Forth of the miln came he,
His bow in hand with him he held
  And shot at him sharply.

He hit the Knight on the breastplate,
  Whereat the shot did glide.
William of Lockwood, wroth thereat,
  Said " Cousin, you shoot wide."

Himself did shoot and hit the Knight
  Who nought was hurt by this,
Whereat the Knight had great delight
  And said to them, " I wis

" If that my father had been clad
  With such armour, certain
Your wicked hands escaped he had,
  And had not so been slain.

" O Eland town," said he, "alack
  If thou but knew of this,
These foes of mine full fast would flee
  And of their purpose miss."

By stealth to work they needs must go.
  For it had been too much
The town knowing, the lord to slo
  For them, and twenty such.

William of Lockwood was adread,
  The town should rise indeed,
He shot the knight right through the head,
  And slew him then with speed.

His son and heir was wounded there,
  But yet not dead at all,
Into the house conveyed he were,
  And died in Eland hall,

But soon he started with a bound,
  And " by the powers " he swore
That whatever Derby offered
  Why he would offer more.

Full fifty years a diplomat
  This wily lord had been,
And he the rise of many a throne
  And many a fall had seen :
Had many a sacred cause betrayed,
  And compass'd all the woe,
Of the noble sons of Poland
  And of Hungary too.

And as he sat—this great man said :
  " This Franchise is a bore,
For give the people all they ask
  They soon will crave for more ;
My order—and the power they wield
  Must soon part company—
Yet though that power must be the price,
  I will the Premier be."

Then up spake he to his valet :
  " I would John Russell see,
And as I cannot go to him,
  Why he must come to me ;
My gouty leg is worse to day,
  But Johnny won't be nice ;
So take this note, and take my coach,
  And fetch him in a trice."

Now, Lord John Russell was a man,
  Wise, honest, and discreet,
A better never lifted leg
  Or walked along a street ;
A plucky body in his youth,
  As ever you could meet,
Could rule the realm, or at a pinch,
  Command the channel fleet.

Soon he and jaunty Palmerston,
  Between them did agree
To grant a six, and ten pound vote,
  If such a thing might be

But members on the hustings pledged
     Were seldom found sincere[2]
And so they toss'd reform about
     For many and many a year.

It was Tory in and Tory out
     Then Whiggery had a spell
And fall five times from Royal lips
     The shadowy promise fell
Until at length the people rose
     Rose like the roaring storm,
And ere a month had passed away
     The Queen had signed Reform.

1. Thus comprising five-sixths of the whole of the British House of Commons.

2. "The House of which you are Premier is rotten to the core. Not 100 members of the House have been sent by the pure votes of electors. There are not 100 honest members in that House."—Mr. Rowcliffe, at Tiverton, March 28th, 1861, when Lord Palmerston presented himself for re-election, having accepted the office of warden of the Cinque Ports.

"He (Mr. Rowcliffe) says there are not 100 honest men in the House of Commons. Well, 100 honest men are a very good allowance in any number of people, and if working together they may do a great deal."—Lord Palmerston at the same time and place.

At the elections in 1859, at least 340 members were returned as good Liberals and sincere friends of Parliamentary Reform, and yet on the division on Mr. Baines's first bill, only 192 voted for it. On the 2nd reading of Mr. Baines's bill in the present year only 216 voted for it. For Mr. Locke King's County Franchise Bill only 227 votes were given in its favor. Why this strange defection?

The Weavers.

Air—O the Roast Beef of Old England.

COME, ladies and gents, I've a song ready made,
And to hear it I'm sure you will not be afraid,
For I'll tell you at once I'm a weaver by trade.

CHORUS.

So we'll sing success to the weavers;
The weavers for ever, huzza!

Some tradespeople always are making a fuss,
But their merits are trifling when talking to us,
And in argument we leave them at a nonplus.

Here are goods every day we're exporting by bales,
And in merchandize ours, as an art, never fails,
For each ship leaving port owes the weaver for sails.

The king in his robes may so gracefully stand,
And his nobles about him may look great and grand,
Still they get all their cloth by the work of our hands.

But for us how your soldier would often repent,
When houseless to sleep on their knapsacks they're sent,
But the weaver, you see, gives each soldier his tent.

If exhausted you feel, and by Morpheus you're beat,
In the heat or the cold a small rest will be sweet,
Then think of the weavers' fine blanket and sheet

The ladies are pretty, as all will confess,
And he's stupid or blind, I'm sure, who says less,
But then to the weavers they're indebted for dress.

Then, since here for mankind, we're sent here to weave
O'er our looms and our shuttles we'll not idly grieve,
But my song is just ended—so I'll take my leave.

And we'll sing success, &c.

The Yorkshire Tyke.

—

Ah iz, i' truth a country youth,
Neean us'd teea Lunnon fashions;
Yet vartue guides, an' still presides,
Ower all mah steps an' passions.

Neea coortly lear, bud all sinceere,
　Neea bribe shall ivver blinnd me ;
If thoo can like a Yorkshire tyke,
　A rooage thoo'l nivver finnd me.

Thof envy's tung, seea slimlee hung,
　Wad lee aboot oor country,
Neea men o't eearth boost greter wurth,
　Or mare extend ther boonty.

Oor Northern breeze wi' uz agrees
　An' does for wark weel fit uz :
I' public cares, an' all affairs,
　Wi' honour we acquit uz.

Seea gret a moind is ne'er confiand
　In onny shire or nation ;
They geean meeast praise him weel displays
　A leearned eddication.

Whahl rancour rolls i' lahtle souls,
　By shallo views dissarning,
They're nobbut wise 'at awlus prize
　Gud manners, sense, an' leearning.

I find this dialectal poem in a work published by Routledge,
entitled "Ten Thousand Wonderful Things." It evidently belongs
to the speech of the Wolds, or the neighbourhood of York ; and I
think it was probably written during the eighteenth century. (See
appendix note 19.)

Natterin Nan :

A PICTUR, BE A YORKSHIRE LIKENASS TAKER.

(BEN PRESTON).

Noa daht ye'll all ev eard abaht
　T' Appolloa Belvidere,
A statty, thowt be some to be
　Fro' ivvery failin tlear.

All reyt an streyt i mak an shap,
  A mould for t'race o'men,
A dahnreyt, upreyt, beng-up chap,
  Nut much unlike mesen.

Nah, thaw ye knaw he's nowt but stoan,
  He lewks sa grand an big,
That little durst ya pool his noas,
  Or lug his twisted wig.

Pratly, reight pratly, ovver t'floor,
  A tep e toas ye walk,
An hod yur breeath for varry awe,
  An wisper when ya tauk.

There's that abaht him, but I knaw'nt
  Nut reytly hah ta say't,
That maks ye feel as small as theves
  Anent a Magistrate.

Yee've seen that dolt o'mucky tlay,
  O't face o'Pudsay Doas,
T'owd madlin's worn it all his life,
  An fancid it a noas.

Yond props is like a pair e'tengs
  O' Sykes's, yet by t'megs,
When he wur souber as a judge,
  I've eard him call em legs.

So heaven be praised for self-consate,
  Withaht it ah sud say
Wee'se hate wursen we all wur meet
  For ivver an a day.

When sitch-like lewks at t'marble god,
  Egoy! ha wide they gape,
An wunder which they favver t'moast,
  A boggard or an ape.

An sum wi envy, and wi spite
  Get filled to that degree,
They'd knock his noas off if they durst,
  Ur give him a black ee.

He sumhah kests a leet on things
  At fowk noan wants ta see,
Thear's few likes tellin what they are,
  Or what they owt ta be,

Wah, wah, perfecshun nivver did
  Ta Adam's bairns beleng,
An lewk at mortals as we will
  We find a summat wreng.

For Adam gate so mesht wi't fall,
  That all o't human race
Grow sadly aht o' shap it mind,
  It karkiss an it faas.

There's noan sa blynd but they can see
  Sum fawts i' other men;
I've sumtimes met wi fowk at thowt
  Tha saw sum i thersen.

An t'best o'chaps al fynd thersen
  At times it fawty tlass,
I've doubled t'neiv, afoar ta day,
  At t'fooil it seemin dlass.

But twarst o'fawts at I've seen yet,
  I' wuman or i' man,
Is t'weary naagin nengin turn,
  At plaged poor Natterin Nan.

I went wun summer afternoin
  Ta see hur poor old man,
An aadly hed i darkened t'doar
  When t'wurrit thus began :—

A wah, did ivver! wot a treat,
  Ta see thi father's sun,
Cum forrad, lad, an sit ta dahn,
  An al set the kettle on.

Nay, nay, ses ah, ah'm noan o'thame
  'At calls at t'time by t'clock,
An bumps em dahn it corner chair,
  An gloars reyt hard at t'jock.

Tha nontkate witta hod the tung,
  He'll sooin be here I'se think,
Soa if thall sit an leet thi pipe,
  Ah'll fetch a sope o'drink.

Owd lass, ses ah, thart hey i bone,
  An rayther low i' beef;
Ah barn, ses shoo, this year ur two,
  I've hed a deal o' greef.

K

Ah'm nut a wuman 'at oft speyks,
　　Ur sings fowk doleful sengs,
Bud ah can tell my mind ta thee,
　　Tha knaws wot things belengs.

Tha noaticed ah noan lewkt sa staat,
　　An ah can trewly say,
Fro t'last back end o't year ta nah,
　　A've nut been weel a day.

An wot wi sickness, wot we greef,
　　Ah'm doin tha may depend ;
Its been a weary moild and tew,
　　Bud nah it gets near t'end.

A've bowt all t'sister 'at ah hev
　　A black merrina gaan ;
Fowk thinks ah'm rarely off, but lad
　　Ah' thenkful 'at ah'm baan.

Wet t'wurld an ivvery thing at's in't,
　　Ah'm crost to that degree,
That mony a time it day ah've pra'd
　　Ta lig ma daan an dee.

What ah've to tak fro t'least it haase
　　Is moar nur flesh can bear,
It is'nt just a time be chonce
　　Bud ivvery day it year.

Noa livin sowl a'top o't earth
　　Wor tried as ah've been tried ;
There's noabdy bud the Lord an me
　　At knaws what ah've ta bide.

Fro t'wind it t'stomach, t'rewmetism,
　　An tengin pains it goom ;
Fro coffs and cowds, an t'spine it back
　　Ah suffer marterdum.

But noabdy pities ma, or thinks
　　Ah'm ailin owt at all ;
T' poar slave mun tug an tew wit wark
　　Wolivver shoo can crawl.

An Johnny's t'moast unfeelin brewt
　　At ivver ware a heead,
He woddunt weg a hand ur fooit
　　If I wur all bud deead.

It midst o' all ah've hed ta dew,
    That roag wur nivver t'man
Ta fotch a coil, ur scar a fleg,
    Ur wesh a pot ur pan.

Fowk ses 'ar Sal al sooin be wed,
    Bud thowt on't turns ma sick,
Ah'd rayther hing hur up by t'neck,
    Ur see hur burried wick.

An if a new a barn o' mine
    Wur born ta lead my life,
Ah suddent think it wor a sin
    Ta stick hur wi a knife.

Ah've axed ar Johnny twenty times
    Ta bring a sweep to t'door,
Bud nah, afoar al speyk agean,
    Ah'll sit it haase an smoar.

An then, gooid grashus, what a wind
    Comes whewin throot doar sneck,
Ah felt it all t'last winter like
    A whittle at my neck.

That sink-pipe, tu, gate stopt wi muck
    Aboon a fortnit sin,
So ivvery aar it day wit slops,
    Am treshin aht and in.

Aw! when ah think hah ah've been tret,
    An ah ah tew an strive,
To tell the t'honest trewth, ah'm capt
    Ta fynd mesen alive.

When he's been rakin aht at neet,
    At mahkit ur at fair,
Sitch thowts hes coom inta me heead
    As lifted up me air.

Ah've thowt, ay lad, when tha cums hoam,
    Thal fynd ma hung by t'neck,
Bud then ah've mebbe thowt agean
    At t'coord ud happen brek.

Ur else ah've muttered if it worn't
    Sa dark, an cowd, an weet,
Ah'd go to't navvy, or to t'dam
    An draand mesen ta neet.

R 2

Its greef, lad, nowt at all bud greef,
    At wastes me day be day;
So Sattan temts ma cos am wake
    To put meseln away.

Towd chap heard pairt o' what shoo sed,
    As he cum clomping in,
An shaated in a red-faced rage,
    Od rot it, hod the din.

Then Nan began to froth an fume,
    An fiz like botteld drink,
Wat then, tha's entered t'haase agean,
    Tha offald lewkin slink.

Tha nivver cums theas doors within,
    Bud tha mun curse an sweear,
An try ta bring ma ta me grave
    Wi breedin hurries hear.

At thee an thine, sin wed we wor,
    Ah've taen no end o' greef,
An nah tha stamps ma under t'fooit,
    Tha murderin rooag an theef.

Tha villan, gimma wat ah browt
    At day at we wur wed,
An nivver moar wi one like thee
    Will ah set fooit e bed.

Here t'dowdy lifted tull her een
    A yard a gooid lin check,
An sobbed, an roared, an rocked hersen,
    As if hur art ud breck.

An then shoo rave reight up be't rooits
    A andful of hur air,
An fittered like a decin duck
    An shutturd aht at tchair.

Aw, Johnny! run for t'doctur, lad,
    Ah feel ah cant tell hah;
Ses Johnny, leet the pipe agean,
    Shool coom abaht enah.

Ses ah, ah nivver saw a chap
    Sa easyful an fat,
Thall suarly lend a elpin and
    Ta lift hur of at plat.

Bud better hed it been for him
  If he'd neer sturr'd a peg :
My garturs ! what a pawse he gat
  Fro Nan rumatic leg.

Sooin, varry soin, sho coom abaht,
  An flang, an tare, an rave,
E sich a way as fu cud dew
  We one fooit i ther grave.

An at it went hur tung agean,
  That minnit sho fan ease,
Tha villan tha, tha knaws the ways
  Brings on sitch girds as theeas.

Aw if thad strike ma stiff at once,
  Ur stab ma to me hart,
A then cud dee content, for fowk
  Ud naw reyt wot ta art.

Unfeelin brewt, unfeelin brewt,
  Ah neer wur weel an strong :
Thears nobbut one thing cheers mah nah
  Ah cannut last sa long.

Ta stand up in a thing ats reyt,
  It isant i me natur,
There is at knaws ah awlus wor
  A poor, soft, quiat cratur.

Wun thing ah can say, if me life
  Ta neet sud end it lecase,
Ah've done me deuty, an tha knaws
  Ah awlus strave for peease.

Ah knaw, ah knaw at ah'm it gate,
  Thas uther otes ta thresh :
So when ah's dun for, tha ma wed
  Yon gooid for nowt young tresh.

Then Nan pool'd summat aht ot drawer
  White as a summer claad :
Ses I ta Johnny, What's that thear ?
  Ses Johnny, Its a shraad.

An t' coffin coom, tu, bud ah sware
  A woddunt ha't it haase :
So, when shoo's muled, shoo sews at that
  As quiat as a maase.

Then Nan lewkt at me we a lewk
  So yonderly an sad,
Thal come to t'berrin? Yus, says ah,
  Ah sall be varry dlad.

An bid the Mother, Johnny cried,
  An ax the Uncle Ben,
For all hur prayers for sudden deeath,
  Sal hev my best 'Amen.'

The name of Ben Preston, from whom I have selected the above, has been a household word in Bradford ever since the year 1844. I have before me the *Bradford Observer* for September 5th, 1844, published in Chapel Court, Kirkgate, in which the editor has compiled, " The Feast of the Poets," which covers a whole page. Among the specimens of local poems, there is one on " Napoleon," possessing great merit, signed P——N. Between 1851 and 1861, Mr. Preston produced his inimitable dialect poems. These are all racy of the soil, and true to the old Bradford life. The dialect is produced to perfection, and the humour will hardly ever be excelled. As a literary curiosity, I will here give the titles.

" A Poetical Sarmon Preycht to't White Heathens o' Wibsay, i' ther Native Tongue, be a Latter Day Saint, 1854 ; " " Natterin' Nan : A Pictur, by a Yorkshire Likeness Takker, 1856." Then followed in 1859, "T' Spicy Man," " T' Creakin Gaat," and " T' Maister o' t' Haase." Of these many thousands were sold. Then appeared in 1860-1, many fine songs and poems in the dialect, which were first published in " The Bradfordian." In 1864 Mr. Holroyd, then of Westgate, made a collection of them ; and again at Saltaire, in 1872. In 1880 Mr. Preston prepared a selection of all his poems, and they were edited by Mr. T. T. Empsall, and afterwards published by the late Mr. Thomas Brear, of Kirkgate, Bradford. This book contains nearly one hundred poems. (See appendix note 20.)

LOVE BALLADS.

York, You're Wanted.

Air—*Bow-wow*.

—

FROM York I comed up to get a place
   And travelled to this town, sir,
In Holborn I an office found,
   Of credit and renown, sir.
Says I, pray get me a place:
   Says he, your prayer is granted;
And when I meet with one that suits,
   I'll tell you,—York, you're wanted.

A gentleman soon hired me—
   I found he was a gambler;
Says he, I want a steady lad,
   Says I, sir, I'm no rambler:
But if you want a knowing one,
   By few I am supplanted;
O, that is just the thing, says he,
   So, Mr. York, you're wanted.

Now, I knew somewhat of a hoye,
   And, master just the same, sir;
And if we didn't do the fools,
   'Ecod' we'd been to blame, sir.
At races then we both looked out,
   For cash each bosom panted,
And, when we thought the flats would bite,
   The word was, York, you're wanted.

A maiden lady, you must know,
   Just sixty-three years old, sir,
Then fell in love with my sweet face,
   And I with her sweet gold, sir.

She said, the little god of love
  Her tender bosom haunted,
Dear sir, I almost blush to own—
  But, Mr. York, you're wanted.

In wedlock's joys, you need not doubt,
  Most happily I rolled, sir,
And how we loved or how we fought,
  Shall never now be told, sir;
For Mr. Death stepped in one day.
  And swift his dart he planted:
I wiped my eyes, and thanked my stars—
  'Twas Mrs. York he wanted.

So, ladies, pray now guard your hearts,
  A secret while I tell, O;
A widower with half a plum
  Must needs be a rich fellow.
With fifty thousand pounds, I think
  I ought not to be daunted:
Some lovely girl, I hope, ere long,
  Will say, sweet York, you're wanted.

                    From a broadside.

Roger and Dolly.

Air—*Calder Fair.*

Down in our village lived a parson and his wife,
Who led a very decent sort o' comfortable life;
They kept a serving man and maid as tidy as could be.
The maid was fond of Roger—and Roger fond of she.

The parson's wife kept Dolly so very close to work,
She might as well have been bred a Hottentot or Turk:
But though she was employed all day as close as close
    could be,
Her thoughts were fixed on Roger, and Roger's fixed on
    she.

The parson was an old man, and would have done amiss,
For he got her in a corner, and asked her for a kiss ;
But she answered to him, as plain as plain could be,
That she wanted Roger, and Roger wanted she.

Cupid, that blind little god, had got so in her head,
That, every night as sure as ever she went up to bed,
Before she went to sleep, she, as pious as could be,
Would pray she might have Roger, and Roger prayed for
    she.

By love and work together, she was taken very ill—
The doctor he was sent for and tried his best of skill,
But she wouldn't take his stuff, though bad as bad could be,
She only wanted Roger, and Roger wanted she.

When the parson found 'twas only love that made her bad,
He very kindly said that she had better have the lad ;
The sight of him soon made her well, as well as well
    could be—
They married—she had Roger, and Roger he had she !

From " The Universal Songster ; or, Museum of Mirth." Printed
at the Ballantine Press, Edinburgh. No date. This little song was
formerly a great favourite in Yorkshire, at all merry-makings.

Jenny! Tak' Care o' Thysen.

WHEN I was a wee little tottering bairn,
    An' had nobbud just gitten short frocks,
When to gang I at first war beginnin' to larn,
    On my brow I got monie hard knocks.
For se waik, an' se silly, an' helpless was I,
    I was always a tumbling down then,
While mi mother wad twattle me gently an' cry,
    " Honey, Jenny ! tak' care o' thysen."

When I grew bigger, an' gat to be strang,
    'At I cannily ran all about
By mysen whor I liked, then I always mud gang,
    Bithout bein' telled about ought.
When, however, I com' to be sixteen year auld,
    An' rattled an' ramp'd amang men,
My mother wod call o' me in, an' would scauld,
    And cry—" Hussy, tak' care o' thysen ! "

I've a sweetheart comes now up o' Setterday nights,
    An' he swears 'at he'll mak' me his wife ;
My mam grows stingy, she scaulds and she flytes,
    An' she twitters me out of my life.
But she may lewk sour and consait hersen wise,
    An' preach again likin' young men ;
Sen I's grown a woman her clack I'll despise,
    An' I'se marry ! tak' care o' mysen.

The Whistle.

—

' You have heard,' said a youth to his sweetheart, who
    stood
    While he sat on a corn-sheaf, at daylight's decline—
' You have heard of the Danish boy's whistle of wood ;
    I wish that the Danish boy's whistle were mine.'

' And what would you do with it ? Tell me,' she said,
    While an arch smile played over her beautiful face.
' I would blow it,' he answered, ' and then my fair maid
    Would fly to my side and would there take her place.'

' Is that all you wish for ? Why, that my be yours
    Without any magic !' the young maiden cried ;
' A favour so slight one's good nature secures,'
    And she playfully seated herself by his side.

' I would blow it again,' said the youth, ' and the charm
    Would work so that not even Modesty's check
Would be able to keep from my neck your white arm.'
    She smiled and she laid her white arm round his neck.

" Yet once more I would blow, and the music divine
  Would bring me a third time an exquisite bliss—
You would lay your fair cheek to this brown one of mine ;
  And your lips stealing past it would give me a kiss.'

The maiden laughed out in her innocent glee—
  ' What a fool of yourself with the whistle you'd make !
For only consider how silly 'twould be
  To sit there and whistle for what you might take.'

The May-pole.

—

COME lasses and lads, get leave of your dads,
  And away to the May-pole hie,
For every he has got his she,
  And the fiddler's standing by ;
There's Willie has got his Jane,
  And Jerry has got his Joan,
And there to jig it, jig, jig, jig it,
  Jig it up and down.

Strike up, says Wat: agreed, says Mat,
  And I prithe fiddler play ;
Content says Hodge, and so says Madge,
  For this is a holiday.
Then every lad did doff
  His hat unto his lass,
And every girl did curtsey, curtsey,
  Curtsey on the grass.

' Begin,' says Harry : ' I, I,' says Mary,
  ' We'll lead the Paddington Pound ;'
' Do,' says Jess : ' Oh, no,' says Bess,
  ' We'll have St. Leger's round.'
Then every lad took off his hat,
  And bowèd to his lass,
And the women they did curtsey, curtsey,
  Curtsey on the grass.

'You're out,' says Dick; 'You lie, says Mick,
  'For the fiddler played it wrong;'
'Yes, yes,' says Sue; 'Oh, yes,' says Hugh,
  And 'yes,' says every one.
The fiddler then began
  To play the tune again,
And every lass did foot it, foot it,
  Foot it on to the men.

'Let's kiss,' says Fan, 'I, I,' says Nan,
  And so says every she:
'How many,' says Nat; 'Why three,' says Pat,
  'For that's a maiden's fee.'
But instead of kisses three,
  They gave them half a score,
And the men in kindness, kindness, kindness,
  Gave them as many more.

Then after an hour they went to a bower
  To play for wine and cake,
And kisses too, what could they do,
  For the lasses held the stake.
The women then began
  To quarrel with the men,
And bid them give the kisses back,
  And take their own again.

Now they did stay there all that day,
  And tired the fiddler quite
With dancing and play, without any pay,
  From morning unto night.
They told the fiddler then,
  They'd pay him for his play,
So each paid twopence, twopence, twopence,
  And then toddled away.

'Good night,' says Harry; 'Good night,' says Mary,
  'Good night,' says Dolly to John;
'Good night,' says Sue; 'Good night,'says Hugh,
  'Good night,' says every one.
Some walked, and some did run,
  Some loitered on the way,
And bound themselves with kisses twelve,
  To meet the next holiday.

MAY-POLE SONGS.

The song sent to Notes and Queries, by "A Claytonian," resembles one which is found in Jewitt's Derbyshire Ballads. It is there entitled "Humours of Hayfield Fair," and Mr. Andrews gave a copy of it some time ago in the *Eastern Morning News*, but the poetry is not so good as the one you have printed. No doubt there are many versions of it in other parts of England. The earliest known printed copy appeared in 1672, under the title of "The Rural Dance about the May-pole." Other versions may be found in "Hutchinson's Tour through the High Peak of Derbyshire," 1809. In "Pills to Purge Melancholy," in "Tixhall Poetry," and in Chappel's "Music of the Olden Time."

The Wanton Wife of Castle-Gate; or, The Boatman's Delight.

To its own proper new tune.

FAREWELL both hawk and hound,
    Farewell both shaft and bow,
Farewell all merry pastimes.
    And pleasures on a row ;
Farewell my best beloved,
    In whom I put my trust ;
For it's neither grief nor sorrow
    Shall harbour in my breast.

When I was in my prime,
    And in my youthful days,
Such mirth and merry pastime,
    And pleasure had always ;
But now my mind is changed,
    And altered very sore,
Because my best beloved
    Will fancy me no more,

I lov'd her and I prov'd her,
    And I call'd her my dear ;
But alas ! my beloved
    Would not let me come near.
I often would have kist her,
    But she always said me nay ;
More as ten times have I blest her
    Since that she went away.

Tinkers they are drunkards,
    And masons they are blind,
And boatmen they make cuckolds,
    Because they're used kind.
But if you meet a bonny lass,
    With black and rowling eyes,
You must kiss her and embrace her,
    You may know the reason why.

There lives a wife in Castle-Gate,
    But I'll not declare her name,
She is both brisk and bucksome,
    And likes a jolly game.
She can knip it, she can trip it,
    As she treads along the plain ;
Till she meets some jolly boatman
    That will turn her back again.

Her husband is a quiet man,
    And an honest man is he ;
And so to wear the horns, sir,
    Contented he must be.
He may wind them at his leisure,
    And do the best he can ;
For his wife will take her pleasure,
    And love a jolly boatman.

At Pomfret clock and tower,
    There's gold and silver store ;
I hope therefore to find her,
    And then, brave boys, we'll roar ;
We'll drink sherry and be merry,
    We'll have beer and ale good store,
And drink to my lass, and thy lass,
    And all good lasses more,

My love she is a fair one,
  And a bonny one is she,
Most dearly do I love her,
  Her name is Mally;
Her cheeks are like the roses,
  That blossoms fresh in June;
O she's like some new strung instrument
  That's newly put in tune.

O my Mally, my Honey,
  O, can thou fancy me?
Then let us home haste.
  Where we will merry be.
For good gold and silver,
  For thee I'll take care,
And for a large pair of horns
  For thy husband to wear.

You young men and bachelors,
  That hear this pretty jest,
Be not of the opinion
  That this couple profest:
But be kind to your wives,
  And your sweethearts alway,
And God will protect you
  By night and by day!

Printed for Alex. Milbourn, W. Onely, T. Thackeray, at the Angel, in Dack Lane.

The Bonnet o' Blue.

AT Kingston-upon-Waldy, a town in Yorkshire,
I lived in all splendour and free from all care;
I rolled quite in riches, had sweethearts not a few,
I was wounded by a bonny lad and his bonnet was blue.

There came a troop of soldiers, as you now shall hear,
From Scotland to Waldy abroad for to steer;
There is one among them I wish I ne'er knew,
He's a bonny Scotch laddie, wi' bonnet so blue.

5

I cannot find rest, contentment has fled,
The form of my true-love will run in my head,
The form of my true-love still keeps in my view,
He's a bonny Scotch lad in his bonnet so blue.

Early in the morning arising from bed,
I called upon Sally my own waiting maid,
To dress me as fine as two hands could do
To seek out the lad and his bonnet o' blue.

So quickly she dressed me and quickly I came
To mingle with persons to hear my love's name,
Charles Stuart they called him, I felt it was true;
Once a prince of that name wore a bonnet o' blue.

My love he marched by with a gun in his hand
I strove to speak to him when down on the strand,
I strove to speak to him, away then he flew
My heart it was with him and his bonnet o'blue.

She says, " My dear laddie I'll buy your discharge,
I'll free you from soldiers, I'll let you at large,
I'll free you from soldiers, if your heart will prove true,
And I'll ne'er cast a stain on your bonnet o' blue."

He says, " My dear lassie, you'll buy my discharge,
You'll free me from soldiers and let me at large,
For your very kind offer I bow, ma'am, to you,
But I'll ne'er wear a stain in my bonnet o' blue.

I have a sweet girl in my country town
Who I ne'er would forsake though poverty frown,
I ne'er will forsake the girl that proves true,
And I'll ne'er wear a stain in my bonnet o' blue."

I will send for my limner from London to Hull
To draw my love's picture out in the full,
I'll set it in my chamber, all close in my view
And I'll think on the lad whose heart has proved true.*

* In another copy it is called "The Bonny Scotch Lad;" and
has this verse additional :—

" His cheeks are like the roses, his eyes like the sloes,
He's handsome and proper, and kills where he goes,
He is handsome and proper, and comely for to view,
He's a bonny Scotch lad, and his bonnet so blue."

From a Broadside, without date or printer's name.

The Disappointed Lady.

—

YE blooming young damsels give ear to my song,
'Tis of a gay lady both charming and young,
She fancied a soldier so gallant and free,
And vowed in her heart that his bride she would be.

When she saw the young man on his way to parade,
She called him aside, and to him she said,—
" I am a young lady, if you fancy me,
Your discharge I will purchase and that speedily,

For you are the man that I feel I adore,
'Tis for you that young Cupid has wounded me sore ;
A lady I am and my fortune is great,
I'll make you the master of all my estate."

" Dear honour'd lady," this young man did say,
" I know not how soon we'll be marching away,
For we must obey, love, when the route, love, does come,
By the sound of a fife, and the beat of a drum."

" I'll away to my halls, and there I will mourn,
Yet, hoping that soon the dear lad will return ;
Neither noble nor squire my favour shall gain,
For my soldier that's absent a maid I'll remain."

From a Broadside ; J. Kendrew, Printer, York.

———

The Farmer's Son.

—

" SWEET Nelly ! My heart's delight !
Be loving, and do not slight
The proffer I make for modesty's sake :
I honour your beauty bright,

S 2

For love, I profess, I can do no less,
 Thou hast my favour won ;
And since I see your modesty,
I pray agree, and fancy me,
 Though I'm but a farmer's son."

" No ! I am a lady gay,
'Tis very well known, I may
Have men of renown, in country or town ;
So ! Roger, without delay,
Court Bridget, or Sue, Kate, Nancy, or Prue,
 Their loves will soon be won ;
But don't you dare to speak *me* fair,
As if I were at my last prayer,
 To marry a farmer's son."

" My father has riches in store,
Two hundred a-year and more ;
Besides sheep and cows, carts, harrows, and ploughs,
His age is about three-score.
And when he does die, then merrily I
 Shall have what he has won ;
Both land and kine, all shall be thine,
If thou'lt incline, and will be mine,
 And marry a farmer's son."

"A fig for your cattle and corn !
Your proffered love I scorn !
'Tis known very well, my name is Nell,
And you're but a bumpkin born."
"Well ! since it is so, away I will go—
 And I hope no harm is done ;
Farewell, adieu ! I hope to woo
As good as you, and win her too,
 Though I'm but a farmer's son."

" Be not in such haste," quoth she,
" Perhaps we may still agree ;
For, man, I protest, I was but in jest !
Come, prythee, sit down by me ;
For thou art the man that verily can
 Win me, if e'er I'm won ;
Both straight and tall, genteel withal ;
Therefore, I shall be at your call,
 To marry a farmer's son."

" Dear lady ! believe me now
I solemnly swear and vow,
No lords in their lives take pleasure in wives,
Like fellows that drive the plough :
For whatever they gain with labour and pain,
    They don't wi't to harlots run
As courtiers.   I never knew
A London beau that could outdo
    A country farmer's son !"

Dialogue songs were formerly greatly in vogue, and this one was familiar to the dwellers of the west and the north of Yorkshire.   It first appeared in the " Vocal Miscellany," a collection of 400 songs, in 1729, but it must be much older.   Mr. Dixon says :—" It was evidently grounded on an old black-letter dialogue, preserved in the Roxburgh collection, called ' A mad kind of wooing : or a dialogue between Will the Simple and Nan the Subtill, with their loving argument.' "

Harry's Courtship.

Mr. Dixon says " this used to be a popular song in the Yorkshire dales."

[We have been obliged to supply an hiatus in the second verse, and to make an alteration in the last.]

HARRY courted modest Mary,
Mary was always brisk and airy ;
Harry was country neat as could be,
But his words were rough, and his duds were muddy.

Harry when he first bespoke her
Kept a dandling the kitchen poker ;
Mary spoke her words like Venus,
But said, ' There's something I fear between us.'

' Have you got cups of china mettle,
Canister, cream jug, tongs or kettle ?'
' Odzooks, I've bowls, and siles, and dishes,
Enow to supply any prudent wishes.'

'I've got none o' your cups of chaney,
Canister, cream jugs, I've not any ;
I've a three-footed pat, and a good brass kettle,
Pray what do you want with your chaney mettle ? '

'A shippen full of rye for to gather,
A house full of goods one mack or another ;
I'll thrash in the lathe while you sit spinning,
O Molly, I think that's a good beginning.'

'I'll not sit at my wheel a-spinning,
Or rise in the noon to wash your linen ;
I'll lie in bed till the clock strikes eleven—'
'Oh, grant me patience, gracious Heaven ! '

'Why then thou must marry some red-nosed squire,
Who'll buy thee a settle to sit by the fire ;
For I'll to Margery in the valley,
She is my girl, so farewell Mally.'

The Garden Gate.

THE day was spent, the moon shone bright,
    The village clock struck eight ;
Young Mary hastened, with delight,
    Unto the garden gate :
But what was there that made her sad ;—
The gate was there, but not the lad,
Which made poor Mary say and sigh,
"Was ever poor girl so sad as I ? "

She traced the garden here and there,
    The village clock struck nine ;
Which made poor Mary sigh and say,
    " You shan't, you shan't be mine !
You promised to meet at the gate at eight,
You ne'er shall keep me, nor make me wait,
For I'll let all such creatures see,
They ne'er shall make a fool of me ! "

She traced the garden here and there,
   The village clock struck ten ;
Young William caught her in his arms,
   No more to part again :
For he'd been to buy the ring that day,
And O ! he had been a long, long way ;
Then how could Mary cruel prove,
To banish the lad she so dearly did love ?

Up with the morning sun they rose,
   To church they went away,
And all the village joyful were,
   Upon their wedding day.
Now in a cot by the river side,
William and Mary both reside ;
And she blesses the night that she did wait
For her absent swain at the garden gate.

    Dr. J. H. Dixon, writing of the above, says :—"One of our most
pleasing rural ditties. The air is very beautiful. We first heard it sung
in Malhamdale, Yorkshire, by Willy Bolton, an Old Dales' Minstrel,
who accompanied himself on the union-pipes ; " and adds the following
account of Billy:—" It was a lovely September day, and the scene was
Arncliffe, a retired village in Littondale, one of the most secluded of
the Yorkshire dales. While sitting at the open window of the humble
hostelrie, we heard what we at first thought was a *ranter* parson, but,
on enquiry, were told it was old Billy Bolton reading to a crowd of
villagers. Curious to ascertain what the minstrel was reading, we
joined the crowd, and found the text-book was a volume of Hume's
"England," which contained the reign of Elizabeth. Billy read in a
clear voice, with proper emphasis and correct pronunciation, interlard-
ing his reading with numerous comments, the nature of which may be
readily inferred from the fact that the minstrel belonged to 'the ancient
church.' It was a scene for a painter ; the village situate in one of the
deepest parts of the dale, the twilight hour, the attentive listeners,
and the old man leaning on his knife-grinding machine, and conveying
popular information to a simple peasantry. Bolton is in the constant
habit of so doing, and is really an extraordinary man, uniting, as he
does, the opposite occupations of minstrel, conjurer, knife-grinder, and
schoolmaster. Such a labourer in the great cause of human improvement is well deserving of this brief notice, which it would be unjust
to conclude without stating that whenever the itinerant teacher takes

occasion to speak of his own creed, and contrast it with others, he does so in the spirit of charity; and he never performs any of his sleight-of-hand tricks without a few introductory remarks on the evil of superstition, and the folly of supposing that in the present age any mortal is endowed with supernatural attainments."

Since the above was penned, both the writer and the minstrel have passed over to the other side. Billy Bolton died on the 1st of September, 1881, and I copy what follows from the *Craven Pioneer* of the 17th of that month :—

The minstrel was born at Gilling, near Richmond, in the year 1796, at which place he was apprenticed to the trade of whitesmith. He afterwards took to travelling the North, East, and West Ridings of Yorkshire in the varied capacities of hardware dealer, knife, razor, and scissors grinder, minstrel-piper, conjurer, "educator and magic expositor." After following this nomadic life for nearly three score years, Bolton settled down in comparative comfort in the pretty village of Burnsall-in-Wharfedale, on a weekly allowance generously granted to him by Mr. Pattinson, merchant, of London, by whose father, the late Rev. W. J. Pattinson, the good rector of Oxwell, the old minstrel had long been known and much respected. During last summer he appeared hale and hearty, and at haytime was occasionally seen rendering assistance to his farmer friends in haymaking. Recently, however, he showed signs of decay, his mental faculties had begun to fail, and he became unsettled in his home, and though far from well determined to be again on the road with his "grinder," though his usual time to take the road had always been in March. So persistent was he in this determination that on the morning of Thursday, the 25th ult., he was up at an early hour and started off at four in the morning, pushing along the road his old grinder, with the intention of reaching Buckden, a village in Upper Wharfedale, four miles distant. He, however, was observed by one or two of the villagers to stop and rest three times in going up the village, and seeing that it was impossible for him to go far in his weakly condition, they at once called up two of the officials of the village, who quickly followed with a conveyance and came up with the old man when near the village of Linton, upon which they conveyed him to the Skipton Workhouse, where he was visited on Saturday by Mr. Bland, and on Thursday, the 1st inst., by the Rector of Burnstall (the Rev. C. H. Carlisle), who ministered to the old minstrel until his speedy death. Bolton's remains were conveyed on Saturday by hearse to Burnsall, where he was interred in accordance with the rites of the Church of England, the rector performing the last sad office. Eight persons of the village attended as bearers, and the funeral was largely followed by the villagers.

Peter King.

A Legend of Craven—By Robert Story.

———

" WAKE, minstrel of Rylstone, arise, and be gone!
Leave thy bonny young bride to her slumbers alone ;
At Kirkstall, this even, a festival gay
Demands all thy music—then up, and away.

The minstrel arose, though the summons but seemed
To his half-sleeping ear as a thing he had dreamed ;
When he saw at the casement, in page garb a youth,
And found in a moment the message was sooth.

He donned his green robe, and his wild harp he slung,
Then o'er moorland and dale like a roebuck he sprung ;
Though ere he reached Kirkstall the summer eve's gleam
Lay rich upon abbey, and village, and stream.

Full gay was the place that received him ; o'er all
A light-flood was cast from the lamps in the hall,
Where the maidens of Aire sat like naiads in ranks,
More sweet than the blossoms that spring on her banks.

And there, too, were youths bent on frolic and glee,
And monks from the abbey the joyance to see ;
(For the priests in that age saw in mirth nothing wrong),
And the night sped away with the dance and the song.

But there was one maiden, unrivalled in shape,
In beauty the rosebud, in ripeness the grape ;
Though sleepy and calm, yet her half shut blue eye
Threw an arrow more sure than the openest by.

The minstrel beheld her, and felt, as he viewed,
Emotions he looked on as vanished, renewed,
Ah, minstrel, beware ! in that glance there is sin,
Thy season is over the lovely to win.

Of his Mary, her love and her beauty he thought,
And her image before him, by effort, he brought ;
The bodiless shape, like a morning dream, fled,
And there stood the beautiful stranger instead !

Why sing then the tale of his fickleness ?   Now
In the arms of a leman forgetting his vow ;
He thinks not, nor wishes, from Kirkstall to roam ;
Nor to soothe the sad heart that is breaking at home.

The news reached that home ; and poor Mary must weep,
But her soul it was high, and her love it was deep,
She saw that dishonour was tracking his path.
And she thought on his state more in sorrow than wrath.

But how shall she act in so piteous a case ?
Oh ! how shall she rescue her love from disgrace ?
Nor kindred nor friends any aid could afford,
And she flew to the wise man, hight Roger de Worde.

The Wizard she found in the Knavey-Knoll Cave,
His stature was tall and his visage was grave ;
But the power lay neither in look nor in form,
That could sink the grim winds or arouse the wild storm !

By the spells which he framed in the Knavey-Knoll Cave,
He could force the strong sprites of the land and the wave,
To veil at his bidding the moonbeams, when bright
They pierced through the sky on a calm summer night.

His answer to Mary was spoken in a tone
That startled the bats from his dwelling place lone—
" I grant thee thy boon, if, *sans* taper or torch,
Thou meet me at midnight in Rylstone Church porch."

Love is stronger than death, and it mocketh at fear,
Yet Mary's heart sunk as the moment drew near,
And she trembled with terror to hear the quick tread,
Returned from the tombstones and graves of the dead.

Half fainting she reached the dark porch, and in sooth
Began to have doubts of the dread Wizard's truth,
When his voice bade her welcome in accents as hoarse
And broken as those of a vivified corse !

" Have courage ! " he muttered, " and soon shall thy arms
Recover thy mate from a paramour's charms ;
Nor ever again, if there's truth in his star,
Shall he leave his fair cottage as *fast* or as far."

"Have courage!" the Wizard repeated; then called
On his aids in a tone that her spirit appalled,
At once growled the thunder, the lightening flashed past,
And she saw the grim Wizard, distinct and aghast.

"Have courage!" the Wizard repeated, again
He called, and the lightning came mingled with rain,
While shapes, as of fiends, she beheld in the light,
And her heart almost died as they vanished in night.

"Have courage!" repeated the mighty De Worde,
"He comes!" The wind rose and a tempest it roared;
Against the church steeple a body is blown,
And it falls on the porch flag, with crash and with groan!

"Foul Wizard!" cried Mary—distracted that hour—
"Accurst be thy kindness! accurst be thy power.
Love faded a space may revive and rebloom:
But where is the hope when the heart's in the tomb?"

Loud laughed the dread Wizard, "Fear nothing for *him*;
My imps have disabled him but in a limb,
Which henceforth will prove an effectual bar
To his leaving his cottage as *fast*, or as far!"

The harp, in the green dales of Craven, no more
Responds to the touch of the bard as of yore:
But our hamlet and towns to the music still ring,
Awaked by the race of the famed Peter King.

I have seen *one*, with violin bag under arm,
Like his ancestor *halting* to cottage or farm:
A warning to *bards*, while the lineage survives,
As a spell-ride they dread to be leal to their wives."

This ballad first appeared in the *Newcastle Magazine*. Dr. J. H. Dixon says that Story has deviated considerably from the Craven version of the legend, where the tale is transferred from Rylstone to Calverley Hall. Dr. Dixon also says:—"Robert Story has never been properly appreciated by the inhabitants of Craven. We say it deliberately. He has found readers amongst the intellectual classes. Men of highly cultivated minds and exquisite taste have ranked amongst Story's ardent admirers. With the masses, the bard (sprung from the

people) has been neglected—aye, looked down upon with scorn.   We
have heard Story's talents disparaged, and the eulogy of his genius
met by remarks on his conduct.   In forming our opinion of Shakspeare,
Burns, or the late Professor Wilson, we have nothing to do with the
deer-stealing propensities of the first, the drunken orgies of the second,
or the pugnacious qualities of the third !   What are an author's foibles
if the moral of his writings be not affected by them ?   Story was a truly
moral writer.   In his works there is not a single improper thought !—
nay, not an *innuendo*, that could be liable to misconstruction.   We
would therefore advise those who shrug their shoulders at the name of
Story, and talk about convivialities at Gargrave, and of his getting
into difficulties, to put all such matters aside.   They should bear in
mind that his latter years were passed in quiet and respectability.   We
have visited his humble cottage at Battersea, and if he were not there,
he was sure to be found at the Literary Institute.   For years before his
death he had avoided all gay or convivial society, and refused to take
even the smallest quantity of intoxicating liquors.   His latter days were
certainly not tinged with any of the faults of the *bon vivant*—using that
expression in its worldly sense.   No one died more respected by his
friends and neighbours.   Let those who survive him, therefore, forget
the follies and faults of his Craven life, and remember only the man of
genius.   We are convinced that the more his writings are examined,
and sifted, and studied, the more shall we perceive their beauties. The
district of Craven ought to feel proud that such a man has dwelt in
one of its most beautiful villages, and immortalised some of our finest
mountain scenery."   (See appendix note 21.)

MISCELLANEOUS
BALLADS.

Jack and Tom.

An Old Border Ballad: Traditional.

I'm a North countrie man, in Redesdale born,
Where our land lies lea, and grows ne corn,—
And such two lads to my house never com,
As them two lads called Jack and Tom.

Now, Jack and Tom, they're going to the sea;
I wish them both in good companie!
They're going to seek their fortunes ayont the wide sea,
Far, far away frae their oan countrie!

They mounted their horses and rode over the moor,
Till they came to a house, when they rapped at the door:
"D'ye brew ony ale? D'ye sell ony beer?
Or have ye ony lodgings for strangers here?"
And out came Jockey the hostler man.

"Ne, we brew ne ale, nor we sell ne beer,
Nor we have ne lodgings for strangers here,
So he bolted the door, and bade them be gone,
For there was ne lodgings there for poor Jack and Tom.

They mounted their horses and rode over the plain;—
Dark was the night, and down fell the rain;
Till a twinkling light they happened to spy,
And a castle and a house they were close by.

They rode up to the house, and they rapped at the door,
And out came Jockey, the hosteler.
"D'ye brew ony ale? D'ye sell ony beer?
Or have ye ony lodgings for strangers here?"

"Yes, we have brewed ale this fifty lang year,
And we have got lodgings for strangers here."
So the roast to the fire, and the pot hung on,
And all to accomodate poor Jack and Tom.

When supper was over, and all was *sided down*,
The glasses of wine did go merrily roun'.
' Here is to thee, Jack, and here is to thee,
And all the bonny lasses in our countrie !'
' Here is to thee, Tom, and here is to thee,
And look they may *leuk* for thee and me !'

'Twas early next morning, before the break of day,
They mounted their horses, and so they rode away.
Poor Jack, he died upon a far foreign shore,
And Tom, he was never, never heard of more !

This ballad was taken down from recitation in 1847, by the late
Dr. J. H. Dixon, and is inserted in " Bell's Ballads and Songs of the
Peasantry of England." Dr. Dixon says—" Of its history nothing is
known. but we are strongly inclined to believe that it may be assigned
to the early part of the 17th century, and that it relates to the visit of
Prince Charles and Buckingham, under the assumed names of Jack
and Tom, to Spain, in 1623. Some curious references to the adventures of the Prince and his companion, on their masquerading tour,
will be found in J. O. Halliwell's ' Letters of the Kings of England,'
volume 2."

Begone Dull Care.

BEGONE, dull care !
    I prithee begone from me ;
Begone, dull care !
    Thou and I can never agree.
Long while thou hast been tarrying here,
    And fain thou would'st me kill ;
But i' faith dull care,
    Thou never shalt have thy will.

Too much care
    Will make a young man gray ;
Too much care
    Will turn an old man to clay.

My wife shall dance, and I will sing,
   To merrily pass the day;
For I hold it is the wisest thing,
   To drive dull care away.

Hence, dull care,
   I'll none of thy company:
Hence, dull care,
   Thou art no pair (peer) for me.
We'll hunt the wild boar thro' the wold,
   So merrily pass the day;
And then at night o'er a cheerful bowl,
   We'll drive dull care away.

This is a very ancient song, and the present copy was taken down from the singing of an old Yorkshire Yeoman. The third verse was never in print until the late James Henry Dixon inserted it in his collection of *Ballads and Songs of the Peasantry of England*. The first two verses may be found in *Playford's Musical Companion*, published in 1687; and also in the *Illustrated Book of English Songs*, edited, I believe, by Dr. Charles Mackay, and published by H. Ingram, Milford House, Strand, London.

Fragment of the Hagmena Song.

As sung at Richmond, Yorkshire, on the eve of the New Year, by the Corporation Pinder.

To-NIGHT it is the New Year's night,
   To morrow is the day,
And we are come for our right,
   And for our ray,
As we used to do in
   Old King Henry's day.
      Sing, fellows, sing, Hagman-heigh.

If you go to the bacon-flick,
   Cut me a good bit;
Cut, cut and low,
   Beware of your maw;

T

Cut, cut and round,
   Beware of your thumb,
That me and my merry men
  May have some.
     Sing, fellows, sing, Hagman-heigh.

If you go to the black-Ark,
   Bring me X mark ;
Ten mark, ten pound,
  Throw it down upon the ground,
That me and my merry men
  May have some.
     Sing, fellows, sing, Hagman-heigh.

Hagmena songs used to be very common in England, Scotland, and France ; and were sometimes sung on Christmas eve, and sometimes on New Year's eve ; and repeated for a few evenings according to the size of the district to be travelled over.   Their origin is lost in obscurity, but some suppose them to be " Holy-month Songs," whilst other antiquaries think they refer in some way to the new year mistletoe.   Those who are curious in such matters may consult " Chambers' Book of Days," and " Brand's Popular Antiquities;" vol. I., page 247-8, Sir Henry Ellis's edition.

Mary, of Marley.

At Marley stood the rural cot,
   In Bingley's sweet sequested dale,
The spreading oaks enclosed the spot
   Where dwelt the beauty of the vale.

Blessed was a small, but fruitful farm,
   Beneath the high majestic hill,
Where nature spread her every charm
   That can the mind with pleasure fill—

Here bloomed the maid—nor vain, nor proud,
   But like an unapproached flower,
Hid from the flattery of the crowd,
   Unconscious of her beauty's power.

Her ebon locks were richer far
  Than is the raven's glossy plume ;
Her eyes outshone the evening star ;
  Her lovely cheeks the rose's bloom.

The mountain snow, that falls by night,
  By which the bending heath is pressed,
Did never shine in purer white
  Than was upon her virgin breast.

The blushes of her innocence
  Great Nature's hand had pencilled o'er ;
And Modesty the veil had wrought
  Which Mary, lovely virgin, wore.

At early morn each favourite cow
  The tuneful voice of Mary knew ;
Their answers hummed—then wandering slow,
  From daisies dashed the pearly dew.

When lovely on the green she stood,
  And to her poultry threw the grain,
Ring-doves and pheasants from the wood
  Flew forth and glittered in her train.

The thrush upon the rosy bower
  Would sit and sing while Mary stayed ;
Her lambs their pasture frisked o'er,
  And on the new-sprung clover fed.

She milked beneath the beech tree's shade,
  And there the turf was worn away,
Where cattle had for centuries laid,
  To shun the summer's sultry ray.

Lysander, from the neighbouring vale,
  Where Wharfe's deceitful currents move,
To Mary told a fervent tale,
  And Mary could not help but love.

The richest might have come and sighed ;
  Lysander had her favour won,—
Her breast was constant as the tide,
  And true as light is to the sun.

When winter, wrapped in gloomy storm,
  Each dubious path had drifted o'er
And whirled the snow in every form,
  To Mary oft he crossed the moor.*

When western winds and pelting rain
  Did mountain snows to rivers turn,
These swelled and roared and foamed in vain,
  Affection helped him o'er the bourne.

Until the last, the fatal night,
  His footsteps slipped—the cruel tide
Danced and exulted with its freight,
  Then lifeless cast him on its side!

How changed is lovely Mary now!
  How pale and frantic she appears!
Description fails to paint her woe,
  And numbers to recount her tears.

Marley is an ancient hamlet on the river Aire, and is about a mile above Bingley. It is a charming spot, and is not far from the far-famed "Druid's Altar." This fine ballad was written by John Nicholson; and John James, in his life of the author, says:—"Almost all Nicholson's pieces were written on subjects which came within the sphere of his own observation. 'Mary of Marley,' 'The Maid of Lowdore,' 'Sally on the Heath-vestured Hills,' had all their living originals, with whom he was acquainted."

 * The "moor" here referred to would be Romilies Moor, or Romalds Moor, as it is now often called, which divides Wharfedale from Airedale. (See appendix note 22.)

Mute is the Lyre of Ebor.

By Robert Story.—1842.

"WE BRING OUR YEARS TO AN END AS IT WERE A TALE THAT IS TOLD."—Psalms.

MUTE is the Lyre of Ebor, cold
  The Minstrel of the streamy Aire!
The "years" are passed, the "tale" is told;
  Prepare the shroud, the grave prepare!

The tale is told—What is the tale?
   The same that still the ear hath won
As oft as in life's humbler vale,
   Genius hath found a wayward son.

First comes the magic time of life,
   When boyhood sees nor dreams of gloom;
And when within the breast are rife
   Thoughts that are made of light and bloom!

When youth is full of burning hopes
   Of fame and glory ne'er to die,
When manfully with fate he copes,
   And will not see a peril nigh.

At length he gives to public gaze
   The transcript of his glowing thought;
And vulgar marvel, high born praise,
   Seem earnests of the meed he sought.

Now round him crowd, where'er he wends,
   His mind yet pure and undebased,
The countless troops of talent's friends,
   Men who affect—but have not—taste.

These bid him press to eager lips
   The double poison of their bowl—
Flatteries that weaken as he sips
   And drafts that darken sense and soul.

O for a voice to rouse him up,
   To warn him ere too-late it be,
That Frenzy mantles in the cup,
   And that its dregs are—Misery!

Days pass—years roll—the novelty
   That charmed at first, is faded now;
And men that sought his hour of glee,
   Repel him with an altered brow.

Where is the bard's indignant breath?
   Alas, the bard, from habits learned,
Is powerless to resent; and Death
   Kindly receives him—spent and spurned!

Talk ye of Fame ? Oh ! he hath borne
   Contempt, alive ; but praise him dead !
Ay, mourn him—whom ye left to mourn !
   Give him a stone—ye gave not bread !

No more.   The old, sad tale is told,
   Prepare the shroud, the grave prepare ;
For mute is Ebor's Lyre, and cold
   The Minstrel of the streamy Aire !

The particulars of the manner in which John Nicholson met his
end, is thus related by Mr. John James, his biographer :—" The evening before Good Friday, April 13th, 1843, he left Bradford for the
purpose of visiting his aunt at Eldwick, and called at several places on
the road.   When he left Shipley time was fast approaching midnight.
He was observed to proceed up the bank of the canal in the direction
of Dixon Mill (the very spot where the Saltaire *New* Mill now stands),
and at this place it seems he attempted to cross the river Aire by
means of the stepping stones there, so as to take the most direct course
to Eldwick.   The night was dark and stormy.   It is conjectured that
in endeavouring to cross the stepping stones, and on reaching the
farther part of the river he missed his footing and fell into the current,
which runs deep and impetuously at that point.   From the appearance
of the place next morning he had been carried away eight or ten yards,
where he caught hold of some hazel boughs, and by a great effort got
out of the water.   Exhausted and benumbed he lay there until about
six in the morning.   Two hours after the poor poet was seen by a farm
labourer, who was proceeding to his work, and upon calling out and
receiving no answer, he ran to inform his master at Baildon, who
instantly returned with him to the place, where they found Nicholson
dead ; but life had only been extinct a short time, as he was quite
warm."   A man had seen him on the bank at six o'clock that morning,
but neglected to give an alarm, or his life might have been saved.   It
is singular that the poet's son Thomas met his death also by drowning
in the river Aire ; and his widow was found burned to death on her
own hearth.

The Jovial Sailor's Crew.

You merchant men in every part,
   To Hull now repair,
You may recreate yourselves with sport
   And view the ships most fair.

Our trading is most flourishing
    As ever I did view,
For there is none can be compar'd
    To the jovial sailor's crew.

So we merry noble sailors,
    That ramble here and there,
When we are in the alehouse
    We drink ale and beer.
We drink our liquor freely,
    Our joys for to renew,
So there's none to be compar'd
    To the jovial sailor's crew.

We sailors are the best of hearts,
    And excel all other trades.
We scorn to sneak to either side,
    We're nobler brisk blades.
We drink our liquor freely,
    Our joys for to renew;
Then sure none can be compar'd
    To the jovial sailor's crew.

When peace it is concluded,
    And war is at an end,
Then, bonny lad, we'll all rejoice.
    When these bad times do mend.
True love will be in fashion,
    Our joys will then renew:
Drink to the prosperity of our trade,
    And the jovial sailor's crew.

Good success unto our ships
    Going out and coming in;
Navigation, it excels
    All arts under the sun.
When our ships they are arriving,
    Looks pleasant to our view,
Our bells they shall merrily ring
    For the jovial sailor's crew.

Come let us drink round, boys,
    Unto the church and king,
And many that do oppose them,
    May they in halters swing!

Likewise unto our merchants,
  Good sir, let me pledge you,
For there's none can be compar'd
  To the jovial sailor's crew.

And now for to conclude, boys,
  Let's merrily drink round,
And stand fast to our ships, boys,
  And ne'er seem to rebound.
So here's a health to all true hearts,
  That ever will prove true,
Since there's none can be compar'd
  To the jovial sailor's crew.

And whilst we have our health, boys,
  Let's ne'er conceit we're poor,
For when that we have spent all,
  We'll to the seas for more.
We'll drink a health to honest blades,
  That ever will prove true,
Since there's none to be compar'd
  To the jovial sailor's crew.

The Dirge of Offa.

See my son, my Offa, dies !
  He who could chase his father's foes !
Where shall the King now close his eyes ?
  Where but in the tomb of woes.

'Tis there his stony couch is laid,
  And there the wearied King may rest—
But will not Penda's threats invade
  The quiet of the monarch's breast ?

No—my son shall quell his rage—
  What have I said ? ah me, undone ;
Ne'er shall the parent's snowy age
  Recall the tender name of son !

O would that I for thee had died,
  Nor lived to wail thy piteous case!
Who dared defy those looks of pride,
  That marks the chief of Wyba's race!

But, O my son, I little knew
  What power was in that arm of might!
That weeds of such a baleful hue
  The laurel's beauteous wreath should blight!

Yes, my son, the shaft that thee
  Transfixed, hath drawn thy father's fate!
O how will Hengist weep to see
  The woes that on his line await!

To see my Offa's latest pangs,
  As wild in death he bites the shore!
A savage wolf, with bloody fangs,
  The lamb's unspotted bosom tore!

Who never knew to give offence,
  But to revenge his father's wrong!
Some abler arm convey him hence,
  And bear a father's love along!

Alas! this tongue is all too weak
  The last sad duties to perform!
These feeble arms their task forsake!
  Else should they rise in wrathful storm.

Against the ruthless rebel's head
  Who dared such laurels to destroy;
To bid each virtue's hope lie dead!
  And crush a parent's joy.

Inter him by yon ivy tower,
  And raise the note of deepest dole;
Ne'er should a friend in deathful hour,
  Forget the chief of generous soul:

And o'er the grave erect a stone,
  His worth and lineage high to tell:
And by the faithful cross be shown
  That in the faith of Christ he fell!

Hail ! valient chiefs of Hatfield Wood !
　　Ne'er may your blooming honours cease !
That with unequal strength withstood
　　The invader of your country's peace.

Now, round this head let darkness fall !
　　Descend ye shafts of thunderous hail !
Ne'er shall be said in Edwy's hall
　　That troubled ghost was heard to wail.

Then with his feeble arm, the sire
　　Into the thickest battle flies,
To die, was all the chief's desire :
　　Oppressed with wounds and grief, he dies.

And let the future love of rhime,
　　If chance he cons of Edwy's praise,
As high his quivering fingers climb,
　　Record, that Mordrid poured his lays !

This ballad is supposed to be sung by Mordrid, chief of the bards,
on the death of Offa the son of King Edwin, of Northumberland. He
was slain in the battle of Hatfield Wood, near Doncaster, A.D. 633.
The ballad was composed by the Rev. Mr. Ball.

The Mummer's Song.

—

You gentlemen and sportsmen,
　　And men of courage bold,
All you that's got a good horse,
　　Take care of him when he is old ;
Then put him in your stable,
　　And keep him there so warm ;
Give him good corn and hay,
　　Pray let him take no harm.
Poor old horse ! poor old horse !

Once I had my clothing
  Of linsey-woolsey fine,
My tail and main of length,
  And my body it did shine ;
But now I'm growing old,
  And my nature does decay,
My master frowns upon me,
  These words I heard him say,—
  Poor old horse ! poor old horse !

These pretty little shoulders,
  That once were plump and round,
They are decayed and rotten,—
  I'm afraid they are not sound.
Likewise these little nimble legs,
  That have run many miles,
Over hedges, over ditches,
  Over valleys, gates, and stiles,
  Poor old horse ! poor old horse !

I used to be kept
  On the best corn and hay
That in fields could be grown,
  Or in any meadows gay :
But now, alas ! it's not so,—
  There's no such food at all !
I'm forced to nip the short grass
  That grows beneath your wall.
  Poor old horse ! poor old horse !

I used to be kept up
  All in a stable warm,
To keep my tender body
  From any cold or harm ;
But now I'm turned out
  In the open fields to go,
To face all kinds of weather,
  The wind, cold, frost, and snow.
  Poor old horse ! poor old horse !

My hide unto the huntsman
  So freely I would give,
My body to the hounds
  For I'd rather die than live :

> So shoot him, whip him, strip him,
>   To the huntsman let him go ;
> For he's neither fit to ride upon,
>   Nor in any team to draw.
>   Poor old horse ! poor old horse !

The above is the song of the " Poor Old Horse," as sung by the mummers in the neighbourhood of Richmond, Yorkshire, at Christmas time. The actor who sings the song is dressed as an old horse, and at the end of every verse the jaws are snapped in chorus. Mr. Dixon was of opinion that the " Old Horse " is probably of Scandinavian origin, —a reminiscence of Odin's Sleipnor.

The Wassail Hymn.

HERE WE COME A WASSAILING.

Christmas time is generally a happy time, and a hopeful time. For hundreds of years the " Wassail Hymn," has been chaunted by English boys and girls, as they trudge along our town streets, and country lanes, in the mire or the snow ; and the good mothers of our blessed land have smilingly opened their doors and welcomed in the Christmas, and the dear children, with their " Wassail Bob," made of rosemary tree. There can be little doubt that these simple lyrics date from pre-Reformation times, and originated in the years between the 12th and the 15th centuries.

> HERE we come a wassailing,
>   Among the leaves so green ;
> Here we come a wandering,
>   So fair and to be seen.
>   For it is now Christmas time
>   When we travel far and near :
>   So God bless you and send you,
>   "A Happy New Year."

> We are not daily beggars
>   That beg from door to door,
> But we are neighbours children
>   Whom you have seen before.
>   For it is, &c.

Call up the butler of this house,
  Put on his golden ring,
Let him bring us of your best fare
  And the better we shall sing.
    For it is, &c.

Bring us out a table,
  And spread it with a cloth ;
Bring us out some mould cheese,
  And some of your Christmas loaf.
    For it is, &c.

We have got a little purse
  Made of stretching leather skin,
And we want a little money
  To line it well within.
    For it is, &c.

God bless the master of this house,
  Likewise the mistress too :
And all the little children
  That round your table go.
    For it is, &c.

And good master and good mistress
  While you're sitting by the fire,
Pray think of us poor children,
  Who are wandering in the mire.
    For it is, &c.

As the above carol differs in almost every village in Yorkshire, I have copied from memory.

A New Fox-Hunting Song.

By W. S. Kenrick and J. Burtell.

From a broadside in the Roxburgh Collection.

The Chase run by the Cleveland Fox-Hounds on Saturday, the 29th day of January, 1785.

Ye hardy sons of chase give ear,
  All listen to my song :
'Tis of a hunt performed this year,
  That will be talked of long.

When a hunting we do go, oho, oho, oho,
And a hunting we will go, oho, oho, oho,
And a hunting we will go, oho, oho, oho,
    With the huntsman Tally, oh.

On Weary Bank, ye know the same,
    Unkennelled was the fox ;
Who led us and our hounds of fame,
    O'er mountains, moors, and rocks.
        When, &c.

'Twas Craythorn first swift reynard made,
    To Limton then did fly ;
Full speed pursued each hearty blade,
    And joined in jovial cry.
        With the huntsman Tally ho.

To Worsal next he took his flight,
    Escape us he would fain ;
To Picton next with all his might,
    To Craythorn back again.
        With, &c.

To Weary Bank then takes his course,
    Thro' Fanny Bell's gill flies ;
In Seymour Car strains all his force,
    His utmost vigour tries.
        With, &c.

To Taunton Nanthorp, next he flies,
    O'er Langborough Rig goes he ;
He scours like lightening o'er the meads,
    More swift fox could not be.
        With, &c.

To Newton, then to Roseberry,
    To Hatton Lockerass gill ;
To Lownsdale, o'er Court Moor we go,
    From thence to Rildale Mill.
        With, &c.

By Percy Cross, and Sleddale too,
    And Pilly Rig full fast,
As fox could run to Skylderskew,
    And Lockwood Beck he passed.
        With, &c.

By Freebrough Hill he takes his way,
  By Danby Lodge also ;
With ardour we pursue our prey,
  As swift as hounds could go.
    With, &c.

By Coal Pits and o'er Stonegate Moor,
  To Scayling renard ran ;
Was such a fox e'er seen before ?
  His equal show who can !
    When, &c.

To Barnby now by Ugthorpe Mill,
  And Mickleby likewise ;
To Ellerby, to Hinderwell,
  Still stubborn reynard flies.
    With, &c.

The huntsman now with other three,*
  And reynard you'll suppose :
Ten couple of hounds of high degree,
  One field now did enclose.
    With, &c.

But now our chase draws near an end,
  No longer we'll intrude ;
For on the cliff, rejoice, my friend,
  Swift reynard there we viewed.
    With, &c.

Sure such a chase must wonder raise,
  And had I time to sing,
The huntsmans deeds who merits praise,
  Would make the vallies ring.
    When a, &c.

Come, sportsmen, all your glasses fill,
  And let the toast go round ;
May each fox-hunter flourish still,
  In health and strength abound.
    When a hunting we do go, &c.

---

* Thomas Cole, huntsman ; the Rev. George Davison, rector of
Cockfield, county Durham ; Christopher Rowntree, jr., and William
Stockdale.

Come to thi Gronny, Doy!

By Ben Preston.

———

Come to thi Gronny, doy! come to thi Gronny,
Bless tha, to me tha'rt as precious as onny :
Mutherless barn of a dowter unwed,
Little tha knaws, doy, the tears 'at ah've shed—
Trials ah've knawn boath fur t'heart an fur t'heead :
Shortness o' wark, ey, an shortness o' breead.
Thease awkud bide—but thau tha't none to blame :
Bless tha, tha browt ma boath sorrow and shame ;
Gronny, poor sowl, fur a two-month or moar,
Hardly kud feshun to lewk aht o' t'door ;
T'nabors called aht to ma, " Dunnot stand that,
Aht wi' that hussy, an aht wi hur brat."
Deary me, deary me, what kud I say :
T'first thing uv all, ah thowt " Let ma go pray."
T'next time ah slept ah'd a dream de'ya see,—
Ey, an ah knew that dream was fur me :
Tears o' Christ Jesus, ah saw em that neet
Fall drop be drop onta one at his feet ;
After that, saw Him wi barns rahnd His knee,
Some on 'um, happen, poor craturs like thee ;
Says ah at last—though ah soarly wur tried—
Suarly a sinner, a sinner sud bide,
Naburs may think and may say what they will,
T'mother an t'dowter sal stop wi ma still ;
Come on't what will, 'i my cot thea sal cahr,
Woe be to thame 'at maks bad into war.
Some fowk may call tha a name 'at ah hate,
Wishin fro t'heart tha wur weel aht o' t'gate :
Oft this hard world inta t'gutter al shuv tha—
Poor little lamb, wi' no daddy ta luve tha—
Dunnot thee freat, doy, woll Gronny hods up,
Nivver sal tha want a bite ur a sup ;
What if ah work these owd fingers ta t'boan.
Happen tha'll love ma long after ah'm goan.
T'last bite it cupbord wi thee ah kud share't,—
Ha ! bud thas stown a rare slice o' my heart ;
Spite o' all t'sorra—all t'shame 'at ah've seen,
Sunshine comes back to mi heart thru thi een.

Cuddle thi Gronny, doy,—
Bless tha, tha'rt bonny, doy—
Rosy an sweet, thro thi brah to thi feet ;
Kingdoms an crahns wod'nt buy tha ta neet.

The Song of the Factory Girl.

SPRING'S early flowers I fain would twine
To deck that open brow of thine ;
But oh ! no garland must I wreathe,
No balmy gales, alas, must breathe :
Within a factory doomed to pine,
No rural joys must e'er be mine.

Ah ! how my throbbing bosom pants
To tread my childhood's hallowed haunts,
Where simplest scenes delight the eye,
And swift the joy-winged moments fly :
Where modest daisies star the ground,
And lovely bluebells nod around.

How oft I muse with gushing tears
On my brief childhood's pleasant years,
For unrestrained I then might stray
Through lane or field the livelong day,
Till evening, and a mother's love,
Recalled me home new joys to prove.

But ah ! too soon those days were o'er,
And pleasure smiled for me no more,
A father's death, alas ! prepared
The path for woes we all have shared :
But I, the eldest, earliest found
This earth was not enchanted ground.

What anguished hours I've passed since then
May not be told by tongue or pen :
Within a factory's gloomy walls,
Which mind, as well as body, thralls,
Through years of toil, of grief, and pain—
With tears I've worn my heavy chain.

For wealth or power I never sigh—
Blest leisure is my deity.
Leisure to read, to walk, to write,
To taste the country's dear delight—
Breathe wholesome air, and gaze my fill
On glen and forest, stream and hill.

How little would my wants supply—
I'd murmur not, though scantily
I fed, and humble was my lot,
To dwell in some quiet, lovely spot ;
Where flowers of every hue might spring,
And welcome birds in gladness sing.

Where I might see the leafy trees
Bend rustling to the healthy breeze,
Might watch birds build and squirrels play,
And timorous rabbits dart away :
Where factory bell I might not hear,
To mar the peace and quiet there.

No more, no more—the dream is past ;
My lot in early life was cast :
Though scalding tears may force their way,
I must my taskmaster obey,
Till some rank churchyard, full of dead,
Forms the last pillow for my weary head.

[The above poem I copied from a slip, apparently from the " Leeds
Times," where it is prefaced by the following remarks !—" These
beautiful lines were written by a factory girl who is now toiling in
Leeds from morning to night, for wages which will scarcely furnish her
with bread. It is our hope that something may be done to get her out
of the miserable place in which she is compelled to reside, and thus to
change her occupation. If any true heart should happen to read this
short preface, and have it in his power to help the person on whose
behalf we plead, he shall have all necessary information by applying,
sending his real name and address, to the editor of this paper." It
would be gratifying to know that help was accorded her in her time of
need.]

The Bradford Scottish.

BRADFORDIAN Scotch! as you revere
Your ancestry and country dear,
Obey the call to volunteer
    Into the Bradford Scottish.

All who their Scotch descent can trace,
Thro' "Sassenach" or Celtic race,
Are welcome to take up their place
    Among the Bradford Scottish.

Perchance a Murray from the Tilt,
Where Celt fought Saxon hilt to hilt!
Then let him don the tartan kilt,
    And join the Bradford Scottish.

If Campbell from the land of Lorne,
With badge of clanship on his "sporan,"
And silver-mounted "Sneeshin-horn,"
    Rank with the Bradford Scottish.

A Struan from the banks of Tay,
If on him your hands could lay,
And put him in the kilt array,
    Would grace the Bradford Scottish.

All the great family of Mac,
Who wield the pen or bear the pack,
Unless they calves or courage lack,
    Must join the Bradford Scottish.

A Bruce or Douglas from the Nith,
Stout of limb and strong of lith,
Let him in gartered hose forthwith
    March with the Bradford Scottish.

Let *any* Englishman *pur sang*
Who for the kilt has a *penchant*,
Go wed a Scottish lass "slap-bang"—
    He's free to join the Scottish.

Let Scotch and English now unite
To uphold Great Britain's might:
If need be, foremost in the fight
    Will be the Bradford Scottish.

(See appendix note 23.)

APPENDIX.

NOTES BY THE EDITOR.

I.—WILLIAM WATKINS was a native of Whitby, and was born in 1755. 'Athelgiva' was written and published in 1778 (pp. 26). He died January 4th, 1811. Amongst his works are "The Sailor" pp. 14, 1782; "The Whitby Spy," pp. 246, 1784; "Anconaliae," pp. 273, 1798; "Original Sonnets," pp. 64, 1799; and "The Fall of Carthage, a Tragedy," pp. 68, 1802.

II.—The following account of William Todd, by W. H. Hatton, F.R.H.S., editor "Bradford Mercury," author "The Churches of Yorkshire," appeared in my "Poets of the Spen Valley," issued in July, 1892. "WILLIAM TODD is one of our Yorkshire poets of humble origin. Horace never attempted to screen the fact that he was the son of an emancipated slave, and Becanger often planted in the face of society his lowly origin. Wm. Todd, even in these days when ancestry counts for a good deal, is none "too proud to care from whence he came." He was born at East Harsley, a hamlet near Northallerton, some sixty-five years ago. He had not the advantage of much schooling, indeed, outside his own efforts, his education was seriously neglected. At eight years of age he was sent into the fields to work, at eleven years of age he was hired to a man who proved himself to be of a most tyrannical nature. Under his control Wm. Todd passed a most unhappy twelve months. As a boy, however, he manifested a great thirst for knowledge. He saved as much as he possibly could from his small earnings, and with his limited capital he purchased useful books. By his own close study he was soon able to spell out the English language. He then made his first purchase, which was Wesley's Notes on the New Testament. He looked upon this book as a rich store of instruction. No miser loved his gold more than William Todd loved Wesley's Notes. He studied them under difficulties, for he had to secretly convey the candle into his bedroom, and b'ind the window in the most careful manner that his master might not detect the light. He often continued his reading until the early hours of the morning. Then he saved sufficient money to enable him to purchase Bishop Horne's work on the Psalms. With this he felt that his store of knowledge was richer still. Persevering with the same policy, he soon became the possessor of "Sutcliffe's Commentary on the whole of the Bible." As he once remarked, "What a mountain of a library I had now." About this time he obtained a situation in a warehouse. His employer ordered him to work on the Sabbath Day. He refused, with the usual consequences. Then William Todd sat down for his "maiden effort"— "Heaven's Boon and Earth's Bliss." His work was favourably reviewed by Dr. Cook in the *Wesleyan New Connexion Magazine*. Thus encouraged, he wrote "The Footsteps of the Deity," which received a flattering notice from the pen of William Petty in the *Primitive Methodist Magazine*. Then followed in quick succession the following poems : "The Yorkshire Ploughman." "The Church." "The Fall of Sebastopol," "The Lily of the Valley," "The Rose of Sharon," "The Flower of Spen Valley," "Moses and his Critics," "A Satire : Jackey Dale." Subsequently William Todd produced a large collection of minor poems, which are too numerous for the mention of each title. Included in his collection are squibs on town matters, and these were often written amidst hard toil to obtain the means of subsistence, and frequently when his mind was troubled with affliction and loss. He has occasionally found pleasure in the study of the Greek poems, but in this relation not very much has come from his pen. When he was twenty year of age William Todd found himself located in Heckmondwike, where he still resides, and in which town all his publications have appeared.

III.—The following authentic account of Hardacre's career appears in my "Poets of Keighley, Bingley, and District," from the interesting pen of Percy Milligan, Esq., M.R.C.S. L.S.A. "JOSEPH HARDACRE, or Hardaker, for he signed his name in both ways, was born at Lees, a hamlet a mile wide of Haworth, in the year 1790. It is not certain that he was brought up to any trade, but the probability is that, as his parents were only poor hill-side farmers, they would have to eke out their living by hand-woolcombing, the almost universal means of existence in the district at that day, and, undoubtedly young Hardacre would have his share to do towards the family purse. Physically he was a poorly, delicate man, of broken constitution : a condition which gave him great and continued mental distress. His parents were Protestants, and Hardacre followed in the same belief until in middle age, he became a Roman Catholic, and died in that faith in the year 1840. He was never married. He was almost entirely self-educated, a capital debater, a dabbler in several of the sciences, and a good speaker. He started the first druggist's shop in Haworth, and by his attention and abilities, soon drew to the place the best people of the neighbourhood : he supplemented this business by acting, during several years, as clerk to solicitors in Keighley, and only relinquished this employment on account of failing health, when he retired to the old home at Haworth to die. His remains lie in the old churchyard.

Old Patrick Brontë, and his son Bramwell, were his friends: indeed, all the best in position, education and wealth of the district took pleasure in honouring Joe with custom and countenance, more, I fancy, for his native talents and evident intellectual superiority, than for the meagre accommodation his shop afforded. He was the author of three volumes of verse: "Poems: Lyric and Moral," printed by Inkersley of Bradford, in 1822, pp. 151: "The Æropteron, or Steam Carriage," printed by Aked of Keighley, in 1830; and "The Bridal of Tomar," printed by Charles Crabtree of Keighley, in 1831, pp. 144.

IV.—SPENCE BROUGHTON was hung at York for robbing the mail-coach on the 14th of April, 1792. The copy—an original broadside—from which this lament is printed has no printer's name attached—and there is no indication in the lines to show any connection with Yorkshire.

V.—Mr. SCRUTON is *par excellence* Bradford's historian—the sketch of the compiler of these ballads is from his facile pen. Mr. Scruton is also the author of "The Birthplace of Charlotte Brontë," "Pen and Pencil Pictures of Old Bradford," and numerous articles on the former Religious and Political Life of Bradford.

VI.—Among my valued Yorkshire literary friends I am proud to claim a personal acquaintance with Mr. WILLIAM GRAINGE of Harrogate. He was born at Castiles farm, in Kirkby Malzeard, where his ancestors had resided three centuries. His birth took place January 25, 1818. His bit of schooling was over when twelve years old, but a love for reading never left him. From early youth he was a gratuitous yet acceptable contributor of history and poetry to the local newspapers. On the death of his father in 1845, he removed to the neighbourhood of Boroughbridge, where he resided for fifteen years, and compiled the history of Aldborough and Boroughbridge for T. S. Turner, bookseller, issued 1853; nearly 200 pages. From this time he appears almost annually as an author, and some of his works are out of print. "The Battles and Battlefields of Yorkshire" appeared in 1854; "The Castles and Abbeys of Yorkshire" in 1855; "The Vale of Mowbray, a Historical and Topographical Account of Thirsk" in 1859; "Nidderdale," published by Thomas Thorpe of Pateley Bridge, in 1863; "The Poets and Poetry of Yorkshire," in two volumes, published at Wakefield in 1868; "Guide to Harrogate," five editions; "A Memoir of Sir W. Slingsby," "A Short History of Knaresborough," 1865, 161 pages, "A Tract on the Geology of Harrogate," "A Ramble among the Ancient British Remains on Rombalds Moor," by C. F[orrest] and W. G[rainge] in three parts: "The Annals of a Yorkshire Abbey," [Fountains,] published by R. Ackrill, Harrogate; 1879, 145 pp., "Yorkshire Longevity," published in 1864, pp. 40; "Memoir of Peter Barker, the blind joiner of Hampsthwaite," 1876, second edition, 16 pages; "Walks and Footpaths round Harrogate," 1874, pp. 73; "The History and Topography of Harrogate and the Forest of Knaresborough," published by J. Thorpe, Pateley Bridge, in 1871;

" Fairfax's Dæmonologia, or Witchcraft as acted in the family of Mr.
Edward Fairfax, of Fuyston, in 1621." pp. 189, 1882. He was a
contributor to Ingledew's Ballads, 1860.

VII.—JAMES HENRY DIXON was a Doctor of Laws of the University of
London. He was born in that city in 1803, and died at Lausanne, near
the shores of Lake Leman, on October 26th, 1876. Part of his boyhood
was spent at Skipton, during which time he attended the Free Grammar
School. He was a "born poet," and his gift was early and vigorously
cultivated. The poet's corner in various newspapers received welcome
contributions from his pen. Dr. Dixon was by profession a solicitor,
being articled to an eminent firm of lawyers in Durham from about
1821 to 1827, after which he commenced practice in London, where he
stayed more than twenty years. Whilst in London he was elected a
member of the "Percy Society," and the works mentioned by Mr.
Holroyd were entrusted to his editorship by the society. For many
years, too, Dr. Dixon resided at Grassington. The doctor also produced "Chronicles and Stories of the Craven Dales," to which he
contributed a number of fine poems, notably "The Boy of Egremond."
He generally adopted a *nom de plume* when issuing his writings, and
when the reader saw "F.Q.M.," "Oliver Cauvert," and Stephen
Jackson, Esq.," appended to different articles, many knew that this
was signature of the genial and gifted solicitor, Dr. James Hy. Dixon.

VIII.—Lieutenant-Colonel Hirst, C.B. J.P. is now residing at Clayton,
taking an active interest in the affairs of Bradford.

IX.—I once had the pleasure of meeting the author of this poem, and I
believe he is still residing in Bradford. Mr. Grainge quotes some of
his poetry on p. 520 of his "Poets of Yorkshire," and says of him "he
has given to the world some genuine poetry." Mr. Holroyd, both in
his "Garlands" and "Spice Islands," gives examples of his muse.
In 1863 Mr. MILNER published a small volume of poems entitled
"Sacred Musings, or Simple Rhymes for Humble Souls." This was
dedicated to the late Rev. J. P. Chown, of Bradford, and the profits on
the sale of the work were devoted to religious purposes.

X.—Mr. JOHN SWAIN is still living, and residing in Battersea, London.
I have frequently had communications from him, and a few months
ago, along with my friend Mr. W. J. Kaye, M.A., the principal of
Ilkley College, who is a distant relative of his, called upon him at his
house in Bridge Road. He was, however, far from well. Mr. Swain
was born at Haddenly Hall, which is situate between Holmfirth and
Penistone, on October 30th, 1815. When between three and four years
of age he was sent to the school at Cumberworth, where he remained
until thirteen. He then went to learn his father's business—that of
cloth finishing—but at the age of twenty-two he became engaged at
Garforth Village School as a teacher. After this he went to London,
where he was examined by the Revs. Dr. Robert Newton and James
Bunting. They, observing his capacity as a tutor, advised him to

enter the Glasgow Training Institution. where he ultimately obtained a Diploma. Whilst at Garforth, he had commenced contributing poetry to the "Leeds Mercury Supplement," which finally brought him an introduction to Sir Edwin Baines, who took great interest in him and introduced him to that noble patron of literature Lord Morpeth. afterwards Earl of Carlisle. His Lordship eventually procured for him an appointment as Inspector of Letter-carriers in the General Post Office. Here, after twenty-one years' service he retired on a well-earned pension which he still enjoys. Many of his volumes of verse were inscribed to the late Sir Edwin Baines, M.P., and some hundreds of his poems have been set to music by eminent composers.

XI.—For an interesting account of JAMES BRADSHAWE WALKER, the reader is referred to page 142. vol. ii. of my "Yorkshire Poets. Past and Present." Walker was born at Leeds in 1806. In addition to being the author of the works mentioned by Mr. Holroyd, he wrote "The Warriors of our Wooden Walls and their Victories," 1853. At one period of his life. Mr. Walker was schoolmaster of St. Luke's, Leeds. On resigning this position, he went to London, where he earned a scanty living as a journalist. For years he held no correspondence with his family at Leeds. Later, he returned to the house of his son, Thomas Percy Walker, North Street. Leeds, at whose house he died. September 28th, 1860.

XII.—For a biography of EBENEZER ELLIOTT I refer the reader to vol. iii. page 68. of my "Yorkshire Poets. Past and Present." Elliott, who was widely known as the "Corn Law Rhymer," was born at Masborough. March 17th. 1781, and died on December 1st. 1849. Charles Dickens said of him: "He was a true poet, whose credentials, "signed and sealed in the court of nature, attested the genuineness of "his brotherhood with those children of song who make the world "holier and happier by the mellifluous strains they bring to us, like "fragments of a forgotten melody from the far-off world of beauty "and love." A bronze statue by Burnard of London, subscribed for by the working men of Sheffield, was erected in the market-place of that town in 1854, to the memory of Elliott. Landor wrote a fine ode on the occasion. The statue was afterwards removed to Weston Park.

XIII.—The writings of WINTHROP MACKWORTH PRAED, the author of "The Battle of Marston Moor," ought to be more widely known. It was not until 1865 that his writings appeared in this country, in a collected form. It is creditable to transatlantic taste that two editions of them had already been published in America. His comic pieces display a playful tenderness that cannot fail to charm the reader. while his ballad metre has the true ring about it, reminding one of Macaulay and Aytoun. Mr. Praed was in the House of Commons, and was some time member for St. Germain. in Cornwall, for Great Yarmouth. and for Aylesbury: and in 1835 he was secretary to the Board of Control. He died of consumption at the early age of thirty-seven in 1839.

XIV.—In the Rev. Baring-Gould's work entitled "Yorkshire Oddities" the following incongruous paragraph occurs:—" Mr. PRESTON is no oddity, but a very remarkable man, whose poems deserve to be better known and more widely read than they are." Mr. Preston is still living in his rustic retreat at Eldwick, and many are the happy moments I have spent in his charming company. He was born in Bradford on August 19th. 1819, and in addition to numerous pamphlets of his poetry, two volumes of his poems have been issued. For an exhaustive account of his career I refer the reader to an article in "The Poets of Keighley and Bingley," written by the Rev. J. W. Kaye, LL.D. Rector of Derrybrusk, Enniskillen.

XV.—For an interesting life of DAVID MALLET I refer the reader to "The Leading Poets of Scotland," by Mr. Walter J. Kaye, M.A. the Principal of Ilkley College, Yorkshire, and the writer of " Some Remarks on Ballad Lore " at the commencement of this volume.

XVI.—Mr. LEATHAM represented Wakefield and the Southern Division of the West Riding in Parliament for some years. He married in 1839, Priscilla, the fourth daughter of Mr. Samuel Gurney, of Upton, Essex. He died on November 14th. 1889, at his residence, The White House, Carleton, near Pontefract, and was buried at Hemsworth Church. For further particulars see my " Yorkshire Poets, Past and Present," vol. iii. page 127.

XVII.—I have, more than once, visited the esteemed Rector of Bulmer, the Rev. James Gabb, B.A. who is a true poet, and the author of several volumes of verse; and he informs me that the house in which Captain Bolton's horrible crime, or crimes, was committed, was some time since pulled down : and happily no trace of it now remains.

XVIII.—Mr. Holroyd is correct as to CHARTER receiving twenty years for these murders. The wretched man is still in gaol.

XIX.—This beautiful little ballad, though written in dialect, is worthy of perpetuating. I should be glad to know the name of its author.

XX.—See Note XIV.

XXI.—See page 152. STORY'S poems may be found in the Bradford Free Library, and, in fact, in almost every free library throughout the kingdom.

XXII.—An exhaustive biography of NICHOLSON from the trenchant pen of Mr. C. A. Federer, L.C.P. together with an autograph, portrait, view of his birthplace, and complete bibliography, will be found in my " Poets of Keighley, Bingley and District."

XXIII.—Mr. JAMES SMEATON, now of Menstone, is the author of " The Bradford Scottish." He lived in Bradford more than twenty years, but is a native of Forteviot, near Cairnie, in Perthshire, and was born December 28th, 1819. He is a talented controversialist and a bard with the ring of true poetry in all his effusions.

INDEX.

WORKS BY

Chas. F. Forshaw, LL.D. D.D.S.

Wanderings of Imagery: *a Volume of Poems.*

Thoughts in the Gloaming: *a Volume of Poems.*

Yorkshire Poets, Past and Present. *Four Volumes.*

Original Poems, pp. 320.

The Poetical Works of the Rev. Thomas Garratt M.A., pp. 368.

A Legend of St. Bees and other Poems. pp. 256.

The Poets of Keighley, Bingley, and District.

The Poets of the Spen Valley.

Yorkshire Sonneteers.

My Little Romance.

Hannah Dale.

The Teeth and How to Save them.

How to Manage Childrens Teeth.

Tobacco and its Effect on the Teeth.

Alcohol; and its Influence on the Body.

Cocaine for Tooth Extraction.

Stammering: Its Causes and Cure.

BRADFORD:
PRINTED BY THORNTON AND PEARSON, THE COLLEGE PRESS,
56, BARKEREND ROAD.

www.ingramcontent.com/pod-product-compliance
Lightning Source LLC
Chambersburg PA
CBHW020953030726
47496CB00005B/1490

* 9 7 8 3 7 4 4 7 7 7 8 5 8 *